BLINK-BLINK

J.P.S. STALDER

J.P.S. Stalder is a California native, who currently lives in the greater Kansas City, Missouri area. A writer and avid reader from a young age, his passion for language, people, culture, and philosophy led him first to a degree studying rhetoric and political science, which was followed by a career in the government sector.

After the passing of his father in January 2023, Stalder dedicated himself to pursuing writing to leave behind something positive for future generations of his family. This story, and those that will follow, are a manifestation of that pursuit.

Other works:

ISBN# 979-8-9927394-0-4 (Paperback)

ISBN# 979-8-9927394-1-1 (ePub e-book)

In loving memory of S.C. Stalder,
an old man, who once lived on a boat,
swore like a sailor, and distrusted powerful people.

~ 1 ~

Why it took three hours to weed Mrs. Marbury's garden beds, she could never figure out. The garden wasn't particularly large, but no matter how much compost she added the past few winters, soil compaction was a consistent problem. The dandelion leaves could always be used for salad, she supposed. But the thistles and the sharp, bladed grasses that continually crept in between the tomato plants were sharp and thorny, even when they were still small. It was worth it for fresh produce she wouldn't have to buy; Mrs. Marbury allowed her half of each harvest in exchange for the helping hand. Nearing eighty, the old widow cared little for her company, but she was certainly fond of the labor.

Finishing the chore took most of the late morning, but with the work complete, her share of the ripe harvest included fresh basil, a dozen plump heirloom tomatoes, six large English cucumbers, and about ten pounds of sweet potatoes that had gone wild with the incessant summer rain they were having. All the bounty was neatly loaded into sacks she placed carefully in the small trailer that she towed behind her rusty, vintage bicycle, where it would be sufficiently secure until her next stop.

Several blocks eastward from Mrs. Marbury's home, she rode easily and carefree through the blocks of old craftsmen homes until she reached the stores that lined the Historic District of Main Street in St. Charles. There, she parked her bicycle in a public lot near Mr. Addison's art supply store, where she would barter a portion of her produce for needed supplies. Mr. Addison, the owner, was especially keen on fresh tomatoes, swearing the heirlooms she traded were far superior to any that could be ordered locally. The exchange took only minutes, and when she exited, she carried with her a half-dozen new tubes of acrylic paint. Gunky Paint, her preferred brand of art supplies, had only recently released eleven new color blends, although she suspected they were older blends that were simply rebranded. Regardless, she desperately needed a new type of teal-green for a project she had in her mind — the color had to perfectly replicate the patina of aged copper. Likely she would need to add gray to get the right tone on canvas, but time and patience would solve that mystery.

From Mr. Addison's it would be a short ride down Jefferson to 7th Street, and then a few more blocks to reach the small blue sided home of the Andover family, and behind it, the similarly painted garage that had long before been converted to a small cottage she called home. The Andover's had been loyal friends of her parents despite their beliefs, and had generously allowed her to live in the small, one bedroom structure even knowing she could not pay. An informal arrangement had been agreed to, exchanging occasional childcare for a roof and place to sleep. While the whole family was fully connected to the feed, their loyalty and love for her and her parents ran deeper than any disagreement over the state of the law or connectivity. The last few years, they had quickly become surrogate parents, and she became the big sister to their eight-year-old daughter, Mia.

When she finally reached the blue cottage, Mia was waiting for her at the door. The young girl greeted her precociously, saying, "You know, Blair, with all the painting you do, you should really paint this door..."

"Is that so?" Blair asked.

"Yes. I think it should be decorated with big, pretty flowers!" Mia answered energetically. "Like BIG ones!"

"Hmm...Well, what kind of flowers should we paint?" Blair asked. Then, squinting somewhat conspicuously, she added, "What are your favorites?"

As Mia pondered the question, Blair turned the key in the lock, and then gestured for Mia to join her inside for further discussion.

"I think big, white magnolias – I LOVE MAGNOLIAS!" Mia added after careful consideration. "We saw them when we went to Savannah last summer - have you been to Savannah?"

"I... I haven't really been much of anywhere, actually. It's a good thing I love St. Chuck so much. St. Louis too," Blair answered with a smile.

"Well, I'm sure there's a whole scroll on the feed filled with pictures of magnolias. You'd just have to – oh, wait. I'm sorry," Mia said, interrupting herself apologetically. Then sounding somewhat contrite, she continued by saying, "Mama says I'm not supposed to talk to you about lenses and the feed and stuff."

"That's okay, Mia," Blair chuckled. "Listen – you're connected to the feed – it's a part of your life. I don't mind if you look; you can even describe them to me. The feed and all that stuff – it's just not for me." Blair then gave her a wink, assuring her no harm had been done by approaching the topic.

With a shrug, Mia popped onto Blair's bed as she put away the produce and her recently procured art supplies. The eight-year-old looked confused by Blair's response, or perhaps it was simply a result of confusing messages between the adults in her life. It occurred to Blair that she may have never considered the possibility that someone could simply not be connected. Nearly everyone older than a toddler was, after all; people grew up with connectivity front and center in their lives. Sensing the tension this confusion had created, she sat down beside her on the bed and tussled young Mia's curly, black hair as she said, "I don't expect you to understand how confusing grownups are. I don't really understand it myself, and I'm much, much older than you."

"How old?" Mia asked excitedly.

"I turned twenty-three a few months ago," Blair responded.

"THAT'S SO OLD!" Mia groaned.

"I know – I know... I'm basically an old lady now, right?" Blair laughed.

As Mia began to blink her way through various threads within the feed, contented to relax in the company of her older friend, Blair turned her attention to the drop cloth covered canvas seated on the easel only a few feet away.

"Can I stay here and watch you paint for a while?" Mia asked suddenly, distracting herself from the barrage of videos and images that flooded over the virtual renderings that appeared in front of her eyes as she lay flat on Blair's small bed.

"Of course – you can hang out as long as you'd like, if it's fine with your mom," Blair responded as she began collecting her paint pallet and an assortment of flat, round brushes she would use from a decorative ceramic vase that sat at the center of a well-worn, wooden table otherwise cluttered with a mess of books, sketches, and vinyl album covers.

Mia lay motionless momentarily and simply blinked her eyes several times. She then blinked again, in multiple short bursts, followed by one final blink-blink. She then pronounced, "Mom says it's ok as long as I go back for lunch when it's ready."

"Then by all means..." Blair answered with a smile.

As Blair removed the large cloth draped over the canvas, she took a moment to kick gently at one of the wooden easel legs, attempting to re-adjust the aged contraption. The easel, which she had salvaged from a dumpster behind Mr. Addison's art supply store, had personality all its own. From the random bolts that were not original and the layers of paint drips, it was clear that years of other artists' efforts left a decorated trail along thin wooden legs and triangular frame. To match its rough appearance, the easel's temperament was also old and crotchety, seeming to take great delight in thwarting her efforts to adjust its height or fix it in place to prevent a canvas from falling out of level. Still, her combination studio, living quarters, kitchenette, and bedroom was a collection of similar personalities, a curated menagerie that had been salvaged or bartered. One couldn't be too picky when the price was right, and being free or near to it was always the right price. Improvisation and adaptation were part of the charm, she supposed.

After several additional gentle kicks to the left and right leg, Blair settled for shimming the back leg of the tripod with a hardbound copy of the complete writings of Jean-Jacques Rousseau. The worn, blue canvas of the cover already had a likely permanent indentation from previous similar use.

"What's this one about?" Mia asked as Blair kneeled down beneath her painting while she repaired the easel.

"What do you think it is? Does anything look familiar to you?" Blair asked as she scrutinized her work.

"It looks like the baseball stadium in St. Louis," Mia answered as she studied the piece.
"But fancy, I guess. It's pretty."

"Well... I suppose it's a success then," Blair answered as she used a fine pointed brush to apply several small touches to the piece.

"I don't like baseball, but daddy does. He'd probably like this one," the young girl answered.

"I don't much like it either," Blair answered with a laugh. "But I hear it's more exciting in person – can't say why – that's just what people say. Anyway, the folks who walk through the art fair might like baseball... or St. Louis... or maybe just paintings. Maybe some people visiting from out of town will want a souvenir of their trip... It might be a pleasant reminder, don't you think?" Blair asked as she glanced over at the young girl.

"Not if they don't like baseball," Mia said precociously.

The honest answer of the young girl made Blair laugh hard enough that she nearly dropped her palette knife, almost unintentionally transferring paint onto the canvas. She shook her head with a broad smile, answering the young girl, "Miss Mia, you are the wisest of us all — truly. If they do not like baseball, this one probably isn't for them."

Blair continued applying the finishing touches, as Mia observed each movement of her hand as she carefully added minute details that brought the piece to life. White hues created contrast with the dark brick tones and deep green steel of the stadium's frame. As she worked, she hummed along to herself for a while, until she quietly sang along to a song trapped within her head. Eventually, she turned to Mia and asked, "Why don't you put a record on? Do you remember how?"

Mia rolled sideways off of the bed, nearly falling onto the floor before she caught herself. Then, dragging her feet forward, she approached a square wooden box with a metal turntable on top. Within a milk crate on the floor beneath the record player, several dozen square cardboard album covers were crammed together awaiting an audience. The young girl flipped through the collection lazily, not knowing who any of the artists were, but after finding a colorful cover, she snatched up one album and removed the black vinyl record from its protective sheath. A short scratching sound later, the small cottage was filled with the sound of delta blues from the 1960s.

"Oh, good choice, Mia," Blair said, praising her young friend. "I love this album."

As the wail of a rhythmic guitar kept tempo, Blair continued, adding small dabs of paint, little by little. By the time the third song had finished, she stepped back from her work and said, "Well...I think that's about it – what do you think?"

"It looks beautiful – if you like that kind of thing..." Mia answered dismissively. Then, with enthusiasm, she asked, "Now can we paint the door?"

Blair laughed once again, but before she could respond, a knock at the door resounded throughout the small studio. Mia, who was still lying lackadaisically on the bed, rose from to open the door, albeit with more grace. Then suddenly she exclaimed, "Mommy!"

"Hey squirt!" Mrs. Andover exclaimed from the other side of the threshold, "Lunch is ready for you on the kitchen table – go eat!"

"Bye Blair," Mia shouted as she ran across the backyard lawn that separated the main house from the cottage. As she did, Blair put down her palette knife and paint and wiped her hands briefly on her overalls as she moved toward the door to give Mia's mother a hug.

"Hey you," Blair said as she squeezed the woman tightly.

"Hi – *other squirt*," Mrs. Andover replied with a warm smile as they embraced. Then, looking at the newly completed piece of art still sitting on the easel, she asked, "Is this the newest one?"

"Yes, ma'am. Just finished it – what do you think?" Blair asked.

"It's marvelous, of course – but everything you paint is... marvelous. I think I'm running out of the right words to describe your work," she answered with a laugh as she brushed her salt-and-pepper colored hair away from her eyes so she could lean in for a closer look.

"I have a few others I've completed over the last few weeks," Blair said excitedly as she moved toward two completed canvases that leaned against the wall near the door. Then, as she moved the piece closest to the wall so that it was visible, she lifted each of them slightly as she identified the subjects, "The Arch and the Old Courthouse down by Kiener Plaza. And then that one of the stadium... do you think... do you think they'll sell?"

"Of course they will – Just don't be disappointed if they don't all sell this weekend. But yeah, they're beautiful. I'm sure someone will want them. What kind of deal did you work out with Tony?" she asked. Then, after pausing for a moment, she interrupted herself saying, "I'm sorry, it's probably none of my business; I probably don't want to know, especially if it's illegal. And I know how much you value your privacy. If you think it's fair, I'm happy for you."

Blair grimaced slightly, sensing the gentle condemnation her friend had often espoused for her less-than-legal bartering of goods. She understood it was Blair's only way to provide for herself, but neither of Mia's parents particularly approved of circumventing the law, no matter how obnoxious it had become.

"Bell..." Blair said gently, "I... I just don't want – "

"No – no, no. Don't say any more. I don't want to know. So long as you're staying safe and whatever THIS is stays unnoticed... I don't want to have answers if anyone begins to ask," Bell said with a laugh that followed a dismissive wave of her hand.

"It's going to be fine – no, better than that. It's going to be great! Just... do me a favor and make me a grocery list of things that you need for the house," Blair responded with a coy smile.

"Right... So, you're now doing the grocery shopping, Miss Unscannable? No – don't answer that either. I don't want to know," Bell said, shaking her head in resignation. Then, as she turned to leave, she again admonished her friend, saying, "Just promise me you'll be cautious. Stay safe... and drop by the house tomorrow afterwards. I want to hear how it all went."

Blair raised a meek hand with a tempered wave goodbye. Finally left to work without spectators, she moved the still drying stadium piece from the easel onto the window ledge, where the warm summer air from the partially open window would allow it to dry quickly. She then removed the cloth cover from a stack of canvases that sat at the opposite end of the room, inconspicuously hidden from any eyes that were not her own. She'd done the work that needed to be done for the art fair that was held on the 2nd Saturday of the month in St. Charles, as it had been for decades. With the bills paid, it was time to work on her passion projects.

With the cloth removed, she lifted the poster size canvas into place and then stepped back to admire the progress that had been made. On the canvas, the image of a dying, bald eagle lying flat and lifeless was painted at the center; its wings were spread open and patches of its skin showed bare as feathers lay at its side. The eagle's eyes were a sickly gray-white tone implying the predator had long been blinded with cataracts, and on the concrete ground surrounding the icon, gold and silver coins had been strewn – one of the gold coins was wedged in the blind birds beak.

Blair found an assortment of round brushes in her ceramic vase and began adding dark shades to the feathers, adding depth and dimension. As she worked, soulful blues rifts played in the background. Into each feather, she carefully applied lines of colors in a variety of tones and shades, a tedious process without which the bird would appear dimensionless and flat.

She worked late into the evening, only stopping when she remembered the vine ripe tomatoes she had brought home from Mrs. Marbury's garden. Blair looked around for the loaf of bread she had bartered for the day before, and then quickly cut the tomato for a late-night sandwich. When a pinch of salt was added, dinner was ready. Blair took her meal to the front door, and while juggling a plate as she opened it, she laughed and said aloud to herself, "This door really would look better with some large magnolias..." Just outside the entrance, an old wooden rocking chair she had inherited awaited her arrival.

The heat and humidity of the night air wasn't pleasant by any means, but it was significantly cooler than the mid-day sun. As Blair rocked in the wooden chair, the flavor of fresh tomatoes exploded in her mouth, tantalizing and decadent. For a girl who lacked the means to pay for anything, the meal and a night alone were a luxury at its finest. "What more to life was there than making art, fresh heirloom tomatoes, and a comfortable rocking chair — who would ever want more?" she asked herself.

With the smooth, raspy voice of a bluesman singing faintly in the background, the slow rock of the wooden chair eased her comfortably as she relaxed and the worries of the day washed away. Without noticing, her eyes closed and the gentle sway of the chair mixed with the warm air to usher into a deep sleep. There she remained, sleeping alone in a rocking chair in the Andover's backyard for hours, until at some point a noise from the street woke her just briefly enough to wander back into her little home and fall into her bed.

The ring of her winding alarm clock felt as if it would vibrate her whole dwelling when it finally sounded, signaling the arrival of morning light that crept into the yard outside of her window. Blair startled awake at the sound, as she had frequently before, only on this morning, rather than sinking back down to the softness of her pillows, she sprang from her bed. On this morning, she had a purpose and place to be, and there was little time to waste lazily preparing. Her long, crimson colored hair was still a mess from the day before, and as she began wondering how to master that riddle, she realized she had fallen asleep in the same bib overalls that she had both gardened and painted in the day before. Scrambling hastily, she quickly changed into a worn pair of jeans that had spent several days folded and sitting on the floor at the foot of her bed. Next, she found an old t-shirt that was mostly paint free and swapped the one she was wearing for the cleaner of the two. Changing took only a minute, after which she left the cottage hastily and made quickly for her bicycle and the small trailer it towed parked next to the old garage.

Still fighting the grogginess, Blair yawned deeply as she quickly mounted her rusty bicycle and made her way toward the front yard of the Andover home. Fortunately, before she left the driveway, she realized in her half-wakefulness she had not loaded her paintings into the trailer. After a quick retreat, Blair grabbed the artwork from the stack near the door; it was only after she caught a quick glimpse of herself in the mirror near the door that she realized she had done nothing with her hair.

There's no time, she thought frantically.

With a twist and a whirl of her hand and the aid of two chopsticks she left in the small organizer mounted beneath the mirror, her long red hair transformed into a messy top-knot. Seconds later, she was once again on her bike and peddling down 7th Street. She turned on Jefferson to head toward the historic district where the market would be held. She peddled hard and, after only a few blocks, quickly passed the stately County Executive office, sitting on a slight hill that was adorned with bronze sculptures and historic plaques. Then, after a quick right on 2nd Street, it was only a few blocks past the hospital complex Tompkins Street, where after a quick left, she arrived at Sweeny's Corner Market, awkwardly located between Main Street and 2nd. She quickly parked her bike and rushed into the store to find a large, older man with a potbelly that was covered by a grease-stained polo shirt seated behind the counter. He hardly noticed her arrival as he continued, busily browsing the feed as he stared off blankly into the emptiness of his small market.

Out of breath, she placed one hand on the counter and steadied herself before greeting the man with a smile, "Hi Tony!"

"You're a bit late there, B," the somewhat slovenly old store owner responded without breaking his concentration from the images that filled his lens coated eyes.

"Sorry, Tony – I promise it won't happen again," Blair answered. "But I brought you some really nice pieces – GREAT PIECES - do you want to see them?"

"No...not really – I know you can paint, kid. You kept it to tourist stuff, right? Stuff folks will buy?" Tony answered skeptically, still fixated on whatever content was crossing his eyes at the moment.

"Absolutely – the Arch, the ballpark, the courthouse – all gems of St. Lou," Blair answered proudly.

"Good... good-good... I'll have Ernie get them all set up on the sidewalk out front..." he answered before turning toward the back of the small grocery store. "ERNIE! Ernie – get your skinny little backside in here!"

Moments later, a gangly teenage boy with an acne pocked complexion sauntered forward from a back area of the store and arrived at the counter. Dressed in a basketball jersey and athletic shorts that hid beneath a dirty, red apron with "Sweeny's" printed diagonally across the center, the teenage boy exemplified a sort of minimum effort standard that had become increasingly prevalent among the area's less affluent residents.

It took the teen several seconds to break away from his own feed, but when he noticed Blair standing in front of the counter, his attention became immediately fixed.

"Hey, what's up, Blair – you lookin' good as hell, girl," the teenager said as he walked up to the counter next to her as smoothly as he could muster. "When you gonna let me take you out for a good time?"

Blair's response was more of an annoyance than flattery, having yet again felt more embarrassed for the young man than by his awkward advances. Every time she came into Sweeny's, his attempts at courtship clumsily made an appearance. The exuding hormones and clunky bravado held zero appeal for her, yet she attempted to remain polite all the same.

"You idiot! Get a clue," Tony yelled as he slapped the counter in front of him to get the young man's attention. "She's way out of your league! Hell – they may all be! Now wake up! And get those paintings set up like I told you."

"Alright... alright... you don't have to be a jerk about it," Ernie answered as he wandered out the entrance of the small market.

"So," Tony said, turning his attention back toward Blair. "I'll let you know how it goes then? And only credit – no cash, just like we discussed. It's only for groceries and such – no booze or junk. It's just cause I'm trying to help you out, is all."

"That sounds great, Tony. Thank you. And actually, I was kind of hoping I could watch for a bit? Like, from a distance - If... if you wouldn't mind. I won't get in the way," Blair pleaded somewhat pathetically.

Her pitiful display must have sufficiently caught his attention, as at last, Tony broke his concentration from the feed long enough to look directly at the young artist, as he said, "Hey, look, B – I'm not sure that's such a good idea. There's gonna be loads of tourists in and out all day... Lots of scanning, buying, selling – I'm not sure someone of your particular... situation... We wouldn't want anyone to get weirded out is all I'm saying."

Blair's face must have revealed her obvious disappointment; she had only wanted to see if there were people who would appreciate her work. Then again, she understood. If someone were to scan her - if they were to notice she wasn't connected – at a minimum, there would be a hassle and calls made. If the police showed up, it would look bad for him, and it would be even worse for her.

The look on her face when he responded must have softened his heart momentarily, as seconds later he let out a deep exhale, revealing just a glimpse of empathy for the young woman. He then said, "I'll tell you what, B. You know Mrs. Lee across the street?"

"The flower shop – of course," Blair said impatiently as she eagerly awaited his pronouncement.

"Well, she's closed right now - away on a fancy trip with her husband – Florida, I think," Tony said reluctantly. "See, I've been watching her cat for days now - and I hate those damn things – plus, I'm allergic. I can't ask Ernie to look after it, because - clearly, he's useless. He's my nephew, so... Well, my sister says working with family is good for him. Anyway, you go look after Whiskers for me, and you'd probably have a view from the window upstairs. Just be non-chal-AUNT...non-discrib... non – just don't be seen, alright? And don't touch anything – you break something, and I'd have to explain why you were there."

The shop owner fumbled around in his pocket for a moment before producing a key attached to a large, neon-pink, fuzzy dice, which he slid across the counter toward her. The look of surprise on Blair's face as she looked at the tacky ornament decorating the key accurately reflected both her level of surprise and disapproval, as quickly Tony interjected, "Hey – it's so I don't lose it!"

"Well... um... I'm guessing it works," Blair answered, wide eyed. "And thank you – really. I appreciate everything you're doing to help me out."

"Nah, don't worry 'bout it. Your folks were good folks – didn't deserve what happened to 'em. Besides, you paint good. Everyone needs a break now and then, right?" the shop owner said with a genuine but rather hideous, yellow-toothed smile.

With key in hand, Blair crossed the narrow street to the flower shop and let herself in through the front door, locking it behind her as she went. In the back of the store, she quickly found the staircase that led to the living quarters above the shop. Minutes later, following the acquaintance of an enormous, long-haired cat, she was seated in a floral patterned, velour chair. Its location near the window provided her with an impeccable overlook onto Tompkins Street and the tables that would display her work in front of Sweeny's market.

Ernie was lazily setting up the paintings, using milk crates to prop the pieces up. The table cloth he had covered the folding table with was a sufficiently pleasant touch. While Tony's willingness to work with her was generous and his efforts to display her work humbling, the lack of refinement was underwhelming; it simply wasn't how she had envisioned her work being introduced to the world. For a moment, she considered possibly going down to assist him in the set-up, wondering if there was something that could be done to improve the awkwardness of the display. After consideration, she eventually thought better of it; she didn't want to anger him. It then occurred to her she could yell from the window if she could open it. Again, remembering his direction to remain unseen, she decided against it. She would simply have to wait and endure the underwhelming spectacle, hoping someone would see her art for what it was, and not the presentation that lessened it.

She sat quietly in the chair, stroking the long fur of Whiskers and watching as the streets filled with hundreds of weekenders and tourists. They wandered down Main Street off to the left of the shop, meandering through the coffee shops and bakeries that hummed with business on a Saturday morning. Sweeny's location off of 2nd Street was less than ideal, and for a while, she felt like she was simply watching a parade pass her by, just out of reach. Without a direct connection to the scroll or help from another shop owner, she knew she had to manage her expectations. She would have no marketing, no agent, no fanfare that would promote what she felt was a significant achievement; she simply had to hope some tourists wandered past the shops far enough to see the meager display that had been created. It was not a great option, but it was the only option available to her. Without an artist license or lenses, it was impossible for her to accept the only legal form of payment, making selling her own work alone a fantasy.

Blair slowly and gently ran her hand down the fluffy coat of the husky feline that had fallen asleep in her lap as she watched the tourists move up and down the red brick streets of the historic district. As Main Street filled, she noticed some people beginning to spill into the side streets more and more, and it gave her hope that perhaps one of the wealthy wanderers would find their way down Tompkins if for no other reason than to escape the carnival like atmosphere surrounding the main offerings of the art fair. As hours passed, Blair waited, staring down at her paintings, and eventually several people stopped and looked. By mid-morning, the street that separated the flower shop and corner market was becoming crowded, increasing her odds and sense of hope. She thought for a moment the surge may have been thanks to the artesian chocolate shop that had just opened, drawing more people towards their end of the fair. There was also a long line forming outside the coffee shop at the corner of main and Tompkins, which was overflowing their way. In time, several latte wielding ladies wearing expensive summer dresses began strolling in their direction, one of which stopped in front of the corner market to admire her work. Then suddenly, a well-dressed man caught up from behind to accompany the woman who was looking at her art, and she could then see him leaning towards her saying something as he pointed at the paintings. The woman nodded her head in agreement, and the man disappeared into the market. Several minutes later, the man exited the small store, followed by Ernie, who stacked her art work one on top of the other, binding them together with what looked like twine or string of some kind. The well-dressed man then gestured toward the canvases, at which point Ernie picked up the bound stack of canvases, and began walking off towards 2nd Street with the man. Only seconds later, an automated driverless vehicle arrived at the parking lot next to the market, and the rear doors opened. Seconds later, Ernie was loading the paintings.

It had all happened so quickly that Blair stood in excitement, waking the poor feline that fell from her lap unexpectedly. She watched closely as the doors to the robocar closed. Suddenly, as if from a dream, they were all gone.

She knew she had never felt an emotional attachment to these particular pieces; they were made to be sold after all. But seeing them go, it was different. There was a sadness that mixed in, oddly indistinguishable from her excitement. Like salt in water, the two blended into something that felt useless to consume, but it was there just the same. It was as if she had lost an acquaintance she had just recently met, and along with the departure, the hope of what could have been. Still, the complicated feelings she struggled with were tempered by the realization she had finally done it – she had sold some of her art.

I guess that makes me a professional artist now, she thought to herself – *if just barely.*

After ensuring the litter box was freshly cleaned and fresh food and water were left for Whiskers, Blair made her way back down the stairs of the flower shop, locking the door behind her as she exited. For a moment, she wondered if she should go check-in with Tony – she desperately wanted to know what her paintings had sold for. But the streets remained full of tourists attending the fair. If she stayed – if she was noticed... it simply wasn't worth the risk. Instead, Blair found her bicycle, right where she had parked it in the lot next to Sweeny's, and after carefully guiding it through the crowds on Tompkins Street, she peddled home.

As Blair parked her the bicycle and trailer on the side of the cottage, she heard the back door of the house open, and the voices of Mia and her mother just behind.

"So... how'd it go?" Bell called out as she entered the yard through the backdoor in the home, chasing Mia, who was steps ahead.

"Can we paint the magnolias now?" Mia interrupted energetically.

"It went well, I think," Blair answered calmly. Then unable to contain her excitement, she suddenly erupted, giddily saying, "They sold! So – yeah, it went well!"

Mia stood frozen in place in the middle of the backyard, staring at Blair as she waited patiently for a response to her own question. When Blair's eyes finally caught hers, the eight-year-old's eagerness was nearly oozing from her face. Calmly, Blair looked at her and gently answered, "It's your mom's house, Mia – we need her permission before we just start painting all over it."

Bell laughed at her attempt to calm the child, and instead, kneeled down beside her as she said, "See – even Blair asks for permission before painting on the house. She doesn't just go drawing or painting on mommy's walls – or doors – without permission. Does that make sense, Mia?"

The young girl nodded curtly, saying, "I just wanted to be an artist – can we paint the door now?"

"Not without painting clothes! Go inside and change really quickly," Bell responded with a laugh. Then, attempting to return to the previous conversation, Bell looked at her quizzically and asked again, "So, you sold them? All of them?"

"Yes! Some fancy dressed people - a lady and a man bought all three of them – all at once!" Blair exclaimed joyously.

As a big smile spread across Bell's face, she gave her a hug and squeezed her tightly, saying, "Oh honey, I'm so proud of you. I only wish your mother was here to share this moment with us."

"I'll write her and tell her ALL about it; I'm sure she'll be excited to hear," Blair answered, examining Bell's reaction. For a moment, she wondered if Bell understood how much seeing her paintings sold meant to her. She didn't want to put the Andover's in a precarious position, should her circumventing the authorized payment methods be discovered. At the same time, she knew she could paint others that would sell as well. At some point, maybe she could even be completely independent and not have to count on the Andovers for a place to live. After a long silence between them, she asked, "So you're good with this, then?"

Bell nodded somewhat hesitantly, "Just so long as trouble stays away... you have my support. But I mean that – don't get caught up in trouble like your parents did... Don't bring trouble our way, and all is well."

"Thank you," Blair said with a sigh of relief. "I'll drop by Sweeny's tomorrow and find out how well we did."

"You didn't set a price?" Bell asked, somewhat confused.

"No – I didn't know what I should ask for them," Blair responded. "Tony didn't have a clue, so we agreed to see what someone would offer – "

"Oh Blair," Bell answered dismayed. "That old crook Tony could tell you ANYTHING – you'd have no way to know what they actually sold for!"

Blair shrugged her shoulders in response, "I don't have a lot of options... I guess I just have to trust that he'll be honest and fair with me."

"Honest and fair? Blair, if I learned anything in your mom's class, it was that people are generally dishonest and unfair whenever it benefits them. I don't know why Tony, of all people, would be any different," she said condescendingly. Then in a frustrated exhale she added, "It's really none of my business – I'm proud of you. You sold your work! We should get a bottle of wine to celebrate!"

"Maybe after we paint this door," Blair laughed. "If we don't get some magnolias on this thing – and quickly – I don't think either of us will ever hear the end of it!"

"Oh, she's been obsessed with them lately!" Bell chuckled. Then, placing her hand on Blair's shoulder, she said, "Let's paint the door. Heck, it'll probably increase the property values once you're a world-renowned artist!"

"I'm not sure they let the children of dissidents become world-famous artists, but I appreciate the vote of confidence," Blair laughed. "And to be fair, Mia's right – that door could use with a touch of personality. What good is having a bright blue cottage if you don't have an obnoxiously cheerful front door?"

Within the hour, Bell had opened a bottle of white wine, while Mia impatiently listened with brush in hand as Blair lectured on composition and color scheme. She then mapped out the door that would serve as their canvas in a grid-like pattern with tape, ensuring the design would read well from across the yard. Using a pencil, she outlined the image of the oversized magnolias flowing down the door, leaving just enough of the door's original orange color for contrast. It took some time, which was prolonged by Mia repeatedly asking if she could start already. But after careful planning and preparation, soon enough, bristles of the paint brushes graced the wooden door in swirls of warms–whites with creamy undertones.

~ 2 ~

"**M**om – MOM! Listen - there's nothing wrong with your feed – I'm almost one-hundred percent certain," he bellowed into the emptiness of his kitchen.

"Oh, but there is, Jaxson! It's never acted like this before!" the elderly woman replied sternly through the link that connected their feeds. "I think I've been hacked!"

"Mom – that's not possible," he replied, exasperated at having to once again explain technology to her. "I've told you before - your lenses constantly scan your retinas – it's a biometric authentication method. There's no known way to hack someone's feed - like globally – it's not a thing!"

"They said the same thing about crypto back in my day – it's a 'decentralized blockchain algorithm based on nonfungible encryptions and it can't be hacked'," his mother answered indignantly. "And we all know how that ended."

"Mom – I'm going to go now. If you think there's a problem with your feed, maybe check in with your caseworker at the Department of Connectivity to see if you're eligible for an update – ok? I'm going now," he responded.

"Isn't there someone I can pay to scoot to the head of the line? Can't Henry make a call to one of his attorney friends?" the elderly woman stammered as the link between their feeds terminated with Jax's blink.

Following the call with his mother, he returned to making breakfast, a soy-egg omelet.

"Guaranteed to be the best tasting synthetic egg product available!" he read aloud from the label. "How do you guarantee taste?"

A light blinking in the corner of his scroll alerted him to yet another incoming call, but this time, it was from a friend. It took him a second to put away the cardboard carton containing the soy-based egg product as he looked for a utensil he would use to flip the omelet once it was ready. As he did, he simultaneously moved his focus diagonally to answer the incoming call, exclaiming, "PARKER! How's it going?"

"Bro, you know how I was telling you my wife's sister was in town, and I was being dragged to that kitschy art fair at St. Charles?" the man said expectantly.

"Yeah... sounds like you survived..." he replied with a laugh.

"Not gonna lie, it was touch and go there for a minute... they were bickering a bit, and her sister kept wandering off... rough," Parker said.

"So you called me to tell me about how horrible your sister-in-law is? Is she cute?" Jax laughed.

"No, I got the better of the two – and no, that's not... Wait, are you looking again? What happened with what's her name?" Parker asked abruptly.

"Eh... I dunno. Just kinda vapid, I guess. Cute, but no taste for art. That woman would have scoffed at Van Gogh but swooned over Kincaid... Just didn't work for me," Jax said as he focused on prying the corners of the omelet in the pan before him to check if it was ready to flip.

"Well, you can't expect all of us to be experts, Jax. That's your thing. I thought she was pretty hot – just don't tell my wife," Parker joked quietly. "Speaking of art and my wife – she fell in love with some paintings at that art fair thing..."

"Parker – I want to remind you how your best friend runs an art gallery. Me - I am that friend," Jax scolded playfully.

"I understand," Parker answered. "Noted."

"Okay – so tell me, why are you letting your wife buy garbage instead of REAL art? Is it because you like throwing all of that IT money away?" he asked. "Because if it is, I can get you a deal on a Caldo or two…"

"Well…I mean… these are actually pretty good," Parker answered, somewhat apologetically. "Hey, I'm no expert, clearly. But Jaxy - there's some talent here… You know I don't get mushy-feely about this stuff, but there's something cool about these… they feel kinda vintage – like I dunno, something from back in the golden age before the internet or something… You could say it better – or at least accurately, I know. Something about these…I just… get it."

Jax groaned loudly at the realization that work would be further interrupting his breakfast. He then flipped the omelet, whether ready or not to buy himself enough time as he answered, "Fine - let me take a look – send them across."

Seconds later, images of three paintings appeared across Jax's feed. All three were local attractions, a prosaic and expectedly dull subject matter. Yet, as he enlarged the image, the brushstrokes and layering the artist used were surprisingly sophisticated. More impressive, the artist's style was beautiful, reminiscent of classic artists that had been famous in the late 19th century up until the middle of the 20th century. There was a certain historic quality to them, albeit with a more modern composition that flowed perfectly, magnifying the illustrative quality. Even with the subjects that had been chosen, the artist had made an intentional, sophisticated decision to focus on a single, ornate quality or perspective rather than trying to cram everything into the scene. Each piece had a sort of intimacy to them, a hidden seductive quality that focused in on a singular, recognizable element of the well-known locations. They were familiar but still new, an exciting, innovative perspective. Whoever had painted them was clearly talented; what stuck him as odd was the notion that someone with this skill set would hock their work for tourists at a suburban art fair.

"See what I mean?" Parker asked after Jax remained silent for several minutes.

"Oh... you really weren't kidding. I'm... I'm actually a little surprised," Jax responded with a laugh. "Who'd you say the artist was?"

"That's the thing – we don't know. They're all unsigned. We ran into them outside of this small grocery store called Swindles or Swearingtons or something. Guy who ran the place was kinda gross and kept going on about it being the oldest Irish-Italian store in the country – like that's a thing in demand," Parker laughed. "Anyway, when I asked him about the artist, he became a little nervous... wouldn't say exactly who painted them."

"Well, what did he take you for?" Jax answered. "How bad?"

"Fifty-thou," Parker answered.

"Each? For this quality... at a local art fair – that's a steal. Frankly, I'd say you scored some really lovely pieces for the price of a nice dinner out! Good find, bro!" Jax responded.

"No, no – fifty-thou for all three," Parker exclaimed.

"Oh, you fleeced him! You bastard!" Jax laughed loudly. "The canvas and paint alone would have cost about half of that!"

"I mean, I didn't mean to low ball him, but I didn't want to spend too much for some unknown – you'd never let me hear the end of it," Parker answered. "I figured for fifty-thousand, if she hangs it up in the basement for a year, I'm good with it. Hell, I might even hang the one of the ballpark in my office."

"What was the name of that store again? I might drop in and make some inquiries. Honestly, I'm sure this kind of kitsch sells well to tourists, but it's peanuts compared to what they could be making. If the artist has some other pieces, there could be some decent money to be made. Especially if they're undervaluing their work," Jax asked as he continued scrutinizing the images in his feed.

"Let me check my transaction history – should have the name of the place," Parker said, somewhat annoyed by the hassle of having to open another link in his feed. Then a second later he said, "Sweeny's Irish-Italian Corner Market... it's off Tompkins."

"Sweeny's... Alright. I'll check it out – hey, I appreciate you, bro-seph," Jax answered with a laugh.

"My brother. Bro-venor of the State of Missouri. Saint Bro-seph! Appreciate me more by taking me next time you go to the stadium – I know you still got those good-good season tickets," Parker chuckled suggestively.

"You got it, bro-ski. Been a while since we saw the birds together... Wait a minute – you manage AI app design for one of the largest feed contributors in the city – you're telling me you can't afford tickets?" Jax laughed.

"Not them old-money, family-heritage season ticket kind of tickets, Señor Bro-sueño. That's what I've got you for!" Parker emphasized.

Jax rolled his eyes before answering, "Fine... Although, I must say, you've gotten awfully particular in your old age."

"Bruh – I'm thirty-two. Which means I'm mature enough to enjoy the finer things in life," Parker answered, before adding, "Peace out, hommie."

Finally able to finish making his breakfast, Jax removed the now overcooked soy omelet, topping it with both spinach and fake-bacon, another flavored crumble that guaranteed all the flavor of real, albeit illegal, animal products. As he worked, he searched the threads within his feed until he located as much information about the small market his friend had spoken of. Then after identifying the route, he used the feed to order a vehicle for pickup, scheduling it to arrive after he had finished breakfast and dressed for the day – his lenses could calculate his daily average and project the time better than he could, anyway. The integrated AI based system served the role of a personal assistant,

studying people's patterns and habits besides their role in transactions, searching for information, and communication. The flaw-
lessness of the small lenses was so accurate that later, when he
took longer shaving than normal, it caused no delay in the arrival
of the automated vehicle. By the time he exited the front doors
of the high-rise that held his loft suite, the vehicle simply pulled
up next to the curb at the entrance. It was complete efficiency,
which was likely the reason the resistance to eliminating private
vehicle ownership dissipated so quickly. Automated vehicles were
cheaper, faster, and usefully intuitive.

After the rear door of the vehicle opened, he hopped into the
backseat as he had thousands of times before. Of course, his destination had already been sent through the feed, so there was
no need for communicating his intentions. The system within
the machine would simply debit his account using the preferred
method that was linked to his lenses, which he would confirm with
a simple blink-blink when he arrived.

As the ride to St. Charles began, geographically located advertisements associated with his location began populating in his
feed, which over the years he had simply learned to ignore. While
a nuisance, it was commonly believed that the revenue from the
advertisements helped to subsidize the government's cost for
standardizing transit. Most people had simply learned to ignore
the adds that appeared as he had. Those who preferred not to look
through the semi-transparent ads could always close their eyes
until they had passed. And once the initial advertisements associated with ride-share had passed, the remainder of the trip would
only be interrupted every ten minutes with a 30-second clip that
were mostly associated with various points of interests, restaurants, and businesses that had paid for promotion in proximity to
the changing location.

When they finally entered the historic district of St. Charles, a
particularly garish ad appeared promoting a swanky, Italian fine-

dining experience. The ad had clearly pulled from the name of his destination, an Irish-Italian market, but in theory, advertisers were not supposed to have access to privately held destinations. Somehow, the feed simply knew, no matter the constraints that were put in place to limit it. With no interest in fine dining, Jax closed his eyes and rested until the vehicle had come to a stop in front of a small brick building, the front of which was adored with a sign that read "Sweeny's" diagonally over the entrance.

As Jax exited the vehicle and blinked confirmation for the cost, a separate message was communicated, asking him what percentage of the fare he would prefer to leave as a tip.

"Ugh," Jax groaned loudly. The tipping culture for AI powered services had only recently been introduced in some areas, especially heavily frequented tourist areas. And while ten percent was reportedly customary, the idea of paying above the standard rate to a driverless vehicle struck him as odd. Then, adding to the injury, he was asked to rate the quality of the experience, another nostalgic holdover from a bygone era when ordinary people piloted vehicles along inefficient routes at varying speeds.

Jax entered Sweeny's after completing the rating ordeal and was greeted by the ring of a metal bell above the door — something he had not seen since he was a child. The old shop looked like a time capsule, something he wasn't sure existed anymore. The floors were black-and-white checkered tile, and the walls held old newspaper clippings from back when media still used paper to communicate newsworthy stories. As he began wandering aimlessly around the store, he casually looked at the various groceries and products it carried. There was no attendant behind the counter, but a checkout kiosk was also missing. There had to be another person around her somewhere, and Parker had even said as much. In most modern stores, the lack of personnel would not have been unusual, as any items he wanted to purchase could simply be scanned and paid for via lenses. But this old shop was clearly not automated; it obviously still relied on a personal touch, a quaint but odd idea that felt out of place and time. For his purposes that morning, that human touch was something that would serve his purpose well, if it was reliable. He had no need to physically purchase and carry home groceries, even the mysterious Irish-Italian kind.

At last, a rather robust older gentleman exited the back area of the store and noticed his arrival. The man greeted him saying, "Sorry, I must have missed the bell - Welcome to Sweeny's – if you have any questions, please don't hesitate to ask. We've been family owned for forty years!"

"Thanks – I'll let you know," he answered. Of course, Jax's feed could provide far more accurate evaluations of any products than the old man could, including user reviews generated globally and price comparisons between this store and what could be purchased and delivered directly through his lenses. Nevertheless, the proprietor's welcome gave him a glint of hope that some small talk might be the path forward he was looking for.

"I heard there was some sort of festival or fair that was held this last weekend," Jax mentioned casually.

"Yes, the St. Charles art market is held on the second Saturday of the month, Spring to Fall, so long as the weather's nice – thinking about checking it out at some point?" the old man asked.

"Oh, no – not personally. A friend of mine came by is all. He was raving about this little Irish-Italian store he found – said I had to come by and see it myself. 'Best Irish-Italian market I've ever seen,' he said. Nothing beats the real thing, am I right?" Jax said with a charming smile.

"That's why we're still around after all these years!" Tony answered proudly. "I keep telling my kids, some people just prefer doing things in person – being personable. Not everything needs to be from a thread or a scroll; sometimes it's nice to just be people around people. You know what I mean? I'm old-fashioned, I guess;

I just miss the days when we used to have to hunt a little for that right jar of balsamic — you know what I mean?"

"Quality is worth the effort," Jax said, nodding in agreement. "So, my friend also said you had some art for sale?"

"Oh that – hey, is your buddy the guy who bought the paintings? They sure were great; I gave him a good deal too," the old man answered, pointing his finger at Jax for emphasis as he spoke.

"That's what I heard! He sent images of them to my feed; I was kind of hoping there might be others I could buy – I was a little jealous, I must say," Jax said, trying to not show too much eagerness.

"Not right now, unfortunately. But next month, I'm sure she'll have others ready to go. After the last ones sold so well, I think we're going to make it a regular thing... I'm Tony, by the way," the old man said as he extended his hand.

"Jaxson," he answered, taking the old man's rough hand in his. "Good to meet you, sir."

"Listen... if you uh... if you have any requests... something you'd like to see maybe? Union Station... or that fancy greenhouse over at Forest Park... the one that's all glass – I forget the name..." the old man said, rambling a bit as he searched his lenses.

"The Jewel Box. I believe it's called," Jax said, nodding helpfully.

"Yeah, that's the one! It's a pretty spot – maybe it'd make a nice painting to hang on your wall? I know the artist – I could ask her," Tony said with a smile.

"Oh, you know her? Well, could I talk to her directly?" Jax asked suddenly. "If you'll pass me her info, I could reach out to her directly – "

"Sorry, sir – she's uh... she's a real private type," Tony interrupted, rather defensively. He then explained, "That's why she's started selling her work through the store, see? She's uh... well, she's not one for the spotlight."

"I see… that's a shame," Jax said, realizing he may have pushed too hard and there was a real danger his trip all the way out to St. Charles may have been a total waste. "I'll tell you what, Tony – I'll send over my information… you should have it now. And if you'd pass that along to the artist, maybe she might decide to reach out if she's interested?"

"Got it – and yeah, I can pass it along," Tony answered with a smile. "Now, if there's anything else I might help you with?"

"Honestly, you've got a lot of really tasty looking Irish-Italian offerings… I'm not sure where to start. I'll confess, I mostly came out here to see about the artist, but I could probably be tempted with some specialty of some kind," Jax answered, trying not to dissuade the man from helping him further.

Tony frowned a bit, but then held up his finger, signaling Jax should wait but a moment. Within seconds, Tony disappeared to the far end of the store, and when he returned, he carried with him a rolled Italian pastry filled with a sort of cream. "The cream in this cannoli is made with real cream… from a cow — none of that fake nut stuff," he said proudly as he handed it to the man. "On the house – if you like it, you know where we are – you come back and order them by the dozen!"

Jax couldn't help but smile at the charm and hospitality of the old man, and took the pastry, saying, "Well, thank you – that's very kind."

The bell at the store's entrance rang the announcement of another customer as Jax said goodbye to depart. As he turned toward the entrance, a stunning, twenty-something redheaded woman caught his attention, having triggered the store's antique alarm upon entering the shop. She too appeared to be in a hurry, as she failed to see him turning the corner of the aisle, nearly knocking him over as she mumbled, "Oh, sorry!" before continuing on with her own business. While she captured his attention briefly, his thoughts quickly returned to the small pastry he had been gifted, fixated on how delectable it looked and eager to indulge as he continued back through the entrance. Real cream was an odd thing to find at such an unimportant, obscure store. He wondered at once where the man had been able to source real cream and what would happen if they were caught. Perhaps no one would care, he considered.

Within a few seconds, the automated vehicle was in front of the store, and Jax began his trip to work, a destination inferred from his lenses based on the time of day and his normal routine. When he reached the gallery, he would no doubt have to explain the adventure he had undertaken that morning to Bruce, his assistant. Owning a premiere art gallery had perks in a city that had recently become famous for the renaissance that had transformed it into a new cultural and commercial hub. Aside from appointments with clients or shows at the gallery, he had the freedom and revenue to operate, however he pleased.

It took half an hour for the ride-share to deliver Jax to the nineteenth century, two-story brick building that housed the Crush gallery. Located in the Central West End, Crush had become a sort of hallmark or centerpiece of the swanky, up-scale St. Louis neighborhood, known for its old money, old mansions, and affluence. To Jax, it was simply where he had grown up; it was home.

As he passed through the entrance to the gallery, his assistant smiled awkwardly rather than greeting him. In a tone reflecting his obvious annoyance, he then announced, "Caldo is waiting for you – in your office. I told him you had been unavoidably detained."

Jax was immediately confused, furrowing his brow as he blinked through the calendar attached to his feed. He had been certain there were no scheduled appointments for the morning. After confirming his calendar was clear, he responded, "Thank you, Bruce – Did Caldo happen to mention why he decided to drop by?"

Bruce forced a fake smile as he answered, "He said something about 'Always being welcome as the top grossing artist in the Midwest' or something along those lines."

Jax rolled his eyes and said, "Great. Of course he is welcome... I'm not sure calling ahead is a big ask, but... it's fine – thank you for making sure that he was comfortable while he waited."

"I was half-tempted to spike his coffee with drain cleaner," Bruce muttered quietly, blinking his way back into the feed.

Jax did his best to contain the urge to laugh as he glared at his assistant knowingly and shook his head. "I appreciate your self-control," he whispered back to the man.

The inside of the gallery looked the part of a fine art museum hidden within an urban loft; its industrial, understated feeling evoked an elevated, opulent ambiance, with just a hint of a hidden grittiness, fitting for St. Louis. Those who frequented the gallery came to be seen. They wanted to be associated with the type of money that was required to be known within the city's art-scene. They wanted edginess and exclusivity. But Jax understood the real culprit of his success was simply a matter of the wealthy patrons competing for the right to brag about owning the next 'it thing'. The fortunes they spent for this privilege set them apart from those who worked for their wealth; the money often felt meaningless to them compared to the reputation.

Caldo had once been that 'it thing', but more recently, the value of his work had plummeted along with demand; half of the old mansions in the Central West End and Clayton had an original Caldo. His artwork was in New York, Dallas, Chicago, and Los Angeles as well, but in St. Louis, there had always been a greater demand, something akin to supporting the local underdog. However, that façade only worked when the local was still an underdog; Caldo had made generational wealth from his paintings, which had been exclusively sold through Crush. As his popularity waned, many of his early patrons had recently started selling their originals at auction to the suburbs, who were no less concerned with flaunting luxuries, but lacked the discernment to remain truly current in the art scene. Jax took the change in the market as a sign his audience was searching for something new. In a way, it was simply the pattern that evolved when the hysteria exceeded the fundamental talent. While Caldo had made his gallery massive profits over his run in popularity, Jax had long suspected the trend would come to an end once people became bored and owning a Caldo piece was no longer exclusive.

As Jax made his way up the shiny, bright-orange painted steel staircase that led to his office, he scrolled through the sales data in his feed to access the latest figures for the artist. Unexpected visits from artists the gallery partnered with were rare, but when they occurred, it was never for the sake of discussing art – it was always about the money.

When he reached the top of the stairs, he noticed Caldo had seated himself on the large, leather sofa that sat center in the open-air office level. Unsurprisingly, the artist was occupying himself by applying a liquid from a small, glass dropper into his eye that Jax instantly assumed must be Plush, an illegal, feed-altering hallucinogenic liquid that was said to make one's scrolling surreal and vivid. Ignoring the indiscretion, Jax greeted him, saying, "Caldo – always great to see you – I wish you would have let me know you were stopping by. I would have prepared some catering or entertainment for you – we could have invited some of your followers..."

"No, no – Jaxson. I am but a humble artist, but thank you," the short and portly man wearing a rough spun tunic answered as he began blinking rapidly to spread the drug across the full surface of his eye. He then began shifting around awkwardly on the couch as he smoothed his long, bushy beard until he had made himself comfortable.

"Well... Caldo... what brings you by Crush today?" Jax asked, getting straight to the point for fear of other clients may assume the gallery was complicit in his illicit activity.

"Jaxson – don't be dull. I have come seeking answers! What does Crush intend to do about this mess we have found ourselves in?" the artists asked. Then showing evidence that the chemicals hit his bloodstream, he began blinking wildly through his feed, suddenly distracted by the sensory inundation that was flooding across lenses.

"What... um... what mess are you referring to, friend?" Jax replied politely.

"Jaxson... Jaxy-Jax-Jax – you clever rascal! Now stop it – I mean, go on. I love these games we play! But stop!" Caldo answered as he careened further into a state of borderline confusion.

Jax sat quietly for a moment, studying the man. He could remember when Michael Caldo had first visited his gallery several years before. The man sitting in his office had been a carpenter, who was painting on the side. When he first saw Caldo's work, he was unimpressed. It lacked refinement and mastery of basic techniques that even the local art majors could achieve. Despite the technical deficiencies, it *did* have a certain dark quality about it he knew would be appealing to some with the right marketing.

Compositionally, the subjects of Caldo's paintings were mostly portraits of unknown, average looking people, but their faces unanimously reflected a distinguishable expression of pain, torment, or rage. They were disturbing in an intriguing way, and after some consideration, Jax decided the gallery would carry a few pieces on a trial-basis. The anguish in the art showed through the work, and it carried an odd authenticity. After some careful marketing and several positive reviews from notable critics, a few of his earlier pieces sold in the thirty-million-dollar range. Within a year, things really took off, with one zealous critic calling him "The greatest post-modernist since that fellow from Mágala in the

1970s." The dozen or so pieces that sold thereafter commanded prices ten times his earlier works.

"Caldo, my friend... I am but a humble servant of your vision. Crush is completely dedicated to ensuring the offers for your work are consistent with the demand. That being said, I think we should both understand a certain ebb and flow to these things is normal," Jax said, attempting to help the drug-induced artist understand the reality of his situation.

"Of course. Sure-sure-sure. I only wonder if perhaps expanding the availability of my work might help ebb that demand. Or flow it. Or something," Caldo mumbled nearly indiscernibly, as slumped back onto the couch cushion and began staring blankly at the ceiling.

"If that is what you want, Caldo, I would have to speak with my legal team – it has been so long, I don't remember all the particulars of the contract. But I'm sure we could come to some kind of arrangement... I would expect some sort of settlement where you could buy-back the rights to distribute your work. Then you could sell those rights to whomever you'd like. Is that what you have in mind?" Jax asked.

"Oh, Jaxson – I hate that it comes to money. I don't want any animosity between friends!" Caldo sighed wistfully as he blinked blindly at the ceiling as his feed swirled and images twisted.

"Of course, not – Caldo. Of course not," Jax replied carefully. He then added, "But if you no longer believe Crush is the best representative for selling your work, I want you to do what you think is best for you."

"It's just that... Well, Crush is so small! Exclusive, but small. I'm just thinking of a bigger, wider audience," the artist answered as he stared off into the void, fixated on the patterns in the tiles that decorated the ceiling. "And I don't want to hurt your gallery, Jaxson – I just think it is time my work is given wings so it can fly about... flapping gracefully into the hellscape that is people's homes. I hope you understand."

"If that is your vision, Caldo – I think you should follow it. I would just need to speak with Counsel – they could reach out –"

"Thirty mil," Caldo said abruptly. "That is what I am willing to offer you for the distribution rights to my work... I need not remind you it is MY work, of course. And I don't want to part ways angrily."

Jax thought for a moment, considering what it would take to get the man out of his office. Thirty million was a fraction of the commission the gallery had made as the exclusive dealer for his work, but with revenue generating, it would likely be generous in hindsight. If Jax had any belief the artist's work would continue selling, he might have hesitated. Instead, he simply said, "For you, my friend – of course. Thirty-mil it is. As soon as the funds have transferred, I'll have my legal team draw something up."

"Oh goody," Caldo replied as his gaze suddenly snapped back from the ceiling toward Jax, who was still seated across from him. "I think it's for the best, my dear friend."

With that, the short, portly man attempted to lift himself from the deep leather sofa he had sunken into. It took some effort and several attempts before he once again found his feet. Then he blinked several times into his feed and pressed his thumb against a metallic bracelet he wore on his left hand.

"There," he said. "All better – the funds will be transferred through my dub account, of course."

Jaxson nodded uneasily, not sure of how to respond. As the man was already quite intoxicated, he thought it best not to argue.

These dub accounts had a reputation as being used by people who wanted to pay for controversial or illicit goods that required privacy to avoid law enforcement monitoring.

"Of course," Jax responded hesitantly, masking his frustration. "I'll make sure that my legal team records the payment as coming from you in the contract changes. That way, there's no question about it later. When everything is ready to go, I'll link over a copy of the new contract for your records."

By the time Jax finished speaking, Caldo was already stumbling down the bright-orange metal staircase and back into the gallery.

$$\sim 3 \sim$$

"**I**s this the one... the special commission?" Bell asked as she looked over the nearly completed painting still sitting on the easel.

"Yup – nearly there," Blair replied, without turning around.

"It looks..." Blair interjected as she looked over the work. "Well... different."

"Different bad?" Blair said, as she finally turned away from the canvas.

"Oh, gosh-no. Good different. I mean, it's still you, obviously. That way that you see things. It's just... is it recognizable for tourists?" Bell responded, "I wouldn't say anyone particular mansion is a real calling card of St. Louis. I mean, there are dozens of them throughout the city. Why this one?"

"I'm not too sure – I guess it's recognizable to someone," Blair replied, completely focused on finishing her work as she removed a small, fine-tipped paintbrush from the front pocket of her paint stained overalls. "I had to ride all the way to the Central West End to study it a few days ago. It was a pain. But I suppose it's a pretty house. And it's what he asked for."

"He... meaning the mystery man that randomly walked into Sweeny's and coordinated a commissioned piece through Tony? And it just so happens he wanted you to paint a house – just a house. You understand how absurd that sounds, right?" Bell said rhetorically.

Blair turned toward her with a goofy smile and shimmied her shoulders a bit as she added, "It's like one of those old spy novels, right? So exciting."

"If by exciting you mean entrapping – then yes. Quite," Bell laughed. "Just be careful, Squirt. Tony exploiting your talent is bad enough... If this is some scheme... I just don't want you to get caught up, is all," Bell said as she moved closer to Blair and put her hand on the artist's shoulder.

"We got a few weeks of groceries out of those first ones... after Tony's cut and taxes. He said we'd get at least one-hundred thousand for this piece alone," Blair replied as she continued adding highlights with the bristles of a fine tipped brush.

"And what's Tony's cut this time? Same deal?" Bell asked. "I know it's not my business – I... I just know how much time and energy you put into these. And then there's all the random jobs you do to trade for the materials to even make them. I just don't want you selling yourself short."

Blair set her paintbrush down for a moment and looked at the woman who had cared for her and watched over her for the last few years. She knew Bell only wanted what was best for her, but if Bell had it her way, Blair would simply give in, get lensed, and go about her life. And she wasn't about to give in – not after all that had happened to her parents. Certainly not after the years she had spent in placement homes, simply trying to survive. She was determined to resist giving in, to find a way – no matter how difficult it would be.

"What would you have me do, Bell? Other than some sort of unconditional surrender – what would you have me do?" Blair asked.

"Well, maybe stop working with these shady, gray-market types like Tony? Maybe there's some way you could sell your work directly to people that we haven't thought of?" Bell said as she searched for answers.

"And the moment they go to pay me – and I'm not lensed – it's the same old story. Even being accused of trying to accept payment outside of the feed is enough to get unwanted attention – you know that. Frankly, there aren't a lot of people out there willing to exchange artwork for food and clothing – that's why we need Tony," Blair answered, returning to the same trail they had traveled down a dozen times in the month that had passed since the art fair. "I know it's not great. And I know you and Zay have been more than generous letting me stay here, or I'd be back on the streets. This is my way to contribute – it's the least I can do."

"Well, then don't do it – any of it. Don't do this for us – you are family. We have plenty," Bell insisted. "If you're going to paint, do it because it makes you happy. Do it because it's all you can think about – because it's who you are. And don't worry about trying to exchange your soul for a week's worth of soy nuggets and a bundle of kale!"

"So, just paint and fill this little cottage with my art?" Blair asked, searching for the answer.

"Well, our house too – probably Mrs. Marbury's and Mr. Addison's too... maybe even Tony's!" Bell laughed, then added, "Well, old Mrs. Marbury is about as blind as a bat now days – I'm not sure she'd really appreciate your work more than it just coming from you." Bell understood the absurdity of her argument even as it left her lips. While she knew the current arrangements that Blair had made were sufficient for the time being, she also knew they wouldn't last forever.

"I'm twenty-three, Bell. How long do you think I can talk people into letting me weed their gardens for some cucumbers? And I don't know of anyone willing to trade some pretty paintings for healthcare or a dental exam. Everything I own either came from a trade or a dumpster, but it can't last forever. And I'm content, for now – I am. I don't need much more. But my life only works because I'm relying on the generosity of the people I care about –

people who are connected to the feed so that I don't have to be. I can't – I can't ask any of you to support me forever," Blair replied emotionally, as her frustration began to take the shape of tears welling behind her eyes.

"Hey – hey, listen, Squirt," Bell said gently. "All of St. Chuck loves you; we have your back – we're going to figure it all out, eventually. I just haven't figured out how yet."

"YOU don't have to figure it out, Bell – although I appreciate you want to help," Blair said as she turned to give her friend a warm hug. "I'll figure it out. Maybe there's someone who'd trade art for like a trailer on some property in the country – I could be like a hip, artist-farmer type thing... I've already got the overalls!"

"Oh, that's a fantastic idea," Bell laughed. "The great artist-farmer, Blair Huxley! Get a painting along with your pumpkins!"

"We could get cool hats!" Blair said excitedly. "Big straw ones!"

"Ok... Ok... I get it. I'll leave you to your work – just let me know when you go down to Tony's?" Bell asked.

"So that you can tell him to stop exploiting me?" Blair asked. "Not a chance – you'll go in there like a steamroller and I'll be out of a job. Heck, I'll probably never be able to work with any of the other local shops again – that'd be super."

"Heaven forbid I ruin your relationship with the fine people running the local black market of goods and services outside of the feed," Bell replied stoically.

"Yes – truly. Heaven forbid it," Blair laughed, glaring at Bell. "They are useful, especially when you're trying to get your hands on vintage blues albums – I'm just saying."

"Stop - I don't want to know any more," Bell responded, holding up her hand. "I'll see you later... just be safe."

"Bye," Blair said before blowing a kiss toward her friend. She then turned her attention back toward the canvas on the easel.

She painted late into the afternoon until she reached a point where her eyes were tired from staring at her work. As tired as she was, she knew paintings came alive in the minutia; she just often forgot to blink while creating these details. In need of a break, Blair decided a walk down to the river would do her some good.

As she strolled down Monroe, she recalled how the homes looked so different in the summer or fall than they did in the spring. Each season of the year cast a different hue of light on the brick buildings. Sometimes they were pink, bright and cheerful. In the fall they changed to orange, peach, and burned tones of rust. And all the while, the buildings remained the same, orange brick construction that had held the test of time. It was only the light that changed, and the brick changed with it, while remaining timeless as it had always been. It was this observation that had influenced the mansion she was painting. Getting the light right for the time of year was critical. It needed to be accurate, and she had spent days obsessing to make sure it would be.

It didn't take long before she reached the river front on the far side of Main Street, which was home to a fantastic, easily accessible sculpture. The bronze piece just down the Katy Trail depicted Lewis and Clark from the Corps of Discover along with a large dog, who had joined them on their journey into the unexplored lands of the Louisiana Purchase. One man wore an absurdly large plumed hat and a military uniform; the other was ruggedly handsome, leaning forward on a bent knee. When she was younger, she had imagined meeting a man as handsome and courageous. She had dreamed of being whisked away to some exotic wilderness where none of the people had much use for modern technology, let alone lenses and the feed. As she matured, she realized she would be lucky to find such a loyal, loving dog. A life for those not connected to the constant feed could be lonely at times, but dogs never seemed to mind if you weren't distracted by the scrolls and threads.

By the time she began her short journey home, the sun had nearly set. With her eyes rested, she left the small park at the riverside and headed toward the sound of nightlife that was just starting in the bars and restaurants along Main Street. She would need to walk a few blocks down Main Street to reach Monroe, and while she typically avoided crowds, the Historic District of St. Charles was well lit and relatively safe compared to walking along the river alone. As she strolled down the distinct uneven brick street, she noticed the distillery had filled with patrons, and several bars were already overflowing their interiors as diners sipped ales on their patios. The liveliness of it all looked exciting, as she walked toward the revelry she had seen from afar dozens of times before. She never really wanted to be a part of it, necessarily. But she also longed to belong somewhere with people she could enjoy an evening with. Her cottage and simple life provided everything she needed, of course, but perhaps because of loneliness, she often felt like there was an entire world waiting to be explored, a world full of interesting people she would never get to meet without lenses. Fighting back against this feeling, these long walks down to the river had long ago helped her to find joy in the simple, small moments that were just hers. Loneliness was tough, but there was no one to make a mess of things. Then again, a little messiness might be a welcome change from solitude.

As she reached the end of the block at the corner of Main and Monroe to begin the walk home, she was suddenly startled by a large crash that rose from a nearby restaurant patio, introducing two men who were grappling with each other as they crashed out onto the street. Blair instinctively took steps back, attempting to avoid the chaos that was sure to follow, as two men began exchanging blows in front of the restaurant. The fight lasted only seconds, and in what felt like only seconds, a uniformed police officer intervened, barking commands at the men to get on the ground. When they ignored his warnings, the officer produced a small weapon from his duty belt, from which he fired what appeared to be electrified darts that struck first one man and then the other, sending them both forcefully to the ground, writhing in pain only a few feet away from her. She didn't know what to do, frozen in place as the fight unfolded, and then suddenly and surprisingly, the officer approached her rather than the two men that had been disabled. He looked directly at Blair and said, "You – stay put. I'm going to need a witness statement."

The officer's command was enough to cause Blair to panic. She had tirelessly worked to avoid attention, especially the attention of law enforcement. Despite the effort, she now found herself in the middle of a situation she hadn't even been involved in and wanted no part of. Still, there was little she could do but wait and comply. After several minutes, black boxes were placed on each of the men's hands, restraining their movement as they lay on the ground, groaning. Another officer then arrived and both of the men were forced into one of the patrol vehicles. She watched as the officers stoically went about their business, and she even considered for a moment whether it would be possible to slip away unnoticed. Out of fear of getting into more trouble, she stayed in place as ordered, trying to think of what she could say.

Once the officers had concluded with the two men, the first officer turned his attention back to Blair, still frozen in place on the sidewalk of Main Street.

"Could you share by sending your information over for the record," the Officer said, more demanding than asking.

"I'm sorry... I can't," Blair said apologetically.

"Oh, so it's going to be like that, huh? What, was one of those bozos your boyfriend or something?" he asked, annoyed by her resistance.

"No – nothing like that. I... I don't know either of them. And I'm happy to cooperate – I'll answer whatever questions you have," Blair said, shaking her head defensively.

"Then please, link me your record information – name, address, and identification number will be sufficient," the Officer responded.

"My name is Blair Huxley... I live at—" Blair tried to explain as the officer interrupted.

"Miss – I said send – not tell. I need an official record," the Officer said in a tone that revealed he was losing his patience.

"Well... I mean... I don't have an official record to send to you – I... I'm not connected to the feed!" she answered louder than she had intended as her own annoyance for a moment got the better of her.

The officer paused briefly, appearing to decide if she was telling the truth. She knew he'd find it suspicious. There was a common belief that the only people who took out their lenses were criminals so that the feed wouldn't have any record of their actions to be used against them. After staring for several seconds and numerous blinks as he searched facial recognition records within the feed, he finally answered, saying, "Miss, I'm going to need you to come with me."

"But... there's no law that says I have to be connected! I haven't done anything illegal – I wasn't involved in this fight!" Blair protested loudly, trying to contain her panic.

"Ma'am, you are being detained on suspicion of violating Section 574.010 of the Revised Missouri Statutes, Disorderly Conduct – now please place your hands behind your back and drop down to your knees so that I can apply restraints. If you resist, it will be an additional charge," the Officer said stoically.

"Wait, what? What did... How... how was I disturbing anything?" Blair stammered as tears poured out of her eyes. "I... I was just walking home!"

"Ma'am, if you resist, there will be additional charges. Now, please drop to your knees or I will use force to gain your compliance," the Officer answered as he reached toward the weapon he had used only minutes before on the two fighters.

Blair fell to her knees, sobbing, and placed her hands behind her back, signaling her compliance. Seconds later, the officer placed a small box over one hand and then the other. When both hands were in the box, she heard a click sound coming from the box, after which it filled with some kind foam that quickly dried around her hands, locking them into place behind her back. As Blair wept on her knees, onlookers stopped and stared. Their faces reflected a certain disgust reserved for villains, and Blair continued her protest through tears, "What have I done? What did I do?" Despite her pleas, her voice fell only on ears that had already found her guilty.

The officer then ran his hands around her waist and torso, searching for weapons or other contraband. When his hand landed on a hard object in her pocket, he must have thought he had found something of importance.

"Ma'am, do you have anything in your pockets that can prick me, poke me, or hurt me? Any drugs – weapons?" the officer asked.

"No – nothing!" Blair cried through her tears.

"Ma'am, I'm going to reach into your pocket to remove an object that my training and experience indicates may be a weapon. Are you certain there is nothing in your pockets that can injure me? If you are lying to me, there may be additional charges," he answered cooly.

"No – I don't even know what is in my pocket!" Blair sobbed, searching her mind confusedly for what might have been left in the pocket of her overalls when she left the house.

The gloved hand of the officer pressed firmly at the base of the pocket over her right thigh, and began pressing firmly in an upward direction, attempting to force the object within to dislodge. Moments later, the bristles of a paintbrush popped up over the seam of the pocket, revealing itself as the mysterious hazard that had caused such concern.

"I'm a painter," Blair said apologetically. "Sometimes I get a little scattered."

The officer remained silent as he removed the brush from her pocket and tossed it on the brick street next to her. He then continued his search until he was satisfied nothing important would be discovered.

After the longest few minutes of her life, a marked police vehicle stopped at their location, and the rear door opened. The officer then directed her into the vehicle, and as she entered, he fastened a harness around her chest until the clasp clicked and locked in place, securing her tightly to the seat. Then the vehicle departed.

When the driverless patrol car reached the station, it parked in front of the booking office, awaiting an officer that would retrieve her. Blair's tears had stopped at that point, replaced by anger at the circumstances she now faced. She had done everything she could to avoid this exact situation, but it wasn't enough. *How she could have fooled herself into thinking she could survive independently of the system*, she wondered. Her nightmare had at last arrived in an unexpected moment of terror, and she was once again alone.

Suddenly, the door of the vehicle opened to reveal another officer, who, after activating the latch on her harness, ordered her out of the vehicle. He then led Blair into a crowded room full of recent arrestees, who were sitting on long, metal benches around the room. Both of the men she witnessed fighting were there; the eye of one of them was swollen nearly shut. Others in the booking room were in similarly rough condition. Dark red blood leaked from the nose of another man. Still another was slumped over, still feeling the effects from a night of partying that ended early, as he dizzily slurred responses to the booking officer's questions.

Blair was directed to a steel bench of her own at the far end of the concrete walled room, where she remained seated for some time, waiting her turn. She watched the numbers turn on an old digital clock that had been placed on the wall many years before. It glowed with red numbers on a black rectangular background and blinked every time a number changed. The sight of the other prisoners only increased her anxiety at the situation she found herself in, and in an effort to remain as calm as possible, she fixed her eyes on the clock, counting as the minutes passed.

At last, a third officer finally came and retrieved her, escorting her first into a small sallyport where she was once again thoroughly searched. She felt humiliated as the female officer ran her hands along every curve of her body as she asked the same questions about drugs and weapons. The female officer escorted her from the sallyport into a large room where other officers were busy with others who had been recently arrested, but rather than being placed in a cell, the female officer walked Blair across the large room to a small office with a door that closed behind her. There, behind a desk, an ununiformed man sat with a tablet and several large screens. As she entered, he motioned to a chair opposite his desk, where the female officer guided her to sit. The female officer took hold of the box behind Bair's back, and after several seconds of awkward contorting, a click came from the box behind her back and the box was removed.

"Thank you, Martinez," the man behind the desk said as the female officer left the room.

Turning to Blair, he began speaking loudly and articulately, "My name is Officer J. Rawlins, St. Charles Police Department assigned to Booking and Inmate Processing. This interview is being recorded for the official record. Anything you say can and will be used against you in court; you have a right to representation. You also have a right to not answer these questions. Do you understand?"

"Yes," Blair answered, unsure of why she was being told she didn't have to answer when she was clearly expected to.

"Good. Feed thread sent over by Officer G. Jones, badge number 847, arresting officer... Officer Jones has indicated the unidentified suspect – that's you – was arrested due to a violation of section 507.010, Disturbing the Peace..." the officer continued aloud, as he recorded the information into the feed. He then looked directly at Blair and asked, "Officer Jones indicated you are not connected to the feed — is that correct?"

"No – I mean, yes, it is correct. No, I am not connected. I don't have lenses," Blair explained uncomfortably. In that moment, she realized she must have stopped crying at some point. The panic had subsided, and what had replaced it was only fear and anxiety coupled with a numbness and embarrassment at her plight.

"How's that even possible now days?" the booking officer muttered with a slight laugh as he continued his recording.

"My parents did not believe it was the right choice for me," Blair interjected abruptly. She had realized the comment was rhetorical, of course. But she felt like she needed to explain. She wasn't some lowlife; she had done nothing wrong. When the man looked in surprise at her explanation, she continued, "See, I was young when the first Blinks came out. My mom and dad were big believers in privacy; they didn't want some company scanning me constantly and gathering data about my habits and interests – tracking my movements. Now that I've grown up, I... Well, I tend to agree with them. It's a choice I've made,"

The man's eyes revealed he held a certain skepticism, or perhaps it was annoyance. After clicking his tongue against his teeth, he stoically said, "Huh... Well, I guess we will do this the old-fashioned way. Can you tell me your name and date of birth?"

"Blair Huxley, July twenty-second, Twenty-twenty-five," Blair responded.

"Standby..." the booking officer answered.

"Ah, here you are... Mother is Dr. Ayn Huxley, incarcerated for felony...seditious acts against the state. Also, felony Safe Speech

Act violations, promoting violence or dissident behavior... father is Dr. Franklin Huxley, deceased – father's record includes charges of felony SSA violations and felony... treason," the Officer said expressing surprise.

"He was never prosecuted," Blair answered defensively.

"Hmm," the man mouthed. "So, it sounds to me like baby-girl is following in their footsteps? Taking up the family business, so to speak?"

"Is that a question?" Blair asked, outraged by his accusation.

"Maybe – are you now or have you ever been involved with any group or groups that are attempting to overthrow the government?"

"No, of course not!" Blair answered, shaking her head defensively.

"Have you been engaged in any speech of any kind that promotes hate or extremism? Have you advocated for extremist views, or views that are encouraging negative or anti-government beliefs?"

"No," Blair said coldly. The answer came out of her mouth before she even considered how her paintings might be perceived. For a split second, she considered whether she had just lied to the man, but dismissed the thought as quickly as it had come.

The booking officer blinked as he stared through her, reviewing feed records as she waited. It took him several minutes of scanning before he spoke again, "Well... Officer Jones says that you refused to cooperate with his investigation into a physical altercation that took place at the corner of Monroe and Main – you refused to provide identification and then knowingly and unreasonably disturbed and alarmed restaurant patrons by making loud, bombastic and-or belligerent noises..." the Officer said argumentatively.

"I did not refuse to provide identification – I just couldn't send him the information through the feed because I am not connected! I don't have lenses. I told him I wasn't, but he wouldn't listen...

He just kept demanding I send over my identification record, but I couldn't!" Blair shouted defiantly.

"Hm," the booking officer grunted. "Well, you couldn't because you're not connected to the feed."

"Yeah – but that's not illegal," Blair answered.

"No, but conducting any business or transaction outside of the feed is – have you bought anything recently?" the officer asked, fishing for some kind of self-incriminating statement.

"No, sir – that WOULD be illegal," Blair retorted, trying to contain her annoyance.

"And how *exactly* do you... live?" the officer asked skeptically. "How can a person eat... pay bills... buy clothing... get a ride – how is it that you... do things? You...do those things, right? You're not a robot? You've got to eat."

"I mostly rely on help from friends," Blair answered truthfully. Saying it out loud only made her feel worse about her living circumstances, and at once her chest felt tight and hot with frustration as she said, "Look, I don't do business. I don't buy things. I don't get rides – I just live. I get by."

"Oh... of course you don't... Of course," the officer answered with an eye-roll, realizing the clumsy trap he set had failed. He then added, "Well, Disturbing the Peace is a misdemeanor – it carries a fine of fifty thousand dollars or three months' jail time. You'll be released shortly, pending a court date. There will be a hearing where you will be presented with charges, and you can tell it all to the judge. If you fail to appear on your court date, a felony warrant for failing to appear will be issued for your arrest. Do you understand?"

Blair nodded her head, but the officer appeared to ignore her response. Instead, he looked directly at her and said, "I need you to confirm you understand out loud – for the record."

"I understand," Blair answered angrily.

"Good. If you could select the acknowledgement in your – Oh, right. Um... wait just a second, he said. He then scrolled through his feed issuing some kind of command, as moments later an officer appeared with a small packet of papers. He laughed as he dropped the packet of papers on the desk, saying, "I didn't even know we had a printer anymore!"

The booking officer seated at the desk laughed in response as his colleague left the room. He then searched through the drawer in his desk until he produced a pen, which he handed to Blair to sign the documents. "We're about done here – is there someone I can call for you?" he asked.

Blair froze for a second, terrified by the thought she would be forced to ask Bell for help. She had tried to avoid attention; Bell wanted nothing to do with her beliefs and the way she chose to live. She respected Blair's decision and even empathized philosophically with her position, but she had been clear she did not want trouble brought to her family's door. *But what choice did she have?* she thought. Even if it means she would have to find somewhere else to live – she had no one else to call.

"Isabella Andover on 5th Street, St. Charles," Blair answered, fighting back tears that once again started filling her eyes.

The booking officer nodded as he searched for information on the Andover family within the feed. Having located it, he motioned for Blair to rise from the chair. He then connected with Bell, and as he walked Blair back to a bench within the booking office, he began explaining through the feed, "Mrs. Andover, this is Officer Rawlins with St. Charles Police Department – I have with me Blair Huxley, who has told us you might be willing to come pick her up... Yes, if you follow the signs to booking, then check-in at reception, we'll escort her out to you... Thank you."

Blair waited on a bench within the main booking area of the jail, hoping to hear news of Bells arrival any second. The officers in booking hardly seemed to notice she was there. Those who weren't busy searching arrestees in the sally port were joking about each other's spouses until the conversation turned to football and some sort of impending draft that Blair knew nothing about. The system was seamless, operating as a well-oiled machine. As she waited, another half-dozen people passed from the sallyport to the office, although most of them were then transferred to the small cells with metal doors within the booking area. It occurred to her she may have been the lucky one to even be going home, an odd sensation given the ordeal she had been through.

At last, an officer from reception entered the booking area and assertively called her name, "Blair Huxley?" When Blair raised her hand in response, the woman said, "This way."

She was then led down a corridor to an entrance lined with glass doors, behind which she could see Bell waiting impatiently. A buzzing sound at the door signaled it had been unlocked, as the woman from reception said simply, "You're free to leave."

Blair exited the jail to find Bell, obviously fighting back tears of her own. Bell took several steps toward her and simply wrapped her arms around her, saying, "Don't say anything – not here."

For several long moments, they simply held each other closely. After a long pause, Bell finally pulled away, nodding her head, and said, "Let's get you home."

An automated ride-share vehicle arrived a few seconds later, and both women entered the vehicle. They remained in complete silence until at last they reached the Andover house on 5th Street.

After they arrived, Bell walked with Blair toward the back cottage as she slowly removed the lenses from her eyes, placing them gently into a case she had kept in her pocket. She and Blair then sat down in chairs in front of the cottage, calmly and quietly in the warm air of the summer night.

"Want to tell me what happened?" Bell said gently.

Blair explained all that had transpired since she left the house, leaving out no details. At several points, she became tearful again, recalling the hands of the man running down her clothing and the humiliation she felt sitting in the room in booking, surrounded by the intoxicated and injured. She explained the charges that had been made against her, and handed Bell the small stack of papers she had been issued with her court date.

"Quite a fix you've found yourself in, Squirt," Bell replied sympathetically.

"I didn't do anything, Bell. You have to believe me," Blair answered apologetically.

"I know, B. I know... I'm not sure that it matters all that much in the end... But we'll get through this. I... I think one of the attorneys at Zay's firm could probably help. They don't really handle criminal stuff, of course. But maybe they know someone... Maybe if we go to the hearing and show that you're willing to fight the charges the DA will decide it's not worth it – with all the crime in St. Chuck and St. Lou I can't imagine they'll want to tie up the courts with something this stupid, especially how shaky it all is. But with your family's background, there could be some political pressure. It's hard to say," Bell said, trying to comfort her friend.

"I'm so, so sorry, Bell – I've tried to be invisible. I've tried to stay out of trouble - I've tried. I don't want to cause any attention to you or Zay – I know you guys have lives to live and an image that you have to maintain – I don't want to cause you any trouble," Blair cried tearfully but still angry at all that had transpired at the difficulty they were all now facing.

"Let's... not worry about all that right now. Let's talk with Zay and see what he says, and we'll go from there," Bell said quietly before adding, "Go get some sleep. Tomorrow's a new day with no mistakes; it will be better in the morning."

As Bell left and returned to the main house, Blair sat for a moment in her favorite wooden chair. It struck her as odd that only a short time before, she had sat in the same chair, relishing her uncomplicated life. In such a short time, everything felt turned upside down.

Then again, she thought, *maybe this wasn't such a big thing – maybe the abruptness of it all had simply scared her and she was being dramatic.*

She had been shaken thoroughly, having never been arrested before. If her mother was there, she was certain it wouldn't have been as dramatic. She could recall being told her mother had been arrested, although she was not there to witness it. She wondered if her mother had cried as she had. While it had been years since she had seen her in person, her memories of her mom were of strength and courage. She was never one to cower in front of the police; her entire career had been dedicated to speaking out against the injustice of the current political climate where rights had been reduced to meaningless words on paper. Blair couldn't imagine the mother she remembered sobbing as she had.

"She was a lion. She would have conducted herself with dignity," she whispered to herself.

It took her a few minutes to collect herself and regain control of her emotions. As she did, she determined in her heart this evening would be the last time she would cower to the police. If she was ever to be arrested again, she would not give them her tears – she would refuse to be weak.

Energized by her resolve, Blair found herself inside her cottage, safe and warm once again. She stood at her easel, and stared at the mostly completed painting of the choking eagle, still sitting in place. Something about the piece made her uncertain, and she wondered if setting it aside might help her think clearly. She needed to begin something new — something raw and powerful. With a cover placed over the eagle, Blair placed a new, large canvas atop the platform. An idea that had lived for so long in her head was finally ready to come to life. So, rather than sleep, she set herself to work.

~ 4 ~

"**G**ood morning, sir," Bruce said as Jax stumbled into the Crush gallery looking half-asleep and holding his morning coffee.

"Morning," Jax answered, attempting to mask his lack of caffeine with a cheerful smile. "Anything new on the calendar this morning?"

"Yes, actually. That um... curious fellow from the Italian market left a message saying the artist would be here at ten... I took the liberty of confirming this morning, based on your calendar," his assistant responded.

"Wait, what?" Jax answered confusedly as he began gulping his coffee aggressively.

"Oh... um... the message said something about the artist personally delivering the piece you commissioned, as per your request," Bruce answered, assuming Jax had simply made arrangements beforehand. He must have noticed the puzzled look on Jax's face as he quickly asked, "Was... that not something... I'm sorry, sir – did I overstep?"

"No – no, no – nothing like that. I asked this guy Tony about this local artist that had been selling pieces through his grocery store, and he was weird about providing more information. So, a few days later, I called and I sort of baited him with a commission of the Wadsworth Manor, saying I'd pay double if the artist personally delivered the piece to the gallery – I didn't think it would actually happen – the whole thing felt a bit off. He said something about how 'she wanted privacy' or something like that; I wonder what's changed," Jax replied with a shrug.

"He didn't provide any explanation, sir. He just confirmed she would deliver the work at ten; does that work for you?" Bruce asked, annoyed he had not been better informed on the situation.

"Ten is great – um... if you can move anything I have between then and lunch, that would help. I have a feeling I'm going to need to take my time with this one," Jax answered.

"Of course, sir," Bruce replied. "Also, the disclosures and releases for Caldo arrived yesterday afternoon while you were at the club with your parents. Would you like to look them over before we send them to the artist?"

"Sure, send them over now – I'll take a look before the thing at ten," Jax answered. Within seconds, the new legal documents from his attorneys appeared on his feed, and he began casually perusing the documents as he found his way up to his office on the upper level.

"In consideration of compensation since rendered," Jax read to himself as he set down his briefcase on the stark desk at the far end of the room. "...Releases exclusive rights to distribution and sales of all works attributed to Michael Caldo, hereinafter referred to as OWNER, to said OWNER, ..." he continued. "With transactional details to be recorded on behalf of OWNER by way of transfer from third-party account on behalf of OWNER..." he muttered as he continued through the contract.

It was as good as a safeguard against an audit as he was going to get, he thought. *It listed his name and the source of the payment. With the timing of the payment and the contract coinciding, it should be enough.*

With a review of the Caldo contract addendum complete, Jax began reviewing accounts and upcoming events. He had spent several weeks planning a gala-esque formal event that would feature several of the gallery's more prominent artists. There was work to be finished on the design of the invitations, but he was still unsure of what to name the event. His mother was intent on calling the gathering "A View at the Lou," while he was more inclined to call it "A Night with Your Crush." The decision needed to be made soon, as the event was about a month away. There were expensive bourbons that still needed to be ordered, invitations that needed to be printed, and a whole host of minor tasks that needed to be sorted out. While not much in the way of revenue generating, his parents enjoyed using the gallery as a pretense to display their cultural sophistication as well to mingle with the other socialites of the city. As they had financially backed the gallery's opening, these little favors were the price he paid for his family name and reputation remaining associated with the business.

At last, a notice came across the feed from Bruce indicating his ten o'clock appointment had arrived. Jax made his way down the orange metal staircase to greet his potential new client and immediately noticed two women wandering through the gallery. One was perhaps in her forties, with graying black hair she wore in a short, modern fashion; she was dressed in simple but professional business attire that she appeared comfortable in. The other was a young woman with long, deep-red hair that flowed effortlessly down her back. She wore a simple, floral-patterned sun-dress that appeared a bit thread-worn and outdated as it hung over her thin frame. But aside from her crude adornment, her striking, natural beauty was immediately noticeable to him, nearly intimidating. As the older of the two women walked carefully through the gallery, the younger of the two moved energetically, rushing enthusiastically from painting to painting. As she reached each new piece, her face radiated an excitement that at once filled the mostly empty gallery.

"Good morning," Jax said to them both as he reached the last few steps.

"Good morning," the woman with short, dark hair replied. The younger woman echoed her greeting, at once appearing altogether shy and out of place. *Maybe she felt embarrassed by her prior enthusiasm, as if she had been caught in an excitement thinking no one had noticed*, he thought.

"So – my apologies if this is a bit awkward, I suppose – I've been trying to find this artist that a friend of mine discovered through Mr. Tony. Um... Tony, who owns the um... Italian-Irish market in St. Charles, just off of 2nd, I believe... Are you... is that...?" Jax said, uncertain of which of the women he should be addressing.

The dark-haired woman then nudged the redhead, who acted momentarily embarrassed. She then extended her hand and smiled as she said, "I'm Blair."

"It's really nice to meet you, Blair. I'm really impressed by your work," Jax said, shaking her hand. "And this is?" he asked, tuning toward the other woman.

"Isabella Andover," Bell said, introducing herself as she shook his hand.

"Ah – your agent then?" Jax asked, still confused about who the second woman was.

"Oh – no...No, she's a friend... like family, really," Blair answered with an awkward smile.

"I see... Well, it's a pleasure to meet you both," Jax answered, still uncertain of why an artist had brought a friend along to their meeting. Then, gesturing to a canvas that had been covered in a sheet and laid against Bruce's desk, he asked, "And I'm guessing this is this the piece I asked for?"

"YES!" Blair said excitedly. "Would you like to see it now?"

"Um... Well, yes – but first, would you both like to come up to my office where we'll be more comfortable? You could bring your piece along, of course," Jax answered with a smile, trying to contain his amusement as her giddiness returned at the mention of her painting.

"That would be great – thank you," Bell interjected as Blair nodded in agreement.

Jax led the two women back up the orange-metal staircase toward the suite above, where he began explaining more about the gallery, the artists it featured, and its general *bona fides* within the community. Both Blair and Bell remained silent as they ascended the staircase. Whether they were intimidated or unimpressed, he couldn't say for certain. The gallery was designed to be impressive, but it could reasonably intimidate to those who were not used to more high-end businesses. She wouldn't have been the first artist to be featured at Crush, who came from a more modest background; several had been undiscovered, debut artists, where notable exceptions were made for truly impressive work.

As his introduction to the gallery concluded, Jax gestured toward the leather furniture in the office, insisting they make themselves comfortable. "Would you care for some sparkling wine, perhaps? Maybe something else? I make a mean mimosa."

"It's... ten in the morning," Bell answered on their behalf.

"Of course it is," Jax answered with a knowing smile. "Perhaps some coffee or tea then, if you'd prefer?"

"Some tea would be lovely," Blair answered for herself, then added, "And thank you."

"I'm fine, thank you," Bell said cooly. "I'm just here for moral support."

"Great," Jax answered. "I believe we have some matcha... some nice oolong... or there're some herbals, chamomile... is there a particular type you'd prefer?"

"Do you have anything British? I had lavender Earl Gray once, and I really liked it... I know that's a bit exotic... if not, any kind of black tea would be great," Blair answered.

"Um... I don't think so... We're more coffee drinkers around here. I think we might have some black tea – I'll ask Bruce to find you something. And you, Mrs. Andover?" he asked.

"I'll have whatever she's having," Bell said, trying not to be difficult.

After taking a second within his feed to request refreshments from Bruce, he seated himself across from Blair and said, "Bruce will be up in a moment with some tea... I just received a lovely order of Youpon Holly tea from Florida – it's light and delightful. He'll figure something out, I'm sure. Now, how about you show me the masterpiece you've created for me?"

Blair beamed with excitement as she carefully removed the cover from her canvas to reveal the intricate painting of an old, orange brick manor house hidden beneath. She then laid the work down on the glass table that sat between them, oriented so that it would face her would-be patron.

"Remarkable," Jax answered breathlessly. He took several minutes examining the composition and thoughtful use of color, contrast, and line evident in her painting. "Truly beautiful work, Blair."

The young redhead's smile grew so broad it was ready to break free from the confines of her delicate face. Her large, brown eyes were wild with excitement and hopefulness as she began explaining what she saw as the strengths of her painting.

"See, it's the brick for me. And the lighting... I've been obsessed with these old homes since I was just a girl – my mother used to take me into town, and we would walk the old streets and marvel at the homes that I was convinced changed colors depending on the time of year," she said, pointing at various aspects of the structure. "And these decorative facades – they're so romantic – the arches always make me feel like the people who built them were giving birth to the building – it's like they loved each brick into place and had to use mortar to keep them there."

Jax struggled to contain his amusement as he admired the work. She must have noticed his expression change, as she quickly added, "I'm sorry – that was... silly. I get carried away sometimes."

"It's beautiful – the work and the sentiment. I'll admit, I've seen this home a million times or more, and I never thought of it that way. You're stunning – your piece – it's marvelous," Jax said, blushing slightly at the slip.

Blair's face instantly blushed, nearing the shade of her red hair as she responded, "Thank you – I'm so happy you like it!"

"I love it – truly," he answered sincerely.

The awkwardness of his exposition was interrupted briefly as Bruce arrived with the tea he had requested. After serving the refreshments, he once again disappeared down the staircase, leaving the trio to further discuss their potential business relationship.

"I have to ask," Bell interjected. "It's none of my business, of course – but the other pieces she's made lately – they're well-known sites of the city. And while these old mansions are sort of a staple, why this one?"

"It's my parent's house," Jax said in a matter-of-fact tone. "My family's, to be more accurate. It's passed down to my father from his father who had it passed from his father and so on... I grew up there."

Blair looked overjoyed, as if her soul was about to leave her body completely, and was visibly forcing herself to calm down as he explained. He genuinely appreciated her talent, and the calming effect of the compliment was enough to cause her body to relax instantly.

"Can I ask you a question?" Jax said somewhat abruptly.

"Um... okay..." Blair said, looking at her painting as if she assumed there was some flaw or error he had found.

"Why... how should I put this..." Jax said, struggling to figure out the best way to phrase his query. "So – Tony, from the store in St. Charles – he was very reluctant to send me your information; if you don't mind me saying, he seems a bit... out of his league when it comes to art."

The comment made Bell laugh abruptly, after which she immediately apologized. Blair's eyes grew wide once again with a growing hesitation. But if anything was to come from this work, he would need to know more about what had motivated the secrecy. He would need candor so he understood what he was working with.

"So, I assumed correctly then," Jax said, smiling. "His cannoli, on the other hand — masterful."

Blair and Bell both nodded in agreement, revealing their familiarity with which the decadent treats had been commonly foisted on many in the community.

"If he gave you one on the house, it means he likes you," Blair answered with a laugh.

"Oh, good to know – the cream filling was magnificent. Honestly, it's been haunting my dreams for weeks now," Jax laughed, which was genuinely reciprocated by the two women. "But... ok – so he knows nothing about art, clearly. Why sell your paintings through him? Why... or maybe how... what's his role in this?"

"We have an arrangement," Blair said cryptically. "He agreed to sell some of my work to tourists, thinking it would drum up business for his store. In exchange, he handles all the transactions for me."

"Well, that would make sense if he was a dealer, or a typical agent, I suppose. But why not a gallery? Why not sell your work for what it's worth?" Jax asked, genuinely trying to piece together the mystery that seemed to evade him.

Blair paused for a moment and looked at Bell, who sat silently staring at her. The older of the two women looked as if she was waiting, unwilling to betray some hidden secret of her friends or not wanting to speak on her behalf. Clearly, coming to Crush to deliver the piece was Blair's decision to make, and Bell must have been simply a support role. But whatever the mystery, it was enough to cause both women to pause as Blair searched for the right words.

"I'm... I have no legal method of conducting transactions," Blair explained delicately.

"What... do you mean?" Jax said as his eyebrows furloughed contemplatively.

"I'm not connected to the feed; I am un-lensed... I don't have Blinks... I don't want them," Blair answered with a heavy sigh.

Jax stood up from the leather chair across from the sofa on which they were seated. For a moment, he began pacing within the room, scratching at the finely manicured stubble of his chin. "Apologies, ladies..." he said suddenly, "I... I just need a moment to process this."

He made several passes back and forth across the office, muttering to himself as he walked. Both of the women remained seated, staring at the spectacle with keen awareness of both Blair's odd circumstances and the unusual reactions it invited. After several more steps, Jax paused suddenly, turned to Blair as if he had something to say, and then sat back down across from her.

"I'm not here to judge you," he said empathetically, as if he had weighed his first words carefully. "But if I am going to carry your work – if you are to be featured at Crush - there are details we will need to consider... things we're going to have to figure out. I have... so many questions."

"What do you mean 'featured at Crush' –" Bell interrupted.

"My apologies. I've gotten ahead of myself," Jax answered, shaking his head. "Blair, I think you're immensely talented – I think there is a strong market for your work in the right circles. There's an honesty to it – an intimacy... But it's not just that – you're talented. I want to show people how talented you are."

Blair looked at Bell with a mixture of both panic and joy, speechless upon hearing his direct proclamation. It had been obvious in his mind, but both women were clearly surprised by the declaration, and neither appeared certain of how to respond. For her part, Bell remained perfectly calm, masking any hint of excitement and refusing to appear overly eager.

"This painting you've made for me – it's my home, obviously. But... it makes me feel *at home* - I'm not sure how else to say it... If you can make that kind of connection with others... I want my gallery to help you make that connection – if you're interested," he said. Then suddenly, he began laughing to himself ever so slightly and added, "It suddenly all makes sense about why you wouldn't just send over your information – why you wouldn't seek better representation!"

Blair inhaled deeply and held her breath for a moment before she responded. The complexity of her situation was obvious, but still very new to him. It was doubtful he understood the full picture, and his suggestion caused her body language to suddenly reflect an anxiety that caused her to shift uneasily in her seat.

"Look, I get it – this probably seems impossible right now – given your... situation. And I have so many questions that we would need to get to before we could agree to anything formally. But I have counsel on retainer that helps with the legal stuff – if there is a way to do this, we can figure that part out," he added sincerely.

Blair's face reflected a certain skepticism as he spoke. She looked both eager and hesitant, conflicted as she shifted uneasily on the sofa. Several minutes passed as she fidgeted, her face reflecting a back-and-forth shift as she considered his proposal. Then at last she buried her face in her hands and let out a sigh.

When at last she spoke, she said only, "I'm... scared."

"Oh," Jax answered sympathetically. "Did I... come on too strong? If you have other offers – "

"No... no, nothing like that. I... I've just spent most of my life now trying to avoid attention; I have my reasons. Now, you're asking me to enter what feels like a spotlight, and I want to – I really do. I want to live – I've only ever known placement homes – I... I don't want to unpack it all on you; I'd just unload all of my drama. It's just not been the easiest for me. And I want to make something of my art – I do. I'm just scared," she said, summoning courage as she straightened her back and attempted a confident demeanor.

"Well... how about lunch, then? We can talk about your concerns; I'll answer any questions you might have – full disclosure. And then take a few days to think about if this is what you want once we've had a chance to really talk things through. You don't need to decide now – I mean, lunch you would need to decide now. But um... whether you want to pursue this, you can take your time," Jax said, trying to ease some of the tension.

Blair looked at Bell for guidance, at which point Bell interjected, "I apologize. I have other appointments I must attend to." In an instant, Blair's face changed to disappointed understanding as she looked back at Jax as if the decision had been made. Bell then continued by saying, "But if I could trust you to ensure she makes it home safely... I don't see any reason the two of you would need me to tag along."

Blair and Jax's faces suddenly and simultaneously changed to reveal a mutual level of excitement. They both wore the look of children whose parents had agreed to some exciting adventure, sufficient to elicit an eye roll from the most senior of the trio.

"I assure you, Mrs. Andover, I will personally see to Blair's safe return," Jax responded without even looking toward the elder of the two women.

"Mmm...hmmm..." Bell murmured. Then, turning to Blair, she said, "Have fun, Squirt." With that, Bell made her way down the orange metal staircase to the ride that waited in front of the gallery.

"Do you have a favorite restaurant? Wherever you'd like to go – just say the word," Jax said after Bell left his office.

She paused and looked somewhat helplessly at him for a moment, gesturing with her hands to imply she had no answer.

"Well, there must be some place..." he answered quizzically.

"When I was young, with my parents... we used to go out to dinner occasionally, but it was so long ago, I don't remember the names of any of the places or whether they were actually good at all," she laughed.

"I see. Is there anywhere you've maybe seen around town you've been curious about?" he asked with a smile.

"I've seen the café at the art museum... I'll admit, I've only ever admired it from the outside, sort of wondering what it would be like to eat in a place that... nice," she said sheepishly.

"Yes, of course! I lunch there frequently - the head maître d is a friend. It's a solid lunch spot, if not a tad casual," Jax said, searching for confirmation. When Blair's eyes beamed with excitement, he ordered the vehicle and placed a last-minute lunch reservation through the feed. Then he added, "Shall we?"

As he escorted her down the staircase to the entrance, he looked at Bruce and casually asked, "Would you keep my afternoon open, Bruce? We're going to visit the museum and may be awhile."

"Of course, sir," responded Bruce from the sole desk in the gallery without distracting himself from his feed.

Once they reached the automated vehicle that awaited, the door opened automatically. Jax gestured to allow Blair to enter the vehicle, after which he joined her. From Crush, Forest Park was only a short distance, mostly the length of the enormous park.

"Do you go to the museum often?" Jax asked as the vehicle pulled away and began winding its way through the streets of the Central West End.

"As often as I can; it's not a short ride from St. Charles, and it's usually difficult to get a ride down here unless someone I know is headed this way. But it is one of my favorite places in the city," Blair answered, trying to contain her excitement. "Usually I ride my bicycle; it just takes a few hours. But it *does* give me as much time as I'd like there, which is usually quite a while. I like to study some of the pieces – the artists' techniques, their perspective..."

"I imagine getting around anywhere is difficult for you," Jax said, nodding his head.

"Well, I enjoy fresh air and exercise," she replied with a smile.

After the vehicle arrived, they ascended the steps together, and Jax looked over at his potential client and asked, "I am assuming you have some favorite pieces you'd like to see after lunch?"

Blair nodded excitedly, "Can we? I mean, if it's not taking too much of your time."

A short walk from the entrance, one of the museum officials greeted them saying, "Ah, Mr. Wadsworth – we weren't planning on seeing you today. What an excellent surprise!"

"Well, I'm trying to impress this young lady in hopes she will become a client; she specifically requested we make a visit," Jax replied with a smile.

"A mark of excellent taste," the curator replied kindly. "Will you be joining us for lunch?"

"Yes – I've blinked ahead," Jax answered, shaking the man's hand warmly.

"Excellent, sir. Please let us know if there is anything you need, and enjoy your stay," the curator answered.

As they walked toward the restaurant, Jax quietly mentioned, "Apologies for all the... attention. My family are supporters of the museum, and regulars at their charity events. I'm guessing word got out of our arrival when I blinked ahead; the curator doesn't usually welcome people personally."

"Ok – I'm already impressed," she laughed. "You don't have to show off on my account."

"Nonsense," he chuckled. Then with a wink he added, "I want to make sure that good impression sticks."

As they entered the small café, the hostess smiled warmly and immediately escorted them to a table upon which a small cardboard sign was sitting reading, "RESERVED." Once they were seated, Jax looked through the wine menu before asking her, "I'm assuming a white?"

Blair nodded and smiled, conveying the same look of helplessness he had seen back in the gallery. Jax simply smiled politely and ordered whatever he thought would pair well with whatever she might order from the menu.

Once the wine was poured, and the server had taken their orders, the young woman wasted no time in attempting to explain the awkwardness of her circumstances, "I want to be honest with you... I'm just not sure you'll like what you hear."

"Blair, I can't help you if I don't understand what we're working with," Jax responded empathetically.

"I'm not sure where to start," she said as she began fidgeting with the cloth napkin that had been laid across the lap of her sundress.

"Well, you said your parents seem to have been some influence behind your... beliefs, as it were. They instilled in you a desire to not be connected, I think you said," Jax answered, trying to get the conversation started.

"My mother was a professor of Criminal Justice at the university in St. Charles; my father too, but he taught American history. That's where they met," she answered as she took a sip from the wineglass in front of her.

"Your parents were accomplished academics – that's fantastic. That will help establish some *gravitas* with some of the more established families that might be interested in your work," Jax said confidently.

"Yeah... maybe not," Blair said with a grimace. "My father was an outspoken critic of the legislation that included the government's standardized transaction policy... the major piece of the Anti-Money Laundering Act. He was... sort of a leader of some of the more vocal groups back during the period of unrest in the thirties."

"Hmm," Jax mouthed, sipping from his glass of wine as he listened.

"Well, it's just everyone was freaking out over the quantum hack that de-encrypted all the banking transactions and the cryptos and everything. And everything was a mess. I was too young to really understand it then, but now it's pretty obvious that the panic is what led to the US digital currency, the AMLA, and the biometric verification in lenses – all of it. My dad was one of the voices against it. I remember hearing his lectures when mom would take me to these big speaking events. He'd get the crowd fired up about how government control of money was the death of liberty and how fear and panic caused people to surrender their rights. 'It's bad for people, bad for business, and bad for freedom' he'd say. He was very vocal about too much control... too much power in too few hands..."

"I see," Jax answered solemnly. "And, may I ask, where is he now?"

"He died in late in '37. From the reel we saw at the trial... I was about twelve then... one of the military drones assisting the police fired into the crowd," she answered. "He had been leading a protest on the mall in DC, and things got out of hand... There was an inquiry afterwards. But nobody was charged because they say he had active warrants related to all his speaking events."

"That's awful," Jax answered sympathetically.

"My mother told me after the trial that the warrants were for Safe Speech violations... and they only came after he was killed. Anyway, it was a long time ago."

"Oh, I'm so sorry – I... I didn't know," Jax said apologetically. "I was in high school back then. I remember my mother not letting us go into downtown because of all the people in the streets. The news had video of people setting banks on fire and throwing bricks at the police. It was a... um... troubled time everywhere."

"Well, that was my dad and his people," she said awkwardly, but not apologetically. "He always spoke his truth; I still admire that. I remember him telling me as a young girl that free speech wasn't given by the government and so it couldn't take it away... As a professor, he was a big deal, and he really felt like he was doing the right thing. Creating momentum with other academics..."

Jax sat quietly, listening. He knew instantly that if he promoted artwork from the daughter of known dissidents, it could create difficulties for both his family and the gallery. There was no possible way his parents would approve of carrying her work once they knew who she was. It would likely ostracize them and their businesses from the type of social circles they moved within. Nevertheless, they were already enjoying lunch, and she was a lovely, talented artist. There was no reason to cut the afternoon short.

"I'm sorry to hear that," Jax said earnestly after taking another long sip of his wine. "His loss must have been difficult on your family."

Blair nodded and added, "My mother... Well, she wasn't the same after that. I remember her sitting by the window in our house, just staring out at the street blankly. She... suffered, but she tried not to involve me, I think. I don't know, they were pretty united in their beliefs."

Jax tried to contain the concern he felt, realizing her father was not the only dissident in her family. Still, he would hear her out, out of politeness if nothing else.

When he didn't respond, she continued, saying, "It took her a while before that grief turned into a drive, I think. After the trial, she started leading her own speaking events, talking about privacy violations and the collusion between tech and government to spy on the people..."

"Um... she... didn't pass as well, did she?" he asked, attempting to convey sympathy without judgement.

"No – no, she's alive," Blair answered.

Jax breathed a sigh of relief, hoping perhaps he had been wrong in his assumption. Then the young woman answered, "She's incarcerated in Greenville. She's been eligible for parole several times, but...no luck, I guess."

The news deflated any remaining hope Jax had of working with the young woman. Talent and beauty were wonderful, of course. But for her work to be marketable, she either needed to have sufficient anonymity or at least be on the correct side of history. As it stood, her pedigree would make her an instant pariah among his family's peers.

"But... you've managed to stay away from that type of... activism – I'm not sure that's the right word for it. But you haven't had any trouble with the law, correct? Maybe there's a way we can frame things –"

"Actually, I was arrested about two weeks ago – but not for any kind of speech crime or extremism!" Blair answered defensively. "I just witnessed a bar fight that ended up on the street I was walking down - it wasn't my fault! The officer demanded I send over my record, but I couldn't because – well, obviously... so they charged me with disorderly conduct when I couldn't do what he was asking me to."

Jax laughed to himself at the absurdity of it all. Then, realizing he was being impolite, he paused momentarily and looked across the table at the young woman with a face that must have conveyed a pure disbelief. It all sounded so outlandish, and Blair must have realized how bizarre it must have come across when she had unloaded her troubles on the man. Until that point, he had been genuinely interested in working with her. She too laughed, ever so slightly.

"I'll tell you what, Blair," Jax said with a chuckle. "Whether we can do business or not, I'll see if my attorney can quietly look into that disorderly charge. Maybe we can help, even if the gallery isn't able to carry your work."

Blair beamed upon hearing the positive news. "You could do that?" she asked, looking like she was afraid to even hope for real help.

"Honestly, it doesn't sound like it would be that big of a deal; there's no law against not being connected explicitly. If it's as simple as you say it is, I'm sure we could at least look into it – I just can't guarantee any results," he answered, trying to manage her expectations.

As lunch arrived, his lunch companion seemed both excited, and a bit intimidated. She was obviously trying to be polite as she quickly changed the subject. "So, what about your family? I can't imagine you have half the drama that I do."

"The Wadsworths?" he asked, revealing a bit of confusion. "I'm sorry – it was arrogant of me to have assumed you would be familiar with the name. We've been in St. Louis for generations; the manor house you painted is a sort of icon of ours."

"Oh... that must be... challenging," Blair said with a smirk.

For a moment, it was as if Jax's inside voice overpowered his rational thinking in an odd, candid way he otherwise would not have verbalized.

"It can be," Jax replied quietly, then, realizing his overt admission, he backtracked slightly. "Of course, there are advantages that come with the name... opportunities afforded to those with influence... But that reputation also has some complications. Maybe 'obligations' is a better word."

"I imagine," she said with a knowing smirk.

"My family has done well in chip manufacturing, real estate, and finance. Honestly, when I chose to pursue a business in art, there was a not-so-subtle sense of disappointment. I was viewed somewhat as the... well... gentle-hearted child. But eventually, it just meant that I would become the focal point for the family's charitable efforts... in particular the arts, which I'm fine with. But yes, I suppose 'challenging' is an appropriate way to describe it. There are certain... expectations that must be upheld."

"Sounds a bit rough," Blair replied empathetically.

For a moment, Jax was taken back by the young woman's response. She had lost those nearest to her, and by virtue of their actions, she would likely never be welcomed in polite society. Yet, despite her misfortune, the look on her face revealed a genuine sense of pity.

"Oh, don't feel sorry for me," Jax laughed, feeling slightly embarrassed. "As a general rule – you shouldn't feel pity for... wealthy people. My family – the people they associate with – they don't have *real* problems. Not really. And my family's name has afforded me a very nice life – I have my own gallery, I can do as I please, I –"

"Can you though?" Blair interrupted with a hint of argumentativeness. Then, shaking her head defensively, she added, "I'm sorry, that was rude of me."

Jax considered for a moment what she meant, and stared deeply into the young woman's brown eyes. It was as if she saw straight through the well concocted and impressive charade he had perfected. Speechless, he simply looked at her, wondering what else she would say.

"The way you looked at me when I told you I was disconnected from the feed... It was as if you took pity on me, like some caged animal," she confided. Then, after a brief hesitation, she said, "While the life I have chosen *does* have its limitations – and they really are numerous – nobody... owns me. There's no feed that tells me what to think. I barter labor and help for the things that I need. It's difficult, but it's my choice. There's a certain freedom to it, I think."

"That's... an interesting way to look at it," Jax responded contemplatively. "I... would have thought the opposite."

"I get that a lot," she said with a laugh. "It can be inconvenient, but it's not impossible... I have my books and my records... I have a life surrounded by friends that carries little distractions... I live in the real world. I have dirt under my fingernails and paint stains on my clothing. My thoughts... my art... they're all mine, and they are real. I'd say I'm free from the sorts of influence that comes with constantly being bombarded by advertisements and the marketing of feed sponsors."

Jax returned his fork to his plate with a feeling of astonishment. He then sipped the glass of wine in front of him, studying her to decipher the truth behind her gaze. Her candor was remarkable, if not exceptionally dangerous. There was something about the way she saw the world – her perspective – it carried a certain allure that he could not deny. Perhaps it was this same perspective, this approach, that made her work so captivating.

"You are... truly fascinating," he said at last, still not entirely sure what to make of her.

After they finished their lunch, they spent hours walking the hallways of the museum. Jax was repeatedly taken back by which pieces she seemed enamored with, with one particular piece being her favorite. It featured a minor Greek goddess that Blair explained was the goddess of starlight and justice.

"It's always interesting to me how the Greeks seemed to have gods and goddesses of such disconnected things," he said after she had explained her views of the painting.

"Maybe not so much this one," she answered. "A light in the darkness... bringing the hidden things to light... justice... it makes sense to me."

Jax was astonished at how she spoke of paintings; it was as if they were kin to her, a family she had adopted with the loss of her own. She knew the artists' meaning behind many of them, but more so, she had studied every brush stroke of her favorites. As they continued through the exhibits, she pointed out facts even he didn't know. This one was painted by a drunk who had been kicked out of a monastery; that artist was famous in his day, but fell out of favor with a certain royal family. She knew many of the stories by heart, and could have rivaled the curator. While Jax knew the stories of many of the artists from his graduate studies, her knowledge surpassed even his, and she clearly wasn't accessing the feed to confirm what she had learned.

They stayed at the museum until it was nearing time to close, and even after hours of walking and talking about the various pieces, there was still so much they had not seen. When they exited the large stone building, the ride-share was already waiting, and true to his word, Jax accompanied Blair back to St. Charles as they chatted about their favorite artists from around the world. When at last the vehicle stopped outside of the Andover house on 5th Street, Jax walked her to the door of her cottage.

"Those magnolias are lovely," he said with a smile.

"Thanks - they were Mia's idea," Blair said proudly. "She's developing quite the eye for composition."

After a brief pause while Blair unlocked the door to her small home, Jax, who had been waiting patiently for her to finish, said, "Listen, Blair - I can't make any promises. Obviously, your family history presents certain... difficulties."

"I kinda figured," Blair said with a laugh. "But you're sweet. Thanks for taking me out. And really... it's okay, Jax. The lunch... the afternoon - well, it's been wonderful. It was great to have met you."

Jax was immediately taken back by how she already seemed to understand his reluctance. The thought of being so predictable and conventional at once made him feel subservient and cowardly, and before he could contain himself, he blurted, "Hey - I'm not saying 'No.' I... just need to see what... if there's anything that we could maybe work around... maybe there's a way."

Blair smiled politely, reflecting the years of disappointment she had clearly known as a result of her convictions. "Sure," she whispered kindly.

"Oh, and um... I don't think we discussed compensation for the piece you brought me. I offered to pay you double for it... for bringing it to me personally," he blurted.

"Consider it a gift – for you and your family. With my gratitude for lunch and the company," she laughed.

"Nonsense," Jax answered, shaking his head. "The canvas... the paint... the brushes – you can't come by those things easily."

"As I said, it's a gift, Jax — you're welcome," Blair emphasized.

"Well... um... thank you – I don't... I'm not sure I can accept this. It doesn't feel right," he said, shifting his weight where he stood with uncertainty.

"You can, and you will," she said loudly as at last she entered her cottage. "Now, if you don't leave, I'm going to have to call the police and tell them there's a strange man lurking outside my home!"

Jax laughed and said, "Okay... fine... It was a pleasure to meet you, Blair. Truly. I... I hope to be in touch soon."

With that, Jax returned to the automated vehicle that awaited him. As it slowly lurched forward, he searched his feed for art stores in St. Charles; Addison's Art Supply was the first result to appear. Moments later, he was on the phone with the manager.

"I'd like to establish an account," Jax said to the man who answered the phone.

"An account, sir?" the man asked.

"Yes, I'd like to establish billing to my feed for any purchases that are made in your store for one of my clients – anything she needs, I want it billed to me directly," Jax answered.

"Um... that's a bit unusual, but I'm sure we can accommodate that," the man responded. "Whom is your client?"

"Her name is Blair Huxley; I believe she may be a regular in your store," Jax responded.

The voice on the other end of the phone paused momentarily, deafeningly quiet. Then, cautiously, he asked, "Are you with the police or any kind of law enforcement? Because I know what entrapment is – you have to tell me if you are – it's the law!"

"What? No – it's nothing like that. Listen, this is Jaxson Wadsworth the fourth; you're probably familiar with my family... we're involved in the fine arts community in St. Louis... I own the Crush Gallery on the Central West End," Jax said assertively. "I am interested in possibly carrying some of Blair's work – I'm well acquainted with her situation. I only want to ensure she has what she needs to produce the work we intend on commissioning without it becoming a hardship on her... given the challenges she's working with."

"I see," the voice answered. "In that case, please link over your information, and I'll be certain all invoices are sent to your feed."

~ 5 ~

Nearly two weeks had passed since her trip to the Crush gallery and the afternoon stroll through the museum that followed. When Blair heard nothing from Jax or his gallery, she assumed she had an answer. Her family's history and her personal choices were simply too complicated for polite society to want to deal with. And so, with gratitude for the experience, Blair continued on as she had, passing her days with odd jobs that she exchanged for various goods and spending her nights painting her passion.

She had nearly completed her painting of the choking bald eagle in the days that followed her adventure with the gallery owner. She wondered how he would react if he were to see this authentic, raw side of her work. This pondering quickly led to her upcoming court date and the pending charges. She didn't know if Jax would come through with his offer of legal help, but the more she painted, the more she simply made peace with the idea she may spend some time in jail. Regardless of what would happen, she would know soon enough, as she needed to be at the hearing by ten o'clock the following day.

The inevitability feeling of what would follow slowly churned in her stomach throughout the day, mixing with the still fresh emotions from the night of her arrest. As she stared at the painting, she remembered the resolve she had committed herself to that night; she had determined to not live in fear. She would not let them see her beg or cower ever again. Then, as she stared at the unsigned work she had spent so many hours on, she realized the first step in no longer living in fear should be to take ownership of her artwork.

I should claim it – loudly and boldly, she thought. *It will be my own declaration of independence from the system, from the feed, from all the world that wanted nothing more than control. If anyone ever sees it, I'll be charged with Safe Speech Act violations, anyway; signed or unsigned. If the police find it here in my cottage, it will mean jail, and they would not be releasing her to Bell.*

"They would say this painting is inciting violent extremism," she said aloud to herself. "They'd have to, or else others might question the propaganda on the feed."

As she looked over the work, she laughed at her own madness as she began speaking in a low, official sounding voice, "Everything is fine; ignore any false rumors that don't come through the feed. We are still free, and to stay that way, we must surrender some of our privacy... That hyperinflation? Oh, it's just a minor thing! It's lingered for thirty years, according to the data! There's no possible way subsidies of Blinks are causing it! All these people talking about the rich getting richer and the poor getting to suck it – well, that's just greedy and selfish individuals who refuse to pay a sixty percent tax on their income! It has nothing to do with all the spending!"

As she contemplated the lie that had become commonplace, the burden of her hesitation in leaving the piece unsigned felt outright fearful and cowardly.

"It's wrong," she said aloud. "Unsigned paintings are fine for the tourist dribble, but not from you sick bird." Resolved, she then carefully placed her mark in the bottom right corner, painting her initials "B.H".

With the eagle painting finally complete, she moved it toward the window to allow it to dry before returning to her more recent project that she had under drawing. The contour line of the woman's dress had proven difficult to get right. It would not lay flat like a dress normally would; she was being pulled – it needed to show the movement. The other challenge was making the iconic old man sufficiently recognizable, but original and interesting. Once completed, it would truly be her most provocative piece, bordering on crude and comical.

She painted into the evening with the only interruption being Bell, who came by after she returned from work. Blair heard her coming through the yard as she spoke with Mia, so she quickly found the cover and draped it over her new project, careful not to reveal its form to her friend for fear of the repercussions for them both.

"You sure you don't want me to come with you? I could give you a ride at least," Bell asked after Blair answered the door.

"I don't want you caught up in all of this – and it's not far. I'll manage, but thank you," she answered.

Bell, who was visibly exhausted from her day at work, lingered a moment and then hesitantly asked, "Anything from Jax or from his attorney?"

"Nope," she answered casually. "But it'll be fine, I'm sure."

Bell sighed, and then unconvincingly replied, "Okay, if that's what you want."

"It's probably for the best," Blair answered.

Bell nodded pensively as she turned to leave. As she did, Blair quickly returned to her painting, not sure of when she would have another chance.

The next morning, Blair left the cottage early. She didn't really know how the legal system worked; she only knew there was to be a hearing. The officer had said something about having an attorney assigned to her, but maybe that was just something she had heard in old movies. Regardless, as she walked down 5th Street, she walked slowly, drinking in the morning air and fresh sunlight. If this was to be her last morning of freedom, she wanted to enjoy each drip of sunlight that would fall on her; she would soak up each moment. After several blocks, Blair turned northward toward the Frenchtown area in St. Charles, and the Courthouse, which was a landmark at the northern end.

When she reached the entrance of the building, it was dated and worn, as if it had not been updated in decades. It was also crowded with people – jurors, attorneys, witnesses, and the others who had business there. She was alone and instantly confused, not sure where she should go or what room her hearing would be in. There were several large screens mounted on the walls that posted hearing numbers and docket numbers, but none of them contained her name. She wasn't sure where to go. Fortunately, because she'd arrived early, she knew there would be some extra time to figure things out.

She looked around the busy lobby area of the building for some clue. A dozen of well-dressed people passed by her without note. Unfortunately, there wasn't an information desk or a place to check-in; she assumed it would be obvious where to go when she arrived. Feeling helpless, she finally approached one of the uniformed officers that was posted at the entrance to a large hallway, just off of the entrance area.

"Excuse me," she said, attempting to gain the man's attention. "My apologies, but I'm not certain where I need to go."
"Ma'am, check your feed; all hearing information is disbursed directly to the interested parties, or otherwise posted on the court's thread. It's part of privacy protections," the officer droned.

"Um... ok... My mistake," she said reluctantly. There was no way she was going to draw additional attention to herself, not right before her hearing. She had virtually memorized the paperwork that had been provided to her at the jail; there was no reference of a hearing number. It only spoke of the date and time that she should be present for court. Of course, if they only sent information through the feed, she wouldn't have received it. And she was doubtful the clunky machine of justice would even know how to mail the paper documents the old-fashioned way. The Postal Service shrunk dramatically in the decades that followed the introduction of Blinks, and was mostly used as a novelty.

Blair froze in place, uncertain of what she should do next. Not knowing, she simply stayed in place, staring at the large screen as it continued displaying hearing numbers and room numbers, cycling through them until the end of the list was complete before starting at the beginning.

As she stared blankly at the screen, she became increasingly anxious, wondering what she should do. Then, appearing from nowhere, a smartly dressed man wearing a pinstriped black suit walked directly up to her. He was likely in his late fifties if not sixties with perfectly groomed hair and with a cleanly shaven, non-nonsense face that was exemplified by terse, cold eyes. "Ms. Huxley? Blair Huxley?" he said after catching her attention.

Having never met the man, Blair didn't know what to say other than, "Yes – that's me... Hi."

The well-dressed man then said, "My apologies for the confusion. Mr. Wadworth had asked me to take care of this matter on your behalf; I perhaps improperly assumed you would not be in attendance. In fact, a week ago, I directed the court to send all correspondence to my office to not bother you. I regret that wasn't better communicated to you."

Blair's eyes widened, uncertain of what to say. She had not heard from Jax or anyone connected with the gallery in weeks, and she had simply assumed she was on her own. As she stood in place speechless, the man continued by saying, "Oh... my manners - My name is Henry Wells, Esquire. I represent the Wadsworth family, including the business of Mr. Jaxson Wadsworth the fourth and Crush Galleries, LLC. Which... as fortune would have it... means that today I am representing you. If you'd care to accompany me, we should have this entire situation resolved momentarily."

The sigh of relief that followed must have been noticeable, as Mr. Wells smiled slightly before extending his arm as a gentleman and guiding the young artist toward the courtroom. Shortly after entering, and once her case was called, the proceedings began. From the dais, the judge read off the docket and hearing number, and then turned his attention toward the man representing the District Attorney's Office, who introduced himself and the charge being filed against the accused. When the judge turned his attention toward Mr. Wells, the old attorney introduced himself and the firm with which he was associated. He then politely added, "Your honor, if it pleases the court, rather than enter a plea, we would ask for all charges to be dismissed."

"Dismissed?" the judge asked loudly, revealing his surprise. Turning to the District Attorney, he waited for the prosecution to provide an answer. For his part, the thirty-something, scruffy bearded representative from the DA asked only, "Um... on what grounds?"

Without waiting for the judge to respond, Mr. Wells interjected, "On the grounds that the threshold for probable cause resulting in an arrest was never reached. In fact, following these proceedings, I will be filing a civil suit against the City of St. Charles Police Department for a wrongful arrest... You see, your honor. My client is accused of disturbing the peace due to 'loud protests', as described in the arresting officer's statement. Any reasonable person could easily conclude there was no peace to be disturbed; that peace was shattered when a violent bar-room-brawl extended onto a public street, landing at the feet of a young woman walking home alone in the dark. Now, there were obviously many loud, disturbing noises at that time, and it's likely my client was the least of these. The officer who arrested her simply did so under this trumped-up charge because my client is not connected to the feed and was thus unable to send over her record to the officer. He was annoyed at the hassle! I submit to you that there is no law requiring her to be connected, and the officer's frustration simply manifested as a bellicose tantrum. But of course, if the District Attorney's Office would like to pursue this matter, we would be more than happy to convene a jury and put this young woman on the stand so that she can tell her peers about the traumatic events of that night. And while such a trial will be quite costly, in the interest of justice, we are willing to see it through."

"Counsels, approach the bench," the judge ordered with a less than pleased scowl.

From the center of the room, sitting behind a small wooden table, Blair couldn't hear all the whispered discussion being held between the attorney from the District Attorney's office, the judge, and Mr. Wells. At one point, she heard the word "Dissident" come from the judge, to which Mr. Wells gave some sort of response that left both the other attorney and the judge less than convinced. After several long minutes of discussion, Mr. Wells turned back toward Blair and gave her a quick wink, unobservable to the others behind him. As he returned to the table where Blair had remained seated, he turned once again toward the front of the courtroom, just in time to hear the judge speak.

"Motion granted," the judge mumbled reluctantly before adding, "Court will take a short recess." In a huff, the robed judge stood up from his chair behind the large wooden bench and excused himself through a doorway at the right end of the room.

Turning to Blair, Mr. Wells said only, "Should I see you home, then?"

"What? Um... sorry! I mean, is that it?" she asked, unsure of what had just transpired.

"Yes. My motion to dismiss the charges was granted – that means you're free to leave," Mr. Wells responded with a cocky smirk.

"Thank you! Thank you so much!" Blair said as she stood from the chair in which she had been seated and impulsively embraced the man.

Taken back by the warm gesture, the attorney chuckled to himself for a moment before saying, "Oh – well, yes, of course. Happy I could help." Then, after a moment's pause, he said, "But do you – need a ride back home?"

"No – of course not. It's only a short walk. You've already helped so much! And I'd really like to enjoy the air of freedom – I was a bit terrified on the way here thinking... Well, thinking I wouldn't get to enjoy long walks alone anymore!" she laughed.

Mr. Wells nodded his head in understanding before saying, "Well then, if you'll excuse me, I have other appointments I must attend to." He ushered her with his arm toward the exit of the courtroom, where he said goodbye. Blair watched from the courthouse entrance as moments later he had entered an automated rideshare and was gone.

It was still before noon, and the late morning sun felt hot on her skin in the humid, late summer air. But just thankful to be free, Blair didn't mind at all. Instead, she nearly skipped down the steps of the old courthouse building as she pointed her way toward home. As she reached the bottom, she paused, and in a moment of frivolity, she said aloud to herself, "Might as well make the most of this unexpected miracle!"

She turned north toward the Frenchtown and its collection of stores that held odd antiques, junk, and an assortment of services that lay beyond. In only minutes, she found herself peering through the window of the pet store, admiring the puppies behind the glass entrance. She stared longingly at the fluffy menaces for some time until at last she was sick with heartache at the antics of a small Pug that would never be hers. So, she moved on.

Wandering down 2nd Street, she passed the coffee and tea shop, where the morning rush had long since ended. A fashionable older woman with large framed sunglasses sat outside the shop and was delicately handling a small cup of espresso, while her miniature poodle wandered about on her feet. Past the coffee and tea shop, she continued on past a massage parlor and spa, heading toward a machine shop that was owned by an old friend and former student of her fathers. The owner, Jed, held a collection of random odds and ends behind the building, and was always excited to barter or otherwise share with her any salvaged treasures he had come across.

Still a few blocks from the machine shop, she passed the old tattoo shop that had sat vacant the past few years, ever since the building on its north side had been demolished, leaving an empty lot. She had never known the previous owners, but had often seen a rowdy crowd gathered behind the glass windows of the store-front. To her surprise, as she passed the front of the shop, a woman was hanging a sign above the door that read "Under New Own-ership." She was older than Blair, but not quite Bell's age, and in the tank top she was wearing, Blair could see colorful artwork that decorated her neck, shoulders, and arms all the way down to her hands. The woman's hair was raven black and tied on the top of her head with a bright red bandana.

Blair rounded the corner of the shop, only to find a heavily tattooed man with a grandiose, waxed, handlebar mustache, who was about the same age. The man stood in front of a barren brick wall that bordered the empty lot. The man was measuring the wall and muttering to himself with a large piece of chalk in hand as he struggled to sketch a design. She believed he was attempting to create some sort of mural to decorate the otherwise rough and worn brick exterior.

With nothing important to do and a day filled with a newly dis-covered sense of freedom, Blair stopped and asked the man, "Do you mind if I watch a little?"

"Not at all – suit yourself," he answered.

Blair found a seat on the curb of the sidewalk that bordered the lot and watched the artist begin his work on the wall. With broad, sweeping strokes, the man used various colors of chalk to create an outline that soon took shape as an oblong skull and a somewhat flat rose. Quietly, Blair continued observing the artist's rather clumsy attempts to correct proportions for the piece, a challenge given he seemed to have no plan to account for his close perspective on a large surface. Likewise, he struggled to create straight, consistent lines, and those he created had varying textures from passing over the brick and mortar. Silently, in her own mind, she began critiquing both his plan and technique; she wondered why he had not created a grid or other reference points he could use to keep the composition proportional. She forced herself to remain quiet, as the man's hand swooshed repeatedly, creating lines she knew were wonky and making the situation worse.

"You know, you could help if you wanted to – you don't have to just sit there stewing," said a woman's voice coming from the front of the shop. Having been so focused on the cascading failure before her, Blair had hardly noticed the tattooed woman from before as she approached Blair's side. Turning to her, Blair blushed and awkwardly laughed, asking, "Was I that obvious?"

The mustachioed muralist turned when he heard the woman's voices and confusedly looked at them both. Whether he was frustrated by the unfolding failure or simply confused by what had transpired behind him, the man joined them, and after dusting the chalk off, extended his hand toward Blair, "I'm Tanner – it looks like you've already met the boss – my wife Lillian."

"Blair," she answered, shaking his hand warmly.

"So... you know anything about mural work?" Lillian asked after pleasantries had concluded.

"A little – mostly from reading," Blair said sheepishly. "I know a good deal about composition and layout...I haven't worked on anything this big, but the approach is the same. Theoretically."

"What approach? You draw the idea. You outline it. You paint it," Tanner responded, argumentatively.

"Well, yeah..." Blair laughed. "But something this big... when you can't reach the whole drawing at once – you have to have reference points for perspective. Or you're going to get all... off. See that top line of your skull there?"

Lillian tried to contain her laugh, which came out sounding more like a failed sneeze. Then, placing her hand gently on Blair's arm, she said, "I told him you can't just 'GO AT IT'... but do you think he'd listen?"

Tanner, who was already frustrated, huffed as he pulled a bandana from the back pocket of his dark-rinse jeans. Then, removing the flap cap from his cleanly shaven head, he wiped the sweat that covered his forehead and face. After glaring at them both for several seconds, he simply said, "Here – you do it then!" He then handed the chalk to Lillian, adding, "I'll go back to working on the inside. In the air conditioning. It's too hot out here, anyway."

Lillian looked at Blair mischievously as she took the chalk in hand, saying, "So you wanna help? I can pay you."

"Do you have any tape? Maybe some scaffolding?" Blair asked.

"Tape – yes. Scaffolding – no. But we have a couple ladders and a stack of two-by-twelve boards – I can't say that would pass a safety inspection, but it should get the job done," Lillian said, turning her attention once again toward the brick wall.

"I've done more with less," Blair responded with a shrug.

Lillian gestured for Blair to follow her as the two retreated into the tattoo shop's interior, where she would retrieve tape and the ladders. Blair had never been inside a tattoo shop before, but became quickly fascinated by dozens of frames that held small, somewhat crude pieces of vintage art that decorated the walls. An old, decorative wood desk sat near the front of the shop, acting as a sort of welcome area, while just behind it, a room not much larger than a bedroom held several folding tables and chairs that were cushioned in a material that looked like black leather. Tanner and Lillian were obviously making some updates to the space, as boxes of new flooring and several gallons of paint were stacked here and there.

"Pardon the mess," Lillian said as she rifled through a box in search of tape. "We bought this place on the cheap, on account of the roof needing some work and it sitting vacant for several years. It's hard times for small business, but we thought we'd make a go of it."

"No boss, no master – makes sense to me," Blair said as she looked around at the art on the walls.

"Exactly," Lillian answered. Just then, Tanner appeared through a door in the back carrying several boxes of the flooring material to add to the stack that he had created in the room.

"Oh no, you two aren't going to come in here and criticize my flooring work, are you?" he laughed in a huff.

"HERE IT IS!" Lillian answered as she liberated a roll of blue-colored tape from the bottom of a large cardboard box she had half-crawled into.

"Just needed tape to get started," Blair said to Tanner, who nodded in reply, pausing near his wife after he set the boxes down.

As Lillian exited the box and found her feet, she greeted Tanner with a kiss on the cheek, saying, "Have fun with the floors."

"Oh, loads," he answered sarcastically, then quietly to his wife he asked. "Can we afford to hire help for this? Did you discuss that with her?"

Lillian shot him a telling glare, answering, "I told her we'd pay her for the help – it will be fine."

Blair didn't know if she should say something, as the couple seemed to have a moment between them. There was no way she could accept payment, even if they had negotiated a specific price for her effort, and she hoped that if she simply didn't bring it up again, they wouldn't either. With her newly found freedom, the idea of making new friends and painting a large mural seemed like a fun way to spend the day.

Moments later, Blair followed Lillian as they exited the front of the shop and returned to the exposed brick side. It took several minutes to pull the ladders to the work area, and several more to add the large pieces of lumber that would serve for scaffolding. Within the hour, both women had managed to create a frame with tape that cordoned the wall into manageable sections, after which Blair retreated to the far end of the vacant lot to check how evenly the plan had been prepared.

"You sure about a skull and rose?" she asked Lillian as she held her hands up with her thumbs pressing together to make a frame.

"Not really," Lillian answered. "It was Tanner's idea – something traditional-ish, but fierce. It's my shop, so I get the final say… Why? Did you have something else in mind?"

"I mean, a skull and rose is certainly traditional… it's just a bit unoriginal. Especially a basic side-profile. I really like the little pieces on the walls of the shop – they've got a certain nostalgia to them."

"Oh, the flash?" Lillian answered. "We do a lot of that stuff. Just bullet-proof, old-school, tough tattoos. You can read 'em from across a room."

"I love that," Blair answered. "I just wonder if a skull and a rose are distinct enough. You could do literally anything in that style – why not be the one shop that has something that stands out?"

Lillian paused for a second, staring at the wall, and considering what Blair was saying.

"It's your shop, boss," Blair said with a laugh. "I was just thinking… And I know nothing about your business or tattoos, so don't listen to my gibberish."

"No, I think you make a good point," Lillian answered. "When you were looking at the flash, did something in particular stand out to you? Anything unique?"

"The picture of the skunk with the boxing gloves made me laugh," Blair said with a smile. "So did the little hippo character with the gold chain... But why pick just one? Why not transform this entire wall into one of those framed flash pictures? A big central piece with little pieces surrounding it – just like the ones inside."

"Paint the entire wall like a flash sheet?" Lillian asked rhetorically as she looked back at Blair. "That... might be genius."

"And it would solve the problem of trying to make the whole wall one big, flowing composition," Blair said, still studying the wall.

"Which means Tanner could help, and we'd have it done faster!" Lillian said, as she climbed down from the makeshift scaffolding and retreated into the shop. Moments later, Tanner appeared beside her, listening intently as she explained the idea. The tape lines that had already laid out neatly divided the wall into four even quadrants, which Tanner suggested might look stale. Instead, he suggested one large central image, with smaller images serving as a border. Without hesitation, Blair used tape to create a large, central square box by removing a portion of the tape at the intersection of the previous four squares and using it to create a frame, and then said, "There! A central piece and room for smaller ones on the corners.

"Dagger... skull... rose?" he suggested, as he began pointing at the corners.

"Or something like that," Lillian gently suggested. "Maybe something that really stands out for the central piece, and then you pick the more traditional, kitsch images to fit the vibe?"

"That'd be cool," he said as he twirled his mustache in his fingers, imagining the completed work. "Why don't you two work on the big centerpiece? Then I'll add the filler and surrounding pieces once the floors are in?"

"An excellent idea, love," Lillian responded as she glanced at Blair with a smirk. "What do you think of that hippo with the gold chain?"

"Lil, you know I've been wanting to blast that on someone for years! For real, though – front and center! Gangster hippo!" he howled excitedly.

"Blair kinda likes the boxing skunk... I was kind of thinking, what if your hippo and the boxing skunk were duking it out?" Lillian laughed.

Tanner's eyes instantly became wide with excitement. "So, Gangster hippo and Stinky Mac in the fight of the century?!" he stammered excitedly, before loudly bellowing, "This is why I married you, Lil!"

"We'll get to work, then," Blair laughed.

The two women began working once Tanner had returned to the floor project. Lillian chatted away about her excitement at opening her own shop, and the years she had spent in the business; it was how she and Tanner met. Blair listened as the woman prattled along, revealing very little of her own story and background for fear of scaring off her new friend. While Lillian mostly assisted, Blair began using chalk to outline the composition, mimicking the traditional tattoo style while integrating her own illustrative style. At some point, Lillian must have ordered pizza through her feed, as by the early afternoon, a delivery drone arrived carrying several boxes, which it dropped off in front of the shop. Lillian then gestured for her to join them inside for a quick meal.

While they ate, Lillian finally realized she had been talking so much that Blair had revealed little about her life or her background in art. Without wanting to pry, she handed Blair a beer she produced from a small refrigerator and said, "So... what about you?"

Blair took a long sip of cold beer as she quickly tried to think of how she might maneuver out of scaring them both.

"Well, I live here in St. Chuck. Some friends of the family have a small cottage behind their place, and they let me stay there. In exchange, I watch their daughter from time to time," Blair answered casually.

Lillian nodded, while Tanner appeared completely oblivious as he devoured his pizza and several beers. She then asked, "So, where did you learn to paint? Are you an artist somewhere or...?"

"My mother taught me the basics when I was younger... I sort of read everything I could find and studied the techniques of other artists to develop my own way of doing things I suppose," Blair answered, attempting once again to be earnest and not cryptic.

"So, you're a professional then – a painter," she answered rather than asked.

"Well, I try to be... It's not that easy, I guess," Blair said candidly.

"I get it," Lillian laughed. "Classic art is tough to sell in times like these; that's part of why we started in tattooing."

"That and the money's good," Tanner chimed in, nearly unintelligibly through a mouth full of pizza.

"You must be doing pretty ok for yourselves – I mean look at this place. It's all yours!" Blair answered, attempting to redirect the conversation away from her own story.

"It's taken a lot of work to get here, but... yeah, I think we can make this place a home," she said with a smile that was aimed at Tanner.

"What?" he said as he gulped down what remained of the bottle of beer he was holding.

"Nothing, babe. Just excited to be on this adventure with you," she answered dryly.

"Love you too, babe... I'm going to get back to the floors," he said before leaving his chair to give her a quick kiss on the forehead.

"We should probably get back to it as well," Lillian said with a deep sigh as she grabbed several more beers to take along with them.

They spent the entire afternoon painting, chatting, and drinking beer in the blistering summer sun. Blair began painting the mural as Lillian assisted seamlessly under her gentle direction. Neither of them seemed to even notice how quickly time had passed until the sunlight hung low in the afternoon sky, relieving some of the heat. By then, the 'Fight of the Century' mural was complete. It was silly and fitting. As the light began to fade further, Tanner finally joined them outside and quickly began laughing when he saw how brilliantly the large-scale flash had turned out.

"You two completely destroyed this, in the best possible way!" he said with an enormous grin.

Lillian answered, saying, "We'll certainly be seen as a flash shop that will do the weird ones – that's perfect for us!"

"This was fun!" Blair said to both of them. "I don't usually get to paint things that make me laugh... not for anyone to see, anyway."

"Well, you should - you're clearly very talented. Probably far too talented to be painting the brick walls of a tattoo shop," Tanner answered. Then, turning to his wife, he said, "I'm surprised this one hasn't tried to recruit you into an apprenticeship."

"I was just about to get to that, dear," Lillian said, rolling her eyes. As she turned to Blair, she asked, "Have you ever thought about tattooing? I know painting is kinda your thing, but obviously you could still paint... Just something to pay the bills..."

"Thank you – both of you – I'm flattered. It's just... um... my circumstances are... difficult," Blair answered apologetically.

"We do difficult – and weird – and everything else. It's the industry," Lillian said with a smirk. "I bet your brand of weird wouldn't be all that unusual compared to some of the others we've worked with."

"Oh, I'd take that bet," Blair laughed. "And I... I don't want to appear ungrateful at all."

Her lack of response seemed to have caught both of their attention, as Tanner's eyebrows furloughed inquisitively. Lillian's head moved slightly cock-eyed, and both of her new friends seemed to be looking for some explanation of what her big secret might be.

Blair considered for a moment the idea that if they were to be friends, they would eventually find out, anyway. Building relationships with people she could trust was how she had figured out groceries, art supplies, and most of her other needs. Although she had no need for tattoos, friends who loved art as much as she did were in short supply.

"I'm not 'lensed'... I can't... um... I have no legal means to accept or send payment through the feed. I... I'm offline – no Blinks. I'm... sort of an anomaly," she relented.

Both Tanner and Lillian froze for a moment, as Tanner looked around to see if others were observing their conversation. He then reached up to his eyes and removed his lenses, placing them into a small case he carried in his pocket. Lillian did the same, almost instinctively.

"Let's go inside where it's more... private," she said quietly, looking around to see if anyone was within earshot.

As darkness enveloped Frenchtown, the three returned to the interior of the shop, Blair began to tell her story. She spoke of her parents, their beliefs, and what had led her to choose a life that was free from the feed. Tanner and Lillian quietly listened without interruption, save for a brief few minutes, where Tanner retrieved a half-empty bottle of bourbon from the backroom and poured them drinks. When she had finished, the three of them sat silently for several minutes. Blair couldn't decide if revealing everything had been the right decision, but learning to trust others with her secret had always been the first step. She had done the same with Tony at the corner market. Mr. Addison had known her since she was a child; there still came a point where she had to confirm for him.

At last, whether from the stare Lillian was giving him or from his own motivations, rather awkwardly Tanner said, "My brother's un-lensed... took them out when he was sixteen and never put them back in. It's some big family secret, I guess... So, now we know your secret, and you know ours."

"What Tanner's clumsily getting at is – you seem like a good person. The decisions you've made and the reasons you've made them don't frighten us," Lillian added, shaking her head at her husband's report.

"Frighten us – I support it!" Tanner said enthusiastically.

"Oh... here we go," Lillian said, rolling her eyes.

"No – listen. They tax the hell out of us to give us the damn things for 'free', and then they monitor everything we look at and say while we're wearing them. The feed gets bigger and richer – and what do we get? Targeted adds based on every conversation they listen to; everywhere we go, they follow us. They know what we eat, what we like – they know everything! And if you take them out, you can't do anything!" Tanner raged, working himself into a fit of frustration.

"Well, why use them then? Why not just keep them out?" Blair asked, trying to sort through the man's paradoxical rhetoric.

"You know why," Tanner responded angrily. "You can't own a shop if you can't make and accept payments. You can't go any-where that's not in walking distance unless you can pay for the ride share. You can't buy groceries! You can't pay rent! So, you take the devil's deal, because without it life grinds to a halt. And then they've got you; you're trapped! Say the wrong thing on the feed, and people show up at your door. Say anything negative about the administration – well, that's inciting extremism and not covered by the first amendment anymore. Say something offensive – well, that's hate speech, and it's not protected by the first amendment! And they hear everything – every word."

"Honey, you're scaring the poor girl," Lillian scolded.

"It's nothing she doesn't know already," he answered dismissively. "Otherwise, she'd be in the same trap we all are. At least she was smart enough to never get on the feed!"

It took Blair several seconds before she noticed her jaw was gaping open in disbelief. While she had often had similar thoughts, she had never heard anyone connected express them out loud. The fact they had removed their lenses granted them openness she had not expected.

As Tanner poured himself another glass of bourbon, Blair considered the implications that there were others not connected. She had developed her own system of bartering locally with people who were sympathetic, but if there were others not connected, maybe there were ideas or tactics they had used that she had not considered. Once he had finally calmed back down, Blair mustered the courage to ask, "So, your brother – how does he manage?"

Lillian and Tanner looked at each other before he responded. While she thought she had been vulnerable with them, she sensed they were equally cautious. It was Lillian who finally answered, as she rather calmly said, "Come back tomorrow. We'll chat some more."

Blair said goodbye to her new friends and began the walk home in the dark. Along the way, she considered all she had heard, and wondered how many others like her were out there. If the brother of a shopkeeper in her own town wasn't connected, there had to be many others, she thought. But what good would it be if there was? They had no way to communicate with each other outside of the feed; they had no network. There could be millions or there could be just one other, and likely the result would be the same, she thought.

When she finally reached the Andover house, she noticed Bell had left the front lights on for her. As she entered the backyard, she noticed her friend sitting in the rocking chair outside of her small cottage.

"Where have you been?" Bell asked, somewhat franticly. "We didn't know if they had taken you to jail – we didn't know what happened at court!"

"I'm so sorry, Bell. I should have checked in. After the hearing, I went for a walk. I made some new friends, and they were working on—"

Bell interrupted her with a hug as she squeezed her closely. "Any other day, I wouldn't have thought anything about it. But with you leaving for court this morning? You may have given me a heart attack – we had no way of knowing where you were, if you were safe, if you weren't coming back!"

"I'm sorry. I... I was just so happy to be free that I didn't even think about how late it had gotten. We got caught up in a project, and I just lost track of time," Blair answered apologetically.

Shaking her head disapprovingly, Bell finally released the young woman from her embrace, saying, "You're a grown woman. You don't owe us an explanation... I was just worried."

"Bell, you've always looked out for me – if ever there was someone that had the right to demand an explanation, it'd be you," Blair answered softly.

"No, no. I probably overstepped. I got myself all worked up!" Bell stammered in annoyance. "So, now I'm going to head to bed! Just don't worry me like that!"

"I promise," Blair answered, turning to open the door of her small cottage.

"Oh, I almost forgot – a package was delivered for you. I left it on the desk next to the door... And a letter from your mother, I believe," Bell said wearily as she entered the backdoor of the main house.

"Who would have sent me a package?" she muttered to herself as she entered her one-room home. On the table near the door, she saw the letter from her mother sitting on top of a small cardboard box. The oddity of having something mailed to her piqued her curiosity enough to put off the letter from her mother.

She looked around the room for something sharp, and in moments found a pair of scissors in the small box of paints. Moments later, the seal of the box was opened to reveal a vintage, silver colored cellular phone with a sticky note on top that read, "Call Jax – my number is already inside."

~ 6 ~

"Mom – I don't understand what the problem is. You said you loved the painting; she's a talented artist!" he said, increasingly exasperated at her predictable resistance.

"Jaxson Joseph Wadsworth! My dearest son - are you out of your mind? Have you completely lost it?" his mother asked. "Do you have any idea how much money our family has contributed to the administration's super PAC?"

"Why does it matter? You loved the painting; we could feature it – it would give the event an authentic, sentimental angle that people would relate to. Why not let your stuffy friends decide how much her family's history matters to them?" he asked rhetorically, as he leaned backward in the sleek leather chair in his office. Of course, he already knew the answer before it came.

"To be seen associating with the child of known dissidents – to appear as though we are condoning their beliefs by supporting her work – it's outrageous!" his mother answered. "It's appalling you would even consider it!"

As Jax walked to the far end of his office to make himself an espresso, he braced for the bombardment of hostility he was about to call down as he defiantly replied, "Well, mom – it's my gallery. It's my job to sell beautiful art, and she makes beautiful art. I'm going to show it."

"YOU WILL DO NO SUCH THING!" she scolded angrily. Then, in a fury, she rapidly unloaded guilt upon him to put him back in his place. "I need not remind you, Jaxson, that this event is about more than just your gallery – it's about our family's place in the community. I should say 'Your gallery that we funded' - this PAS-SION of yours is tolerated because it benefits our family – let's not pretend otherwise!"

"How could I forget my obligation to the family?" Jax shouted sarcastically. "How ridiculous of me to even consider the possibility! I genuinely appreciate the reminder of your absolute control over my life!"

"Now, don't be like that, Jaxson!" his mother answered tersely. "You have a privileged life because of this family. Expecting gratitude and a little cooperation is perfectly reasonable. We're not telling you what art you should like or not like – we're not telling you who you should sleep with or spend your time with. I am telling you unequivocally that you will not openly feature the artwork from the child of a known dissident. There is too much controversy!"

"Understood," Jax seethed bitterly through his teeth.

"Jaxson – I want to hear it from you," she demanded.

"I will not *openly* feature artwork associated with *known* dissidents," Jax answered through the feed. "Happy now? Because I still have final details to sort out before the gala."

"Yes. I'm content now. Let me know if you need any help deciding on table linens or centerpieces; the company you used last time left the tables feeling so... provincial," his mother replied as her tone of voice returned to only mildly unpleasant rather than threatening.

"Bruce is looking over the last details now – if you're really interested in supervising the choice of table linens, call the gallery. He can link you the images. Now, I really have to go," Jax answered as he cut his mother's link in his feed.

In the immediate days that followed meeting Blair and receiving the painting he commissioned, he had presented the painting of his childhood home to his parents. While Blair had made it a gift to him, he, in turn, made it a gift to them, hoping to buy some goodwill and tolerance for her. At first, both his parents were elated. His mother went as far as to demand Jax provide her with Blair's contact information so that her friends could commission the artist to paint their own estates. His father had inquired about whether she was interested in portrait work, as they were seeking a founder's portrait for the grand entrance of the new Wadsworth office tower near the old football stadium on the northern end of downtown. The interest in her work was precisely what he had imagined it would be until he had to explain why he could not send her contact information through the feed. That conversation led to another regarding her family's history, and immediately the mood soured. What followed was an hour-long lecture from his father about how the Anti-Money Laundering Act had reduced drug-trafficking at the border, reduced drug-related crime across the nation, and prevented terrorist attacks. The notion that any sane person could oppose the standardized payment provisions of the AMLA was unfathomable – it was ludicrous. And if privacy needed to be sacrificed on the altar of safety, of course, everyone should be forced to make that sacrifice. It was necessary for the common good.

Of course, Jax wondered how much of their very audible protests were the result of their feed being closely monitored and how much was what they actually believed. In the end, he supposed it didn't matter. Much as he suspected, they would not support the gallery carrying Blair's work. And yet, he still very much wanted to.

Ten days had passed since their initial protest against carrying Blair's work. The conversation with his mother that morning had only confirmed their minds had not changed. Fortunately, Jax had already put a plan into motion, one that began at the first signs of their resistance. Buying a working cellular phone took some do-ing, and after receiving the device, he needed to have the device configured to be able to call into the feed. While the feed used the infrastructure of the old cellular network, telephone numbers had long since become obsolete. The solution came from Parker, who used AI to write an app that created numbers that would pass from cellular signals directly into the feed by assigning a hidden phone number to a feed contact. When at last the cell phone was ready, Jax programmed his number and sent it via courier to Blair's home. By his estimation, it should have arrived yesterday. He would only need to wait for a call to find out if there was any chance she would be interested.

While Jax sat in his office overlooking the invoices Crush had received for the upcoming gala, it was Bruce who eventually interrupted his work.

"Sir, your mother has selected the table linens she prefers; I'm sending the invoice to you now," he said.

"Thank you for... accommodating her," Jax said as he finally looked past his feed to the man standing in his office. "Was there something else?"

"Um... yes. That young woman from a few weeks ago is downstairs. She does not have an appointment, but insisted you wanted to speak with her," Bruce answered, looking to Jax's facial expression for some indicator of whether he should welcome her in or present some sort of scheduling conflict.

Jax paused for a moment, wondering if there might have been some sort of mistake. Many people came in and out of the gallery on a weekly basis, and while Blair had been on his mind frequently, he didn't want to assume his boyish infatuation had suddenly and unexpectedly arrived in his gallery. "When you say 'young woman from a few weeks ago', who exactly – "

"The um... redhead, sir. The one you seemed *particularly*... interested in," Bruce responded, as he made overly subtle, exaggerated gestures toward the downstairs portion of the gallery.

"Thank you, Bruce," Jax responded abruptly as he leaped out of his chair and toward the staircase, nearly running over his assistant.

"Of course," came Bruce's amused response from behind him as he descended to the lower level of the gallery. Confirming his surprise, there she was, looking closely at a Caldo piece that hung from the far wall in the gallery. For a moment, Jax panicked, uncertain of what to do or if he even remembered how to talk to a beautiful woman without making a fool of himself. *They had talked before, and he did fine,* he reminded himself. But this fascination with her had only grown since their lunch date, if he could call it that. Mentally, he had prepared for a call, practicing a script he had in his mind of how it would go. He had even gone to great lengths to make such a call possible and convenient. Yet despite the efforts, Blair Huxley stood in his gallery like a delicate flower that miraculously appeared on his freshly mowed front lawn.

He walked up beside her without interrupting and stood there for a moment, saying nothing. She must have heard his footsteps, as when he came closer she whispered, "I can't say I'm a fan of this one."

"What about it don't you like?" Jax asked quietly, trying to calm himself so he didn't seem too excited.

"She's in pain... the woman, or despair," Blair responded, matching his quiet tone.

"Yes... Caldo's pieces frequently reflect dark and primitive emotions. Pain... anguish... fear... it's what he's known for," he answered softly, as he began feeling more calm discussing art rather than his romantic interest.

"Oh, I understand *what* he painted... I could even guess as to *why* he painted it. I just don't think it's beautiful. Maybe it's important to reflect on our darker emotions... maybe the painting is exploiting her pain... It's just a portrait of pain. A woman in pain. That's all there is to it... and you could see that walking down several streets in this city. Are the kind of people that buy his work so disconnected from real life that they need to be reminded that pain exists in the world? Is that it? Some need to feel alive again?" she asked, studying the piece closely.

"That's an interesting interpretation," Jax answered, uncertain of what else to say. After allowing a few moments to pass, he summoned his courage and added, "It's good to see you again, Blair."

His words were enough to break her attention from the painting as she turned to him with a smile. She then held up the cell phone he had sent to her and waved it gently in her hand.

"Right," he said when he noticed the phone. "It was so you could call me – you didn't have to come all the way down here."

"I thought about it," she said, brushing a lock of crimson hair that had fallen out-of-place back behind her ear. "I've seen how these things work in old movies... I just..."

Jax couldn't tell what she was trying to say as his eyebrows furrowed, reflecting his confusion. She blushed when she saw his confusion and said only, "Well, after not hearing from you for a few weeks... I just thought if you were ready to break the bad news to me, that I'd rather hear it in person."

"Huh," Jax grunted involuntarily. "How about some tea?"

"Yes, please," Blair said with a smile. She then followed him to his office upstairs. Jax gestured for her to have a seat as he began preparing a lavender infused Earl Gray tea he had recently bought, in hopes the young woman might at some point be in his office once again.

As he poured the hot water into the infuser, the office filled with the soothing aroma of lavender and slightly bitter black tea. He then placed the cup with the steeping tea on the small table beside her and sat down across from her.

"You went to an awful lot of work to find my favorite tea..." she said with a hint of embarrassment.

"Nonsense – you have exquisite taste. I wanted to try it for my-self," he demurred.

Awkwardly, Jax looked about for the cup of espresso he had made for himself earlier, which was still sitting atop his desk. It took him an awkward moment to realize it was behind him, but after locating the small cup, he quickly retrieved it and then sat back down as he finally took a sip. The now cold coffee left a distinctly unpleasant impression, causing his face to twist and distort momentarily, as he quickly set the cup down.

"Now then," Jax said. "You came all this way to be let down, then?"

"Mmmhmm," Blair uttered with a nod as she reached for the small cup of tea on the table beside her. "I got the impression from our last meeting there was no way you'd be able to carry my art. And I... made peace with that. But then your friend Mr. Wells appeared at my court hearing out of nowhere and saved the day... and... You kept your word. That means something to me. So, I also wanted to say thank you – sincerely. And I... sort of figured if you wanted to talk to me, I owed it to you to thank you face to face."

Jax wasn't sure what to say. Of course, he recalled asking his attorney to assist, but like so many similar things, he hardly considered the impact of the insignificant gesture. After a brief, silent moment of consideration, he answered, "I'm glad we could help."

Having noticed the tea in the small glass in her hand had sufficiently steeped, Blair removed the infuser and set it gently on the small plate that held her cup. She then took a small sip from the cup, testing its temperature. Feeling it was still too hot to drink, she rested the cup once again on the plate and looked at Jax asking, "So... you asked me to call... And now I'm here. What's on your mind, Jax?"

Jax shifted uncomfortably in his seat, uncertain of where he should start. Then he took a deep breath and began explaining, "My parents loved the painting you made of their home – they really loved it. But, just as you've already guessed, your parents' history... they are forbidding me from openly featuring your work in the gallery."

While Blair had previously assumed finally hearing the news would send her into an emotional tailspin, when at last her fears were confirmed, all she felt was relief. The anxiety of waiting to be disappointed had finally come and gone, and at least she had an answer. *It's better than false hope*, she thought. As she once again tested the temperature of her tea, she took a deep sip and then placed the cup gently back onto the saucer that carried it. With a polite smile to her host, she stood up from the leather sofa on which she had been seated, intent on leaving the gallery with her fears confirmed.

Jax noticed her movement and abruptly intervened, standing to look her in the eye as he said, "Wait – Blair, please."

She paused for half a second, shaking her head and reassuringly said, "No, that's fine, Jax. That's fine. It's what I expected. I'll just be going – I don't want to take any more of your time.

"I have an idea!" Jax interjected, attempting to salvage the meeting from the freefall it was quickly turning into.

"Jax..." she answered, trying to fight back the tears that were forming as her disappointment set in. "I... I won't compromise my beliefs for the chance at success... I don't want you to do anything extraordinary to try to... I dunno... find a way to make this work. I understand the situation you're in. It's... fine."

"Well... can I ask you a question before you storm out of here angry at me? If you say no... I won't bother you again. I promise," he asked, trying to convince her to hear him out.

"Sure," Blair said curtly.

With an unexpected boldness, he hastily asked, "Would you care to be my date for an upcoming gala here at the gallery?"

"What?" she asked, startled by the question. "Your...date?"

"Let me explain," Jax said, as he raised his hands slightly and motioned for her to return to her seat. "My parents have forbidden me from openly featuring the work of the child of dissidents... but you never signed the piece you gave me. We can have the plaque read, 'Anonymous'... or something like that. Authors have pen names. I'm not sure why artists can't – we'll put whatever you'd like! Then you could come to the gala with me – they don't get a say in who I date, that's a firm boundary even they won't cross. And... you'd get to see your work... in a gallery... being admired by people who love art."

Tears filled Blair's eyes to the point where she had to fight to keep them from running down her cheeks. She was momentarily successful, fighting diligently to dam the wells of her lower eyelids. Then, at once, a single tear broke free and ran down her cheek. Then another followed. "I'm sorry," she said, as she looked around for a box of tissues.

"Why are you crying?" Jax asked, now terribly confused by what had just transpired.

"Why would you do this for me? What... why do you care about me seeing my work in a gallery? Why – why go to all this trouble?" she said, wiping her eyes with the sleeve of her shirt in the absence of tissue.

"Hey... hey," Jax said sympathetically. "You're a talented artist. I want everyone to see that – don't you? Even if they don't know you painted it? Even if they don't know who you are – don't you want people to see the beautiful result of all your effort?"

Blair shifted uneasily, half nodding and half trying to contain her emotions. Then finally she answered, saying, "I... I think every artist wants their work to be appreciated. It's just, I don't belong with fancy people at fancy parties... I'm just a girl that loves to paint. I'm not like you and your family. I don't know how to be that."

Jax immediately felt as if his plan had been so foolishly conceived that any idiot would have known his attempt was doomed to fail. He wondered to himself how he could have been so blinded by the impossibility of his request and how much it required of her. Then at last, almost apologetically, he answered, "I don't want you to be anyone other than who you are – not for anything. Not for this gallery, or my family and their friends. I only want to share your gift with others who will appreciate it."

"I'm... I'm just not sure I would fit in. I've never been to a formal party before; I don't have anything to wear that doesn't have paint on it," she laughed.

"If that's what's stopping you, let's solve that. If you showed up to an art galla covered in paint, people would figure things out pretty quickly," Jax said half-jokingly. "I promise, if you choose to come with me, I won't ask you to be anyone other than you."

"But not me, right? Because if they knew who I was, I wouldn't be welcome," Blair said, seeing through the false promise that even Jax hadn't realized. She picked up her teacup once again and drank a long sip from the tea, now perfectly cooled to a gentle warmth.

"You've got me there," he said with a sigh. "But that's not the same as asking you to be someone you're not. I'm not asking you to pretend. We'd simply have to not reveal too much; concealing your name would be the cost. Otherwise... absolute hell will break loose with my parents."

Blair laughed as he spoke, trying to convince herself this was something she could not do. It went against her entire strategy of remaining unnoticed, but as a counterpoint, so did her desire to have her paintings seen at all. She knew deep in her heart, she wanted her work to be appreciated, and with that desire came risk. Whether this was the right risk and the right crowd to take a risk with, she wasn't certain.

Finally, after staring at the teacup in front of her for several minutes, afraid to look Jax in the eyes, she said, "So, you care this deeply about my art?"

"Well, yes. I think you're talented. I... also *like* you. You're a gentle, honest soul... I'd like to spend more time with you," Jax said quietly, wondering if his admission was enough to break her fixation on the teacup.

Looking up to meet his gaze, Blair smiled, suddenly feeling shy and awkward, as if she had forced the man into revealing his true intentions that she had only half suspected. Then she said quietly, "I guess it's a date, then."

Jax breathed a sigh of relief, instantly relaxing as if he had reached the other end of some tightrope walk between jagged cliffs.

"Thank you – I mean, I'm glad you'll come," he said, finally relaxing into the deep leather chair that until then he had been sitting on the edge of. "I will try to make it as safe and, um... *not weird* as I can for you."

"Promise?" Blair laughed. "What if your parents hate me? What if nobody likes my painting? What if – "

"You're perfect, Blair. Don't worry about any of that; you don't need to impress anyone. You've already impressed me. And I'll have you on my arm the whole evening, or at least nearly. I'll be a shield for you," he reassured her.

Having committed to the adventure, Blair felt uneasy but excited. Maybe it was her sense of vanity that had won out over her reason. It would only take one curious person to ask for her info before she would be exposed. She had dodged many such situations in the past, using an arsenal of excuses or verbal distractions to avoid awkward confrontations. But in consideration of what she had agreed to, she knew she was willfully inviting such confrontations rather than avoiding them. There was also an issue of what she would wear to a formal event; most of her clothing came from bartering or hand-me-downs. She would stand out awkwardly. And while it was easy for Jax to say they could simply solve that problem, without being able to buy a dress, shoes, and cosmetics, the problem seemed to her to be much larger than he assumed.

Seconds later, Bruce appeared at the top of the staircase and said, "Sir?"

"Bruce, would you mind taking Ms. Huxley on a bit of a side-quest for the afternoon?" Jax asked, turning toward his assistant. "I've sent some of the particulars to your screen – whatever she needs for the gala. Just have Jacque's invoice me; I'll see to it."

"I'm certain we can manage, sir," Bruce answered in a tone revealing a mixture of amusement and mild annoyance.

"Jax, you don't need to... I can find something to wear," Blair protested.

"No, no – it would be asking too much of you. Let me do this for you. Please?" he responded, searching for her consent.

"But... my bike... I can't just leave it," she answered, searching for a polite excuse to remove herself from her benefactor's generosity.

"I'll put it in a ride-share and have it sent back to your place. Or, you're welcome to ride home after you've found everything you need – your call," Jax said.

Blair let out a deep breath of resignation and said, "Ok – looks like you've won this round. I'm all out of ideas on how to get out of this."

Her response caused Bruce chuckled slightly to himself, as he struggled to regain his composure. After she joined him at the stairs and as they descended, Jax could hear his assistant say, "Oh, honey – don't worry. You're already a knockout... I was a fashion design major at Washington, and I have excellent taste! You're in expert hands."

Jax spent the next several hours finishing the preparation work for the gala. It was late in the day, nearing the finish of his work, when an interruption came in the form of Caldo, calling through the feed. Not wanting to upset a still important client, Jax set aside his work to take the call.

"Jaxy boy, you handsome devil – what is this I'm hearing about a soirée being held at Crush? Why haven't I received my invitation yet?" the artist asked as soon as Jax answered the feed.

"Caldo – it's great to hear from you. There was a mishap with the printer, but the invitations are going out today – you should receive it shortly," Jax answered.

"I have to say I am a bit disappointed that I was not asked to be the feature for this event, Jaxson. I would have thought that given our relationship, my work would have been the obvious favorite," the artist said through the feed, revealing a mild annoyance.

"I'm sorry. Was that a question or a statement?" Jax asked, trying to put his finger on exactly what the man was asking.

"Neither... and both, of course. I'm just having a conversation with my favorite art dealer in St. Louis," Caldo answered obnoxiously.

Jax sensed there was something he expected he lacked the courage to demand, perhaps considering the recent change in their business dealings. *Whatever it was, it would be better to see any potential trouble coming; there were enough landmines to navigate with his parents*, he thought.

"Well, Caldo... I'm not sure what to say. You asked to be released from the exclusivity clause in our contract. You can now show your work at any of the galleries here or elsewhere..." Jax answered, still uncertain of the card being played.

"Oh, of course... of course..." the artist answered. "Forgive me, I had simply assumed I was the biggest name carried at Crush; I wanted to make sure I was available to you if you needed me present for the event."

"Certainly, we're hopeful you can attend. You are definitely the highest profile artist in the gallery... for this gala, we're taking an approach of trying to highlight all the local talent... create some familiarity among some of our lesser-known artists. You know, the people hiding in that great shadow cast by the name 'Caldo'," Jax answered, attempting to assuage the man's obviously bruised ego.

"Ah, of course. I see," he answered magnanimously. "It's like a charity event for the struggling artists of the city – your family has always been so generous with the needy."

"Something like that," Jax answered, attempting to ensure his eye-rolling would not be visible through the feed. "Allow me to assure you; your invitation will be hand delivered this evening, straight from the printer by courier. It will have all the pertinent information, and we would be honored if you would join us. I'm sure the lesser-known artists would be grateful for the crowd your name will draw... unless, of course, you have prior obligations."

"We will see, Jaxon. I will do you this favor if I can – I've been so busy lately," Caldo answered smugly.

Jax knew the artist's release from the exclusivity had already backfired. With the decrease in his popularity being widely known, several other local galleries had declined to contract at all after being offered terms that were nearly extortionary. Likewise, while Crush would still carry his work, the terms of his own contract with the artist were quite favorable compared to the terms being offered to other galleries. There was nothing to lose by continuing to carry a select few pieces, aside from gallery wall space.

"Well, do what you can, Caldo. I'm sure my parents would love to catch up. But if you can't, I will convey your regrets, loyally as ever," Jax answered.

"Good-good, Jaxson. I'll be looking forward to it," the artist answered, then terminated the feed.

Following the call, Jax briefly glanced at the remaining arrangements and contented himself with the fact he had made as much progress as he was going to. With no other appointments on his calendar, and Bruce away from the gallery, he thought it best to simply close the gallery early and head home.

As he exited the gallery, Jax issued the voice activated command that locked the doors, and just as he was about to enter the rideshare for his trip home, noticed Blair's bike, resting on the edge of the exterior wall next to the gallery. He then recalled he had promised to have it sent on her behalf, and decided he would simply drop it off and save having to call a separate ride. Through his lenses, he relayed his intent to Bruce, who was still busy outfitting the young artist who would accompany Jax to the gala. It took some clumsy effort before he had the bicycle loaded into the empty vehicle, which held six passengers comfortably but one full-size bicycle and one passenger rather uncomfortably.

The ride to St. Charles was awkward but otherwise uneventful, save for the new ads that appeared in his feed, beckoning him to their catering services, party rental services, bicycle shops, and even an app for a virtual DJ, all the result of his daily activities. While the ads had become a daily part of life and easily ignored, for a moment, he considered what it must be like for Blair, living free from the feed. While terrifying, there must be a certain peace to not have every moment of life monitored and recorded, he thought. In that moment, a novel idea suddenly struck him, and with little deliberation, Jax removed his lenses and placed them in the small case that he kept in his pocket. The next few minutes were both terrifying and exhilarating – everything felt quiet and surreal. No calls or messages beamed into view; the eeriness of the empty vehicle in which he was riding suddenly seemed out of place. After only a short while, the uneasiness became too overwhelming, and Jax quickly returned his lenses to his eyes. In an instant, his feed came alive once again with advertisements, messages, and headlines from the day's events.

When the rideshare finally reached the Andover house, Jax instructed the virtual driver to remain momentarily until he returned. Upon exiting the vehicle, Jax retrieved the bicycle, twisting and pulling to free it from the interior; the wheels and handlebars seemed to resist his efforts. Just then, a voice from behind him called out, "Need a hand there?"

Jax turned his head toward the voice, only to find Blair's dark-haired friend whom he had met weeks before. "Um... I think I've got it. Maybe."

"Doesn't look like it," the woman laughed. "Let me help; I've done this trick a time or two."

In an instant, Bell could be seen at the far side of the vehicle with the door open. With her assistance maneuvering the handlebars, the bicycle quickly came free, falling smoothly toward Jax and the sidewalk near the house.

"Thank you," he said, wiping a bit of sweat from his eyebrows with a handkerchief.

"Happy to help," Bell answered before adding, "So, I see the bicycle, but not the rider."

"Ah, right – she couldn't call to let you know," Jax said, shaking his head with a new appreciation for the limitations she faced. "I... Well, I've asked Blair to join me at a gala being put on at Crush; she's going to be my date."

The look on Bell's face could hardly hide the wave of distrust that quickly came over her. "Your date? At a formal event?"

"Yeah, my family likes to use the gallery to... well, promote itself, I guess. It'll feature local artists," Jax said, attempting to ease the woman's concern.

"And Blair is one of those artists?" Bell asked skeptically.

"Well – no. Not exactly. Given her family history, my parents say I can't really feature or sell her work. They're worried about the potential implications of being associated with an artist whose parents were known dissidents," he answered defensively.

Upon hearing confirmation of her suspicions, Bell rolled her eyes and began shaking her head, showing her annoyance. "Dissidents? That's funny," she said sarcastically. "They used to be called professors. In fact, her mother, Ayn, was one of the best criminal justice professors I ever had. She cared about the principles of truth and justice, not just the words. And her father held multiple doctorates. He wasn't just some college professor. He was a well-respected voice in his field nationwide. They were good people – brilliant minds. They were principled. Treating them like traitors because they were vocal in their disagreement with policy was... Well, it was wrong."

"My apologies – I meant no offense. Try to understand, my parents care about the optics. And from a current perspective, they only see them... in their way. It's just, our family has certain ties to certain centers of influence in DC – to policy makers. Not in a way that they set policy, really. More in a way that they get invited to the right parties and donate to the right causes... I suppose they're not willing to risk having their name anywhere near those who aren't currently in favor with the administration," he answered, taken back by her forwardness.

"But you are? You're taking Blair with you, but not featuring her work." Bell replied rhetorically.

"That's the plan – I have her out with my assistant now, finding a dress and what not for the occasion... I'm trying to not make this a burden for her," he said earnestly.

"Hmmm..." Bell answered. For a moment, she studied the man, wondering if his apparent sincerity was an act to disguise some hidden agenda, "Why don't you stay a little while; call another ride when you're ready?"

Unsure if he had passed the test, and suspecting he was walking into an interrogation, Jax was leery of accepting the invitation. Trying to excuse himself politely, he said, "No... no, I couldn't. I don't want to interfere."

"Please – I just opened a bottle of red. If you're going to be taking Blair out, at least allow my husband and I to put a face to the name, so to speak," Bell answered as she gestured toward the home.

Not wanting to be rude and understanding this request was a more polite demand, Jax agreed, shutting the door of the rideshare behind him. Moments later, he was up the steps and through the front door of the small home. As he entered, he heard a man speaking with a young girl from the direction of the kitchen, just beyond the living room at the entrance to the home. It was clear he had stumbled into dinner preparation.

"Honey, who's that with you?" the man called out.

"It's Blair's boyfriend," Bell called out loudly.

Jax's heart dropped for a moment as he quickly tried to decide if he should correct the accusation or simply let it pass. Realizing he had already been outmaneuvered, he remained quiet. As he entered the kitchen, he extended his hand toward the man at the stove saying, "I'm Jax – I'm a friend of Blair's."

"Xavier," the man replied, setting a wooden spoon down on the pot of boiling water. "And this is our daughter Mia – say hi Mia."

"Hi," the girl responded. Then immediately, she asked, "Are you really Blair's boyfriend?"

The remark caused her father to grin mischievously, while her mother made a visible, valiant effort to keep herself from audibly laughing.

"Oh, no – I think your mom was just teasing me," Jax chuckled. "But I am a friend of hers. And I am a big fan of her paintings. I really love all kinds of art – hers especially."

"I do too! Especially the one with the big bird on it!" Mia exclaimed.

Not knowing what exactly she was referring to, but having seen only a few of Blair's pieces, Jax shook his head in agreement before replying, "She's a very, very talented artist."

"Mia, honey – why don't you go get in the bath while daddy finishes up dinner," Bell said as she placed her hands on her daughter's shoulders.

"But mom! I want to stay and talk with Blair's boyfriend!" the young girl responded.

"Now please, Mia Elizabeth," her mother replied assertively.

"Fine," the young girl grumbled, dragging her feet behind her as she departed the kitchen.

"So, Jax... you run an art gallery?" Xavier asked, with his attention once again focused on the pot of boiling pasta on the stove.

"Yes, the Crush Gallery," Jax answered politely. "I'm the owner, in fact."

"Good for you!" Xavier replied genuinely. "It's hard to be a self-made business owner these days, what with the inflation and what not."

"Ha," Bell laughed involuntarily, only to cover her mouth in a bit of horror at her own voice. "Sorry," she said sheepishly.

Xavier's face suddenly changed to confusion that Jax quickly remedied, "My family owns several businesses in St. Louis. Your wife's um... laugh... Well, let's just say 'self-made' is a bit generous."

"Well, you can't fault him for using the advantage he was given, Bell – we would do the same if we were in his position," Xavier responded casually.

"Of course, dear," came Bell's voice rather monotone. Then, after removing a few wine glasses from the cabinet, she removed the cork from a bottle of cabernet that had been sitting on the counter and poured a glass for each of them. The first she handed to their guest, and the second she handed to her husband, who took the glass in hand while he continued to stir the pasta. With the third cup in hand, Bell's demeanor changed to be slightly more serious. She gestured to seats at a small table in the dining nook attached to the kitchen, and after they were seated, she began her interrogation in earnest.

"How much has Blair told you about her past?" she said casually.

"Well, I've heard a bit about her parents, but you know that already," Jax answered honestly.

"And obviously that gives your family some reservations... but not you?" she asked.

"Honestly, I'm not sure. I... don't involve myself too much about politics. When all the riots and unrest happened – when things got bad – I was pretty young. My family was pretty shielded from it all; I stayed out of it," he said.

"Hmm," Bell grunted with raised eyebrows, reflecting a subtle measure of surprise. "I would have thought your parents would have been more... involved. Given the... influence you mentioned."

"If they were, I'd be really surprised. My family has done well by being uncontroversial; we've, um... prioritized backing the winning side – no matter the situation," he said.

"Some people would call that wise," Bell said, taking a sip of the dark red wine in her glass. "That's what gives me some pause about you now taking Blair as your date to this party you're having."

"Wait, what now?" Xavier asked from the other side of the kitchen, suddenly becoming acutely aware of why the man was seated in his kitchen.

"Didn't I mention that, honey? Jax's taking Blair as his date to a gala at the gallery. 'Galla at the Gallery' – that's a got a ring to it," she said with a laugh.

"I wish I would have thought of it," Jax laughed. "We settled on 'An Evening with Your Crush', I'm afraid."

"It's got some whimsy to it," Xavier said with a smile. "Especially for a date night event – the play on words – I get it."

"A little on the nose, though," Bell mumbled.

"Well, my mother suggested 'A view of the Lou' or something to that effect. It had... weird bathroom connotations... a bit cheeky," Jax said with a smirk.

The last part of the comment resulted in Xavier chuckling to himself from his place near the stove. Bell simply rolled her eyes and redirected the conversation to the previous topic. "So, high-profile event – the city's premiere fine art gallery – an army of your family's friends, and you're forbidden from featuring her work? Does that about summarize it?" she asked.

At that point, Xavier turned off the burner and removed the pot of cooked pasta from the stove, emptying its contents into a colander in the sink. Once the noise had dissipated, he leaned against the counter of the sink and simply waited for a response.

"I... There's a nuance to that," Jax said, somewhat defensively. "I was forbidden from featuring the art of a child of known dissidents. I will date whomever I choose; my family gets no say in that – only business. And there was nothing in the threat they made about featuring an artist anonymously."

"So, you're working a loophole?" Xavier said with a smile.

"Don't encourage him, Zay!" Bell said, only half-seriously.

"Yes... I guess," Jax answered. Then, joggling his head as if he was uncomfortable with the way his intentions were being characterized, he began attempting to explain. "Look, Blair's talented. I want to show her work," he said, still uncomfortable with how the topic was being framed. "And I like her – she's got an odd mix of innocence and honesty – a boldness. I... I don't know that I've ever met anyone who was so truly... her own. I mean, the way she lives – she doesn't seem beholden to anyone. Well, maybe you two, of course. But it feels like it's a choice; it's a decision she's made. That you all have made. It's radical, obviously. But she doesn't apologize for who she is or the decision she's made. She accepts it; I respect that. It's refreshing."

Bell nodded her head, evaluating what he had said. After considering his motivations for a few seconds and taking a large gulp of her wine, she said, "When her parents weren't around anymore... the State put her into foster care – 'placement homes' they call it now. She bounced around the system for several years – house to house because while people think they can be ok with it, the umm... being off the feed, being disconnected... it gets old for people who don't understand it."

"Heck, it gets old for us, and we *do* understand it!" Xavier interjected suddenly.

"Look – I don't know what you guys want me to say. It's a date. It's just a date. I'm not saying I won't get tired of it too; I don't know. But I *do* respect her decision and her lifestyle. And it certainly makes things with my family a bit complicated – no doubt. But I'd like to spend more time with her; I'd like to see more of her work. Maybe it's just the one date, and that's all there is to it. Who knows?" Jax said, trying to be honest without being overtly defensive.

"That's fair," Xavier said, nodding his understanding. "We just don't um.... trust people easily. We've been trying to look out for her since she got out of the system. Bell felt like we owed that to her parents; they were friends of ours."

"Just... tread gently, please," Bell said quietly. "She's got a noble, sincere heart."

Jax nodded, hoping he understood whatever it was they were trying to convey. While he had no intention of causing Blair harm, the oddness of the interaction left him wondering what unspoken commitment they were expecting of him. After finishing the last of his wine, he simply said, "Well, thank you for the wine. I'm... not sure if there's... I don't want to be rude, but – "

"Of course, no. Don't let us keep you," Bell answered.

Xavier simply extended his hand, saying, "It's good to meet you, Jax. If you ever need any legal help, let me know. And uh, if we're ever in the market for some art –"

"You'd do well to check with the source living in your backyard cottage," Jax laughed to the reciprocation of his hosts.

"Of course – Well, it's good to meet you all the same," Xavier answered.

As Bell escorted him toward the front door, Mia came bounding down the staircase, saying, "You're not staying for dinner? I wanted to tell you more about MY art!"

"Next time," Jax answered with a smile.

~ 7 ~

"**O**uch! Easy Lil!" she squealed, squirming in the black leather chair of the tattoo shop.

"Think this is bad, and you're going to have a rude awakening when I finally get you under the gun," her heavily tattooed friend replied.

"Is it supposed to hurt? Serious question – I've literally never had my eyelashes curled before," Blair asked, attempting to conceal her discomfort.

"Dudes can't even tell – I don't know why you bother," Tanner interjected without looking up from his work.

His response caused Blair to sigh heavily, which was quickly met with a gentle slap from her friend.

"You move again and I'm going to rip these eyelashes off – like gone. You'll just be that girl with no eyelashes. Is that what you want?" Lillian asked, still standing over Blair holding the small, metal curling device.

"She could probably pull it off," Tanner interjected with a smile, as he continued carefully working on the shop patron laying prone on an adjacent chair.

With the shop's recent opening, business was just starting to pick up. When Blair had asked for Lillian's help with her hair and makeup, Lillian volunteered happily, eager to exchange a favor for all the help Blair had provided in preparing the shop for opening.

"There! Done!" Lillian said as she removed the contraption from the young woman's eye. "Now the other one!"

"Really?" Blair asked, somewhat horrified.

"What? Do you want to go with just one eye's lashes curled? People might think you've had a stroke," Lillian laughed.

"Or you're sleepy," Tanner's patron laughed over the hum of the tattoo machine.

"Only half sleepy!" Tanner retorted as he paused to wipe the freshly applied ink.

Moments later, the handheld curler was applied to Blair's other eye, as Lillian held it in place, slowly counting to herself as she paused. After a long minute, she again released the clamp on the small machine and Blair was free. Looking at Tanner, she asked, "What do you think?"

"I already told you – dudes can't tell. Ya'll do this torture for your own reasons," he said, shaking his head slowly in confusion.

Turning to Lillian, she said, "So...Yes?"

"Yes," Lillian answered. "Just the mascara now."

Blair responded by opening her eyes as wide as she could, and then held in place as still as a statue while her friend applied the eye makeup. Fortunately, the tar-like substance went on easily, and without discomfort.

"Okay – what's next?" Blair asked.

"Get your dress on, and then we'll do your hair," Lillian answered, pointing to the door of the shop's restroom and the mounted hook upon which a long, black garment bag hung. Blair quickly slid off of the tattoo chair and disappeared into the restroom. After a long delay, she once again appeared, adorned in a long, sleeveless black dress that was cut low around her chest, hugging her torso down to her waist and thighs, where it opened slightly, allowing the dress to drape down to the floor where it stopped just above her bare feet.

"Phwwwwwhhht Phew!" whistled Tanner as he glanced up at the spectacle.

Lillian rolled her eyes and responded to him by saying, "Hey – eyes over here, husband!"

"I was just being supportive, Lil," he said with his head back down, staring into his work.

"You look stunning, B!" Lillian said with a smile, then added, "Now, hair!"

As Blair once again found her seat in the tattoo artist's chair, Lillian pulled the chopsticks from the messy pile of red hair that had been haphazardly mounted atop her small head.

"Just – don't overdo it. I... I want to look like me," Blair said appreciatively.

"Absolutely," Lillian answered, fingering through the delicate strands until it lay neatly into sections. As if from the ether, a curling iron suddenly appeared in the tattooed woman's hand, at which point she wielded the device to each of the separated strands, one at a time. As she did, she asked, "You gave him this address, right? He's picking you up here?"

"Yes," she replied, then sarcastically added, "I was going to walk home in this thing and have him pick me up there, but the heels..."

"Really?" Lillian asked, suddenly pausing with the curling iron.

"No! Of course not – but again, I really appreciate all your help," Blair responded genuinely.

"You'd look better with a half sleeve... I have an opening Saturday afternoon," Tanner muttered as he again wiped the back of the shop patron at his station.

In response, Lillian simply rolled her eyes and reassured her friend, "You are the epitome of perfection, just as you are. Don't listen to him."

It took another ten minutes of applying the curling iron before the task was complete. Blair's long hair flowed gently down her back with long loose waves showcasing an effortless elegance. That left only lipstick and heels to be added to the equation before she was ready. As a fortunate coincidence, the rideshare arrived just as Blair stepped into the second of her thin, black heels. Seeing the vehicle arrive out front, Blair squeaked with excitement and headed toward the front entrance of the shop, saying over her shoulder as she left, "Thank you-thank-you-thank-you! And wish me luck!"

"You don't need any, doll – you're stunning!" Lillian shouted.

"Have fun!" Tanner added.

As Blair approached the vehicle, the door automatically opened to reveal an empty interior. She had hoped Jax might greet her in the vehicle, but knew he was probably busy greeting guests at the gala. While feeling disappointed for a moment, the thrill and anticipation of the evening that would come quickly overcame any reservation she had about riding alone to her destination. Then, as soon as she was seated in the vehicle, she noticed that across from her seat, a small velvet box with a note on top was waiting, along with a glass of champagne that had recently been poured.

As the vehicle departed, Blair opened the note, which read simply:

My sincere apologies for not attending to you personally. I would be greatly pleased if you would accept this small gift as a token of my appreciation for joining me this evening.

Eagerly awaiting your arrival,

– Jax

Inside the small velvet box, a delicately thin, lustrous, silvery-white colored chain perched on a small velvet pedestal holding a small pendant shaped like a paintbrush. Blair had not even considered jewelry, aside from the diamond studs Bell loaned her for the occasion. Wasting no time, she quickly removed the necklace from the box and carefully fastened it about her neck; the pendant fell gently to the center of her chest, stopping just above the line of her dress.

The ride to the gallery was quiet and peaceful as Blair sipped the glass of champagne that had been left for her. After only a few sips, she suddenly noticed the marks of her lipstick that had been left behind, and quickly began looking for something with which she could wipe off the glass. Seeing nothing, she awkwardly put the glass down in the holder from which she had retrieved it, afraid of making a further mess. Only a few minutes later, the vehicle turned onto the street where the Crush Gallery was located. To her astonishment, the entrance to the gallery had been blocked off to allow only one vehicle at a time to pass. The rideshare then pulled into line behind two other cars, and Blair waited until at last it moved in front of the gallery.

As the door to the vehicle opened, Jax's face was the first she saw. Dressed in a finely tailored black suit and tie, he held out his hand to assist her in climbing out of the vehicle, which at once was more of a struggle than she had expected because of the pointy footwear she had chosen. Once standing with him in front of the gallery, Jax continued to holding her hand and said, "You look absolutely radiant."

He then turned to the others standing at the entrance and said, "May I present to you, Mrs. Blair Huxley, my date for the evening."

The elderly woman and man looked at each other for a moment with a brief, uncertain glance that Blair couldn't quite make sense of. It lasted only a second, and it was quickly replaced by forced smiles and extended hands.

At once, Jax moved her hand to the crux of his arm and seemed to abandon his duty greeting guests. He walked alongside her through the entrance, where she immediately saw four of her pieces mounted on a temporary exhibit wall at the center of the gallery. There, admiring her work, was another man, about Jax's age, who, upon seeing them both, extended his hand to her and greeted her, saying, "I'm Parker — a friend."

Jax leaned closer to her and added, "He's safe. And I'm sorry, I need to return to greeting the other guests... only for a few more minutes. Parker will be right here with you – just for a few minutes."

While uncomfortable with being so quickly abandoned, Blair smiled warmly and let go of Jax's arm. She then turned to Parker and said, "So, friends then?"

"Since high school," Parker answered casually. He then continued by saying rather quietly, "It can be difficult to find good people in this crowd, but he's one of them. When he told me what was up, I volunteered."

Blair nodded uncomfortably, uncertain of how many other people Jax had explained her situation to. The idea that everyone at the party knew she was un-lensed made her feel queasy, whether or not Jax would act as a shield. The look on her face was sufficient for Parker to notice the change in her demeanor, as he suddenly interjected, "Oh – I bought your paintings. The ones in front of Sweeny's Irish Italian Market!" Then, pointing at three of the works on the wall, he added, "Those ones! I loaned them to the gallery for this exhibit. That way, all four could be featured!"

Still unappeased, Blair began looking about to see if any of the other guests were staring at her, or if she had somehow been found out. Then gently and calmly, Parker placed his hand on her forearm and added, "I also helped with that old cellular phone... I'm a big fan of yours – my wife Jessica is too - Nobody else... um... knows. The tags all say '*Omnis Nemo*' – 'Everyone' and 'Noone'. It's clever, right? It's just a few of us that know otherwise."

Blair breathed a sigh of relief, attempting to calm herself down from the anxiety that was overtaking her. As she did, a lean blond woman approached both of them and wrapped her arm around Parkers.

"Blair, this is my wife, Jessica – Jess, this is Blair," he said calmly.

"Blair... like THE Blair?" Jessica said excitedly.

"Yes. But tonight, she's going by 'Omnis Nemo'," he said with a smirk. "Maybe just 'Omnis'... 'Nemo' makes me think of that book with the submarine."

"I see," she laughed. "So mysterious! I'm a big fan of your – I mean, Omnis Nemo's work. It... makes me feel like... I don't know. Warm. Like Christmas morning, I think. Like the world is peaceful and happy. Like home."

"That's incredibly kind of you," Blair responded as she turned a new shade of red. While her new acquaintances seemed genuine and kind, it was difficult trying to relax and to become comfortable with her unusual surroundings.

"How about some champagne?" Jessica said, suddenly. Then, with a broad smile, she added, "We should celebrate your work, even if we can't 'openly feature' it."

"Champagne sounds great," Parker responded. Then, raising his hand into the air slightly, he was quickly greeted by one of the catering staff, who carried a silver tray filled with champagne flutes. After one was handed to each of them, Parker raised his glass to both women and said, "To unappreciated geniuses, silenced prophets, and the others who have been jailed for speaking their truths."

"Parker!" Jessica responded with an elbow that nudged him firmly in the side. "He's incorrigible – I think he just enjoys feeling like a rebel."

Blair lifted her glass in response, uncertain of his intentions but somewhat refreshed to hear someone who was like-minded speak openly.

"Oh, don't worry – we took our lenses out before you arrived. Jax said he did as well; it's a new sensation for him, to be honest. But nothing we say amongst ourselves tonight will get recorded. We just need to say it quietly and away from the others," he said in a voice just above a whisper.

"I see," Blair said, finally dropping her guard for a moment. She then added, "I hope... I'm sorry you had to go to such trouble on my account."

"Not at all," Jessica interjected. "Parker works on the feed – he's an app developer. We have a strict 'No-lenses at home between 8pm and 6am' rule; just don't tell that to anyone else here. They'd think we were lunatics."

"I know the feeling," Blair said, taking a long sip of her champagne.

Her uneasiness had settled a little from just minutes before, where she looked like she was ready to flee the event altogether. Still, everything about the situation set her nerves on edge. With a big swallow, she finished her glass of champagne, and Parker already had a second waiting for her, exchanging the empty flute for one newly replenished.

"Better?" he asked.

"Uh... maybe," she said meekly.

"Let's talk about something fun, then," he responded. "What do you think about AI and art? That puts me at an even playing field with you."

Blair laughed at the suggestion that they were on level footing, given how awkward she felt in the moment. But thinking about something other than her terrifying surroundings would likely be a way she could calm down and turn her mind to something positive, she realized. Deciding to engage in the exercise, she said, "Well, I think this whole mess started with AI algorithms that facilitated the feed, the digital currency, the biometrics — perfectly reasonable, rational, and repressive."

"No doubt," Parker said with a laugh. "I mean, with art specifically, do you think AI will ever be able to replace actual human artists?"

Blair thought for only half a second before responding with a clear, "No."

Surprised by how quickly she had answered, and certain there was more explanation that would be forthcoming, he asked, "Well, why not?"

"AI... computers... well, they make images on a screen. They may be beautiful images, but they're not art," she said, suddenly amused by how anyone could think otherwise.

"What's the difference?" Jessica asked, curiously.

"Art is something you can feel... what the computers make – it isn't real. There's nothing moving about it; there's no humanity – no illusion, no lies," she said, turning her attention toward her own work for a second, searching for an image that reaffirmed what she was saying.

"Well, what if AI could paint with a brush, just like a human? AI has its own goals; it has its own intentions, if you count following those goals and its other programming. Does that count as enough illusion?" he asked.

"Still no," Blair laughed clumsily, brushing a wayward strand of her long, red hair back behind her ear nervously.

"But AI would be a perfect execution of the artist's vision — technically perfect, like only a machine could be. Why wouldn't that be more marketable than human painted art?" he asked, thoroughly absorbed in the rebel's deviant assertion.

For a moment, Blair paused, looking at Jessica and the large diamond ring that sat on her finger. She then asked, "That's a beautiful ring. Is it real?"

Jessica looked immediately taken back, as if she had been accused of wearing something cheap. Not sure if Blair was simply being rude, or trying to make a point, she simply answered, "Of course it's real!"

"But something created in a lab would technically be perfect, right? I'm sure AI could make a diamond that is flawless, likely in any number of unusual or original shapes, if that's what you wanted. But nobody with taste would actually want it," Blair said with a wry smile.

"Oh, she's good," Jessica said, gently patting her husband's arm.

"So, it's the fact that it's real that makes it valuable?" Parker asked, searching for the definitive answer.

"If by real, you mean it is perfectly imperfect, then yes. It's human in an absolutely imperfect and astonishing way," she answered.

"Interesting," Parker responded. "Although to most people who can't tell the difference, I'm sure the perfect stone would be preferable."

"To some... to people who only care about the shiny perfection rather than the beauty of something real... Show me AI that can cry and laugh and sing the blues. Where's the computer program that can dance naked in a studio? What machine drunkenly paints gold chains on hippos with boxing gloves at sunset? Find me a computer that can, and I'll turn in my brushes!" Blair laughed.

"Not saying I disagree with you, but you *do* realize that sounds more like insanity than artistry, right?" Parker said, chuckling softly to his wife.

"Well, smart people buy what they like – they buy what moves them, what makes them feel something. Only fools pay for what they're told is good art. That feeling – that sense of being moved, even to tears by a beautiful painting you know nothing about – isn't that insane? It sounds like madness to me," she answered.

"I don't know," he responded, shaking his head as he turned toward her work, hanging on the exhibit wall. Until the day before, the painting of the stadium had been hanging in his office, but he had never considered whether the painting held any secret level of insanity within it. "So – are you *mad* then? Is that what all this is?" he said, gesturing to her work.

"The hours spent obsessing about brushstrokes, studying those of the masters and trying to replicate them, only to watch yourself fail over and over again. The fanatical pursuit, the tireless attempts to create something that you can be satisfied with... I mean, I'm sure there are doctors who would call that a compulsive disorder, right? Maybe, in a sense, that's all people who love art are really drawn to – maybe buying art is simply buying a beautiful symptom of the madness that engulfed someone when they were trying to make a hallucination in their brain become a reality. Maybe we're all crazy!" she laughed.

"Poetic," Jessica said with a smile.

It was at that exact moment that Jax appeared once again, having abandoned his duties near the entrance. "How are you all getting along?" he asked with a smile as he handed a glass of champagne to Blair with one hand and another to Jessica.

"Bruh! You gonna leave me hangin' like that?" Parker said, conveying a silly look of annoyance.

"Ladies first, bro-chacho," Jax answered with a grin.

As he began looking for the server carrying additional flutes, a sharp dinging sound resonated from the far end of the gallery.

"Friends, welcome to 'An Evening with your Crush'," the immaculately dressed elderly woman from the entrance announced as the attention of the crowd turned toward the sound. "On behalf of the Wadsworth family, and our son Jaxson, the owner of this gallery, we would like to humbly thank you for your support of the arts. A toast – to artistry, ingenuity, and the beauty that comes from their tireless effort!"

Then, after taking a very dainty sip from her champagne flute, she added, "Please enjoy yourselves this evening."

Blair looked at Jax, who was leaning toward Parker. She could barely make out Parker's words as he said, "Had to be the center of attention, huh? Couldn't even let the owner give the welcome speech?"

"It's fine," Jax whispered back to him, adding, "Bigger battles tonight." From the corner of his eye, he noticed Blair was observing their whispered conversation, and he excused himself from Parker, saying, "Thank you for keeping her company." Then, turning his attention back to Blair, he said, "I have to say... again... of all

the beautiful visions in this gallery, you are by far the most captivating. You... look absolutely, jaw-dropping... Shall we walk around
a bit?"

Blair blushed in response, uneasy with the attention she was
receiving and how to respond to it. Uncertain of what exactly to
say, she quietly said, "Thank you – I hope you like the dress. Bruce
said it was a winner – Oh, and thank you for this," she said, gesturing to the necklace and pendant hanging around her neck. "I don't
think I own any silver jewelry that wasn't my mothers."

"He has excellent taste," Jax laughed warmly. "And you're very
welcome. Thank you for agreeing to all of this. Platinum suits you."

"So, where to?" she asked after they had ambled aimlessly
through the crowded party for only a short time.

"I don't know," Jax said sincerely. "I just enjoy having you here;
I thought you might like to see some of the work from the other
artists? Maybe see what catches your eye?"

Blair smiled in response, having greatly enjoyed their last so-
journ experiencing art together at the museum. As they moved
deeper into the gallery, Jax showed some paintings by a Latin
artist named Ramon who had recently moved to St. Louis from
the Austin area. His work was colorful and abstract, reminding her
of work she had seen from Rothko, but with a bold fluidity that
was reminiscent of Franz Kline. Next, they viewed several pieces
by a woman named Deidra, who worked out of Birmingham. She
painted a style that could have been mistaken for American pas-
toral folk art from the eighteen hundreds in both composition and
style, but the subjects of the paintings mostly featured 21st century
urban decay – high rises and bridges that had fallen into disrepair.

Fascinated by Deidra's work, Blair became elated when Jax offered to introduce her to the artist. Moments later, an elderly
woman with cotton white hair and a dark complexion was shaking
her hand, following Jax's introduction. She had been standing
nearby and overheard Blair's rather vocal raving about her vision

and technique. The three chatted briefly, with Deidra adding that she was looking forward to following Blair's career with great interest and thanking her for her generous compliments. While exceedingly kind, it struck Blair as somewhat odd that the old woman seemed to know rather instinctively that she was an artist. But with little thought, she simply dismissed the comment, assuming something she had said in their exchange had revealed as much.

As they continued their saunter, Blair noticed fewer people were circulating through the gallery. Instead, a large group had gathered in the central area near the entrance. This too seemed odd, as she didn't recall there being many paintings there, other than her own.

At last, Jax and Blair reached a wall with the name "Caldo" painted boldly above five of the artist's more recent paintings. Each depicted a human figure in his familiar state of distress, conveyed through brush strokes that appeared in her eyes to be rushed and reckless. While she politely looked over each of the paintings, her inner monologue critiqued every brushstroke of each composition. Jax stood silently at her side as she carefully looked over the paintings, already familiar with her lack of appreciation for the artist. When she finally finished, he asked, "Still feel the same?"

"No," she responded quietly. "Yes, but no. It's certainly Caldo. It's just... I've seen several of his paintings now... And I can't but help but feel sad for him."

"Interesting," Jax responded. Then a smirk crept across his face as he added, "Although, I do recall us having a conversation before about why it's silly to feel bad for wealthy, accomplished people."

"Oh, I remember," she laughed. "But I can't help it. I get the feeling he's not a very happy person; that's sad."

Jax nodded his head, understanding what she meant. His recent interactions with Caldo had all but confirmed as much. While Blair had not been a part of those interactions, she seemed to infer something about the man through his work. While he generally considered it positive when one of his artist's pieces spoke to someone on an emotional level, her words and the uncomfortable change in her body language upon seeing the paintings conveyed only unease.

When at last they returned to the central area of the gallery, Blair noticed that the small crowd had only grown. Well-dressed men and women holding champagne flutes were gathered around, but their attention was near universally fixed on the makeshift exhibit wall that contained her work. While they whispered quietly amongst themselves, most of the guests stared at her paintings contemplatively.

"I'm not sure why he'd have these front and center in the gallery without identifying the artist," he heard one woman say to the woman standing next to her. "I mean – why all the cloak and dagger? How are we supposed to make inquiries? Why make it difficult?"

"Shelly – you know Shelly who lives down in Forrest Park – Well, she told me these aren't for sale," the other woman whispered back. "Something about them being painted by a friend of the family or something. I'm just going to call the gallery in the morning."

"I was born and raised here in St. Louis – I lived here before its renaissance. I love this town, and I don't care who the artist is. These are just little love letters to my city. I'm going to have one above our mantle just as soon as I talk to Jax," the first woman said in agreement.

Jax led the artist closer toward her four paintings, gently easing through the cluster of people until they were near the front, where Blair could hear an older man explaining to a younger woman standing at her side. "It's Latin, dear... It's a pseudonym meant to convey the artist wishes to remain incognito."

As Blair listened quietly to both critics and admirers of her work, the voice of a chubby man with a bushy beard seemed to increase in both volume and aggressiveness near the edge of the crowd.

"*This* parochial swill is what has everyone all worked up?" he roared.

It was then that Blair noticed Jax's father speaking in hushed tones to the man in an obvious effort to convince the man to calm down.

"No, Jaxson. No – I won't have it," the man argued, brushing the elder Wadsworth aside. "This gallery has clearly fallen into a state of ill repute!"

As the argument continued, a short distance away, a murmur began growing within the surrounding crowd with the words "Caldo" and "Plush" being whispered several times by people nearby. At last, the confrontation ended when the bearded man rudely forced his way through the crowd to stand directly in front of Blair's paintings.

For a moment, he simply stood there, eyes only inches from the canvas as he scrutinized the work closely. He then turned to the crowd and rolled his eyes with a loud sigh, saying, "How good of Crush to provide a place honoring our new, local art students, am I right?"

While one woman in the back of the crowd started to clap in agreement, when no others appeared to join her, the noise ended as quickly as it had begun. Instead, the heads of various men and women appeared to be leaning toward those around them and subtly whispering comments about the man's outlandish behavior.

Oblivious to the foolishness of his own spectacle, Caldo once again began rudely forcing his way through the crowd toward the gallery entrance. When his eyes locked on Jax's, the bearded artist forced a sarcastic smile and then continued along his original trajectory.

In a near consensus condemnation of his absurd behavior, the room full of guests parted, making way for the man, who stumbled as he reached the doors to exit the gala.

As the entire episode unfolded, Blair simply froze in place. She knew better than to speak up in defense of her work; she also had nothing to say. If Caldo didn't appreciate her work, that was fine by her. His actions only reinforced the misgivings she had about the man. And truth be told, all of the artwork on display was, in fact, paintings she had made purely to sell. They were her art, to be certain, but none of the pieces spoke with her voice. Instead, she thought of them more as warm hugs she gave to the kind strangers she had met. If others appreciated her work at all, she was glad for it, but these certainly weren't the masterpieces that moved her.

"Well, that was something," came the familiar voice of Parker from behind her.

Jax, who had remained calm and stoic throughout the interruption, breathed a visible sigh of relief upon seeing his friend. Jessica, who was right alongside her husband, then slid gently next to Blair and whispered, "How's it feel to be the hit of the gala?"

Blair didn't know what to say. Sure, she had heard some people compliment her work, but there were many talented artists present. Deidra's paintings were marvelous, and in Blair's opinion, they were far more interesting than her own four paintings. Not wanting to overthink or dramatize the events of the evening, she simply said, "Thank you, Jessica. That's incredibly kind of you to say."

"I let it slip that we own three of those," Parker interjected. "I've had a dozen people make offers to buy them from me – outrageous offers. People are getting emotional about it – seeing the city they love depicted so beautifully. I'd say 'hit' was exactly the right word."

Jax smiled upon hearing the news and gave Blair's arm a gentle squeeze. He then leaned toward her and quietly said, "Take in the moment; this is how it starts."

As the next hour passed, Jax and Parker discussed baseball, a topic particularly boring for her, but she smiled politely and listened. Jessica made for good company and prattled on endlessly about an upcoming trip she and Parker were planning to Costa Rica, which Blair knew nothing at all about. And while the conversation was exceedingly boring and un-relatable to her, she smiled and nodded politely, engaging with Jax's friends as more champagne and hors d'oeuvres were presented by the servers.

When at last it appeared the excitement of the evening was coming to an end, one final surprise emerged as Jax's mother, who abruptly approached her, greeted her with an unanticipated hug and a kiss on the cheek as she said, "Blair, darling – you look absolutely magnificent! Stunning, indeed - I can see why my son is so fond of you."

The gesture was so unexpected that a wave of fear once again flooded over her, as she felt the instinctive urge to run for the door. However, this time Jax, who had remained steadfast at her side interceded, needling his mother with the retort, "I'm so happy she was able to join us this evening – I'll admit, I was a bit nervous her presence wouldn't be... welcomed."

With a perfect riposte, Mrs. Wadsworth responded, "A beauty of her caliber should never be hidden, Jaxson. It's a wonder why she isn't streaming across every feed in the city! Excluding this young vision would have been absolutely scandalous!"

Having observed the awkward and poorly veiled antagonism, Parker and Jessica both appeared just as frozen and speechless as Blair. Thankfully, Jax countered by answering, "Not appreciating everything about her certainly *would* be scandalous."

Blair couldn't help but want to interject that she was standing right there; it was weird that she should be the topic of their spat, in her presence. Yet, despite the slight, she sensed the exchange was likely more of an ongoing power struggle between them, having little to actually do with her. Instead of speaking, she simply smiled generously as she wrapped her hand once again around Jax's arm.

Finally, after droning on about the success of the art and remarking briefly on the poor decorum of certain other guests, the elderly woman excused herself under the pretense of attending to other guests.

After she left, Jax leaned to her and said, "If you'd like to stick around a while longer, we can. Otherwise, I have something else in mind."

Blair looked at him awkwardly, not knowing exactly what he intended. It was their first date together, besides being the first actual date she had been on in quite some time. Her eyes widened as her head tilted, uncertain of his meaning, at which point Jax laughed and said, "Come on, then!"

Moments later, they exited the gallery into a rideshare and were on their way. Once they entered the vehicle, Jax was instantly, visibly more relaxed. He loosened his tie at the collar and unbuttoned the top button with a look on his face that spoke of having achieved a great victory.

"Where are we going?" Blair asked playfully as she looked out the window at the lights glinting from the buildings near Forest Park.

"It's not far," he answered with a smile.

The vehicle rounded a final corner before it pulled up slowly in front of a vintage neon sign advertising a local type of frozen custard. The two exited the vehicle and approached a small window, behind which a teenager with an acne pocked complexion and dirty white uniform waited.

"Do you like cookie dough? Or maybe peanut butter cups?" Jax asked as he looked over at her.

It was then she noticed the teenager behind the counter was also staring at her, presumably due to the formal wear they both remained dressed in as they stood outside the dingy, frozen custard shop.

"I like both – you pick," she laughed cheerfully.

Turning to the teenager, Jax said simply, "You heard the lady – both. The blended ones, I can never remember what they're called – the ones with the hot fudge in the middle. Please."

She couldn't help but giggle to herself as they awaited the announcement their orders had been completed. The absurdity of her dress, her makeup, and her shoes; Jax in his exquisite suit – the silliness of it all made her feel valued in a sincere, authentic way she had not felt since she was a child, since before the cares of the world weighed heavily enough to crush her dreams.

"You... laugh all you want, Miss Blair Huxley – this is the spot. I'd bet my life on it. Best frozen custard in the city!" he pronounced confidently. "They use a variety of nut and soy milks to make the custard – it tastes almost like the real thing!"

"Order four-one-two," came a voice over a speaker above them. Jax immediately scampered toward the window, and when he turned once again toward her, he held two large paper cups with bamboo spoons harpooned in their centers.

The two found a seat on a low cinderblock wall that overlooked a nearby street with automated cars passing by. They ate their desserts as they reminisced about the evening, laughing about his absurd mother, Caldo's drug induced behavior, and the odd pretenses and protocols of high society. Nearly halfway through his own treat, Jax suddenly became quite serious. He then asked, "So? You think you'd be willing to try it again sometime?"

For a moment, she was uncertain what exactly he was asking, but she assumed he was asking for a second date and answered, "Sure, I'd like that."

Showing a confusion of his own, Jax answered by saying, "I'm just not sure the peanut butter cups and the cookie dough go well together. It's kind of an either-or thing for me."

Blair laughed wildly at his assertion, suddenly understanding he had been referring to the frozen custard. Realizing his miscommunication, he simply added, "Well – that too! I've enjoyed spending time with you this evening."

"For me, it was the frozen custard that sealed the deal," Blair said facetiously.

With a smile, he said, "Like I said – it's the best in the city!"

~ 8 ~

"You cannot be serious, Jaxson," his mother said disapprovingly as she stood in his office glaring at him.

"And why not? Frankly, I think the mystique has actually made her work more desirable! I've been getting inquiries all day. Anyone with money is asking me 'Who is Omnis Nemo?' and 'Where can I get an original?'" he answered incredulously.

"Fine, good for you and well done. She's a lovely girl, Jaxson – but how long do you think you can keep up this charade? How long until the Jennings or the Thompsons discover the piece of art on their wall was made by someone like her?" she asked, attempting to reason with him over the risk posed by his recklessness.

"Someone like her? Oh, you must mean someone incredibly beautiful, talented, and smart? Someone who speaks with her own voice, even when her opinion is unpopular?" he asked rhetorically.

"You need to stop thinking with your manhood and start using your brain, for God's sake!" his mother shouted loudly enough for anyone downstairs in the gallery to hear. "She's un-lensed! The only people who aren't connected are criminals – robbers and drug dealers and rapists! The only reason to disconnect is so you can do evil without anyone noticing! And the fact that you made me take out my own lenses to have this conversation is proof of that."

"Oh... Well, I suppose you're right – Blair must be some kind of druggy-robber rapist kind of evil," he snapped back sarcastically.

"Clearly that's why she isn't connected... I should probably cancel our date this afternoon. She might rob me... or worse."

"You're impossible – I thought I raised you better than this!" she screeched. "Her parents were dissidents – they incited extremism against the administration! That's why she isn't lensed – why is this difficult for you to understand? She's their progeny! She's one of them! And that makes her worse than some low-level thug – she'd happily bring back the riots and the violence, all so she can paint her pretty little paintings! And that may not mean much to you – you were still in college during the years of unrest. But for those of us that are old enough to have really lived through it, you can't possibly imagine how terrifying it was! We were afraid to even leave the house – you couldn't even stream the news without seeing buildings on fire – death and destruction all over American cities like we were some banana republic or something. We are better than that!"

"Mom, listen to me carefully," he said in a sudden, serious tone. "Your fear – everyone's fear – it's no excuse to demonize people who disagree with you... it is impossible to control everything and make the world completely safe – even with the feed and its propaganda! Now, I know you can't hear this, and I can respect that you are in a different place because of what you went through. But you have to accept that you can't control everything; everyone has a voice. She's an artist; art is her voice. Her parents were educators. And sure, they disagreed with the administration's policies. But whatever happened to art being a vehicle for expressing a person's truth? What happened to ordinary people being allowed to speak their truth?" he asked. Then, after pausing briefly to see if his message was receiving any traction, he continued saying, "Your generation built this system – this feed that monitors everyone's movements, every message, and every purchase. No doubt it's had some benefits to reducing crime – I'm not saying otherwise. But this... illusion of stability your generation created... the feed... it can just as easily be used as a cudgel to crush innocent people! Don't you get that? You act like if you just control enough people around you, if you just force them to agree with you blindly, somehow human nature will just suddenly evolve. People don't work like that."

"No, that's where you're wrong. For the most part, it has worked – the riots ended! Conviction rates soared! There is peace in the streets, and this country is more unified than ever. It's my generation that brought about that change, Jaxson – and it's precisely because we won't tolerate the intellectual contagions coming from uneducated people spreading dangerous ideas! Your generation's success is possible because ours created hope. We rebuilt from the ashes that were leftover; we recreated this country, unified and safe!" she answered, her emotions fluctuating between anger, defensiveness, and guilt.

"And the price for this safety – for this unity? The price is what exactly? Our freedom? The end of privacy? Do we have to silence our artists and our academics to be safe?" he asked.

"Everyone must sacrifice for the common good, Jaxson. Everyone. Even you. Even Blair and her parents – everyone. Without control, there is only chaos and misery. And until you've lived in that chaos, you will never understand!" she answered tearfully.

Not knowing what else to say, he simply shook his head, exasperated.

"You do whatever you want, son," she said at last. Then dramatically turning towards the staircase to leave his office, she looked back briefly and added, "You seem intent on breaking your parent's hearts regardless of what I say... You're going to do whatever you want to do anyway, and it's far passed time that your father and I let you live with the poor decisions you're making!"

"Hey – that's not fair and you know it," he answered. "I'm not trying to hurt you or dad – I'm not trying to hurt anyone! I simply cannot understand why you need to control me, my work, my gallery. I don't understand why trying to remove your hands from my neck is hurtful to you. There are limits."

"Oh, yes - there are limits – And you're about to discover those limits, I promise you that!" the woman spitted venomously as she descended the staircase to the gallery floor below.

"Ok – that's fine. Good talking with you, mom – I really appreciate your support in all this," he said dismissively, more to himself than to her.

Leaning back in his chair, he took several deep breaths and held his face in his hands, forcing himself to calm down. A short while later, Bruce arrived at the top of the staircase, only to find his head buried in his hands, sitting behind his desk. Silently, Bruce walked over to the espresso machine and soon thereafter produced two small cups of thick, black coffee, one of which he placed in front of Jax. He then seated himself on the leather couch in the center of the loft and waited for his boss' attention.

"Thank you, Bruce," Jax muttered as the coffee was placed in front of him. The aroma from the small cup drifted upwards until at last he gave in and gently picked up the small mug. Moments later, he joined his assistant on the sofa, ready for the conversation he knew was coming.

"So, Caldo's pissed," Bruce declared matter-of-factly.

"He's an ass," Jax retorted as he lifted the small mug of espresso for a sip. "I'm also not sure his little fit at the gala did anything to help the price of his paintings."

"You'd be right about that," Bruce said as he sent sales data across the feed to Jax's lenses. "Overall prices are down twelve percent in the last three days, and obviously there are several recordings of his little outburst that have been circulating the various streams. My favorite one was the reel from a substance abuse disorder specialist, who pointed out the known symptoms of Plush addiction...four-hundred thousand views last I checked."

"It's not our business what he puts in his body," Jax responded, brushing away the concern.

"You think?" Bruce asked, implying he might want to reconsider his assertion.

"Ok, fine. When it happens *in our house*, it makes us look negligent or possibly enabling him. Maybe we need some kind of statement or presser denying our knowledge... or maybe speaking to the end of our exclusive distribution of his work on account of conflicting priorities... something like that?"

"I'll reach out to the marketing and media contractor – they can figure out how to spin it," Bruce said, blinking through his checklist of items requiring attention. "Mr. Wells sent a note regarding the paperwork for the dub account you asked him to create. Apparently, it's been a week, and he hasn't heard anything back from you."

"I'll look at it today and get back to him... I'm not even sure she'd be willing to use it, but it's the only way I can think of to make this work," Jax answered, closing his eyes as he took a deep sip of his espresso.

"You mean Ms. Huxley," Bruce said.

"Well, yeah – it's not for me! I'm getting calls near constantly asking about Omnis Nemo's work, wanting to commission her – we have to have some way to pay her. I don't know how else to approach it," he answered. "I'm about out of ideas."

"Honestly, boss – everyone is using dubs these days. Well, maybe not your generation, but it's fairly common with the younger crowd," Bruce said, attempting to assuage Jax's frustration.

"Bruce, I'm thirty-two – I'm not that old," Jax said with an eye roll.

"But also... not really that young anymore either... and still a bachelor," his assistant answered smugly, as he continued moving through the checklist.

"Oh, not you too," Jax exhaled. Then, more speaking to himself, he added, "Well, hey – everyone has an opinion on the matter. Why not you too?"

"Hmph," Bruce uttered disapprovingly as he continued blinking through his list. "All of Deidra's works sold just after the gala, but her people say she'll have new pieces ready by the end of the month... And lastly... I spoke with a Captain Daniels from that women's prison you mentioned – the one in Greenville, Illinois. He said that all records related to prisoners were confidential, but he mentioned the facility was open to visitation on Tuesdays and Saturdays. He was a pretty direct fellow – kinda mean, but professional. Otherwise, no appointments for the afternoon – everyone who has contacted the gallery directly has declined scheduling an appointment until new Nemo pieces are available."

"Thank you, Bruce – if I haven't said it recently, you deserve a raise," he responded.

"A big one," Bruce laughed. "But if you keep giving me raises, I'm going to get audited. I already make too much for an assistant."

"Fine – no raise. Maybe a bonus then," Jax laughed. "I really appreciate your help with the dress and Blair – she one-hundred percent looked the part. And I know we have you to thank for helping figure that piece of it out."

"Oh, I know – she looked fabulous!" Bruce said with a flicker of pride. "I saw some clips from the gala – what a heartbreaker! You'd better play your cards right with that one – she's the complete package."

Bruce then stood from the couch and confidently strutted toward the staircase to descend to the gallery floor, only to hear Jax's answer behind him, "You're right – as always. But enough patting yourself on the back. You crushed it; we all know it. Maybe a bonus AND lunch is on me for the next month?"

"Only if I get to pick – that means no more soy burgers," Bruce said from over his shoulder.

As soon as Bruce had left the office, Jax blinked to his contact list and selected the contact information for Wells and Associates, and in seconds he was connected to his attorney's feed.

"Henry, tell me you have good news?" Jax asked hopefully.

"Jax – why do I even go to the trouble of preparing briefs for you when you just call me, anyway?" Wells answered, somewhat annoyed at the interruption. After an audible exhale, he relented, adding, "Look, I'm just about to head into a meeting for a civil action case we're preparing for your father..."

"Hey, I'm sorry – I know you're busy. And I'll admit, I haven't read the brief. But I'm on my way to pick up Blair – I just need to know if it's possible – then I'll leave you alone," he replied hastily.

"Well, anything is possible – at least, maybe possible. But strictly speaking, not legal," Wells responded with another audible sigh. "The problem is that even dub accounts have to link to a member of the financial cooperative. Ms. Huxley isn't on the feed at all – how would she become a member? How would she access the cooperative's network? Even if she could, how would she spend any of the proceeds? A dub might make some of her potential patrons feel more at ease paying for her work discretely, but it can't receive transactions – it only sends them. And that's all assuming someone at the gala doesn't poison the well, so to speak."

"Poisoned in like, someone leaks that she's the child of known dissidents?" Jax asked, confirming what he was hearing.

"Yeah, let's say her family information was leaked... if buyers could still make payments anonymously, that might ease anxiety about the optics. But Jax, that still won't give Blair the ability to receive any of the proceeds. Without some connection to the feed, she'd need a third-party to accept payment on her behalf. In other words, it would completely violate the Anti-Money Laundering Act – but it may be possible."

"I see," Jax said, discouraged.

"Hey Jax, for whatever it's worth, she seems genuine – sincere even... If you have any other ideas, let me know. I'd be happy to help," Wells answered as he ended the feed.

"Well, that's one way it won't work," Jax muttered to himself as he sat alone in his office. Looking through his calendar, he confirmed what Bruce had explained previously about there being no new appointments.

Before leaving the gallery for the afternoon, he spoke briefly with Bruce confirming he'd be available if needed, but otherwise to give a stock answer that the gallery was working on making arrangements for Omnis Nemo pieces.

"Not telling you how to run the business, boss, but is that wise?" Bruce asked as he crossed the threshold of the exit.

"No – you know what, just tell them the artist isn't yet a client, there aren't pieces available. Let's not commit to anything – I haven't figured out how we can legally pull this off yet. Just something noncommittal, ok?" Jax asked, still standing in the gallery's doorway.

Bruce nodded in agreement, and as he turned toward the curb, the automated rideshare vehicle was already waiting for him just outside.

As the trip progressed, Jax made preparations for seeing Blair again, which comprised smelling his own breath in a cupped hand, fixing his hair, and removing his lenses. Removing his lenses at the gala seemed to have put her at ease, and ever since, he had been practicing taking longer and longer breaks from the feed. If he was to spend time with her, it would be safer for them both if there was no record of what transpired between them, romantically or professionally.

In the first and only time Blair used the cellular phone he had given her, she asked him to meet her at a tattoo shop in French-town that belonged to a friend of hers, the same location where he had sent the rideshare to pick her up for the gala. She mentioned that this was where she could be found most afternoons over the past few weeks, after she tended to Mrs. Marbury's garden and whatever other local help she had arranged. When Jax suggested a date that might include seeing some of her noncommissioned, original pieces, she seemed hesitant, insisting he should just drop by Thursday. As the day finally arrived, the anticipation of seeing her grew at nearly the same pace as his excitement at seeing the pieces she painted for herself. Still uncertain of why she would ask him to meet her at a tattoo shop, he figured if it made her more comfortable, there was nothing to lose.

With late afternoon traffic, the trip to Frenchtown took longer than expected, and while dropping by was never fixed to a particular time, he felt late all the same. When at last the rideshare pulled up to the brownstone shop front, a short line of people had been created, filling the entrance and spilling over into a vacant lot next door. The wall bordering the vacant lot held a freshly painted mural, featuring caricatures of a hippopotamus with a gold chain and blue boxing gloves squaring off with a smaller skunk wearing red gloves. Something about the painting reminded him of Blair's landscapes that he had seen, which was odd. Tattoo art wasn't Blair's iconic style, of course, but the composition, rendered with a sort of Americana illustrative quality that conveyed something familiar. He wondered if she had had a part in it, as he took a moment to appreciate the execution of the work, besides the silliness of the subject matter.

Attempting to avoid the loitering crowd of patrons, Jax made his way to the front of the line, excusing himself as he sidestepped his way around patrons to the small shop's entrance. Murmurs arose from several discontented customers at the front who must have assumed he was intending to cut the line, at which point Jax simply turned with a smile and said, "Sorry – I'm not here for a tattoo! I'm just here to see a friend. I'm not – um, I'm sure they'll be with you shortly."

From the back of the room, Blair's voice suddenly sounded over the quiet hum of tattoo machines within the shop, "Jax?!"

"Hi – you said to just drop by – Thursday, right?" he said somewhat apologetically.

"Yes!" she answered, as she took off her gloves and set the tattoo machine gun down. Then, giggling excitedly, she said, "Sorry for all the hub-bub. Lil put out a flyer saying the shop was doing a few cheap tattoos to get her new apprentice some experience – I'm the new apprentice!"

"I... um... I didn't know you were interested in tattooing..." he said, confused by the revelation.

"Oh, well, I'm not really. But hey, you don't know if you like a thing until you try it – it's art. Just on skin," she said playfully. Then suddenly, a bit more seriously, she added, "There's a bit more blood involved than I was prepared for."

"I see – well, I don't want to interrupt your work... You had just said to drop by on Thursday, so," he said.

"Let me finish this one – it'll just be a few minutes. Then we can hang out?" she said, offering a glimmer of hope to her would be suitor. "That ok with you, Lil?"

From the other side of the shop, a heavily tattooed woman with raven black hair tied up in a red bandana looked up briefly at him and shouted over the machine she was holding, "Sure – Tanner and I can handle the other walk-ins." Then looking over at Jax, she said, "You're just lucky we're so busy today – otherwise you'd probably get sucked into hanging out in a tattoo shop all night so we could interview you."

"I can think of worse things," the heavily tattooed man at the back of the shop said loudly as he used a paper towel to wipe the arm of the man he was tattooing.

"Interview?" Jax asked, confused by the remark.

"Just to see if you're good enough for our Blair," the heavily tattooed man laughed.

"Oh, well, I assure you, I'm trying to figure that out myself. Another time, maybe," Jax answered with a polite smile.

Having never stepped foot inside a tattoo shop before, the foreign environment made him feel out of place, as if he were an astronaut making first contact on some remote alien planet. His black suit and tie made his presence even more conspicuous. As he waited for Blair to finish, he attempted to occupy himself to better blend in, and while the art on the walls was interesting, it was far from anything he would put in a gallery. It felt so... common. That Blair could be lured into wasting her talent in such a place was disconcerting, but if these people were friends of hers, they must know about her circumstances. If so, they were likely good, compassionate people, which made them sort of allies, even if their tastes in art were radically different from his own.

Jax paced around the shop's reception for several minutes, looking at the different flash sheets that decorated the room. Ironically, it was the woman with the bandana who approached the counter first, rather than Blair. After she provided some brief aftercare instructions to a customer, she looked at him and said with a smile, "Well, come on then – you're here to see her! There's no reason to wait up here like a lost little puppy." Then, with a nod in Blair's direction, she walked him back toward the table upon which a shirtless, beer-bellied man was patiently waiting as Blair carefully applied shading to the freshly outlined bald eagle she had tattooed on the man's back.

"Remember – whip it! Whip that shading to get that peppery effect – it's not a paintbrush. You have to work it in," she said, approaching Blair.

"You sure she knows what she's doing?" asked the man, who was face down on the table.

"Of course she doesn't know what she's doing! That's why you're getting a deal – it's an apprentice tattoo, dummy! You knew what you signed up for!" Lillian laughed.

"Oh... great," the man groaned.

"If it's any consolation, this kid is a generational talent - one of the best I've ever met," Lillian responded. "Years from now, you'll probably be telling your friends how you got an original piece from her when she went through her tattooing phase."

Suddenly amused by the absurdity of the situation, Jax couldn't help but laugh. He then asked Blair, "So, what's *that* like?"

Blair looked up for a second and said, "If you can imagine trying to paint a portrait with a vibrating brush on a spongy, piece of hard tofu - it's a bit like that."

Lillian laughed at her remark, adding, "That's vivid – but yeah, it is a bit like that."

It took only a few more minutes before Blair finished shading the eagle, and after briefly examining the piece, he saw it looked just like a piece he had seen on one of the many framed sheets of art decorating the wall in the entrance. She then used a squeeze bottle filled with some sort of antiseptic solution to clean the piece, after which she applied a palm-sized piece of plastic that adhered to the man's skin, framing the fresh tattoo, which Jax assumed was meant to protect it. Why the little piece of artwork needed protection, he wasn't quite sure, but he guessed it had something to do with keeping it from becoming infected. From what little he knew of tattoos, he was certain they were permanent; it wasn't going to fall off. But there must be a reason for the ritual, and being out of his element, he waited patiently until Blair had finished removing her gloves.

"You can send payment to me," Lillian said to the man as he put his shirt back on. "Apprentice tattoos get paid through the shop."

The man simply nodded as he blinked through his feed initiating payment to the shop owner. He then thanked them and headed toward the entrance. As he did, Blair finally turned her attention toward Jax and said, "So - you're here!"

"It sure looks like it," Jax replied with a smile.

"Well, yeah – it sure does. Let's um... get out of the shop so we're not in the way," she said as she took his arm and ushered him toward the door.

"You two have fun!" Lillian called out before turning her attention to the next customer in line.

Once they were back onto the street, they walked together for a few moments in an awkward silence before Jax asked, "So tattooing?"

"Oh – yeah, it's a bit of a story, I guess. I helped them with the mural and we became friends, I guess. I've been helping out at the shop for a few weeks, and Lillian helps me with odds and ends I need. Sort of a friendly exchange type situation," she answered. "I don't think I'm really interested in doing it for real. Lillian just wanted to get me some exposure to it. And hey, why not try something new, right?"

"Ever the free-spirit," he laughed with a shrug.

"So, what would you like to do this evening?" she said after they passed the first block, meandering aimlessly westward.

"I... I didn't really make a plan, so to speak," he said. "I was sort of hoping you might show me some of your work... maybe we could just spend some time together? Or we could test my theory on the best frozen custard?"

Blair laughed at his suggestion as she turned to him. Then her face changed to reflect a certain seriousness. She paused for a moment as if searching for the right words, then at last said, "Jax – what are you doing?"

Suddenly unsure of himself and what she meant, he asked, "What do you mean? I – I like you. I'd like to spend time with you. I think you're a great artist – I – "

"That's not what I mean," Blair interrupted. "You know my... situation. I'm never going to be the kind of person – the kind of artist – that sells paintings for bazillions of dollars in your gallery. I couldn't be that person even if it's what I wanted!"

"I'm working on that," he said energetically. "I've been talking with Wells, and... we don't have a plan yet, but we're going to sort something out. We're going to find a way for people to be able to buy your art; we'll find a way for you to be able to use that money to live however you want!"

Blair looked at him skeptically and said, "You're sweet." She then impulsively pulled his arm toward her and wrapped her arms around it as they walked.

"I'm not sure what that means – 'sweet'. Sweet like an older brother – or like a fluffy puppy?!" he said in a playfully antagonistic tone.

"You are sweet for wanting to help me sell my art and to work out a way to make all *this* work... I just don't know how it *does* work," she replied.

"Do you need to? Do you need all the answers now? Or... can I selfishly ask to spend time without being able to offer you solutions?" he asked sincerely.

"Hmm..." she responded, considering his question. "I think you like the idea of me – you like the paintings I've made of the city, and they've gotten a lot of attention. And all that's great! It's just – those were things I painted to barter for grocery money so that I'm not constantly draining Bell and Zay. I'm not – sorry, I'm just conflicted."

"About?" he asked.

"Painting what other people want to see... it just feels soulless to me. It just feels empty," she answered.

"I get that," he said, then asked, "So then show me what you love to paint?"

"I can't!" she stammered.

"What? Why *can't* you?" he asked as he turned to her, suddenly confused.

"Because you're going to hate me! If anyone sees my actual work – if anyone sees the things I love to paint – they'll be at my door in minutes!" she answered as her eyes suddenly filled with tears.

"I'm sorry," he said suddenly, "I'm REALLY confused here."

Blair gently pulled his face close to hers and looked carefully at his eyes, trying to determine whether he was connected to the feed. She had already taken a chance by suggesting her passion projects might be illegal, and before she said more, she had to be certain their conversation wouldn't be monitored. Misreading the gesture, Jax assumed it was an invitation. So he kissed her.

Instantly, Blair froze in place, uncertain of what to do. It took a few seconds for the fear to subside before she wrapped her arms around him, actively engaged in the romantic moment. When finally they separated, she blushed, and pulled away for a second before asking, "You're not connected, right?"

"No – after the gala – I just thought you'd be more comfortable if our conversations weren't... Well, if they weren't on the feed," he said.

"Thank you," she said with a sigh of relief. Then, tugging gently on his hand with hers, she added, "Well, come on then."

"Where are we going?" Jax said as he followed.

"I'm going to show you my illegal art," Blair said with a laugh. Then added, "Just... if you're not good with this – if I can't completely trust you to keep this between us – say so now. I'm happy to go out to dinner with you and smile and play the part. I'll even paint a few paintings for those gallery people if you want. But this is something I need to be private – really, truly private."

"I promise you, it will stay just between us. I want to see the real stuff – the stuff that makes you love painting. I want to see the work that moves you; I've seen the fluff," he said with a note of apprehension. "It's superb fluff, but it's fluff."

"I'm serious, Jax," she exhaled cautiously as they walked. "My art - the paintings... I make them for me... I'm pretty sure they'd be flagged by the monitors the moment they hit the feed. You know they lock up people for smaller violations of the Safe Speech Act – just for saying things that are critical of policy on the feed. I'm pretty sure my work would be 'triggering' for at least half the country, including your parents."

"I understand," he answered. "And I promise you, you are safe with me. Your art is safe with me."

After another ten minutes, they reached the magnolia covered door at the entrance of Blair's cottage. Fumbling in the pocket of her overalls for a moment, her hands trembled slightly as she fit the key into the lock and opened the door.

As he entered, Jax found her small studio to be almost humorously consistent with what he had envisioned it would look like. A record player sat in the corner, which Blair was quick to approach and add a black vinyl record to. He found a seat in a small wooden chair at a table in the middle of the room. Atop the table was a smattering of books, and at a glance he noticed several titles that had long before been added to the prohibited reading catalogue, which seemed fitting, given he was about to see paintings that she herself had described as illegal. As the soulful tones of southern delta blues began to fill the cottage, he looked around the humble surroundings, thinking she had done surprisingly well for herself, considering it had all been obtained illegally. Moments later, Blair was standing in front of a large stack of what he assumed were canvases that had been covered with a large sheet.

"Where do I begin?" she muttered to herself nervously. Then, carefully removing the sheet, she revealed a painting that had recently been completed. It depicted a woman who had obviously been beaten and was since being dragged away by an old man. The woman was adorned with a starburst crown, and her torn, copper-green dress exposed a bare breast as she attempted to resist the old, white-haired man in a comically patriotic suit.

Jax couldn't help himself as he suddenly stood from his chair, a look of shock and fascination flooding across his face. Then, moving closer toward the painting, he kneeled beside it and studied both the composition and technique, both of which were exquisite. He then responded, "Well, yeah – Uncle Sam forcibly dragging Lady Liberty... with a not-so-subtle suggestion of sexual violence having taken place – it's provocative, that's for sure. It would DEFINITELY get you arrested."

Blair flinched at his reaction, as she quickly grabbed the sheet and moved it back over the painting. "See – I knew... I'm sorry. I shouldn't have –"

"Shouldn't have what? It's a masterpiece, Blair. It's stunning, thought provoking, truly brilliant – this is what art is supposed to be. There's nothing to be ashamed of here!" he answered.

She looked down at the floor for a moment, shaking her head defensively as she said, "No – no, it's um... it's too much. Too on the nose, I think. Too obvious."

"It's brilliantly illustrative – a bit reminiscent of Rockwell mixed with Mucha... but distinctly... Blair Huxley," he said with a wide grin.

"Thank you," she said in a breathy whisper.

"Would you be willing to show me more?" he asked.

Blair removed the sheet once again and took a second to move canvases until the paintings were side by side. Each piece was uniquely her work, a collection of mostly illustrative but painterly works that gushed with a romantic, vintage voice that sung loudly of by-gone Americana imagery in each brush stroke. And yet, several of the pieces were funny – a hen with the coloring of a bald eagle, struggling to lay a rotten egg. There was homage to James Montgomery Flagg's iconic "I Want You" recruiting poster, only in Blair's depiction, Uncle Sam was a rotting, zombie figure with a worm crawling out of its eyes. Another depicted a sickly bald eagle posed similarly to the nation's seal, but the bird was choking on a large, gold coin. Another depicted a prairie field, filled with the rotting corpses of American Bison and the bodies of protestors still clutching signs with slogans as drones flew above. The two remaining were smaller pieces, which Blair explained were some of her earliest works that she had kept. One was a portrait of a Native American princess, complete with headdress and war paint, only her eyes and mouth had been sewn shut with barbed wire. The other depicted human like caricatures of an elephant and donkey, kissing passionately and locked in an intimate embrace as they stood atop a pile of gold coins and jewels in a large treasure vault.

A long silence passed as Jax examined the paintings, marveling at their perfection. Blair fretted, fidgeting as he looked silently on, unsure of what to say. After several minutes of awkward quiet, she finally blurted out, "You hate them – I get it. It's too much. Too... um... base."

"Nothing about these... there's nothing 'base' about it," he replied calmly.

Several more minutes passed in silence before she awkwardly poured herself a glass of water at the small sink below the window that faced the Andover home. The slow rhythm of blues guitar sounded through the small cottage as she guzzled the water, and she trembled with the realization that she may have lost him by revealing too much. The thought of ruining their relationship and his eventual absence from her life pulled her spirt down like an anchor. Finally, she turned to him and said, "Well – you've seen them. This is me – this is who I am. You... can't hang any of these paintings in your lovely gallery. You can't show them to your clients –"

"Of course not," he laughed with a melancholy tone. "But they are brilliant, regardless. Even if having them would get you arrested, or me seeing them meant I was arrested – they are masterful pieces, Blair."

"I feel like when you asked me before – at the gallery – you asked if I had been involved in any dissident acts... or whatever. I probably should have just been straightforward with you back then and saved you all the time and effort," she said as she nervously brushed her hair out of her face.

"Blair – " he began to say, before she nodded her head and interrupted him.

"No – I should have just told you everything," she stammered hesitantly.

"Your father was killed in a drone attack during a riot, and they imprisoned your mother for speaking out against these policies. I think it's reasonable for me to infer that would cause you – well, that it would show up in your work. I mean, it's understandable..." he answered, losing his words as he continued staring into the dark, visceral artwork.

"They murdered my father," she snapped, correcting him. "And they locked up my mother for protesting that murder — don't you see? Don't you understand how UNJUST this all is? And they'd lock me up as well if they saw any of these. So, I'm sorry I can't be your arm decoration and play the part for your wealthy friends. It's fun for an evening, but when they find out I am exactly who they fear I am, I can't. You can't – it would ruin you!"

He turned to her to see the tears welling up in her eyes, and he couldn't think of anything she said that he could dispute or argue. She was right in every aspect, and the thought of it both saddened and sickened him. Lacking any retort, he hurried toward her and wrapped his arms around her in a warm embrace. It wasn't a romantic gesture, so much as an understanding she needed to be comforted. She needed to know he understood her fear, and he simply would not walk away, leaving her defenseless.

For a brief moment, she resisted his arms, wanting to blame him or someone – anyone – for the world, it's problems, and the voice inside that told her these problems were destined to be silenced. Yet, as she broke down and began to cry, his warmth felt like safety when the rest of her life felt so abysmally alone. She let him hold her there as the minutes passed, staining his fine white dress shirt with her tears.

When at last she pulled away, he wiped her tears with a handkerchief and said, "I'm never going to ask you to be anyone other than who you are. You are brilliant. You're bold, and you have an earnest sense of right and wrong – there's nothing about YOU I am afraid of."

"My art – these paintings – they are me! They are what burns inside me in my secret, innermost heart," she said defensively.

"And I'm not afraid of them either – I AM afraid of the world that would receive them, and what they would do to you – to me too!" he answered.

"So, what then?" she asked, unsure of what would come next between them.

"I... I don't know. Obviously, we can't share this work at the gallery – the blowback from even having you at the gala was... severe. My parents are already on the warpath," he laughed rather melancholically, as he recalled the conversation he had with his mother earlier that day.

"Obviously," she answered, nodding her understanding. "I can still paint pretty things – the houses and the landmarks – you could sell those for your gallery if you wanted to."

"Is that what you want?" he asked, earnestly trying to understand her intentions.

"I don't know," she answered. "I... I was thrilled to see people love my paintings at the gala. And you've already done so much for me, I feel like I owe it to you to at least... I dunno, paint some pretty things that would help your gallery."

"You don't owe me anything, Blair," he said, suddenly serious. "I mean that – the pleasure of your company is more than enough. Your work is amazing – I wanted to share it. But I understand now how much of a risk that is for you. Too many questions – too much attention... if anyone discovers these pieces..."

"I could destroy them – throw them out. Nobody needs to know – I painted them just for me; it was a way to express my frustration with everything. I – "

"Don't you dare!" he said in a panicked voice. "These are genius - you can't just destroy your work because we haven't figured everything out yet!"

She held out her hands, exasperated by his reluctance as she replied, "What then? What's the answer?"

"Let's... just slow down for a minute, okay?" he answered calmly as he placed his hands gently on her outstretched arms. "I have an empty storage unit for the gallery – we can keep them there for the time being. It'd be safer than having them here, where someone could accidentally find them."

"Well, it's not like I have them hanging on the walls! And nobody even knows who I am!" she whimpered.

"After the gala, the feed in the art community is buzzing with the anonymous artist. Everyone is asking where they can get an original Omnis Nemo work. If someone who knew you were the artist were to out you... If someone came looking and found them – if the police searched the place... or a nosey neighbor peered through the windows and saw something... or whatever. What I'm getting at is, Bell and Zay and Mia would be caught up – not just you. It's not fair to them, either. If we move them to somewhere safe and out of sight, it would give you some time," he answered, reassuring her.

"Time for what? You can't sell them; I can't show them to anyone. It's too dangerous to keep them here," she responded, frustrated by the lack of options.

"I get it – you have every right to be frustrated – but you can't just destroy them! I'd sooner throw a bag full of diamonds into the muddy river!" he replied. Seeing he had yet to put her at ease, he continued by saying, "Maybe in time, things will change; maybe the laws will change. I can't see the future, but shouldn't we hope? And even though they can't be sold here, there could be foreign buyers at some point – people who care about art who aren't bound by the Safe Speech Act. I don't know if you'd even want to part with them, but shouldn't we keep our options open?"

"Fine," she surrendered. "But I want the key – it's the only way I'll know they're safe."

"Done – easy. You'll be the only one with access; I'll give you the key. Your name won't be anywhere near it. Do you have anyone you trust to help you move them?" he asked.

"Lillian or Tanner would help," she answered, a glimmer of hope returning to her voice. "They're safe – I'm one-hundred percent sure of it."

"It sounds like we have a plan then, he said as he stroked his hands along her arm. He then added, "We're going to figure this out. You're too talented to hide from the world. If you want to paint for the gallery's clients – we can find a way to make that work, I'm sure of it. Or if you don't want to, that's fine too. It's up to you."

The sound of the record on the turntable skipping provided a timely distraction from their intense conversation, as Blair sighed with exhaustion. In seconds, she provided attention to the vintage device, removing the needle from the record and replacing it with another, whose cover depicted a collection of classics from Motown.

Jax smiled as he held out his hand toward her, inviting her to dance. She grasped his hand and pulled herself close to him as they began slowly swaying to the horns and the smooth rhythmic sounds that filled the cottage.

"I wish my mother was here," she whispered as she held her head against his chest.

"When was the last time you saw her?" he asked, cradling her as they rocked.

"I was just a girl... I write her letters, and she writes back. Pieces of them are blacked out, of course, so I have to fill in some of the blanks in my mind. But... we stay in touch as best we can," she replied, drying what remained of her tear-soaked cheeks on his shirt.

"I... have a confession to make," he said as they danced slowly, alone in the small cottage. "And I'm sorry if it was too forward of me...but I asked Bruce to make inquiries at Greenville."

A look of confusion suddenly filled her face as she pulled away slightly to look into his eyes as she asked, "Why?"

"I just thought... Well, I remember you saying that's where they were keeping her. The women's prison there. I sort of assumed you weren't able to visit much because of the transportation involved... I guess I was just thinking you might want to see her," he answered, as he continued to sway to the music.

The thought of being able to see her mother brought new life to her eyes and the warmth again returned to her face as she pulled herself back to his chest like a warm blanket, squeezing him tightly as they rocked. After several moments, she asked, "You'd... really do that for me? It'd be a really expensive trip in one of those robocars to get all the way out there – I don't want to... I mean, I don't have any way to pay for something like that."

"The look on your face when I even suggested it tells me just how much it would mean to you. Visiting hours are on Saturday," he answered warmly, still holding her as they moved to the music.

"I... I don't think you should come," she said rather abruptly. "I mean, I'd love for you to come, but if your parents found out you were going to visit –"

"I'll send the ride for you – no obligation to drag me along," he chuckled quietly. "I'd be happy to."

~ 9 ~

The ride to Greenville was shorter than she had expected. In her mind, anything she could not easily bike to might as well have been on the opposite end of the country. To her surprise, when the automated vehicle stopped outside of the visitation center in just over an hour, Blair wondered how her mother could have been so close for the last few years without her finding a way to visit.

From her first view of the prison, it looked more like a high school than a facility for housing society's dangerous women. The entrance to the tan colored brick building was decorated with numerous flagpoles, each adorned with a different flag. Passing through the entrance to the information desk, she asked the officer where visitation took place, only to discover women were housed at a minimum-security camp next to the main facility that housed male prisoners. Fortunately, the women's camp was only a short distance to the north.

Blair walked the several hundred yards down the grass lined road until she found the parking lot of the camp, along with a large sign posted outside of the building that read "Visitor's Center." As Jax had instructed, the automated vehicle remained at the entrance of the main building where she had been delivered. She had no way to communicate to it otherwise and thought it best not to try.

Once she entered the building, several uniformed officers were present, processing visitors through a machine she assumed was scanning them for weapons or drugs. Another officer was performing searches of any items the visitors were bringing into the facility. She had nothing with her, which made passing through the line relatively painless, but she was dismayed to discover it was possible for visitors to bring certain gifts and items for the prisoners they were seeing. These tokens weren't big things, but the list on the wall providing instructions included books, lip balm, hairbrushes, and other personal care items within strict size limits. Blair hadn't known she could bring anything with her, not that she would have been able to. But she was sure her mother would have appreciated anything, having been alone for so long.

After passing through the search area, she was ushered into a large, open room, wherein a series of tables with attached benches were arranged. A series of vending machines lined the wall, mocking her inability to purchase even meager snacks for her meeting with her mom.

"Ayn Huxley from fourteen for visitation," came a voice from an overhead speaker.

Blair found a seat at one table and waited; she wasn't sure exactly what she should expect. The notion that such visits were so commonplace that everyone else in the room seemed to understand the rules when she didn't only aggravated her feeling of guilt. The round mechanical clock on the wall ticked away as she waited, as each minute felt agonizingly long. As the time passed, she wondered if she would even recognize her mother after so long; she wondered what she would say. She hoped her mother wouldn't be angry or disappointed it had taken so long, but she knew she wouldn't blame her if she was. There was so much to say – so much that couldn't be transferred into words on a page. With each tick of the clock, her anxiety increased, somehow suddenly afraid, wondering if she had made a mistake in coming.

At last, the latch on a large metal door clicked, and one of the uniformed officers opened the door wide to reveal a woman with stone gray hair, dressed in an orange jumpsuit. When she stepped into the visitation room, her eyes suddenly came alive as she recognized her daughter, seated at one of the small tables. The older woman's eyes instantly burst with tears as she rushed toward Blair, who at that point had nearly jumped out of her seat to run toward her mother.

"Oh, my lovely one," Ayn said with a cracking, tearful voice as she embraced her.

"Oh, mama – I'm so sorry it's taken me this long to come see you," Blair said tearfully.

"Never mind that – I understand how hard it must be for you," her mother answered. "Now, let me take a look at you – it's been years!"

Blair pulled away briefly and smiled, but couldn't resist the urge to return to her mother's warm arms. They stood there, holding each other for many minutes until others in the visitation room looked at them strangely.

"Let's... sit down, love. Before we cause a fuss," Ayn finally said, rubbing her daughter's arm as she gently pulled away.

The two women returned to the small table Blair had previously occupied, and immediately, Ayn began trying to catch up on the years that had passed between them, saying eagerly, "Tell me – everything!"

"Well, I don't know what to say that I haven't put in a letter," Blair laughed awkwardly.

"It doesn't matter, honey – I still want to hear it. I just want to hear your voice and take in the sight of you!" her mother answered, still tearing with joy at being reunited with her daughter.

Blair started by telling her mother about Bell, whom she remembered from her teaching days, as well as her husband Zay and their daughter Mia. The Andovers were regularly present in her letters, of course, and while none of the information was new, her mother didn't seem to mind. Next, she began telling her about her new friends at the tattoo shop, while her mother listened intently and smiled.

"They sound like good people," she said at last. "I always wanted to get one of those things, but your father... Well, it wasn't really his thing, I suppose. He didn't think it was fitting for professors to be seen with tattoos like their students."

"I miss him," Blair said, after hearing mention of her father. "Terribly. Every day."

"I do too, love. He was the best man I've ever known," Ayn answered sweetly. "What else? Tell me about your art."

She started by telling her story of the night of the gala at Crush, but then jumped backwards to explain how her paintings had been sold through Tony's store in a sort of agreement they had made. As she did, her mother placed a single finger over her mouth and said, "Easy on the details, kiddo."

Blair nodded, seeming to understand her mother's desire for discretion, given the atmosphere. She talked about her dress, the necklace that Jax had given her, and his love for art — her art.

"He sounds like quite a catch," Ayn said with a wink.

"He's... too good for me," Blair laughed, shaking her head.

"Don't you ever say that, Blair Huxley!" her mother scolded playfully. "You are beautiful, talented, and most importantly, you have a wonderfully big heart. I only wonder if he is good enough for my daughter!"

Blair blushed at her mother's pride, but the sweetness of having affirmation from the woman meant everything in that moment. It had been so long since she felt her mother's genuine love, rather than constantly feeling like an inconvenience her friends were dutifully tolerating. While she knew the Andovers were loyal and loved her, the immensity of the burden she placed on those around her was a constant regret she hadn't figured out how to solve.

"There are other pieces that I've made... pieces that aren't a good *fit* for the gallery. But I think you and dad would appreciate them," Blair said cryptically.

Nodding her understanding, Ayn said simply, "You have to be careful with that."

Blair shook her head in agreement and added, "I will. I just... I don't know what to do. I paint with heart first. You know?"

Ayn nodded again, showing she understood the topic weighed heavily on her daughter as she said, "I *do* know... And I want you to know... it was never our desire for you to get caught up in any of... this. Our day came and went; it's over now... I don't want you to lose yourself in a lost cause like we did."

Blair paused for a moment, shaking her head in confusion before she answered, "Want it or not – this is my story too. What you're going through – what they did to dad... "

"Let's change the subject, sweetie," Ayn said in a voice just above a whisper.

"No – I can't. I won't! This is my life – it's the result of everything that's happened. I can't just pretend like everything is ok!" Blair whispered back defiantly.

"Good," Ayn whispered with a smile before adding, "Then you own it now – it's your choice."

"I... just wish it was all different – I wish he was here. Well, not here-here. But with me – both of you," Blair answered.

"Wish all you want, but you'll never stop the sun from setting or the moon from rising... Darkness has a way of finding us all at times. It's the nature of this world, I'm afraid," Ayn replied in a serious, hushed voice.

"What do I do then? What do I do in a world full of... darkness?"

"Well, have you tried turning on some lights? A candle? A campfire? Anything? When you shine a little light, even in the darkest places, folks tend to stop banging their heads against the walls so much," her mother laughed somberly.

"And... what if that fire burns down everything around me? What if we're all consumed by it?" Blair asked, searching for some kind of concrete reassurance everything would be well in the end.

"Then it consumes us all," Ayn answered. Then loudly she added, "Your father and I always believed it was better to be consumed by the flames than to live as beggars, pleading for our rights on our knees!"

Moments later, one of the Correctional Officers approached their table and stood next to her mother as he said, "Time's up Huxley."

As the old woman stood from the bench, Blair rushed to embrace her one last time. As she did, the older woman whispered into her ear, "Shine your light brightly, my dear. Just make sure those who walk into the flames alongside you do so willingly. How all of this hurt you is my only regret."

"Let's go, Huxley," the Officer said sternly.

"I love you, mom," Blair called out as the guard walked her back toward the steel door that led to the interior of the prison.

"I love you too, Blair Bear – with all my heart," Ayn replied as the door closed.

The short walk back to the waiting vehicle felt impossible, as with each step she left behind a tiny morsel of her heart like a trail of breadcrumbs. She didn't know the next time she could visit; she couldn't say for certain if she ever would. As meaningful as the moment had been, the experience was entirely too short to be satisfying. Her mother was close enough to touch, but that made the letting go even harder. By the time she reached the vehicle, tears began streaming down her cheeks as she silently boarded the vehicle. They continued to flow along the brief journey back toward St. Louis, ceasing only as the vehicle eventually crossed over the bridge spanning the mighty river that separates Missouri from Illinois.

Eventually, the autonomous vehicle delivered her safely to the Andover home, just as Jax had instructed. While she knew Bell, Zay, and Mia were home, she knew if she checked in with them, they would spend hours discussing her mother, father, and all the emotional turmoil that would come with it. Instead, feeling the need to be with friends, she decided to walk down to the tattoo shop in Frenchtown. Tanner and Lillian would, no doubt, be booked with appointments, and she knew her help at the shop would be welcome, having spent many afternoons there in the previous weeks. A lighthearted change of scenery would help ease her mind.

As she entered the shop, both of the tattoo artists were busy working on projects with their clients. The few chairs in front of the counter that acted as a waiting room were also full, and needing to distract herself from the emotionally charged visit, Blair fell into the same routine she had grown accustomed to when helping at the shop. The next appointments needed to check in, and there were forms that needed to be completed within the feed. Of course, she couldn't accept any of the forms or verify the client's identification, but she could provide direction. More importantly, she helped those next in line understand the process, as well as what would work from a compositional standpoint.

"I really want a dragon – like a Japanese one! But I want him sitting in a recliner and smoking a pipe... like an old man pipe... because that's what my grandfather did. And I want the whole thing set in space... like the universe," a husky, long-haired young man said excitedly when Blair finally signaled it was his turn.

Managing the expectations of wide-eyed clients was where Blair's understanding of art ended up saving Tanner and Lillian time and effort. With nodding affirmation, Blair tackled the confusing request with precision, saying, "That's an interesting idea... tell me, how do you see all the dragon's legs and tail all fitting in a recliner like that? I just want to make sure we understand your vision."

"Hmm, well... I figure the artists will know how to make it work – I mean, it doesn't have to have a lot of legs, I guess," the young man replied.

"I see... Have you looked at any of the dragons on the flash?" she asked, guiding the young man over to a particular sheet of art that depicted a long, traditional Japanese dragon.

"Yeah – totally! That's what I want!" the young man said excitedly.

"Well, Tanner could tackle that and make it really killer – I just don't know that it would work... like sitting in a chair, ya know? The really cool thing about dragons is the flow of their bodies. You don't really want to squish them all together in a chair, do you?" she asked.

"Umm... Well... I guess not," he replied as he stared at the piece of flash on the wall.

"He could probably add a pipe to a dragon like this one. So, instead of a puff of smoke in the front, you could do that... And while he could do some kind of cosmic background, it might be cleaner looking to use the smoke from the pipe as an intentional element to help frame the piece," she suggested, pointing to the image on the wall to help him visualize how it would look.

"Yeah, that would be sweet!" the young man replied.

"Great – so all you need to do is send the form and your feed contact to Tanner, and I think you're up next. Shouldn't be too long," she responded before excusing herself to give Tanner the details on the next piece.

In the back of the shop, Tanner was busy putting the final touches on a large black and gray floral piece that, while beautiful, seemed a bit of a cut-and-paste type piece she had seen a dozen times already in the few weeks she had helped at the shop.

"What'd he settle on? Did you do your magic?" Tanner asked without looking up as he whipped in the final shading.

"Japanese traditional dragon with a new-school twist of a smoking pipe. And you can use the smoke for framing and background," she said casually.

"Easy-peasy," Tanner responded before adding, "I was worried that kid wanted to put ten pounds of tattoos in a five-pound bag."

"He did, but we're good now," she laughed.

While Tanner finished his piece, she checked in with Lillian, who had clearly spent the better part of the day on an intricate and large, traditional-style depiction of a playing card, the Jack of Diamonds. The outlining had taken hours to put in, and it was clear the piece wouldn't be finished in a single session. The thirty-something man whose back would host the piece looked as if he was ready to tap out, and Blair could see him wince each time she wiped away ink and blood from his skin.

"That's going to be awesome when it's finished," Blair said as she watched Lillian work.

"Long way to go still," Lillian said with a sigh. "But yeah, I think it will look tough as nails... so long as Corey here doesn't puss out and stops moving!"

"Dude – six hours is a long time to sit with you torturing me," the man replied, face down on the black tattoo table.

"It's a back piece – what did you expect?" Lillian said to the man with a chuckle. "Quit being a big baby!"

The man only groaned in response as Lillian continued working away. After pulling several more short, bold lines along the interior of the playing card image, she looked up at Blair briefly and said, "How'd it go?"

"Good," Blair said, shaking her head in affirmation. "It was really good to see her."

"Good... good-good-good," Lillian answered as she continued her work.

"Hey... after you guys are done for the day... I was wondering if you could help me out with something?" Blair asked apprehensively.

"Girly, we owe you after all the work you've put in here. We'd be happy to," Lillian answered without reservation. "Hear that, Tanner?"

"Uh huh," her husband responded without looking up. "Happy to help, Blair..." he said as he placed several small highlights on the floral piece.

"Thank you," she said to Lillian before turning to Tanner as well. "Both of you – I appreciate it."

"You bet," Lillian responded as she continued working.

It was at that moment that the floral piece was finally finished, as the client finally stood from the table so that Tanner could clean up and apply the protective film that would cover the piece. Once he had finished with the client, he looked over to Blair and asked, "Wait – so what kind of help are we helping with?"

"Oh, I just need a hand moving some things to a storage unit... and wheels to get us there. Can you swing that?" Blair said cryptically.

"Sounds easy enough," Tanner responded before heading to the front of the shop to greet his next client.

The afternoon passed slowly in the shop as both artists worked on their pieces. What little conversation passed between the three of them was mostly light and superficial, as Tanner and Lillian focused on the work at hand. Blair kept herself busy consulting with clients that waited as well as booking appointments with those that walked in. When she wasn't busy with clients, she went about the normal chores of the shop, cleaning every surface with a bleach solution and antiseptic to ensure it sparkled impeccably. When they finally finished with the last clients of the day, it was Lillian who brought up Blair's request first.

"So, what is it we're moving?" she asked casually while she put away the last of the supplies and prepared her workstation for the next day's appointments.

"Just some of my paintings... I was counting on your... discretion. Well, you and Tanner's discretion. There just not... um... I don't think Bell and Zay – "

"Now I'm intrigued," Tanner interrupted suddenly. "Sounds like we get to see some of the highly sought after originals!"

Lillian smiled when she heard her husband's excitement, but reassuringly answered Blair, saying, "Don't mind him. We've just been eagerly waiting for you to invite us to see your stuff... after hearing all the fuss your boyfriend made about it and what not."

"Well, he's not exactly my boyfriend," Blair responded defensively.

"Oh... sure. Of course not," Lillian laughed. "Just obviously completely smitten with you, but hey – you call it whatever you want."

"Lead the way!" Tanner interjected as he grabbed the keys to the shop and began shutting off the lights.

The three walked in the cool night air of early fall, passing quickly through the several blocks of Frenchtown until they reached the historic district. It occurred to Blair that she had not previously invited them over, which may have been an unintentional slight. She said as much as they walked the last few blocks.

"We get it, B – you live in a shoe box. No room to host and all that," Tanner said dismissively.

"I would have brought wine – fancy wine," Lillian added to the conversation.

"You still can!" Blair laughed. "Just... maybe hold off until you've seen the place. I'd gladly have you both over if you don't mind standing the whole time."

At last, they reached the Andover home, and thereafter Blair's cottage behind the house. She fumbled for her keys as she said, "Again, thank you both for being willing. And... I probably don't need to say it, but if you can keep these paintings between us, I'd appreciate it. Oh, and if you could take out your lenses... Um... I can't have them scanned and end up on the feed."

Tanner and Lillian looked at each other, puzzling over the great mystery their friend was conveying. But with a keen understanding of Blair's circumstances, neither protested removing their lenses, and it took only moments before both had secured the devices in small cases they placed carefully into their pockets. Only a few minutes later, they discovered inside the small cottage what had caused Blair's paranoia and cryptic request surrounding her art.

"Blair – these are really, really good," Lillian said enthusiastically when she saw the first of the pieces. Then, teasing her friend, she added, "You're definitely going to jail!"

"Agreed," Tanner said loudly, through a mischievous grin. "It all makes sense now – you're a revolutionary!"

"Shhhhh!" Blair insisted defensively, as her eyes grew wider. "Nobody knows about these – if they did, there'd be trouble for Bell and Zay too! I just need to get them to the gallery's storage unit – I have the key. It just seemed like it'd be better to do it at night, so no one will see."

"This one – the Native princess – absolutely gorgeous! My favorite, for sure. And it's probably ambiguous enough to not draw any attention... the rest are probably too critical for the monitors' taste. Are you sure you need to store all of them? Maybe the others, but this one?" she asked pleadingly.

"I think my wife is interested in your work, Blair," Tanner laughed as he elbowed her gently. "Although, I'm not sure we can afford you from what I've heard about the demand for your work."

"I'll make it a gift to you both – there's no way you could pay me, anyway. You just can't say it came from me," Blair answered as she pulled sheets back over the remaining paintings. "That is, if you're sure you won't get in trouble for having it."

"This is stupid," Lillian interjected abruptly.

Tanner and Blair both looked at her, confused by the sudden outburst. It was then that Blair noticed how emotional her friend had become as she looked deeply into the painting of the Native woman.

"It's really a beautiful piece, Blair. Masterful... Provocative... Engaging. But honestly... they all are," Lillian said as she explained. "And you don't have to give it to us – I'm sure we can work out some way to exchange something meaningful for it – but I'm not.... It's not that. It's stupid. You shouldn't have to hide these! I'd be proud to have one of your original pieces – I think any *sane* person would. This whole idea of hiding your work - it's stupid! These deserve to be everywhere – on the feed, in museums, in front of millions of people that these pieces will speak to! We shouldn't be afraid to hide your talent and your voice – we shouldn't! It's ridiculous!"

Blair shook her head nervously, blushing at the compliment, but certainly there was no way her work could be displayed to anyone she didn't personally know and trust. "I can't, Lil! You know what will happen! Even being caught in the same room... they'd charge you with inciting extremism or whatever other Safe Speech violations they come up with."

"I agree," Tanner said quietly.

"See, he gets it," Blair said, pointing at her husband, who was twirling his mustache in his hand pensively.

"No – with her. I agree with Lillian. You can't hide this from the world, B. For your sake – for the world's sake. It'd be worth a risk to put it out there," he answered.

Blair was taken back for a moment, feeling as if her friends were teaming up in a way that made her feel vulnerable and uneasy. "Look, for tonight, we just need to get these paintings out of here," she said, somewhat dismissing their input.

"Listen, doll – we'll help you – we're good," Lillian answered reassuringly. "Just give it some thought. There might be a way. And I'm serious about this painting with the Native girl, if you're willing to part with it. We could hang it at the shop for a few weeks and test the waters... I don't think it violates any speech laws directly. And you haven't even signed any of them – how could they pin it to you?"

"I signed one of them... that one," she said, pointing to the painting that depicted an Uncle Sam figure forcibly dragging the woman resembling Lady Liberty.

As Lillian and Tanner looked closely at the painting, they saw the BH in the bottom right corner. Tanner continued twirling his mustache as he examined the mark, studying it briefly. He then randomly announced, "Have you ever seen us fix a bad tattoo?"

Blair looked confused by the question, and shook her head, showing she had not. Lillian moved even closer to the work until her eyes and nose were only inches away. Staring at the mark, she said, "Hey, what was the name they used for you at the gallery? That anonymous name they listed your paintings under?"

"Omnis Nemo", Blair responded, still confused by what was being suggested. "Why?"

Lillian glanced at her husband briefly, who simply nodded with a smile, who simply nodded with a smile. He then responded by saying, "If she's thinking what I'm thinking... to me... it looks like those initials could have been an error... just like someone did a bad tattoo and we have to fix it... that 'B' can become an 'Θ' and the 'H' could become a 'N'. You know, for *Omnis Nemo*? That would... um... shield you a bit, right?"

Then Lillian turned her head from the painting and looked at Blair somewhat suggestively, saying, "And if you signed each of these with 'ΘN', you could even deny it was the same *Omnis Nemo* who was featured at Crush... layered deniability."

"I never signed any of the paintings they showed at Crush... it was just a tag they placed under my work for the guests," Blair responded, suddenly understanding what was being proposed.

"Even better," Tanner laughed.

"I mean, anyone whose seen your work would know it was yours – your look, your style – it's very you. But you could at least deny making it if you had to... You could give yourself enough space to stay off their radar..." Lillian added.

"But once it hits the feed... I mean, if enough of my paintings were on the feed, wouldn't the algorithm do the work of connecting the dots for people?" Blair asked hesitantly.

"Maybe..." Tanner responded.

"Maybe not!" Lillian answered. "If the dozens of different people scanned enough of your work, the AI might have trouble associating the paintings with the artist. It would certainly attribute the work to 'ϴN' if you go that route – but what does that even mean? There's no user profile; it's not a known alias or username for anyone. I'm no expert, of course, but I think, worst case, 'ϴN' gets some attention. I'm not sure how the feed could trace it back to you when you're not even connected."

Blair looked at each of her friends, uncertain of her next steps. The words of her mother that morning still pulled on her heart, encouraging her to bring her light into the darkness. But how could she when she was completely disconnected from any meaningful method of communicating with people lost in the same darkness? She had lived so much of her life in fear of being discovered that the idea of taking such a bold step was terrifying, leaving her with an ache in her stomach that was both nauseating and exhilarating.

"Let's take a pause for a second," Blair said as she sat down at the small table in the center of her cottage. As she did, Tanner sat down beside her on a small stool, while Lillian found a place sitting on the edge of Blair's bed because of the lack of seating. After several seconds weighing what was being suggested, she began sorting through the competing ideas as methodically as she could, saying, "First – we need to get the paintings out of here. We can all agree on that?"

Tanner and Lillian nodded their heads in agreement, her conclusion being obvious and uncontested.

"Okay then – second, we could move them to the storage unit easy enough, right? Except for the Native girl," Blair asked, looking to Lillian who had been the force behind the issue.

"If you are willing to part with it, B – I'd love to have it in the shop. Sign it or don't – it's up to you," Lillian replied earnestly.

Tanner nodded in agreement as he finally stopped fidgeting with his mustache. He then interjected himself into Blair's reasoning by saying, "Thirdly, if I may, the question is whether you should even put them in the storage – if that's what you want to do – but only you can answer that."

"Well, of course I don't want to put my paintings in storage – but where else will they go? What else can we do with them?" she asked. "Look, if you guys have a better idea, I'm all ears. Jax and I discussed it at length. I don't know what else to do."

"Hmm... I might have an idea," Tanner answered, looking at Lillian to measure any hesitance from his wife.

"You're not thinking Blaze... you're not serious," Lillian answered, confirming his fears.

"No... of course not," Tanner replied in a dismissive tone. "I mean... I was just thinking. But you're right."

"Whose Blaze?" Blair asked, confused.

"Trouble," Lillian answered sternly. "Let's focus on the task at hand. For now – I think you're right. Let's move the paintings to the storage unit – just like we agreed. Tanner?"

"Yeah... of course," he responded.

Not fully understanding what had transpired between them, Blair let out a deep sigh before asking, "So – how about I sign the princess painting, Lil? Just one of them out there couldn't hurt anything, right?"

"I'd love that, B," Lillian said with a smile. "And it's not a gift – you're already too generous with your time and help around the shop. We're going to find you something worthy of trading for this – I promise you."

"That's really not necessary, Lil. I'm happy you love it; I'm happy it will have a home in the shop! Honestly, I'll just love seeing it on the wall when I go to the shop!" Blair answered. Then, in a sudden flash of movement, she was ducking down, searching through a small wooden toolbox next to her easel, where shortly thereafter she produced a small paintbrush and an accompanying small glass bottle of black paint. Moments later, the signature 'ΘN' was applied to the portrait of the Native princess.

After signing the first, she looked at the collection of paintings and noticed the other that was still marked with a 'BH', which she quickly painted over the top of, replacing her previous signature with 'ΘN'.

"How's that, then? Look convincing?" she asked rhetorically.

"Sure," Tanner responded, then laughing he added, "Honestly, that's a much easier fix than trying to correct 'Daddy's little angle' or 'No regerts'."

Blair moved her face close to the newly applied paint and blew gently on the new signature, hoping to entice each painting to dry quickly so that smudging wouldn't occur when they moved them. Then rather impulsively she declared, "It looks weird only having two of them signed, when they're all mine... If I'm going to be ΘN, I should just commit."

Moments later, she applied the same two letters to each of the paintings, signifying their creator in the unlikely event an observer would not know. "There," she said, having completed the small task. "Now they're finished. Let's just give them a few seconds to dry."

"Do you have more sheets?" Lillian asked as she searched for a means to cover the piece that would return with them to the tattoo shop.

Blair held up a single finger as if to show she either did or had an idea. After carefully washing her brush, she returned it to the ceramic base before placing the bottle of black paint back into the small wooden box, which she then shoved under her easel, creating extra space at the foot of her bed. Then, lifting the quilt that draped over the bed to the floor, she pulled out a cardboard box in which a stack of old linens had been stored. "We can probably fit two or three under each sheet if we stack them. So... maybe three, then?" she asked.

"I'll get it back to you," Lillian laughed. "Looks like you're in short supply."

"I work with what I can find, Lil," Blair chuckled knowingly.

They waited about thirty minutes for the newly added signatures to dry before they adorned the stacks of paintings with the supply of sheets that would cover them for the journey. Tanner then used some twine to tie the sheets tightly around the paintings, preventing them from slipping off while they traveled, and once everything was secured, they moved the artwork to the curb in front of the Andover house in three sets, including the single painting that would go to the shop.

"I'm going to put my lenses back in to get us a ride," Tanner announced, making sure Blair was aware of his intent.

"Just make sure you take them out again before we get to the actual unit. We can't have a record of where exactly they're being stored," she responded.

Within a few minutes, the automated vehicle arrived. Carefully, the three artists loaded the paintings into the vehicle before attempting to squeeze in beside them. While the car had been built to accommodate four adults, they soon discovered three adults and six large paintings was trickier than they had expected. For several minutes, they shifted the paintings that had been loaded first, first to one side and then the other as they attempted to create room for each adult that climbed into the vehicle. By the time Tanner boarded, so little room remained inside the car that the only obvious remedy was having Lillian sit on his lap, sandwiched on all sides by paintings, door, husband, and car ceiling. Then, just when they thought they were ready to depart, the voice of the automated vehicle sounded over a speaker built into the ceiling, repeating the same message, "All passengers must be seated in approved seats with safety devices fastened."

Frustrated, Tanner contorted his head to lean toward the side of his wife, still seated on his lap, as he asked, "How about you go with Blair, and I'll walk the one painting back to the shop?"

"In the dark – alone?" she asked, somewhat skeptically.

"I'm tough!" Tanner answered in a bristly, comical voice.

"Ok, love – you're right. I'll meet you back at the house when we're done," Lillian answered.

What followed was a reversal of the initial tedious process of loading paintings and people, when it was quickly discovered that the single painting was in the center of the three separate sets of paintings. By the end of the exercise, all three were giggling at the circus they had created, shuffling people and paintings in and out of the robocar that was parked and waiting under a dimly lit street light.

"Now then!" Tanner said, having finally extricated himself from the confines of the car with the single painting wrapped in a sheet tucked under his arm.

"Bye, love," Lillian laughed with a graceful wave.

~ 10 ~

"Jax, it's Lillian, Blair's friend," came a voice through an unidentified link in his feed.

"Of course – Lillian! How are you?" Jax asked as he scanned images of new pieces recently sent over by Deidra's people for a newly expanded exhibition wall.

"Good-good... good. So, um, question for you?" the woman asked hesitantly.

"Shoot," Jax replied, half listening as he worked.

"What's one of her original pieces worth?" she asked abruptly.

"Uh... that's an odd question, Lillian, if you don't mind me saying so. But short answer, it's worth whatever someone is willing to pay for it," Jax answered cryptically. Then, having considered the oddity of a question from a woman he had only spoken with a few times, he dug a little deeper, "What's on your mind? What... brought all this up?"

"So... I kind of talked Blair into giving me one of her pieces," Lillian answered.

"One of the, um...the special ones?" Jax stuttered as his voice became hushed.

"Well... I think it's special," Lillian laughed.

For a moment, a flood of panic washed over him, concerned primarily for Blair's well-being, should any of her more controversial pieces become publicly visible. Then, of course, there was also the issue of transactions that could subject them both to impromptu audits, which could just as easily land either of them in jail. Sitting at the desk in his office, he weighed carefully how to provide as much guidance as he could through the feed without revealing too much. Finally, he answered as carefully as he could, "Well, you know I'm not a lawyer, so I can't give you any official legal counsel. But my understanding of AMLA is that gifts are permissible within normal limits, Lillian. Now, I can't say for certain what exactly any particular piece would go for on the open market, and none of her pieces have been on the open market. That helps. So potentially, if she gave it to you, then it's yours. There's obvious... considerations... precautions, if you will, that may be prudent..."

"Oh, no – I'm not worried about that. I want to get her something – a gift, as it were. We do, Tanner and I... something equally nice... I suppose. But a gift... because Christmas is only a few months away!" she answered, trying to emulate his cryptic caution but struggling, given her normally straightforward demeanor.

"I think I understand," he answered. Then, with a casual laugh, he continued, "Well... it's a bit strange for me to act as an intermediary in gift giving. I can tell informally based on offers that have been thrown out to the gallery to commission her, my estimate of current demand, etc., I would place an approximate value of an original piece around one to two million. But it's difficult to say, as we don't have any we can sell to test the water with."

"Wait – you're serious?" Lillian asked in a doubtful tone.

"Yeah – well, that's probably conservative. I've had commission offers come in for her, offering one-point-five, but those are for specific landmarks that people are asking for. That might make the price higher, but it could also make it lower, depending on the buyer. Some people really want the artist's original work. So, I'm broad ranging it there," he answered, trying to simplify the complexity of his approximation.

"That's like half of what we spent to buy the shop. For a painting," she answered, shocked by his evaluation.

"Lillian, listen," he answered. "You know as well as I do – Blair doesn't care about any of that. She wants her work to be appreciated; I think we can both agree it should be appreciated. I wouldn't worry too much about trying to find something worthy of her... gift. If you want to do something nice for her, do that. Something that will make life easier... maybe safer for her," he encouraged.

"Well, I mean... we can't afford to buy her a house or an art studio," Lillian chuckled. "But we have an idea... might require a little help with the details on your end, if you're willing."

"Sure," he responded, somewhat hesitantly. "I'm happy to help however I can. A bit more detail might help me know what I'm getting into."

"Swing by the shop when you're done for the day? Blair's already here; she said you were planning on coming over anyway, right?" Lillian asked. "You'll know more this afternoon."

"Alight – I can do that," Jax responded. "I'll have things wrapped up here in the next hour or two and I'll head over."

"Great! Oh, and Jax... bring flowers! Girls love flowers!" Lillian said abruptly as she canceled the link.

"I know she likes flowers! I was planning to bring her flowers!" he stammered defensively to the empty office around him. He then immediately contacted the florist used by Crush for all of their events and ordered a bouquet of magnolias to be delivered urgently.

It took several more hours for him to go through the new paintings that would arrive from Birmingham. Deidra's perspective on the old city was masterful in its approach, while simultaneously evoking a sense of melancholy at what had once been a beautiful city, now fallen into severe disrepair. That was the nature of her work, of course, but each of the scans would need to be catalogued and assigned coding for billing and accounting purposes. Likewise, the size of the paintings played a role in how they would be displayed in the gallery; he needed to ensure there was sufficient room on the exhibit wall that was planned and determine the best configuration for displaying the pieces.

As he returned to the gallery floor down the stairs from his office, he noticed the flowers that had been delivered from the florist sitting atop Bruce's desk, and he was immensely grateful they could accommodate his last-minute request. For his part, Bruce seemed to admire the freshly cut bouquet, humming to himself as he worked in their shadow.

"Oh – they're not for me after all!" he said sarcastically when Jax picked up the small, lilac colored vase that held the bouquet.

"Not this time, my friend," Jax laughed. "I've been given strict orders."

"Seems like Miss. Huxley is already bossing the job – as it should be," Bruce smirked.

"Oddly enough, it was her friend. But yeah, same thing, I suppose," Jax answered.

"She deserves it – do as you're told, sir," Bruce responded, returning to his work.

Moments later, Jax was on the curb in front of the gallery, bouquet in hand, awaiting the automated rideshare that would deliver him to St. Charles. Oddly enough, it occurred to him in that moment the vehicle had not anticipated his departure, as it was not ready. Just then, a stranger approached, seemingly out of nowhere.

"Jaxson Wadsworth? Of Crush Gallery?" the man asked.

Immediately, Jax knew something was not right; the man's threadbare suit and hardened demeanor gave the impression his question was more official business than courteous.

"I am," Jax responded cooly. "How can I help you?"

"My name is Detective Hernandez. I'm with the St. Louis Police Department," the man said casually as he blinked his contact information over to Jax's feed.

"Yes, Detective – is there something I can do for you?" Jax answered calmly and politely.

"I'm looking into some allegations surrounding an artist known as 'Caldo' that involve improper payments... certain violations of the AMLA. Do you have a minute to spare?" the officer asked.

"Actually, I'm late for a date," Jax responded apologetically. "But my attorney's name is Henry Wells – I can send you his information. If you'd like to set up an appointment through him, I'd be happy to answer whatever questions you have."

"I see..." the officer answered. "You know, having to make this an official conversation... through an attorney and all... it's not a great look for the gallery," the officer said suggestively.

For a moment, Jax paused to read the man, wondering how much he should take into consideration the veiled threat. Then very carefully he said, "Good look or not, when it comes to allegations and potential violations of the law that may have been committed by a well-known client of ours, having counsel present seems... pretty reasonable to me."

The Detective's facial expression gave the impression he understood there wouldn't be any additional discussion on the matter. Instead, he simply responded by saying, "Have a good afternoon, Mr. Wadsworth."

As soon as the officer walked away, the automated vehicle pulled up to the curb for Jax's ride to St. Charles. After securing the flowers on the seat next to him in the vehicle, Jax called his attorney through the feed. Unfortunately, the call went directly to an automated response that was initiated when the recipient was occupied or otherwise not willing to receive calls.

"Figures," Jax muttered. He then recorded an audio message that could be sent to his attorney once he became available. "Wellsy – Giving you the heads up. I was just contacted by Detective Hernandez of St. Louis Police regarding allegations surrounding Caldo and suspected AMLA violations. The Detective's contact information will follow... Looks like we're going to need a meeting, as they have some questions. I provided your contact info to the Detective and told him I would need counsel present – just as you've always instructed. Just let me know what you want to do with this one."

As the vehicle rolled on through the northwestern corner of the city, Jax's mind raced considering what trouble Caldo may have dragged him and the gallery into. It was likely the gallery was only tangentially connected to whatever mess the artist found himself in, but given this particular artist's personal habits and known indiscretions, he could never be certain.

Nearing St. Charles, Jax quickly completed what had become a ritual, removing his lenses before meeting with Blair. While a mild inconvenience, he had noticed how much quieter the world seemed without a constant bombardment of messages, calls, and advertisements beaming into view. When the vehicle finally came to a stop in front of the tattoo parlor in Frenchtown, he found himself calm and collected, excited to see Blair.

Moments later, upon entering the tattoo shop, his jaw dropped as he noticed a familiar painting hung center on the rear wall of the studio, greeting visitors from a distance.

"That's... surprising to see here," he announced, nodding toward Blair's painting on the wall. "Although, out of the lot, you probably picked the... most discrete."

"Blair, your 'Not boyfriend is here'," came the voice of Lillian from a tattoo table to the left of the painting.

"Not boyfriend?" Jax asked with a look of confusion as he glanced deliberately at the artfully assembled bouquet of magnolias he was holding.

"Ah, you see... we referred to you as her 'boyfriend' a little while back, and she was quick to correct us. So, you know what *that* means..." replied Tanner, who was face down at a small table, drawing on a tablet.

It was then that Blair appeared from the small backroom, at which point she beamed as she rushed towards Jax, nearly jumping onto him with a warm embrace.

"Again – not boyfriend?" he chuckled as he squeezed her closely.

"Well, I... I didn't want to assume..." she blushed.

"I mean... I assumed we were adults, and I didn't need to propose any sort of formality...But that's what happens when you assume, I suppose," he said apologetically. Then, dropping to one knee, he set the bouquet down beside him and took her hand, melodramatically saying, "Miss. Blair Huxley, will you take me, Jaxson Wadsworth the fourth, to be your formal boyfriend? To have and to hold from this day forward until you are sick of me, or otherwise find someone more to your liking..."

"Oh, shut up!" Blair squealed in embarrassment. "I... I just didn't want to put you on the spot! You are too much!"

As Jax returned to his feet from his submissive posture, he retrieved the flowers next to him and produced them before her. "So that's a 'Yes' then? Or should I get more elaborate? I can do more elaborate!"

"STOP!" she laughed, kissing him gently as she wrapped her arms around his neck. "They're beautiful – thank you."

"You can put them over there, B," Lillian replied, having clearly stopped her work to witness the grandiose, romantic gesture. She then looked over at Tanner and asked, "Why don't you ever propose to me like that?"

"We're married, dear. I did. Flowers, dinner, the whole lot," Tanner replied, shaking his head at the absurdity of the display. He then set down the tablet and turned off the light at his workstation to join them at the front of the shop, while his wife continued working on her client, who remained face down and asleep on her table.

"So – we did a thing," Tanner said as he approached the gushing couple.

"Oh, a thing, huh?" Blair laughed. "What kind of thing?"

"A gift thing. For you, Blair. It was Lillian's idea, but I had a hand in it," Tanner said with a smirk.

"I told you both, you don't need to do anything for me – ," Blair answered.

"No, no. I love it; Lillian loves it," Tanner interrupted, careful to not publicly name her as the artist who created the painting now hanging as a centerpiece on the shop's wall. "Frankly, even the street urchins that walk-in here talk about it, compliment it, and ask where they can get a print... We wanted to do a thing for you," he said as he produced a small key from his pocket.

"What's... what is this for?" Blair asked, looking at the brass-colored key.

"Head northwest from town a few miles to the part of the river where it's still running east-west before it wraps around the bend that runs to the south. It shouldn't take long, even on your bike. You're looking for a place called Southshoal... It's out by the Ma Belle if you know where that is. And it's number 26; my brother is up there, getting it ready for you. If you go now, you'll catch him," Tanner responded, smiling as he revealed the big secret he had been keeping for days.

"A boat?" Jax responded. "You're giving her a boat?"

"A shallow-drafted ketch; it's double-masted, a forty-three-footer with a fiberglass hull. She's older than me – been in my family for years," he said, beaming with pride. Then, with the precision and care a father would show for a child, he continued by explaining, "Now, she needs some work and a new motor. The interior hasn't been touched since the nineties... so it's as old as she is. The linens and lines are all only a few years old, and they've been stored away. So, she'll sail well enough, but you'd have a heck of a job getting her out of the marina without the auxiliary motor. But

I haven't had time or the money to keep pouring into her, what with opening the new shop and all... What I'm getting at is don't get too excited until you see her."

He then removed an envelope from his back pocket, handing it over to Blair as he said, "Old enough that the title is still on paper, you see. It's all signed over to you – legal like. And we'll cover the slip fees and shore power costs until you figure that part out; it's not much. But it'll give you a place of your own that's private. Everything's all hooked up, or should be by the time you get there. You could live on it full time if you wanted... It's all yours."

Tears welled up in Blair's eyes as she bounced around the counter to hug the man.

Then grabbing him, she squeezed him tightly and said, "Thank you – both of you. This is too much..."

"Nonsense," Lillian laughed, still working on her sleeping client. "It's a gift, B – with our appreciation for all of your help at the shop, for your art – for everything. We wanted to do something nice for you. Besides, I've been trying to convince my husband to sell that thing for years."

Tanner's smile felt pasted to his face as he radiated joy at how excited she looked, adding, "Well, go on then — go take a look at her!"

Blair looked at Jax, shocked by the spontaneity and unexpected generosity of her friends. She realized the event may have derailed the date they were supposed to have and took a moment to check with him, asking, "Would you mind terribly?"

"Would I mind? I think Lillian may have made me a silent co-conspirator in this adventure!" he laughed.

"You can borrow my bike, if you'd like, Jax," Lillian answered. "Blair rides her bike here sometimes, so like a good co-conspirator, I brought mine along, just in case you might need it this afternoon."

"Thanks... I don't actually remember the last time I was on a bicycle... I'm sure we'll sort it out," Jax laughed.

Outside of the tattoo shop, the sun was hanging low in the western sky, but there was still plenty of time before it set. With the marina only a few miles away, the bike ride would be short, he knew. Still, upon mounting the contraption, the awkwardness of having not ridden in so long quickly set in.

Blair stared at him with a mild delight as she watched him struggle. After an initial failed attempt, which resulted in him nearly falling over, Jax loosened his tie and tucked the pant legs of his lacks into the tops of his socks. Then, carefully, he placed one foot over the crossbar and steadied his feet on both sides.

"Okay – I'm ready when you are," he announced confidently.

"You sure about that?" Blair answered with a smile.

"Yes. Positive this time – just go slowly. It's been a while," he said, attempting to maintain a serious expression.

With an urgent push, he peddled forward, and after only a few feet, his childhood instinct of how to maneuver the vehicle returned, if only enough to stay upright and continue at a steady pace. The two riders passed slowly and methodically through the busy afternoon swarm of automated vehicles delivering commuters until they passed the university. From there, they zigzagged along the grid patterned streets until they cleared McNair Park and then St. Charles West High School. From there, they continued north through neighborhoods of St. Charles until they were riding along the country streets of the rural area between town and the river.

The entire journey took about an hour of easy riding, and when at last they arrived at their destination, the gate to the marina entrance had been left open. Just past the gate, a historic marker pointed the way towards the wreck of the Ma Belle, at which point, Blair exclaimed, "This must be the place."

A sign outside riveted on the wall of a large metal building read "Office", but whether from enthusiasm or ignorance, Jax followed as Blair simply peddled on, skipping past the office completely. Both riders examined their surroundings for any sign or marking or sign that would point the way to the dock containing slip number twenty-six. As they continued, a brief distance down Lakeview Drive, the wrecked hulls of several destroyed boats decorated the side of the road, accompanied by several other vessels that remained under covers. It was obvious to Jax that Tanner wasn't exaggerating when he said it was private; they didn't see another soul.

At last, they spotted two large marinas with metal roofs that covered rows of large boats beneath them. When they neared the entrances, the first was adorned with a small metal sign that read "1-30", which seemed as good enough of an indicator as any to park their bicycles and investigate further. No sooner did they drop the kickstands on the bikes than a man appeared, walking toward them from the long floating walkway that intersected the slips of boats in the marina. He was about Jax's age, average height, and wearing a captain's hat over black hair that matched in color with a bushy, well-kept beard. Through his beat-up tank top, Jax could see a collection of tattoos along the man's arms and shoulders, and thought there was a better than fair chance he was related to Tanner. Fortunately, the man waved as he closed the distance up the ramp, eliminating any doubt, until he reached a barred metal door that acted as a gate.

"It's locked, see?" the man replied from the other side of the door. "I'll give you a key when we're all set here. Tanner said he didn't have a spare, and he gave me the one he had a few days ago when I came out here."

"You must be Tanner's brother," Jax said, extending his hand to greet the man politely.

"Blaze," the man answered, shaking Jax's hand.

Blair paused for a moment, as if uncertain of something and seeming to have recognized the name. When he noticed her reaction, for a moment, he assumed she had heard Lillian and Tanner discuss the brother from the shop. But the look on Blair's face said something more, as if she was puzzled or searching to place the man in some context she couldn't find.

"Blaze, huh?" Jax said casually. "Is that a nickname?"

"It beats Bartholomew... and it sounds cool," the man answered with a grin. "After that cartoon that ran for a million years, I can't go by 'Bart' – it's ruined."

The remark made both he and Blair laugh a bit, which eased the tension, after which Blaze simply gestured as he spoke, "This way then... I'll show you around."

The ramp into the marina was gradually sloped and textured, making the descent easy enough. When they reached the boat slips, he noticed markers on the electrical connection pedestals outside each of the boat slips. Most of the slips were occupied with various boats, mostly yachts and speedboats, but a handful were empty.

"Do, um... many people live here full time?" Jax asked as he looked around at the rows of covered boats.

"A few," Blaze replied. "There's showers up in the lot near where you parked your bikes. The key to the gate will get you in. And if you're wondering about safety, I wouldn't."

"Well... while I appreciate your perspective, I just want to make sure Blair will be safe down here, if and when she's alone," Jax replied.

"Understood," Blaze answered without turning around as they continued down the pathway between the boats. Then abruptly he stopped and pointed out a medium-sized power boat on the right and said, "That one belongs to Old Mr. Agnew... he's tough as nails and armed to the teeth – I've seen it. I don't think he sleeps much, heard him say it was on account of several tours in 'Rough

Bush'. Anyway, that old pirate's got the whole marina wired with cameras – he takes his security pretty serious, even if he's a bit paranoid. Then again, who can blame him these days. It's not official-like, but it's full-time, unpaid security if you ask me."

"Ooooh, pirates!" Blair laughed, as Jax's eyes grew wider, uncertain of how he should respond to such a motley security system.

"Look – nobody comes down here except people with boats, and they leave each other alone. I've never even heard of anyone having a problem or break-in or anything," Blaze responded. "It's pretty chill."

Finally, Blaze stopped at the end of the dock where the electrical pedestal held a reflective tag with the number 26 freshly applied.

"This is it," he said, pointing towards the large sailboat with two masts that had been dropped and covered with fresh, blue canvas. It was older, just as Tanner described, but it appeared to be clean and well taken care of.

Moments later, he helped each of them up a small stepladder and onto the deck of the vessel. Looking at them both somewhat skeptically, he then said, "I'm not sure if either of you knows their way around a sailboat – if you plan on taking her out... or..."

"I sailed in college," Jax answered, which produced a look of surprise from Blair. "What? I was on the sailing team!"

"Of course you were," Blair laughed, shaking her head.

"Great – shouldn't be too much trouble. The main mast and mizzen are in good condition, as are the sails. Canvas is new. It's the outboard motor that's kept her in dock," Blaze continued, ignoring Blair completely as he directed his information to Jax. "We've been working on her off and on, but with a boat this old, it takes time. I'm not sure that the motor can be salvaged."

"I see," Blair said, interjecting herself back into the conversation. "I'm sure we'll figure out something."

"Sure," Blaze said, nodding with skepticism. "Let me show you inside."

Just in front of the helm, Blaze slid a wooden cover out of place before parting two wooden doors, which covered an opening to below decks. After they descended, he flipped a switch nearby to turn on the light, revealing a larger than expected interior space complete with a kitchenette, a seating area, a forward cabin, and a small bathroom. All the interior upholstery was quite old and sun bleached, with tears visible in many of the cushions. Jax did his best to remain positive, unaccustomed to things that were not immaculate and pristine. When he looked at Blair, all he could see were glassy eyes and a sweet smile that reached ear to ear.

"It's marvelous!" she said excitedly.

"She is," Blaze responded with a grin. "I was shocked Tanner said he was willing to part with her, after all these years. But he said something like, 'If there was ever a cause, this is it.' Or something like that."

"Will there be enough room for you to work?" Jax asked, sounding as positive and nonjudgmental as he could muster.

"Yes, of course! I'll cover the upholstery on that side of the seating with tarps – it's nearly the height of my easel! And – I bet this place is easily as big as the cottage!" she continued excitedly as she began looking around through the interior of the vessel.

"Well, take good care of her," Blaze said, somewhat saddened at the thought of parting with the ship. "Oh, and you'll need to rename her, if 'Trident's Envy' doesn't suit you. It's good luck for a new owner to give their vessel a proper christening, if you believe in that sort of thing."

"We will see to it," Jax answered politely as he shook Blaze's hand once again before he departed. "Thank you – we appreciate you showing us around."

"You bet – Tanner's family. Blood is thicker than... well, most things these days," he said suggestively.

Jax simply nodded in response as Blaze excused himself. They could feel the vessel rock as his weight shifted until he had disembarked. When finally alone, Blair beamed with joy as she looked around, wiping aware tears of joy.

"You've got generous friends," Jax said suddenly, breaking her attention away from the surroundings.

"All my friends are generous – I've been fortunate to find the right people in life. That's why they're still friends and not strangers," she answered. "You're not bad yourself, though."

"Well, I try," he said, pulling her close and wrapping his arms around her. "I *do* have one serious question – do I need to call you 'Captain'?"

"The term 'Skipper' will suffice – for now," she answered as she kissed him.

They held each other for several minutes, content in the moment and happy to be alone in her new home. Eventually, it was Jax who spoke first, "It's getting pretty late... the bikes are here... it's going to be a long ride back."

"You're leaving?" Blair asked with a coy smile. Then suggestively, she said, "I was thinking maybe we could stay here... see what kind of mischief we might get up to..."

"Oh... well, I suppose I could order some take out for delivery. Maybe a bottle of wine or champagne?" he asked.

"Champagne feels more boat-y," Blair responded facetiously.

"Well, boat-y is certainly what we're going for these days, and I wouldn't want to kill the mood," he laughed.

~ 11 ~

"I don't know why you're so eager to move out of the cottage; I thought you were happy and comfortable there," Bell protested pensively.

"I have been, Bell. And I'm eternally grateful for everything you and Zay have done for me," Blair answered as she looked directly at her friend to show she was being earnest in her appreciation.

"So, you've been happy, but you still want to move?" Bell asked, uncertain of what had changed that might be motivating the decision.

"Well, it's a place of my own – like really mine," Blair explained. She had been packing up her art supplies when Bell joined her to help, but the reluctance of her friend to watch her leave was making the transition increasingly difficult. "It's just, I feel like I've been enough of a burden on you guys for years now. I just – "

"You stop right there, Squirt. You have never been a burden on us. Having you stay in our little cottage has been wonderful. We love you dearly and wouldn't have it any other way. But if this is what you want – if it's what you think is best, we support your decision. Just don't do this because you think you're putting us out. Mia was devastated when I told her we were losing you," Bell responded.

"She can come visit! And when the boat gets fixed up... and I learn how to sail... maybe we could all go out on the river. It could be great!" Blair answered in a hopeful, optimistic tone.

Knowing there would be no arguing with her and having said her piece, Bell helped her place the last of her things into several boxes Zay had scrounged from around the office. She didn't have much, of course. Save for her record collection and art supplies, there wasn't much help that was needed with the move that Jax had not already helped with.

"So, this is it – you're going to tow all this in your little bike trailer?" Bell asked, already knowing the answer.

"It's not too far – just a few miles. And it's still early. I took care of Mrs. Marbury's garden at dawn – literally. All so I could have the entire morning to paint. And I don't need to be at the shop until lunchtime. Jax's got some big meeting with this lawyer that he has to get ready for... So, that leaves me hours and hours to paint and get settled," Blair laughed.

"Okay then," Bell sighed reluctantly. "Let me know if you need anything? I'd be happier knowing you still needed us occasionally – even if it's just a cup of sugar or something..."

"Bell, I'll be a few miles away. And I can't bear the thought of not seeing you or Mia regularly – Zay I could live without," she answered sarcastically.

"He's an acquired taste, true enough," Bell chuckled. "A good man can be hard to find these days... speaking of which... how is Jax?"

"Good... he's good," she answered with a smile. "The gallery keeps him pretty busy, but he's great. He makes time for me. It's all so stable and boring in the most wonderful way!"

"I'm glad," she answered. "I was a little iffy on him, to be honest. Rich guy from a wealthy family suddenly takes an interest in a former foster kid... You are gorgeous and you're talented, love – who wouldn't be interested? It's just... it felt like he was trying to prove something to his family more than he was interested in you. Or something like that, I don't know."

"He can't help who his family is any more than I can," Blair answered somewhat defensively. "And maybe he is trying to prove something to them; I'm trying to prove something to my parents as well, in a different way, I suppose. I'm proud of who my parents are and what they stand for. I think he's always lived in his family's shadow... His interest in art... his passions... who he is or was supposed to be could only ever be seen by them as an asset to the family. They didn't... see him, not the way I do. So, now he's defying them a bit, but I don't think that means he likes me any less."

"Meaning? Defying how?" Bell asked, trying to be careful not to pry too much.

"Oh, you know... there was some push back at the gala... then his mother, who can be a real delight, made some kind of veiled threat..." she answered, moving the last of the moving boxes into the small trailer attached to her bicycle.

"A threat? About what?" Bell asked in a mildly disdainful tone.

"Me, mostly. Who my parents are... their reputation. Ironically, I think it's his parents that feel threatened. I don't know, it's rich people stuff," Blair answered dismissively.

"And he keeps coming around, huh?" Bell asked rhetorically.

"For now, at least... although, I think if I don't learn to cook a proper meal pretty quickly, that might all change," Blair joked. "Suffice to say, the delivery drone has had no trouble finding the entrance to the marina."

"One cannot live on take out alone," Bell laughed as she closed the door to the cottage behind her.

Before mounting her bicycle, Blair took a moment to give her friend a warm hug, adding, "Thank you – for everything. Zay too, tell him I said so?"

Bell laughed, "I'm going to tell him you think he's a bit sketchy!"

"Oh, he already knows," Blair chuckled loudly. "Okay. For real now."

"Bye," Bell answered with a wave.

By the time she cleared the Andover's yard, Blair was so excited to bring the last of her belongings to her new home she peddled her bicycle as fast and as hard as she could until her legs burned and her lungs gasped for air. For the first time in her adult life, she felt truly free. The place she was headed was a real home, and it was hers. As much as it was a gift, for legal reasons, to her, it meant that a person out in the world loved her art more than they loved that boat. And even though that person was a friend, it made no difference. Friends don't just casually give each other boats.

She arrived at the marina in less than the forty-five minutes it had taken on her previous trip, setting a new personal best time at thirty-four minutes flat. It took her a moment to gather the boxes from the trailer after she parked her bike and locked it. But she approached the gate that led down to her boat slip with full arms and had to maneuver acrobatically in order to produce the key and unlock the metal door without dropping anything.

Halfway down the ramp, the voice of an old man called out, "Hey kid! You need a hand?"

"Sure," Blair responded blindly as she tried not to stumble down the ramp. A few short moments later, the top two boxes levitated in front of her, removed by old, weathered hands that had met her midway down the ramp.

"I gotcha, kiddo," the old man replied in a gruff voice.

"Thank you. I really appreciate the help," she responded. To her surprise, she had not seen the man before on the many trips she had made to the boat over the previous week. He was easily in his sixties from the look of his sun-leathered skin, and he wore a knitted beanie from under which thin silvery hair was attempting an escape. He was every bit the image of the 'old pirate' that she had imagined when Blaze spoke of him before.

"I'm Miller Agnew, your neighbor of sorts," the old man interjected as they walked with her boxes.

"Blair – pleased to meet you, Mr. Agnew," she answered politely.

"Pick one or the other, kiddo — either Miller or just Agnew. Everyone else just calls me 'Agnew' or 'Old Man Agnew'; it's been so since my days in the Corp. No need to be so formal with an old salt like me," the old man said with a gruff laugh.

"Thank you, Agnew. I was imagining these boxes would have me blindly wander off the dock!" she laughed.

"Straight into the drink, as they say," he replied.

Once they at last reached Blair's slip, the old man waited for Blair to climb aboard and set her boxes down before handing her the ones he carried. She thanked him again, and just as he was politely excusing himself, she abruptly asked, "I'm sorry if this is forward – I know we just met... but I've got to know?"

"What's that, my dear?" the old man asked.

"Are you really a pirate?" she asked slyly.

The grizzled old sailor squinted for a moment, looking at Blair intently as he studied her. He then looked up the boat ramp towards the entrance, attempting to determine if any others were nearby to hear him. Then with a wink he answered, "It's not just dead men that tell no tales, deary."

Blair's eyes grew wide with excitement as an illustrious smile grew across her face. "I knew it!" she shouted.

"Just keep it between your ears, kiddo. Don't want the riff raff to know where I keep my gold," the old said, smirking as he waved goodbye. And then, as quickly as he had appeared, the old sailor ambled off towards his own slip.

With some bending and carefully maneuvering, she moved the remaining boxes into the cabin before latching the opening behind her. She was alone in the privacy of her own space, a place more private than she had ever really known. For a moment, she considered whether she should put things away and tidy up, or whether she should set straight to painting. After several seconds of looking at the newly delivered boxes, she looked over to her newest piece, only under drawing on canvas, sitting on an easel that she rigged to sit on one of the padded benches.

"There's plenty of time to tidy up later," she said aloud to herself as she abandoned her chores for the pleasure of her art.

After rifling through the still partially packed cardboard box that held her brushes, pallet knives, and paints, she quickly produced several brushes, which she then laid in front of her workspace. She returned to the box to remove several tubes of acrylic, a small jar of mixing medium, and a thin, plastic palette that would hold the paint as she worked. After donning a paint filled apron she had previously hung from the edge of an easel, she was ready to work.

The landscape of Mount Rushmore was iconic, of course, but as was true for all the prominent symbols she painted, most people had seen the moment enough times to not pay much attention to it. If she could achieve what she envisioned, she knew anyone who saw the work would certainly notice some changes.

She began with the underpainting, using the blocking in tones that would form the heads of the presidents into focus. It took hours to add layering of mixed colors to build dimension into the work. The light source shone brightly on Washington's forehead, which meant she would need to build up the darker areas around Roosevelt, Jefferson, and Lincoln, leaving the forehead of the first president nearly white at the top left corner. As she put down her brushes to allow the piece time to dry, she glanced up briefly at the clock on the wall and noticed it was already three o'clock in the afternoon. While not technically on the payroll, she typically arrived at the shop a little after lunch; she had simply lost track of time painting.

Hastily, she threw the apron back onto the edge of the easel, and began washing her brushes to ensure they wouldn't be ruined. She then grabbed the boat's keys and an old denim jacket she hung on a peg by the door as she hurried out of the boat's interior and onto deck, locking the cabin behind her.

As she raced down the dock to the ramp, she took only half a second to wave to her new friend as she passed. "Have a good afternoon, Cap'n!" she exclaimed before lunging up the metal ramp to the gate.

When she reached her bicycle, she realized she still had the small trailer attached, and with no time to disconnect the contraption, she thought it best just to leave it attached for the several mile trip down to the shop. It was empty, she reasoned. It wouldn't add too much effort to tow it along, and she didn't want to waste time dragging it down to her slip and storing it on her boat.

Moments later, she was peddling hard with the trailer in tow as she exited the marina, heading south towards Frenchtown. The jean jacket she had grabbed before leaving quickly became too hot in the afternoon heat, and as she held the handlebar with one hand, she began wiggling her free arm to remove it. Once the precarious maneuver was completed, she was left trying to steer a bike, trailer in tow, down bumpy, poorly maintained country roads, while holding a jean jacket under one arm.

"Way to leap before looking once again, Huxley," she muttered to herself and she clumsily peddled on through the ordeal. Only a few blocks from the historic district of St. Charles, the challenge became even more awkward once she contended with the unmanned robocars that filled the side streets. The autonomous vehicles were courteous enough drivers, and they seemed to go to great lengths to ensure they did not collide with pedestrians. Unfortunately, she was not a pedestrian, and the vehicles whizzed past her without hesitation.

She had navigated these streets hundreds of times before, and on dozens of such occasions, she had towed the contraption behind her as she went. Yet in none of those instances had she been rushing while clumsily steering while juggling a jacket with a trailer in tow.

Whether because of her overconfidence, her clumsiness, or the poor programming of the autonomous vehicle, only a few blocks from the tattoo shop in Frenchtown, suddenly, a silver vehicle abruptly turned right from a perpendicular path, and then immediately braked to avoid some unforeseen obstacle on the road. Blair squeezed the brake on her bicycle's handlebars as hard as she could, and as she did, the back of the bicycle lurched forward, breaking free of the trailer and sending it careening to the side of the road. Simultaneously, her body lurched forward over the handlebars and slammed into the back of the vehicle.

The unexpected jolt of slamming her face into the rear bumper of the robocar sent a shockwave of pain through her whole body, causing a sharp, stinging sensation all the way down to her toes. For a moment, she laid in the street, shaken and woozy from the impact. Then, gradually, she began to move, trying to get to her feet. The vehicle she had rear-ended pulled forward several feet only to stop, at which point its passenger, who had seen what happened, exited and rushed over towards her.

"Oh my gosh – oh my gosh! Are you ok?" the woman screeched as she ran up to her.

Blair groaned for a moment as she continued trying to find her footing. She pushed herself up off of the asphalt to her knees and began to sway.

"I'm calling 9-1-1," the woman said energetically as she began blinking through her feed for the emergency contact.

"No – no, I'm fine," Blair mumbled.

"You're far from fine; you just face planted into the back of a car!" the woman exclaimed.

"I'm fine. Please, don't call anyone," Blair groaned.

"You're delirious," the woman answered, her tone suddenly changing to one of concern and empathy as she took Blair's arm, attempting to hold her steady as she struggled to her feet. "There you go – easy, now."

Only seconds later, emergency medical drones from the nearby hospital appeared in the sky overhead, and Blair could hear as they began slowly descending towards the scene of the accident.

"Thank you – but I really need to go," Blair said as she staggered away from the scene of the accident.

"Where are you going? At least let them scan you for injuries!" the woman called out as Blair nearly fell over herself, attempting to escape.

"Wait a minute... Miss... the Medicopters are almost here!" the woman shouted as Blair fled into the alley that separated some of the historic buildings.

Using the walls to support her, she zig-zagged through the labyrinth of stone and old wooden structures of the Historic District as the medical drones whirred overhead, searching the scene of the accident. After several left turns and a few right turns, she found herself on Main Street, surrounded by the afternoon crowds of tourists. Without hesitation, she immediately walked up beside one of the small groups that was headed towards Frenchtown, attempting to blend in with the group as they passed. They continued north for several blocks before one at the head of the group of tourists pointed towards a nearby shop, at which point Blair lost her cover.

While she couldn't hear the drones anymore, she knew they were in the area and there was a good chance they knew what she looked like from the images captured in the woman's feed. Fearing repercussions if they attempted to scan her and found her unable to pay for the costs of the emergency medical response, Blair fought pain and nausea that had followed her accident and pushed on towards the tattoo shop and the safety that would come with her friends.

When she finally stumbled through the door, she realized she must have looked far worse that she had imagined.

"Oh my god, Blair – what happened?" Lillian exclaimed loudly.

"It's nothing... I just crashed my bike. The stupid robocar braked hard, and I was towing the trailer and – "

"Come sit down before you fall down," Tanner said from the back of the shop.

Holding onto the counter at the front of the shop, Blair did as she was told, making her way towards the back of the shop until she found the nearest chair she could fall into. As luck would have it, the shop was unusually quiet that afternoon and completely empty. In a few quick seconds, Lillian arrived with paper towels coated in the disinfectant they used for their tattoos. She then began gently wiping Blair's face and chin, which revealed small amounts of blood and gravel.

"You must have had quite a spill there, doll," Lillian said as she cleaned the wounds.

Blair groaned and winced with each wipe, answering, "I was rushing because I was late to get here... and then the next thing I knew I was ass over handlebars going face first into its bumper and then the ground... Honestly, it probably would have been hilarious to see if it weren't so... painful."

"I bet!" Tanner laughed discreetly, catching a mean glance from his wife in reply.

"I wish we would have known. I would have told you to stay and paint – it's been dead all afternoon," Lillian answered as she wiped away the last of grime and gravel that clung to Blair's wounded face.

"Ah well... it may pick up all the same. It's still early," Blair said. "I'd hate to think I went through this whole ordeal for nothing... and after running from those hospital drones, it's probably best to lie low for a while."

"Ever the outlaw," Tanner laughed as he looked up from his tablet. "Oh, don't worry, neither of us is connected right now. It's just us."

"Speaking of which," Lillian said as she turned towards her husband.

"What?" Tanner said dismissively.

"Outlaws, babe. Blaze. You said he was coming by. Remember?" she pestered. "I'm going to go get a bag of ice from the freezer."

"Well, it's hardly a good time to get into all this right now, Lil," Tanner answered, gesturing towards Blair, who was half sprawled out in a tattoo chair.

Confused by what they were getting at and seeing Tanner imply it had something to do with her, Blair asked, "What am I missing?"

"You remember Blaze... Tanner's unlensed brother... the guy you met at the marina?" Lillian asked.

"Oh, yeah, of course! Now that you mentioned it, I DO remember you telling me your brother wasn't connected, and I remember meeting Blaze, of course. How am I just now figuring out HE is the brother you were talking about?"

"Beats me," Tanner answered. "We figured you two would be well acquainted by now, being in the same... circumstances. That's why we sent him to meet you at the boat; I figured you guys would just know... or something."

"Well, that's the thing, Tanner – when you don't have lenses, you can't scan people to see if they don't have lenses," Blair said sarcastically.

"Well, I don't know!" he responded.

"So, he's coming here to... hang out? I mean, you know I have a boyfriend," Blair asked sternly.

"No – it's not like that," Tanner answered defensively.

"We're not trying to set you up with him," Lillian interjected from the back room, trying to help clear up the confusion at a distance.

"Then...? I mean, it's your shop. He's your brother..." Blair said. "Still not sure what that has to do with me."

"Well, he is unlensed… yes. He's also a printer, by trade. He's managed to work out a living, somehow avoiding the feed. And he's old school – no scans, no feed – completely offline," Tanner explained apologetically. "I mean, I didn't want to just assume you'd be interested, but Lil and I were discussing prints for the shop. It's a common thing for tattoo artists to make prints of their work and sell them to clients who want to hang something on the wall. So, Lil and I were talking with him recently about making prints of the "Fight of the Century" mural outside, and it sort of came up we should ask you if we could get prints made of the Native girl painting… It's the most popular piece we have in the shop, and people keep asking. But it's your work, and so we won't reproduce it if you don't want us to…"

"Wait… so you want to sell prints of my painting to people who come into the shop? But you guys would still have the original," Blair asked, trying to understand exactly what he had in mind.

"Only if you're open to it, B," Lillian answered as she returned with a bag of ice that she placed on Blair's forehead.

"And Blaze's situation makes him… discreet. There' no digital scan that links to him or you. It's all old school computers. They scan the image and physically print copies on paper," Tanner interjected.

"I'm just confused – it's probably the accident. I gave the painting to you, Lil. That makes it yours. If you want to make prints, make prints. It's your call," Blair said, trying to cipher out what the big fuss was all about.

"It's a copyright thing, B. You gave us the original painting, but you still own the rights to reproduce it. That's how original art works," Lillian explained.

"Huh," Blair shrugged. "I'm sure Jax would have known that stuff. I just paint. I'm not quite sure how the rest of it works, but if you can sell copies and it would help the shop – great. I'm just glad people like the piece as much as they do."

"Well, it's not all that simple, Blair. We can reproduce it with your permission, but you're entitled to compensation on the sales," Tanner added, trying to help her understand how it all would work.

"Right, and there's not much I can do with compensation," Blair laughed. "Maybe it will help cover some of the slip fees and what not you guys are already footing the bill for? That seems more than fair to me."

Lillian shrugged in resignation, frustrated by Blair's ambivalence towards the business end of art. While Blair understood she didn't know how it all worked, she also wasn't interested in trying to become wealthy from her art, even if it were possible to do so in her circumstances.

As they continued discussing the painting and the process they were proposing, Blaze arrived at the shop. He was expected, but with no connection to the feed, his timing was always a bit of a mystery. He immediately noticed Blair, sprawled out on one of the tattoo chairs, clutching a bag of ice she was pressing against her forehead.

"Woah, what happened to you?" he exclaimed abruptly.

"I rear-ended one of the robocars with my bike," Blair groaned, shifting the bag of ice to a new position on her face.

"Ouch," Blaze responded casually. "You… didn't get caught up with the police or medics or anything, right? We're not expecting the authorities to…"

"Our girl, Blair? Talk with the cops?" Tanner asked rhetorically with a chuckle. "Nah, bro – she beat feet and hightailed it out of there."

"Anyone see you? At the accident?" Blaze asked, exhibiting an overly abundant amount of caution for some reason unknown to Blair.

"There was a lady in the car who helped me up. She called emergency services... there were drones, but I lost them going through the alleyways," Blair answered stoically.

"Right... so they likely have an image, but you're not on the feed, anyway. So, they won't know where to come looking unless they picked up your scan in Lil' or Tanner's feeds. But then they'd have to know where to look. And you don't actually work here, so... hopefully it's not a thing," he said as he talked himself through the scenario, weighing the likelihood of incidental contact with the authorities.

"Probably not," Blair sighed. "I've managed to stay off radar my whole life; I'm not a rookie at this."

"If you say so," Blaze answered sarcastically as he joined them in the back of the shop, where he found a free seat next to his brother. Then, looking up at the painting of the Native princess that hung on the wall behind him, he asked, "That's it, huh?"

"That's the one," Tanner answered.

"And you painted it? You're the artist?" he asked, looking over to Blair, who nodded quietly.

"Easy enough," Blaze said before walking over to the painting and removing it from the wall. "I'll have it back here in a few days."

"You... actually need to physically take it with you?" Tanner asked, suddenly unsure of the decision he had made.

"Well, yeah – I mean, I obviously don't have my setup here," Blaze responded. "The dinosaur type computers and printers take up space, lots of it. And it takes a few hours; it's manual. After I use a big scanner to image it digitally, I'll do some test runs from the proof to make sure it renders correctly. But for a minor inconvenience, there's no trace of the job, the printing, or the image anywhere on the wire. It's all offline – don't sweat it."

After removing the work from the wall, he began securing it for what Blair could only assume was a long walk to wherever his shop was located. The bushy bearded brother wasted no time in finding some brown construction paper leftover from the renovation in the backroom, after which he began cutting pieces large enough to cover the work discreetly on both sides.

At some point, while he worked, he casually asked Lillian, "So, why a Native American woman? Why the mouth and eyes all sewed up?"

"Ask her, she's the artist – I just like it. It's beautiful, and it makes me kind of sad for her. But it's beautiful," Lillian answered, reflecting on the painting as it lay on top of Tanner's desk to prepare for being moved.

"Oh, I just like painting my take on American icons... Lady Liberty... Uncle Sam... stuff like that," Blair answered ambiguously.

"Huh," Blaze grunted as he looked at the painting one last time before placing the final brown paper over the front of the piece. "I wouldn't have got an American icon vibe from this..."

Blair looked at both Tanner and Lillian apologetically, the same look she had when she asked them to remove their lenses when they helped her move her paintings to storage.

"What?" Tanner answered gruffly.

After fidgeting several seconds, she explained, "Sorry, you're just... you're about to find out how nerdy I really am. So... you've heard of Columbia, right? The District of Columbia, the Columbia River, et cetera. It's just that the first images of Columbia were paintings of a Native American princess... My dad loved history, and he used to tell me about how the early colonists had a complicated relationship with the indigenous people on this land... as much as they sometimes fought with them and often treated them horribly, it was more complicated than that. It wasn't all violence; not all the colonists were cruel. Most just wanted to live free – that's why they came here. Some even respected Native values... their sense of freedom and independence... their ability to survive in harsh conditions. If you look at the really early iconography in the colonies, when they started making early images of Columbia... they were of a Native princess. Actually, a lot of the earliest symbols were sort of borrowed from Native American icons... The bundle of arrows on the seal are there for the same reason – it's like a forgotten piece of who we are now... blinded and muted by the official story."

Lillian and Tanner looked at each other silently as Blair explained. As much as Lillian loved the painting, she said she loved it for what she saw in it. It moved her. Neither of them had ever asked her what motivated her to paint the piece or what she saw in it. They simply loved the art for its own sake. Having heard Blair's explanation, she sensed they suddenly understood its meaning, conveying a forgotten piece of our history that was blinded and silenced. In that moment, she wasn't sure if they liked it more, or if they would have preferred the ambiguity that made it feel more legal.

The room stayed quiet and still for some time as they simply looked at the painting while Blaze stood quietly, holding the large piece of paper that would cover it. Blair felt awkward, not sure if she was being stared at or judged but feeling both. Had the pain in her face and head not been worse, she likely would have felt more uncomfortable, but the pain radiating through her body seemed to dull her concern over her awkward lecture. Eventually, it was Tanner who finally broke the silence, saying, "Well, you suddenly just became a whole lot more interesting, didn't you?"

~ 12 ~

"For the official record, it is October 20th. I'm Detective Pietro Hernandez, St. Louis Police Department, interviewing Jaxson Wadsworth, the fourth owner and manager of Crush Gallery. His counsel is Henry Wells, Esquire, attorney at law... Also, for the record, I am advising you that this interview is related to potential criminal proceedings and as such, any information provided could be used in said proceedings. Do you understand?" the detective asked as he turned his attention away from the feed scrolling through his lenses and looked directly at Jax.

"I understand," Jax responded stoically.

The small interview room was cramped and gloomy, and the whole situation felt overblown for what was supposed to be a meeting related to an investigation of Caldo. With the three of them crowded into a large shoebox, Jax did his best to take the situation seriously and overcome the irritation the spectacle provoked.

"Can you please tell me your relationship with Michael Caldo, also known simply as 'Caldo'?" the detective asked, appearing aloof as he worked his way through the questions he had prepared.

"Caldo has been a client of Crush for several years now," Jax answered.

"Uh... huh... what's that mean... when you say he's a client... how does that work?" the detective asked, focused on recording responses accurately in his lenses.

"Well… simply… the gallery houses pieces for clients until we find buyers. We negotiate the sales of art on behalf of our clients, for which we receive a commission," Jax explained.

"Is that all you negotiate for them?" the detective asked cryptically.

"Can you be more specific, detective," Mr. Wells interjected. "Is there some specific item or term you are interested in knowing if we negotiate for our clients?"

The detective thought for a moment before continuing, at which point he said, "Do you facilitate your client's transactions directly?"

"No," Jax answered. "We negotiate a price; money doesn't flow through us between artists and buyers. That would be a violation of the Anti-Money Laundering Act provisions requiring end-user to end-user payments."

"Never?" the detective asked.

"Never. We only 'sell' paintings in a sense that we provide the space and the audience for buyers, and we negotiate the purchase price for the artists. That's it," Jax answered.

"I see," the detective answered, still occupied by the scroll of notes that beamed across his lenses as he sat at the far end of the table in the sterile, cold interview room of the police station. "Do you ever procure services or products on behalf of your clients?"

"What kinds of services or products are you referring to?" Mr. Wells interjected as he placed his hand over Jax's arm, signaling he should remain silent.

"Any kind, I suppose? I've been told you like to throw parties at your gallery… do you buy refreshments for these parties?" the detective asked.

Before Jax could answer, his attorney put his hand on Jax's arm, indicating he should stay silent. He then responded on behalf of the gallery, "Only those types of refreshments that are prudent and necessary for the purposes of the event being hosted. Crush does not procure supplies or other goods for clients outside of what is available to anyone attending our events... or otherwise coffee, tea, or the occasional professional lunch meeting. Only the products and services that are ultimately for the benefit of the gallery.

"What is this all about?" Jax suddenly interjected as he instantly felt his attorney's hand squeeze his arm where it rested, urging him to remain calm and silent.

"Oh, I thought I had been clear, Mr. Wadsworth. We are conducting a criminal investigation. Your answers are intended to help with that investigation," the detective said as he finally turned his attention away from his scroll and looked at Jax directly.

Jax took a deep breath, frustrated by how pointless and time consuming the endeavor seemed, but understanding he had little choice in the matter, he focused on remaining calm and expressionless during the exercise.

The detective shifted uneasily in his seat as he returned to the questions he had prepared. Then he asked, "Please tell me the nature of your relationship with Ms. Blair Huxley."

Jax's eyes widened with shock, as he had not expected the interview would have anything to do with Blair. Before he could say anything, his attorney once again interjected, "Ms. Huxley is my client's girlfriend. Of what relevance is her relationship with my client to this interview?"

"Allegations have been made that your client acted as an intermediary in transactions for Blair Huxley, circumventing AMLA. That your client facilitated the sale of these works and received compensation for the works, after which he compensated Ms. Huxley in-kind," the detective answered directly.

"That's a lie!" Jax said angrily.

"Hmm," the detective grunted, remaining completely calm and composed. "Our source says differently."

Once again, Mr. Wells squeezed Jax's arm gently as he answered on behalf of his client. "No paintings signed or attributed to Blair Huxley were featured or have been featured at the Crush Gallery for the purpose of being sold. Certain works from an anonymous source were recently exhibited at a formal event hosted by Crush, but at the artist's request, these pieces were attributed anonymously – they were never for sale. No paintings were bought or sold from the anonymous artist who contributed the work. The paintings were being exhibited solely as a courtesy to the artist and in appreciation for the quality and craftsmanship of the artwork. That's it."

The detective's face remained emotionless as he listened. Stoically, he then asked, "Transaction records have shown several trips recently – one to a correctional facility in Illinois, the same facility where Ms. Huxley's mother is incarcerated. Can you tell me anything about that?"

Henry paused momentarily, looking at Jax to answer, as he wasn't aware of the trip. Jax casually explained, "I wanted to treat my girlfriend to a visit with her mother; I paid for the trip."

"I see," the detective answered. "And how was the correctional facility? How did you find it?"

"Don't answer that, Jax. It's subjective and has no bearing on this interview," Mr. Wells interjected.

"Hmm," the detective grunted again. "Your feed records indicate you did not go on the trip. Instead, you paid for a rideshare to pick up Ms. Huxley and to deliver her to the facility in Greenville, only to return her later on."

Jax listened quietly and said nothing in response.

When he failed to respond, the detective added, "So you're not denying it?"

"Listen," Mr. Wells interjected, "If that's the best you've got to show that my client is circumventing AMLA – buying a ride-share for his girlfriend – tell the DA to go ahead and file. We'll see you in court. Otherwise, I think this interview is over."

"Well, you are not officially being detained at this time," Detective Hernandez answered with feigned empathy. "But I have to say, the pattern isn't looking good here. There's an art supply store in St. Charles that is billing Crush monthly for art supplies, and the invoice of record indicates it is for a client – not a girlfriend. Of course, your services, Mr. Wells, are available for clients of the gallery – presumably not girlfriends. Did you not represent Ms. Huxley on a legal matter? Was your time billed to the gallery, for that matter?"

"At the time, Ms. Huxley was a prospective client of the gallery," Mr. Wells responded carefully. "She still is, for that matter. Should she decide to comply with the legal requirements for payment as specified in the AMLA, she may still choose to and her work would be welcome. While Crush does not normally purchase art materials for its clients, the minor costs involved in this area do not differ from paying for lunch or other pleasantries associated with building a good business relationship. As her attorney in the matter, I cannot speak to specifics related to her case, but in my capacity for Crush, I can say that I was working in the best interest of the gallery. And if you'd rather put that in front of a judge and let them decide, I'd be happy to."

"All I'm saying is it looks like your client has been spending a good amount of money wining and dining this woman, who is known to be associated with dissidents and in contact with a convicted provocateur. One could argue that your client is effectively facilitating her ability to live outside of the law – that isn't behavior commonly associated with intimate partner relationships, is it?" the detective asked assertively.

"I imagine it would be for anyone when one partner chooses to not be connected," Jax muttered sarcastically.

"I've got records that show trips, food, clothing and jewelry... all of that could be easily enough attributed to a girlfriend... sure. But there's also multiple requests for commission for Ms. Huxley's artwork that the gallery hasn't responded to... or at least the response has not been recorded," the detective explained calmly.

"Jax, let's go – there's nothing illegal about buying art supplies and meals for your girlfriend. The AMLA clearly excludes transactions on behalf of intimate partners, and he knows it. The rest of this is just fishing," Heny said as he stood up from the table.

He took a moment to adjust the knot on his tie and smirk at the detective incredulously before standing alongside his attorney. The detective stayed cool and calm, carefully observing the two men as they left the interview room.

Jax and his attorney walked quietly through the police station until they had reached the exit. In moments, an automated vehicle approached for them, and they were quickly on the road. Once aboard, Jax had thought it safe to debrief the situation, saying, "I should have told you –"

"Stop. Not another word. Not yet," Henry interrupted.

The vehicle drove on for some ways until it finally reached its destination, a bustling lunch spot that had been a longtime favorite of the attorney's. Then, as soon as they exited the vehicle, Henry removed his lenses, motioning for Jax to do the same.

"Now then," Henry answered. "That could have gone worse... Not much worse, but, hey." Then, after taking a deep breath and patting Jax on the back, he added, "Look, don't let them get to you. Nobody is going to file charges against you for buying a pretty girl art supplies – it's ludicrous."

"I'm sorry – I should have told you," Jax responded apologetically.

"No, you shouldn't have. What business is it of mine what you buy her or don't buy her? The AMLA is a joke, and it's been used too many times now as a political weapon to get at people who *they* don't like," Wells replied dismissively.

"'They'?" Jax asked. "Starting to sound a bit paranoid, aren't you, Wellsy?"

"Don't be naïve," his attorney scoffed. "You think it's a big coincidence that the government subsidizes Blinks at full-cost? We don't pay a thing for access to the feed – we can't. It's all handled through the Department of Connectivity to make sure no one gets special access... but those Department of Connectivity dollars - those tax dollars – that's our money... There's what, four major service providers that operate the feed, collecting everyone's content and data and selling it back to the government? And coincidentally, they justify turning over any traces of discontent or any negative criticism of the government because it's not safe speech – because they're literally selling people out. They make a profit off of the data, the services, and the hardware - they're making a killing! And it's all totally legal because you consent to having your data monitored when you use the feed. We are literally paying taxes to buy our own chains. Do you get that?"

"So, you... really think there is some big, nefarious group of 'They' out to get us then?" Jax laughed sarcastically.

His lawyer looked at him with a bit of a side eye before answering. "You're smarter than that, Jax - at least I hope you are. Why do you think so many people are using dub-accounts for big purchases?"

"I thought it was Plush... drugs... other illegal stuff. It all sounds seedy," Jax answered.

"Or maybe just people, seedy or not, who don't want their purchase history used against them. The immense power of the feed backed by quantum computing and AI – the data it stores – it's god-like power. And it always seems to come down to a few, well-placed people who can use that power however and whenever they like. Who's going to stop them? Now, whoever those people happened to be at any given time..." Wells answered with a shrug, suggesting he didn't know more.

"No, I'm serious," Jax answered. "Blair's paranoid as hell that something or someone out there is coming to get her because she won't connect. And then there's her parents and... If they knew what she really thought — "

"Don't say anymore," Wells replied candidly. "I don't want to know, even offline. If I'm asked, I want to say your girlfriend is some quirky artist – that's it."

"Well, she is – and I love that about her. She's one-hundred percent committed to what she believes in, to hell with the convenience of modern civilization... It's just more complicated than that, Henry. She's never going to give in and connect. It goes against everything she is – everything she believes in," Jax said reflectively.

"Look, I like the girl. She's really lovely and seems like a kind and innocent soul. And what you've shown me of her artwork – she's got a genuine talent. Heck, I like her work more than a lot of the others you've worked with... but there's never going to be a place for her work in the mainstream art community," Henry replied, trying to give his client some perspective. "Now, I'm speaking frankly here for good reason. We're not being recorded. If you're asking for my advice, I'd say don't wear those things anywhere near her. You'll get both of you in trouble. Hell, don't wear them any more than you have to at this point! You have to respect her beliefs for what they are. And clearly, someone out there is looking for a reason to come after you or her or both. Who knows? Otherwise, why was that entire investigation about you and her instead of Caldo and his drug use?"

Jax took a moment to consider what his lawyer was trying to explain, but he couldn't help but be astonished at how paranoid his legal counsel appeared. When Jax didn't say anything, this attorney placed his hand on Jax's arm and looked at him directly as he said, "You must have really pissed someone off. I don't think Caldo has enough influence to stir up this kind of attention. Until you know more, you need to be safe about all this. Everything you buy, everything you say, everywhere you go with those things on – it all gets recorded. Typically, that doesn't matter so much... until it does. Until someone starts paying attention. Whatever you're doing may be innocent enough, but if they're motivated, whoever stirred up this hornet's nest will start taking these little breadcrumbs and try to create a whole loaf of bread. And that's my professional advice to you – Stay out of sight. And get a dub account – make fewer crumbs."

"That's a lot easier said than done running a business, Wellsy. I've been taking my lenses out around Blair – for her sake. But I have a life – how does one simply stay out of sight? Heck, how would my house even know what groceries to order if the fridge can't communicate with my lenses? How would I get a ride anywhere? How would I do anything?" Jax asked rhetorically.

"Maybe ask your girlfriend – she seems to be figuring it out," his lawyer laughed. "Now, I'm late for a lunch appointment, but if that Detective Hernandez shows back up, you let me know first. You don't answer questions; you don't explain anything. You just shut your mouth and you contact me, understood?"

"Yes, sir," Jax replied with a mocking salute. Then, more seriously, he added, "I really appreciate it, Wells."

"That's what you pay me for, Jax – take care," his attorney answered, before darting quickly into the restaurant.

After re-inserting his lenses, Jax was immediately greeted by a busy screen offering reservations at the same restaurant; absent the context of what had just transpired with his lawyer, the algorithm assumed he was there for lunch. However, it took only moments for Jax to dismiss the notification and order a ride. Only seconds later, the autonomous vehicle pulled up directly in front of the restaurant, right where his lawyer had left him. Soon enough, he was headed back to the gallery.

Halfway to the Central West End, the urge to see Blair began nagging at him. Of course, he should go back to the office. But if the police had been monitoring him, they might have been keeping tabs on her as well, which could be problematic, depending on how closely they're looking.

With a few short blinks, he changed the destination of the ride-share vehicle to take him to Frenchtown, assuming Blair would be hanging out at the shop with her friends. After changing the vehicle's route, he removed his lenses, just as Wells had recommended. Although it occurred to him that having made it a custom to remove them prior to seeing her, the recommendation seemed redundant. Maybe Wells was just being a touch paranoid. That being said, there certainly wasn't harm in using the feed less; it was better for Blair, at least. And if he was going to attempt leaving them out on a more regular basis, he knew he would need to get used to the quiet.

After a long, quiet ride staring out the window of the vehicle blankly, the automated car stopped in front of the tattoo shop in Frenchtown. He paused after exiting the vehicle, second guessing himself about arriving unexpectedly. Of course, he had no way to let Blair know he was planning to drop by, given her reluctance to use the cellular phone he had bought for her. Then, when the thought of the phone came to mind, he panicked for a moment, realizing that once the police saw transcripts or a recording of the feed-link he had with Parker about customizing an old cell phone to circumvent lenses, he'd probably have even more questions to answer.

As he entered the shop, Blair ran up to him unexpectedly and greeted him with a squeezing hug as she said, "Babe! You didn't say anything about coming by today – I thought you had that meeting with your attorney all day?"

"Sorry for just dropping by," Jax said, looking over at Tanner and Lillian as he spoke. Both were face down in pieces they were busy with, and neither seemed to pay much attention to his arrival except for politely waving and exchanging greetings. "And yes, we had the meeting... it happened."

"That's... spooky sounding," Blair said with an odd look.

"It's... um... I'll need to explain more later. I just wanted to check on you," he said. Then, seeming to just finally notice the scratches and bruising on her face, he suddenly stepped back and asked, "Hey – what happened here? Are you ok? I mean, really – you ok?"

"Oh, yeah," Blair answered with a dismissive smirk. "Like an idiot, I crashed my bike into the back of a robocar and it sent me flying over the handlebars. I got a little banged up."

"You should have called me, or had someone call me. I would've rushed over here to take care of you!" he said, exasperated at the idea of having only just discovered she had been involved in an accident.

"She was too busy running from the cops," Tanner interjected with a laugh as he continued working on the arm of the client at his station.

"A regular outlaw," Lillian added.

"I'm... totally confused now," Jax laughed. Then, turning suddenly serious, he quietly asked her, "Really? – you were running from the cops?"

"No, it's not like that. The lady in the car called 9-1-1, and the hospital sent out drones. I was worried they would scan me, so I just ran – bleeding and half-conscious like some crazy drunk woman careening through the streets of old town," Blair laughed. "I mean, it wasn't funny at the time, but that was a few days ago. We've all had a pretty good laugh about it since."

"That could have been really serious, Blair," Jax said tensely. "I mean, they probably are looking for someone that matches your image – it could be trouble."

"They would need to know where to look," she answered calmly. "And they don't. I'm sure a few days after the fact, they have more important things to do... I'm fine."

"I'm sorry... I just worry about you. And after the day I've had, I wanted to check in on you – just to make sure you were alright," he responded tenderly as he brushed her hair out of her face.

"See that, Tanner – he's checking on her just to make sure she's alright. Why don't you ever check on me to make sure I'm alright? Huh?" Lillian exclaimed loudly.

"I literally live with you, woman; I sleep next to you. I could set my watch to your bowel movements; if there was something wrong with you, I'm guessing I'd know," Tanner answered equally loudly without looking away from his work.

"Well, maybe it would just be nice of you to ask me occasionally, huh? Maybe I'd just like you to ask!" Lillian answered loudly.

"You good, babe?" Tanner shouted loudly toward his wife on the other end of the shop.

"Yup – thanks, babe," Lillian laughed.

All the shouting had transpired over the din of tattoo machines busily humming away, but it was enough to make both him and Blair laugh at the exchange. It was after witnessing their antics Jax noticed her painting was missing.

"So... um... what happened to the Native princess painting?" he asked curiously.

"Ah, well, Tanner's brother is getting prints made for the shop. But it's cool – I gave permission. I kind of like the idea of my work being out there for people to see. It's nice. I'm becoming St. Louis area tattoo world famous, I think," Blair said proudly.

"Right... I mean, that's what I'm instantly concerned about," Jax replied.

"It should be fine. Blaze is doing the printing – you remember Blaze? Big bushy beard, kind of an ass – Tanner's brother. We met him at the marina," Blair said as she tried to jog his memory.

"I remember him, sure. I'm not sure why that makes it better," Jax answered as concern visibly grew in his eyes.

"He's not lensed either," Blair whispered close enough for only Jax to hear. Then, in a normal voice, she added, "Well, he's a printer. He's got all the old computers and scanners and what not, and so nothing will go on the feed from him or me or Tanner and Lil – it's all just paper."

"Interesting," Jax answered, as he understood the precautions she appeared to have taken. "So then, when someone asks who the artist is?"

"It says so right on the painting, Jax – some Swedish dude named 'ΘN'! He even signed it," Lillian said facetiously, above the humming of her tattoo machine.

"I thought ΘN was Danish – I thought you said Danish," Tanner said loudly over the hum of his own machine.

"Danish... Swedish... something Scandi-ish. I don't remember," Lillian laughed.

"Well, it might be a bit risky for ΘN, if people start asking questions. Don't you think?" Jax asked, revealing he wasn't nearly as amused by their cleverness as they were.

"Nah, nobody here will set them straight. We're all same-page about it," Tanner said, looking up briefly as his machine stopped so that he could catch Jax's eye, making certain he understood they were serious about protecting her. He then added, "My word and life on it – that's as good of a promise as I can make."

"Ooooo... hey, babe - you're kinda... kinda sexy when you get all serious and protective-like," Lillian said as she moved her eyebrows suggestively.

"Thanks, babe," Tanner smirked proudly.

With little more to be said about it and the decision already made, Jax understood there was little he could do or say, even if he was inclined to. Ultimately, Blair had to make decisions about how she wanted her art shown, and it was her decision to make.

"I appreciate that, Tanner. But please let me know if things get... weird. Or if there is something you need from me to help... facilitate, I suppose," Jax said. Then turning to Blair he said, "Now then... if your fellow troublemakers can do without you... I was kind of hoping I could steal you away for the afternoon?"

Blair looked at Lillian hopefully, seeking a sort of blessing before leaving.

"You don't work here, B – you just hang out. Go – have fun. Be wild and passionate young people!" Lillian answered with a smile as she returned to the tattoo in progress before her.

As they exited the shop, Jax thought about calling another ride so they could go somewhere romantic and private, but the idea that the transaction and location data would most likely be recorded made him hesitant.

"Let's just walk for a bit?" Jax said abruptly.

"Sure," Blair answered with a smile.

As they left Frenchtown, they followed the road down toward the river as they strolled towards the historic district, enjoying each other's company. At some point, Blair began pointing out various buildings.

"That used to be an art gallery, back in the day – at least that's what my mom used to say. This town has a long history of being connected with the art scene," Blair said casually as she pointed at an old industrial building that appeared as though it had been renovated many times from its original, antique purpose.

As they continued on, she pointed to another and said, "There's a plaque somewhere that says that one used to be an Opera House back in the early days..."

Jax listened intently as Blair gave him an unrequested, brief tour of town, likely an effort to make conversation that wasn't related to the prints of her work or the potential trouble that would follow. He had been to St. Charles many times over the years, and he'd even walked through it with Blair several times previously. But not wanting to make things more tense than they already had been, he listened quietly and tried to enjoy simply being with her.

It took several more buildings with interesting historic facts before Blair inferred there was something on his mind.

"What... what's all this grumpiness all about?" she teased.

"Ugh," he groaned. Fumbling for words for several yards, he began trying to explain all that had happened in their meeting earlier that day. "There's this detective, and he's been in all my records. He was asking about the gallery and my relationship with you... trying to make a case that we were violating AMLA by buying you art supplies – it was garbage, but it got me all worked up."

Blair paused in the middle of the sidewalk and looked at him as she said, "That *does* sound serious. What did you say? Was Wells there?"

"There's nothing to worry about. Buying things for your girlfriend is exempt from AMLA and the cops don't have a leg to stand on... it just got me feeling paranoid, I guess. Wells was sounding paranoid," he said, attempting to calm the anxiety he saw rising in her to match his own.

"For 'nothing', you seem concerned," she observed.

"I am, of course. I'm concerned about you. I... want to protect you... as best I can, anyway," he answered, downplaying his efforts.

"Hey... I appreciate all that you do for me – how kindly and thoughtfully you treat me, how romantic you are when you get all chivalrous and protective of me – it's sweet. But I can't hide forever, you know that, right?" she said earnestly.

"Why not?" Jax asked rhetorically. "You've done a pretty good job so far."

Blair nodded with a smirk as she answered, "Well, you keep saying I'm 'so talented' - I guess I'm really just multi-talented, if you count hiding from society. Maybe I should have been a spy or something!"

"Nah, you're too good at painting to waste your life in government work," he answered as he suddenly pulled her closer to him and kissed her sweetly.

"Seriously, though... I keep thinking about what my mom said... about shining my light in the darkness of this ugly world. About the fire in me consuming those around me... I don't want you to get in trouble because of what I paint or what I believe," she said, trying to convey her seriousness in the middle of the romantic moment.

"With the craziness of the meeting today and how paranoid I'm feeling right now... I may be just about ready to join you on this holy crusade of yours," he laughed in response.

"Hey, be serious," she said, pulling him close to her. "Eventually word is going to get out – I almost want it to. I don't want to hide what I believe – art should move people. It should make people uncomfortable! I don't care if it triggers people in power."

"I get it... and I agree. It's just all happening quickly. And I'm having a difficult time trying to figure out how I can keep you safe when you seem intent on lighting this fire," he said, mirroring her seriousness.

"I don't think you can... not really. I'm not signing my own name; I'm not promoting my own work. I'm taking precautions... but there's enough data out there that eventually someone could come looking. I don't want you to get dragged down with me," she answered.

"How about – right here and right now – we both commit to neither of us getting dragged down? Would you be willing to do that?" he asked.

"Sounds lovely, but how do we pull that off?" she asked. "I won't stop painting, and I'm not going to change who I am or what I believe. And of course, they won't stop watching everything we do…"

"Maybe it would be a good idea to have some kind of plan," he suggested. Then, with a sort of silly, dramatic tone, he added, "You know, just in case the FBI ends up raiding my storage unit as a part of this investigation…"

"Don't even joke about that!" Blair demanded as she tried to contain her laughter. "We'd both be goners."

"Exactly," he laughed. "And while I don't think it's likely… they don't have any record of me even going there in months and they certainly don't have any records on you, not from the feed anyway."

They continued along for a while, contemplating the seriousness of the predicament they were in as they tried to enjoy each other's company. It was obvious to Jax that it weighed on her as much as it had him, and despite the danger involved, she was really and truly committed. The fear simply wouldn't shake her from this course.

"Was the meeting with the police that bad?" she asked after another block of walking in silence.

"Not yet, but it could be. It depends on a lot of things – who it is that's making these accusations, whether there are enough breadcrumbs… as Henry put it. All the same, maybe you should move your other paintings onto the boat? You have a bit of room there now."

"It would probably be for the best," she answered, taking his hand in hers. "I don't really like having them so far away… it kind of felt like losing friends having them locked away."

"Would Tanner and Lillian help you move them again?" he asked as their clenched hands began swinging with a childlike frivolity. "I know you don't have a bike anymore or your little trailer.

And I probably shouldn't have any record of going there and then to the marina; it would be too obvious."

"I'll ask. Although, I feel like I'm constantly asking friends for help... like I'm putting everyone out," she said.

"I suppose that comes with the territory," Jax shrugged.

"But I want to...," she stammered as she stopped walking and began searching for the right words. "I need to do things for myself. I need to be able to live my life without constantly having to ask others to help me. It's... I feel trapped by it all."

"Henry was saying earlier that I should start using my lenses less... just with the risk of the data being tracked and the recent attention. He also said I should get a dub account so I can start paying for trips to see you and what-not more discreetly. It should help, I guess. But it also got me thinking about how difficult managing basic life stuff must be for you... Frankly, I don't know how you do it."

"It's certainly not convenient, that's for sure," she laughed before becoming distracted by some Halloween decorations that were waving in the shop window behind him.

The thought of the challenges she faced brought about the thoughts he too would continue to face so long as they were together. The struggle of a life disconnected entirely made him feel uneasy, even if it had a certain appeal. He felt as if he was standing on the edge of a cliff, looking into a chasm that lay before him; there was this odd urge to jump, even when his mind knew it would prove fatal. At some point, he feared he would have to test how committed he was to that future, as it was clearly inevitable for Blair. For that matter, he needed to decide if she was going to be a part of his future, or if this relationship simply wouldn't work because of this issue they couldn't reconcile. The seriousness of the thought weighed on him, and while he truly believed he loved her, without saying as much out loud, the weight of the costs to be with her was heavy when he considered his family, his business, and all that he had built. While he agreed with her in principle, the cost of living that principle could be unbearable.

Even if at some point they went their separate ways, he was genuinely concerned for her safety and well-being. He certainly admired her courage and commitment, even more so than he appreciated her beauty or her talent. Whatever may come, if he could, he wanted to make sure she would be ok.

"Hey... so random question... do you have a plan?" he asked, interrupting her amusement at the décor in the store window.

"For?" she asked, only turning her head briefly from a dancing skeleton robot in the shop window.

"I'm just thinking... with the recent interest from the police in the gallery... the um... resistance from my family and the obvious challenges your situation puts things in... if everything goes sideways, do you have a plan?" he asked. He gently placed his hand on her arm, trying to hold her attention for at least a few seconds as he mentally continued searching for some positive result that would reassure him all of this effort held meaning that outweighed the struggle they were facing.

"My plan is to live my life... make my art... and go on as I have until something happens where I can't anymore," she answered, finally turning away from the distraction of the store window. Trying to be sincere and honest, she brushed his concern aside, asking, "What more of a plan do any of us need?"

"Well, yeah – I get that. But if this investigator showed up at your boat... Let's say they searched it and they found your art. Then they arrest you for inciting extremism or some other Safe Speech violation. What would you do?" he asked.

"Go to jail, most likely," she laughed. "Thought that was pretty obvious."

"Okay, but assuming you'd prefer NOT to go to jail... maybe we need an escape plan or something – a plan for somewhere to go that isn't jail?" he asked. Then, second guessing his own words, he added, "I don't know. It all sounds so dramatic and far-fetched right now."

She paused for a moment, staring blankly at him and wondering how seriously he was taking all of this. "Obviously, we would just sail in the Sea Smudge... head to Africa, maybe! Somewhere where they don't have a feed and Blinks or any of it," Blair declared triumphantly. "We could live in the jungle in a treehouse!"

"The Sea Smudge?" Jax said. "Seriously?"

"It's a... working concept... I haven't christened her yet! The old name has been staring at me every time I look at the stern," she said defensively.

"Stern?" he asked dramatically. "Look at you with the nautical terminology!"

"Captain Agnew says I'm quickly becoming seaworthy... although we haven't taken her out yet.... He used to teach classes that certified people to sail, and he's started teaching me the theory and concepts. He even says he'll take me out on the water once the motor is fixed... we've mostly just talked about it. Also, he may just be being nice to me," she answered.

"A lonely, old veteran enjoys nautical chats with an attractive young woman? I'm shocked," Jax laughed facetiously.

"I've been reading too!" she said, slapping his arm gently. "I'm learning all I can while she's stuck in dock."

"Well, in that case, I'd be honored to be your first mate, skipper!"

~ 13 ~

"**I** really appreciate your help, Blaze," she said as they loaded the last of the paintings into the vehicle waiting outside of the storage unit.

"No problem," he answered as he slid closed the metal accordion door with a rattling clang. "Although, I've got to say, when Tanner asked if I could pitch in, I didn't really know what to expect. After seeing the painting in the shop, I expected something.... I dunno."

"Expected something... what?" she asked, searching for his meaning.

"Well, it's just... I guess I wasn't prepared for how... raw they are. I don't know if that's the right word," he answered pensively.

"Raw?" she asked, confused.

"No... Sorry. They're good. Raw like... brutal. Thought provoking. I mean, think a lot of people would see these and identify with them. We all feel like this, I think. At least I do. You just seem to have put it into paintings in a way that is in part funny and another part tragic..." he answered, peeking underneath the sheet once more, as the vehicle Tanner ordered for them began its trip to the marina.

"Well, that's the point, I think. Art is an expression. My family's story can't be too different from what other people experienced. A lot of people have it rough..." she responded.

They drove for a while in silence, each of them lost in thought, until at last Blair said, "I think... maybe I hope there are people out there who still believe in truly free speech and the importance of having a voice against power... the powers that be... My father believed power rested in the hands of the people. The people were the ones who had to hold the government accountable. My mother too."

Blaze looked at her for a moment, studying her as if weighing her words, if not whether she truly believed what she was saying. After a deep breath, he began whispering into her ear as the vehicle continued along its path, "I believe you're right... I have friends that do as well."

Blair's face reflected her surprise at his pronouncement. She had only met Blaze a few times, and while she knew he was not connected to the feed, her knowledge of his beliefs and view of the world had until that point remained a complete mystery to her.

"Hmm," she mouthed in response, not sure of what else to say.

Then, leaning uncomfortably close to her, he again whispered, "What if... we take these paintings to my shop instead of your boat?"

"Why would we do that?" she asked skeptically, unsure of what his intentions were but feeling like he was trying to get something from her.

"So that I can print them," he answered. "Thousands of them."

Fear suddenly flooded over Blair's face in a wave of panic and excitement. As the seconds passed, she could feel her heart throb in her chest, beating wildly at the idea of her artwork suddenly having a massive audience – suddenly being seen for what it was, no matter the consequences.

"If anyone found out..." she said apologetically.

"If anyone finds out, they'll be looking for ΘN... some German guy, right?" he whispered back.

"But if they somehow connected them to me... I mean, where would I go? There'd be no chance of hiding," she responded.

Blaze slowly bobbed his head side to side as if he was dramatically weighing the possibilities. He then added, "It so happens these friends of mine have some means... maybe in exchange for letting us make the prints... we fix your boat up and put some spending money in your pocket in case you need to go some-where."

"Spending money? You know I'm not connected to the feed," she answered dismissively.

"Not that kind," he chuckled quietly. "The old-fashioned kind. The kind that still gets spent in every corner of the globe..."

"Euros? Aren't they digital too?" she asked, confused.

"The yellow, shiny kind..." he said. Then, sensing her continued confusion, he added, "The metal... kind."

Blair's eyes grew wide once she realized what he was referenc-ing. She hadn't considered the possibility of trading her work for a commodity like gold; its use in place of currency was an explicit violation of the AMLA. Then again, any of her paintings could just as easily banish her to some dark cell.

"That's... possible?" she asked.

Blaze shrugged noncommittally, seeming to be overly elusive or perhaps defensive rather than providing a straight answer. Af-ter a long pause between them, he quietly added, "You... *do* want your art... out there, right? I can't believe you'd paint these just for you. If I had to guess, you want the world to know about what they did to your family – to your mother and father. You want to rage and tear this police state down to the ground with a tomahawk – isn't that the point of all these?"

"Maybe," she answered, suddenly looking away in embarrass-ment at her own admission.

"Thought so," he whispered as he too turned his attention to the window.

The rest of the trip to the marina passed quietly, while two dis-connected people stared out the windows imagining what would come of their conversation. When at last the automated vehicle arrived, Blaze helped Blair remove the paintings from the vehicle.

Carefully, they carried the two stacks of paintings down to her boat, where he helped her bring them into the cabin.

As soon as they entered, Blaze noticed her newest work, still sitting atop the easel, uncovered and nearly finished. The painting depicted the busts of the presidents of Mount Rushmore. Only each of them appeared to have been physically beaten and bruised, appearing almost comically so. Washington looked unconscious or dazed, while Roosevelt was grinning with a black eye and missing teeth. Jefferson's face was angry as blood ran down a nose that had been grossly disfigured, and Lincoln wept over purple and black bruising that covered his face.

"Like I was saying…" Blaze said emphatically as he moved to look at the most recent work more closely.

"No matter what you say, I DO paint them for myself. I think it's kind of therapy for me in a way," she answered indignantly.

"Maybe it's a bit of both," he suggested. "You can't possibly want to keep THIS one hidden – it's the best of the lot!"

"I'm more partial to the eagle, myself," she answered. "But… yeah, Rushmore it makes me giggle."

"That toothless grin on Roosevelt – hilarious!" he laughed.

"Thank you," she said. "But… I'm just not sure about… making all of this… public… out there for everyone."

"Maybe just one, then… another trial balloon of sorts. I'll show it to my friends and get a commitment to getting the engine in this tub replaced, or I'll bring it right back, no harm no foul," he offered, sensing they had entered some kind of negotiation.

"And then?" she asked.

"We'll make prints… distribute them through our network. It won't take long for the lenses to have them world-wide…" he said.

"And THEN?" she asked, trying to figure out what more he had planned.

"And then nothing, if you don't want anything more. But if I had to guess, people are going to want to see more from ΘN. And we'll print another on terms we can negotiate – gold, equipment, whatever you have in mind. And either way, we'll just be paying for the right to print them – you keep the originals. We just get to use the image," he answered, sensing a deal was near.

Blair thought for a moment, and suddenly embarrassed at having not covered her work before she left, she quickly pulled a sheet back over her interpretation of Mount Rushmore. Then, after fidgeting and pacing for several minutes, while Blaze sat quietly, she finally relented.

"Fine – one painting. The eagle choking on the coin. I think it sets the stage for the body of work," she answered.

"You're the artist," he said agreeably.

"And if your friends aren't willing to do the engine, the whole engine – brand new parts, top of the line, and someone to install it all – no deal. Oh, and you bring it back to me discretely, safe and sound," she said, extending her hand for him to shake.

"Deal," he answered with a large, clumsy grin that amplified the width of his already bushy black beard.

It took only a few minutes before Blaze had secured the painting of the sickly eagle with a sheet, knotting the strands of twine to secure it. Blair watched as he tenderly covered her work, feeling as if a child that had just come home was once again leaving. The thought made her uncomfortable, but deep inside, she knew the opportunity had arrived for her light to shine. The sensation terrified her, but she also felt if she did not at least take a chance, she would never find the courage. This was her legacy; it was her voice put to the same song sung by her parents. And of course, perhaps it wouldn't come to anything. Maybe Blaze's friends wouldn't like her work or think it was as important as he did. Anything was possible, but certainly, nothing would ever change if she kept her art to herself.

"Ok then," she said, seeing he had finished securing her piece.

"Okay," he replied. "I'll make sure this gets back to you safely."

"Please do. Otherwise, my friend the pirate will have you sleeping with the fishes," she laughed.

"Old man Agnew?" he asked with a wry smile. "He's a friend of mine too – I'd go as far as saying we play for the same team, so to speak. Although, I'm not sure how much he likes art. He's a big fan of freedom, though."

Blair looked at him quizzically, not sure of what exactly he was implying. Of course, the weathered old veteran had hinted several times previously at a certain discontentedness with the state of the world; she had never assumed it was anything more than the grumblings of an old sailor.

"I'll see ya then," he smirked as saw himself out of the cabin and left her alone on the boat.

After he left, Blair uncovered the piece on the easel and was once again amused by how well it was coming along. Over the next few hours, she added some highlights that were missing and then studied the work to decide whether she felt it was complete. Her work was interrupted by a muffled popping sound that seemed to come from several boats down in the marina. Needing a break, she decided to investigate.

As she exited the boat and began walking down the marina, she heard the sound again – a muffled POP sound, only this time it sounded considerably closer than it had before. She then noticed the sound was coming from "Betty's Bannermaid", the pleasure cruiser owned by the old sailor.

She followed the short pathway that intersected the main walkway between Agnew's boat and his neighbor, only to find the old pirate sitting on the back patio area of his boat and holding a long rifle mounted on a bipod behind which he sat in a camping chair. Having never been around guns before, the sight of the weapon made her uneasy and for a moment she froze dramatically, uncertain of what to do.

"Ah, I'm sorry, love. I didn't mean to scare you," Agnew said after moving his head away from the cheek rest from which he had been peering through the scope.

"I... I didn't mean to interrupt," she apologized hurriedly.

"Not at all," he laughed. "Just... skeet shooting, as it were."

"Skeet?" she asked, confused.

"Sorry, that joke's probably lost on you. Skeet are those round, clay discs folks shoot with shotguns at country clubs and the like," he explained.

"Oh, I see. So, you're shooting skeet then?" she asked, trying to understand his meaning.

"No," he said. "Drones. That was the joke."

"Drones," she repeated uneasily.

"Well, they should be minding their own business," he laughed. "Three hundred yards away... under cover... with a suppressor... they'll never even know. They'll probably assume the damn things malfunctioned, as they're prone to do over marinas."

"Why are they prone to malfunction over marinas?" she asked, certain she knew the answer this time, but playing along all the same.

"Mostly this marina, I suppose," he chuckled. "Must be something about this place."

"Must be," she laughed uneasily.

Then, carefully, the old sailor picked up his rifle, and collapsed the folding bipod mounted on its forward grip, placing it carefully into a nearby hard-sided plastic case on the ground beside him.

"There – all better. No more guns, then. I never much liked the things anyway," he said with a smile.

"I thought you were in the army?" she said argumentatively.

"Marines," he answered. "It's like the army, but tougher. And we like boats more."

"I see," she answered. "And Marines don't like guns? Didn't they make private ownership of firearms illegal?"

Old Mr. Agnew simply smirked as he held a single finger over his mouth.

"They'll never hear it from me," she laughed in response.

"There's a good girl – my best girl in the harbor, if you ask me," he laughed.

"Now, if you keep talking like that, Jax's going to get jealous," she said coyly.

"Ah, let him! An old man needs to have his fun, now and then," he said with a dismissive wave. Then, reflecting for a moment, he said, "So it's Jax still? I thought I saw young Blaze passing through here earlier... thought for a moment you'd switched things up – Not that it's any of my concern, mind you! Just need to make sure I'm aiming at the right one if it comes to that!"

His protectiveness made Blair giggle as she answered, "No, it's still Jax – he's away with work right now. Blaze was just helping out a bit."

"Ah, I see... I see. Well, I hope your fella isn't jealous. If I had a gal as lovely as you, I wouldn't let another man within a hundred yards of her!" he answered in a fatherly tone.

Not knowing exactly how to respond, she simply laughed and said, "I'll make sure he knows."

"That Blaze is a good one, though. Has his head on straight, unlike most people running around these days with those microchips in their eyeballs. He told me you weren't one of them before you ever moved in, which is why I gave him the green light to having you stay here," he declared.

"Is that so?" she asked.

"Of course," the old man answered. "Can't run the risk of those cameras telling the authorities where I've hidden my treasure."

"Well, it's a good thing I'm on team pirate," she said with a smirk.

"That you are, that you are," he nodded in agreement. "Otherwise, none of this would have worked. As it is, I'm glad for the occasional company from someone equally disinclined to have their brain poisoned."

"I couldn't have asked for a better neighbor," she responded generously. "Although, I can't speak as to any of the others out here... I haven't met anyone else."

"On account of owning the marina, I've taken the liberty of screening anyone who plans on staying here full time — don't you worry. The weekend crowd is a different story, but for the few of us who sleep here, you've nothing to fear. We share some... common values," he answered.

"Hmmm... I didn't know," she said. "So, this is sort of a safe-haven, then?"

"As long as I'm here it is," Old Agnew declared with a wink. "I should say, though... most of us still have the damn lenses. We just don't use them for anything other than ordering groceries or parts or what not. Not sure I've ever met anyone to just go cold-turkey like you."

"It's... challenging sometimes. But I've had help from friends and kin and so on. I exchange help here and there for the things I need... it works out, mostly," she said, shrugging as if her situation was not the burden everyone assumed it would be.

As she finished speaking, the old man's eyes flashed to some-thing over her shoulder, further up the boat ramp.

"If you'll excuse me, love. I don't have the patience to speak to the police today," he said, nodding toward the gate that led down to the marina.

Just as the old man opened the door to the cabin of his boat, Blair could hear heavy footsteps walking down the metal ramp to the marina. Quickly, she left the small walkway next to Agnew's home, and there along the main walkway nearing the end of the ramp was a middle-aged man dressed in an old suit and a clip-on tie. When the man saw her, he called out, "Ms. Blair Huxley?"

"That's me," she responded. A moment of fear flashed over her, causing a tingling sensation from her toes up to her shoulders. It appeared the old sailor was right.

"Courage, Blair," she whispered to herself as the man closed the short distance between the ramp and her position midway down the walkway between the boats.

"My name is Detective Hernandez. I'm with the St. Louis Police Department... I was wondering if I could have a word with you?" the man asked as he extended his hand to shake hers.

She shook the man's hand confidently, determined not to shrink under the weight of fear. She would be bold, like her mother was; she would not let them see her cry this time.

"A word about what?" she asked with a polite smile.

"I'm investigating a matter regarding an artist known as Caldo and his dealings with an art gallery named Crush – are you familiar with either?" he asked.

"Both, actually," she answered confidently.

"Great – perfect then. Is there somewhere more private we could... um... sit down, perhaps?" the detective asked.

"Actually, I was just on my way to see some friends. I can answer whatever questions you might have here," she answered politely.

"Okay," the detective answered hesitantly. "So first, what is your relationship with Caldo?"

"I have no relationship with Caldo; I only know he is a painter. I've seen several of his works at the Crush gallery," she said honestly.

"I see," the detective answered. "And, I assume your art goes through the same gallery – is that the connection?"

"No, I'm afraid not," she answered. "I'm not connected to the feed; I don't have a way to sell my artwork legally."

A faint look of disappointment flashed across the detective's face only briefly, a rare break in his otherwise stoic demeanor. "I see," he answered. "So, your relationship with the Crush gallery is... what, exactly?"

"I don't have a professional relationship with Crush; Jax, the owner, is my boyfriend. That's how I'm familiar with it," she said truthfully. For a moment, a surge of energy passed through her, replacing the fear. The empowerment she felt from having not melted when he began asking questions was exhilarating. While she thought it probably would have been better if Jax's lawyer had been there, she had no way of calling for help. Even if she could, there was no guarantee he would be able to help. Instead, she thought it best to simply answer the man's questions without revealing anything that would make either of them sound guilty of something.

"That's interesting, because a source has told us that some of your artwork was recently featured at a gala that was hosted at Crush – can you tell me anything about that?" the detective asked.

"I was at the gala," Blair responded cooly. "Although I don't recall seeing any artwork with my name on it, your source may have been mistaken."

"Interesting," the detective answered as he blinked through his feed, capturing notes on their conversation.

"Are you familiar with an artist named *Omnis Nemo*?" the detective asked.

"I *do* recall seeing art at the gala where the little cards said they were by *Omnis Nemo* – I assumed that was like a pseudonym or something," she answered, trying to be as honest as possible without revealing more than she had to.

"And you don't know who Omnis Nemo is?" the detective asked directly.

"Is *Omnis Nemo* in some kind of trouble?" she deflected. "I have my suspicions, but... I don't run the gallery. I don't work there or really know who they work with. I think I personally only met Deidra during the gala, and she signs her paintings. But I could ask Jax for you, if you'd like?"

Another flash of emotion swept across the detective's face, only this time it appeared to be anger rather than disappointment.

"Let me be frank with you, Ms. Huxley," the detective said assertively. "Our source has made sworn testimony that YOU are the artist Omnis Nemo, that the gallery is selling your work on your behalf in violation of the Anti-Money Laundering Act, and that the funds generated from these sales are being used for illicit activities."

"Wow!" Blair exclaimed with a chuckle. "That's a whole lot to take in – I can say confidently I have never sold any artwork through Crush. I can also say that when I was at the gala, many people were speculating about who Omnis Nemo might be, and to be fair, I think several people assumed it was me."

"Why do you think that? If it's not true, why would people assume that?" the detective asked.

"Well, I was on Jax's arm that evening... and Omnis Nemo's paintings seemed to be getting quite a bit of attention. Caldo seemed pretty upset by it; I got the impression he was used to being the center of attention at these things. So, I was wearing this... um... sorry, it's a bit embarrassing – this kinda sexy dress and getting a lot of attention. And I think I stole the spotlight at the owner's side. And those Nemo pieces were getting a lot of attention - maybe people just assumed? I can't say for certain," she explained.

"So, you deny being Omnis Nemo then?" the detective asked directly.

"Detective, 'Omnis' is Latin for everyone; 'Nemo' is Latin for no one. In that sense, aren't we all *Omnis Nemo* in a certain way?" she answered with a wink. She then quickly added, "I think the real question is whether Omnis Nemo did anything illegal by just existing... I don't think she did."

"Don't play games with me, Ms. Huxley," the detective answered, now visibly frustrated by her evading answers.

"What games am I playing, Detective Hernandez?" Blair answered defensively. "Listen, if I could paint as well as *Omnis Nemo* – if my paintings were so good that they made a world-famous artist like Caldo nervous... an artist who's made millions and millions... don't you think I would have cashed in? Shouldn't I be in some beach house or mansion or something?"

"Hmmm," the detective responded, contemplating her reason. He then answered, "If you were connected to the feed, sure. But you're not."

"So, you really think I'm some diabolical mastermind that would give up wealth and fame all because I don't want to connect to the feed that ninety-nine point nine-nine-nine percent of people are using?" she asked in a mocking tone. "To be fair, it's easy to stay principled when you have nothing to lose. And I'm poor, so it works."

"It does seem... implausible. If you were, it might make you one of the most committed and perhaps dangerous people in the country," the detective suggested.

"Dangerous for painting... you really think?" she again asked, mocking his assertion. "I mean, every once in a while, I sit down, forgetting I have a brush in my pocket and it stabs me in the leg; that's about as dangerous as it gets for me."

The detective paused for a moment, studying her. She was dressed in her typical paint covered denim overalls with messy hair rolled up in a top-knot, held together with chopsticks. She certainly didn't look the part of some criminal mastermind.

"Thank you for your time, Ms. Huxley," the detective responded.

"Sure thing," Blair answered as she tried to control the adrenaline that surged through her arms and legs. She felt in control; she had resisted, just as her parents would have. And while concerned about how the detective had found her, she felt she had won this round, at least.

"Um... one more thing," the detective called out as he made his way up the metal ramp towards the gate.

"What's that?" Blair answered loudly.

"There are several... um... broken police drones up here in the parking area. It looks to me like several of them crashed and shattered in close proximity to one another..." the detective said casually.

"Really?" Blair asked, pretending to be surprised by the revelation.

"So... you don't know anything about that?" the detective asked skeptically.

"Sorry, no ... I can't say I've ever used one of those drone thingies; they're too complicated for me," she answered apologetically.

"I see," the detective said stoically. "Thank you again for your time, Ms. Huxley."

~ 14 ~

It had been about ten days since he had seen her, by the time he finally returned from traveling. When the automated vehicle finally delivered him to the marina, the sight of Blair waiting by the gate sent shivers of excitement down his spine. She too was excited, visibly so as she bounced with eagerness, clasping her hands together as she energetically hovered in place. As soon as he exited the vehicle, she lunged towards him, wrapping him in her arms and kissing his face aggressively. For a long moment, Jax forgot anything else existed outside of her arms and the gentle touch of her lips against his.

"So, how was the conference?" she asked once she finally pulled away.

"Boring at times. Exciting at times. It was an art history conference, so a bit of a mixed bag. But Istanbul is a beautiful, ancient city…How were things here?" he asked. With Blair's near complete refusal to use the cellular phone he bought for her, the ten days alone had felt agonizing. And with the added concern of snooping authorities just before he left, the anxiety of being apart from her left him distracted during much of the trip.

"I have a surprise – a big one," she said suddenly, grabbing him by the arm and pulling him towards the gate. "Actually, a few!"

"Let me grab my bag really quickly. I came straight here from the airport," he said as he reached back into the automated vehicle that was still waiting with the door open. After retrieving a small leather duffle and a large, monogrammed garment bag, he was ready. Blair quickly took hold of the garment bag, swinging it around her shoulders with one arm and wrapping her other arm around his, grateful to once again have him close.

"This way," she giggled. "Come on!"

"Okay, okay," he implored, scurrying through the gate and down the ramp beside her. Midway through the marina, Blair suddenly called out, "Good morning, Cap'n!"

"Well, good morning, young lady," the old sailor responded with a generous smile. "I see you finally found that missing man of yours."

"Yup! Safe and sound back home with me where he belongs," she laughed as they passed the old sailor by, still hurrying towards her boat.

When they finally reached the large ketch, Blair boarded first and then took Jax's other bag, moving quickly to lift both bags onto the deck, where she left them in her excitement. As he followed, she abruptly blurted, "No – not yet! First surprise is out here!"

"First surprise? There's more than one surprise?" Jax answered quizzically.

"YES!" she laughed.

In a flash, she had descended below decks and then just as quickly returned, squeezing around him as she once again descended the stepladder to the dock.

"Where are you going?" he asked, still puzzled by the mystery and her excitement. While the idea of surprises seemed fun, after a late-night flight and a long trip, all he really wanted was to hold her in his arms and take a long nap. All the same, Jax played along as Blair scooted quickly to the far end of the dock, near the back of her sailboat. She then stood there, with her hands on her hips, gesturing with her head towards the rear of the vessel.

Jax followed her down the stepladder and towards the end of the dock. Narrow as it was, it provided a good excuse for him to wrap his arms around her waist as he peered at the sailboat's stern to witness the surprise, a beautifully painted script that read "Astraea's Muse".

"Forgive me... I'm trying to remember which one she is," Jax said as he squinted at the name, trying to recall.

"Supposed daughter of Zeus, known for purity even though she's usually painted in a sort of see-through negligee... carries a torch to light the way of justice..." Blair said, holding her hands out to express her surprise. "I was sure – "

"I remember now, yes, of course! A fitting moniker for a vessel carrying a princess," he jibed.

"Well... not sure about the princess part, but thank you. Felt cute," she smirked.

Then suddenly, she grabbed his arms, gently removing them from her waist, and hurried back to the stepladder. "Wait... right there. Don't move!" she exclaimed excitedly.

In a flash of energy, she flew up the short ladder and into the cabin of the boat. Moments later, a brief churning sound arrived, followed by bubbles and a low rumbling from beneath the vessel's stern. Shortly thereafter, Blair slowly exited the cabin of the boat, a look of pride beaming across her face as she walked past the helm directly to the stern above the place where she had left Jax.

"You got it running?" he asked, suddenly confused at the revelation.

"IT LIVES!" she screamed loudly into the morning air, thrusting her hands into the air in a victorious pose as her shout echoed under the metal roofs of the marina.

"That's fantastic, babe," Jax said, suddenly at a loss for words. "But... how did you? Who... how did this happen?"

"I traded for it," she said in a matter-of-fact tone, as she lowered her arms slightly to flex like a bodybuilder. Then, in a wave of overwhelming silliness, she grunted loudly and exclaimed, "Ugh! Intimidating, right? Watch out world, I'm comin' for ya!"

"Terrifying," Jax laughed. Then, thinking for a moment, he asked, "Traded... what exactly?"

Blair's triumphant pose fell as an insincere, nearly apologetic smile spread across her face, "Just some... reproduction rights."

"Wait...What?" Jax stammered, now completely confused.

"Oh, no – not that!" she laughed, suddenly understanding how poorly chosen her words were. "The rights to reproduce one of my pieces."

"I'm not sure that makes it better!" Jax responded in disbelief.

Blair suddenly rushed to the edge of the boat and sat down at the wire railing so that she could look him in the face as she explained. "Well, you've always said it's up to me what I want to do with my art. And I've thought about it... for months. I hate that it's been locked away; I'm tired of living in fear!"

"Honey, I understand that, believe me. I'm not happy about any of this either, but are you serious right now? With the investigation they're doing – is this really the best time?" he asked, taking her hands in his through the ship's railing.

To calm him, she tried again to explain her reasoning, saying, "Listen, I spoke with the detective – he came here, and –"

"Wait what?" he exclaimed. "He came here? How did he find you here?"

"I'm not one-hundred percent sure on that; I'm guessing you've ordered enough takeout and trips here... I'm guessing they put two and two together. Or maybe they found it through the registration on the boat? It was all paper, but if they were looking, they would have found this as my address," she explained calmly and rationally, trying to ease his concerns.

"But they came here - Detective Hernandez came here looking for you?" he asked more aggressively, still fixated on unraveling the events that had transpired in his absence.

"Yes. He was asking about *Omnis Nemo*, and whether I was *Omnis Nemo* – and whether Crush had sold any paintings for me. He asked about Caldo; he wanted to know why people thought I was *Omnis Nemo* after I sort of denied it. Then he left. He's got nothing; we have done nothing wrong!" she answered, matching his energy.

"Well, I mean – you've just got ship repairs in exchange for the rights to reproduce artwork that will be considered subversive. Whoever this is that you're working with is going to reproduce your paintings – likely a lot of them. And they're paying you for that right. You understand how that violates both the Anti-Money Laundering Act payment provisions AND the Safe Speech Act, right? It's like a two-for-one," he asked rhetorically.

"I'm not an idiot," she answered angrily. "But I am very much tired of living in fear that someone will find out who I am and what I believe. I'm tired of being told that I have to surrender to constant surveillance if I want to buy anything that I need! I'm tired of not being able to take care of myself simply because I won't wear those damn lenses! And that's just it, Jax – I won't. I'll never give in to the people – the system – the whatever THIS is!"

"I get that. I know it's tough for you," he said defensively. "But right now, the police are investigating my gallery, trying to make the case that I'm using it to launder money to extremist groups. And now you've sold the rights to reproduce your work – which is clearly very critical of government policies – and magically, your boat has a new motor... just coincidentally."

"They can't prove otherwise," she responded hastily, now thoroughly annoyed at his critical tone.

"YET – they can't prove anything yet. But somewhere in the feed, there's a record of that motor being sold to someone. I'm sure it has a serial number. They could find it here and start connecting dots – don't you see?" he asked, trying to reason with her. "What happens when your paintings start showing up on the feed? I can guarantee you they will get a lot of attention – I know how good you are! People are going to start looking very carefully at who the artist is – even if they're all attributed to 'ΘN' – how long does that cover last?"

"ΘN is a ghost... a phantom. There's no link to me..." she said, shaking her head defensively.

"I don't know – I'm not sure it's a big leap between 'Omnis Nemo' and 'ΘN' – and the police already seem to think that's you. So..." he said slightly mockingly.

"Then I'll go to jail, Jax!" she answered angrily. "That's not going to hurt your precious gallery."

"You honestly believe that you going to jail because of your work won't impact me? The gallery? What do you think happens when people find out I'm dating a dissident? That I featured her work – that I did it all knowing who she was and what she believed in?" he asked, exasperated and frustrated at what had transpired in his absence. "Blair – I don't like this system either. I hate it, but it IS the world we live in. And some of us rely on the feed for our business – for managing our whole lives! What am I supposed to do? Am I supposed to just walk away from my entire life?"

She stood there before him, shaking as she fought away the tears that were welling in her eyes. She must have known how much the decision would cost him, and that eventually it would come to this. He had hoped they could find a path between their different worlds, but in that moment, he considered if that hope was simply dreaming.

"I think you should make a decision about what really matters to you, Jax. And it's not fair of me to expect you to be... okay... with my decision," she replied with a quivering voice. "But I made my decision because I had to; I have to live my life, no matter the consequences. And if being with me is such a threat to you, maybe you shouldn't."

"What are you saying?" he asked, searching her tear-filled eyes for what she really meant.

"I'm saying I don't know how else to be. This is me; my art is my voice – it is my truth. I'm not going to suddenly be someone else. I can put on a pretty dress and shake the hands of your friends for an evening, sure. But... that's not who I am, as fun as it was. At the end of the day, I'm still the daughter of a man who was murdered for speaking the truth. I'm the daughter of a woman who was locked up, likely forever, for saying that the murder was wrong. I'm a woman who has a voice, and I will not be quiet just so I don't cause trouble."

"Blair... I don't know what to say," Jax answered in frustration.

"Say that this business of yours... this life you've built is enough," she answered in a calm, serious voice that quivered as she spoke. "Say that this life you're living makes you happy, and it's all you need. If you think you can wake up in twenty years, content because you followed all the rules and did what you were told, then you've already made your decision. For me, hiding who I am is not enough."

He paused for a minute, hearing what she said and wondering if it *was* enough. With certainty, he knew the road ahead with her would be anything but certain. And while he loved her, he didn't know if he could walk the same path she was taking.

She watched him thinking silently for a while, uncertain of what else she should say. When he didn't answer, she finally said, "Goodbye, Jax," and then left the deck to return to the cabin below deck.

Not knowing what else to do or say, Jax retrieved his travel bags and walked back up the main walkway of the marina. After he passed through the gate, he removed a small container from his pocket and placed his lenses back into his eyes. It took several seconds for his feed to recognize his location, but within a few minutes, an automated vehicle arrived.

He was exhausted from the trip and needed rest, but how he had left things with Blair weighed on him heavily. Whether he could sleep if he tried, he wasn't certain. So instead, he had the vehicle take him to his gallery. It was closed, so it would be quiet at least. Work would provide a needed distraction, or if not, a place to think without the distractions that would come from going home.

As the vehicle departed St. Charles, a regular stream of advertisements poured across his lenses, with other notifications asking him to leave reviews or comments about his experience at various restaurants and landmarks. Quickly blinking away the ads, he scrolled through the open threads that filled his eyes until he found local news events.

The local baseball team had made it late into the playoffs before falling short of the series. In the business of all that had transpired the past few months, he realized he had never taken Parker to the game like he promised. There was always next season, but he could at least send an apologetic note.

Another story reported an increase in vandalism throughout the St. Louis metro that was causing a stir as the acts had not been captured on the feed. Apparently, the police were investigating, and the mayor was promising swift action to protect businesses. Other than other minor crimes, the city seemed to have continued on as it always had in his absence.

When the vehicle eventually pulled up to the gallery, the weight of his travel and the argument with Blair made him feel more tired than he had in some time. He slowly climbed out of the car, fumbling for his keys as he made his way to the door. Once inside, he went directly to his office, not even bothering to turn on the lights in the lower level. Each step up the stairs felt heavy, like he was pulling himself forward wearing concrete shoes until finally he reached the second floor. There, he set his baggage down and plopped onto the leather sofa to briefly rest his eyes.

He awoke hours later, having slept uncomfortably in his travel suit, sprawled out on the sofa. Likely, he would have slept longer were it not from a call from his mother that came across the feed.

"Jaxon, are you there? Why haven't you been answering?" she demanded.

"I just got back into town, mom. It was a long conference, and when I got back, I fell asleep in my office," he groaned as he rubbed the exhaustion from his eyes.

"Oh good, dear. Listen, I wanted to talk to you about Caldo," she said abruptly.

"What? What about Caldo?" he asked groggily.

"Well, I thought you would have heard, darling. He was arrested for using that eye-dropper drug, you know the one," she replied. "The poor man is sick and needs help."

"I... I knew he had a problem, but I had not heard he had been arrested. First thing tomorrow, I'll have Bruce reach out to the marketing team and get a presser distancing us. Okay?" he responded.

"No, no, dear – that's not what I'm asking. See, your father and I... well, all our friends too... we've invested heavily in his work. We all own original pieces, and if this situation isn't handled properly, I'm afraid our investments will be nearly worthless. It would be quite embarrassing for us, as all of them bought his artwork through the gallery, understand? No, right now, what we need is some solidarity. We need to make it clear to the public that the gallery is helping the artist work through his issues, and that he is still a prized contributor to Crush and the national art scene," she said, rambling so quickly he had trouble keeping up with what she was demanding.

"His work has been tanking for the better part of a year, mom. The Plush... the arrest... I mean, all that isn't going to help the price of his work. It's going to decline regardless of what we do," he answered stoically.

"See, that's where we need to focus our efforts, then. Maybe we spotlight some of his latest, more innovative pieces. I'm sure you can reach out to the people at that fine art journal you're always going on about and convince them to do some sort of... I dunno, tortured genius type piece – think you can do that?" she asked.

"Look, mom, I don't wish the man any ill will – he was great for business in his prime. But I can't put my name and reputation behind his work when it's failing; I'd look like a fool," he insisted.

"Of course you can, dear. People trust your opinion, and if you say he's still the phenomenon that everyone believes he is, people will still buy his work. People don't know what they want," she said in a tone that revealed her request was more a directive than a request.

"No, I can't, especially right now. There was a detective that was asking about Caldo a few weeks ago; I got the impression he was implicating the gallery in some illegal activity. I can't now come out and defend a known drug abuser – it will only make us look like we're enabling this," he emphasized.

"I wouldn't worry about that, dear. These things come up from time to time, and so long as you're not doing any business with that dissident girl, I'm sure there's nothing for you to worry about," she said dismissively.

"Wait, what?" he asked. "I said they were investigating Caldo – I didn't say anything about Blair. What would make you think they were investigating anything related to her?"

"Oh, it's nothing, dear. You father and I met with Caldo recently. There were some sore feelings after the gala; he was feeling replaced... forgotten. And he's more than a client – he's a friend of the family. He's made a name for himself," she answered, downplaying her involvement.

"So, a known drug user gets angry that he isn't the prized pony anymore and throws a fit at one of our formal events, and you and dad did what exactly?" he asked, suspecting there was more to the story.

"Nothing... absolutely nothing..." she said cryptically. Then, after a brief pause, she added, "We merely suggested that if he cooperated with law enforcement on more serious matters, it's likely they wouldn't even pursue the drug charge. Besides, I told you working with that girl would be nothing but trouble; you needed a little encouragement. A bit of scaring straight is good for you."

Anger within him welled until in an instant he felt as though he might erupt like a volcano filled with a molten lava of rage. It took every ounce of self-control he could muster to calm himself enough to speak, and when he did, he said, "Did you... talk to the police about my business? About my relationship with Blair?"

"Well, that's not really the point, Jaxson," she answered sternly. "The point is, we all need to do what we must to protect our investment – our award-winning artist, the gallery, the family name. These are all much more valuable than some fling with a redhead, especially with who that young woman is."

"Did you talk to the police?" he asked again, only more assertively, as the anger within him broke through his effort to remain calm. "It's a 'yes' or 'no' question, mother."

"Your father and I did what was best for you, for your gallery, and for our family. I'm not going to apologize for that," she said indignantly. "Besides, nothing bad happened to you because of it. You either did nothing wrong, or you were smart enough to not get caught. There's no harm done."

"I'm going now," Jax raged, cutting the feed abruptly.

Having paced back and forth across his office for several minutes, working out the anger he felt for his parents, he knew something needed to change. He then trudged down the staircase that led to the first floor of the gallery and simply looked around at all he thought he had built. The nagging suspicion that his success was only a product of his parents crushed his spirit, filling him full of doubt.

What good is success if it's not mine? He thought to himself. *How would I even know how much of this was because of my effort, and how much they could take credit for?*

Then it occurred to him, the art in the gallery belonged to the artists; it was only the walls that were his. Those walls were meaningless without art filling them. All that he owned and all that he thought he had built was simply hollow; the only value he contributed was connecting artists with people who loved their work. He was a conduit, a matchmaker. In that way, he might as well have been the Eads Bridge, spanning the Mississippi to connect St. Louis to Illinois. There would always be customers willing to buy beautiful paintings, but without the artists – without the art – he was nothing. And what good was it to perform that function if it simply made him a tool his parents could use for their purposes?

"Is it enough?" he whispered aloud to himself as he stood alone in the gallery. For the first time, he thought he knew the answer.

~ 15 ~

She waited patiently on the cold, stone steps of the Old Post Office on Main Street. Why he wanted to meet her there, she couldn't say. Word had been passed along through Tanner the day before when she was helping at the shop, but Tanner only said Blaze wanted to meet with her at 10 o'clock the following day.

That morning, Main Street in the historic district was ever the bittersweet place it had always been for her. While the coffee shops, chocolatiers, and bakeries perfumed the air with enticing aromas, enjoying any of their offerings was always out of reach. Still, the old buildings with recently added holiday décor, and the tourist filled streets made it scenic. As she waited, she recalled how so many of the stone and brick buildings had lasted through decades of floods and storms, reinventing themselves in each new era and aging with grace to become far more beautiful than their original, practical purpose. Even the OPO, where she waited, had originally been a courthouse before the civil war. Sitting atop a small incline a few dozen yards from the street, the stone walkway that led to the old building had long served as a meeting spot for tourists and locals alike. In time, all things changed and evolved, she supposed.

As the time finally came, Blair studied the faces of the tourists as they passed, searching for the familiar face of Tanner's brother. Then suddenly, from behind her, the infamous bearded man approached unexpectedly and sat down at her side.

"Good morning," he said murmured nearly indecipherably.

"Hi!" Blair responded, a bit startled by his unannounced entrance.

"Sorry about that. I just thought it would be better to be out in the open... somewhere you're not normally spending time... somewhere they weren't monitoring with the drones and what not," he suggested.

Blair paused for a moment, wondering what had transpired that led to the overabundance of caution from a man known for being cautious, but she assumed he would explain once she discovered more of what he wanted.

"Well, anyway, my people love your work," he said awkwardly. "I... I should clarify. I think most of the city has now seen that first one we printed. No, probably much more than that... It's all over the feed. It's everywhere."

"Everywhere how... the feed?" she asked.

"Some of our connections began physically pasting the paper prints to walls of prominent buildings... like they did back in the first war before radios and television and all that. It's... old school," he explained.

"Go on..." she insisted.

"Well, it just means that people saw your work, and they scanned it, searched for it, or at least information about it into the feed... and then their networks had it and shared it... and all the while, none of it is linked to my... group. We've got clean hands on the whole thing," he answered with a smirk.

"I didn't know you were planning... it sounds like this was what you wanted from the beginning," she answered.

"Didn't *you*?" he asked.

"Yes... I guess. I... didn't expect it to be so sudden. It's just one painting," she said, somewhat conflicted by the unexpected success.

"Well, you're not connected. You don't have any idea of how quickly these things go viral. Local media is already running a blitz campaign with the Mayor of St. Louis promising to crack down on incidents of vandalism. The FBI is investigating a suspected foreign-born terrorist; they think some Scandi-nationalist is trying to promote extremism... Something like that."

Blair's eyes became wide with shock at hearing the news. "So – ΘN?"

Blaze simply nodded his head as he nervously stroked his long, bushy black beard.

"We need to tell Lil and Tanner – they have one of my paintings in the shop. I'm sure people have scanned it!" Blair said as she stood from the steps in a surge of adrenaline.

"Already taken care of – shops closed today. Indefinitely, really," Blaze said quietly. "Hey, they took your painting with them when they left - at my insistence. Sit back down and relax. Even here, we don't want to draw attention – calm and cool."

Blair froze in place and then calmly did as she had been instructed. As he once again sat on the cold stone steps, her hands trembled. For a moment, she wondered if it was fear and nervousness or if she was simply shivering from the cold. Not wanting to admit she was afraid, she banished the notion from her head, ascribing her unsteady hands to the weather.

"I didn't mean for this to hurt their business," she said reflectively. "I never would have... I mean, I love Lil and Tanner. There's no way I could have known."

"In the middle of the night last night, someone went to their shop and cut a giant hole in the exterior wall to remove the mural... thieves, from what I've heard from folks who saw the video on the feed. They literally stole a brick wall from a building. From what I can tell, some thread made the connection between your painting in their shop, the mural and ΘN. That mural is an, even if you only did part of it – even if it's not your signature style. It's likely the only original work available on the market..."

The absurdity of what she was hearing left her feeling skeptical of what he was saying, and for a moment she squinted as she looked at him trying to determine if he was being serious or this was some kind of elaborate lie he was manufacturing.

"Hey, honestly, I don't think anyone saw THAT coming," he responded. Then, laughing a bit to himself, he added, "Who steals a wall? I... I kind of respect that dedication to the hustle."

The remark made Blair laugh under her breath, but the hysteria she was only just learning about tempered any humor she found. After a few minutes of silence between them, she asked, "So... where do we go from here?"

"THAT is the right question," he responded. Then, as he continued to stroke his beard anxiously, he added, "ΘN is already being hunted. Obviously, they're suspicious of you, or were. But there's no harm in printing the rest of the paintings now... if they catch you, they'd likely lock up for the rest of your life anyway. 'In for the penny, in for the pound,' as they say."

"Are you serious?" she asked him. "You want to print the other paintings?"

"Well... not just me. My people... the group I'm with. They would like to buy the rights to printing your work – everything you have on the boat," he answered calmly.

"I... that's a big ask," she said, shaking her head with uncertainty.

"I understand... but think this through. With as much as this whole thing is blowing up, you'd be wise to take a long vacation... somewhere without Safe Speech laws, AMLA regs...extradition... You're going to need money – the kind that spends anywhere in the world. We can help with that," he answered confidently.

As she thought about his proposition, a family of tourists stopped immediately in front of them on Main Street. Their youngest, a little girl with a pretty ribbon in her hair was complaining of needing to use the bathroom, which had clearly become the mother's problem to solve as the father was attempting to corral their son who was intent on running up and down the steps of the OPO.

"What about my mother? I can't just leave the country with her locked away," she retorted desperately.

"She will be locked away, whether you leave or not. I don't see how joining her there will make it any better for her," Blaze said a bit dismissively.

"And Tanner and Lil?" she asked.

"That boat of yours takes more than one person to sail..." he answered immediately.

"Given this some thought, have you?" she said, surprised by his instant response.

"They can't stay here – they've had an ⊖N painting hanging on their wall for months. And it didn't matter a week ago. They were selling prints of it. But after the new prints... I'm one-hundred percent sure the police are already looking for them. Both have cut feed since last night," he said calmly. Seeing the look of concern on her face, he added, "Look, they are tattoo artists – they can do that anywhere. You can paint anywhere. Hell, anywhere BUT HERE, you could even sell your work without being afraid of being arrested. With the wall damage to the shop, they'll get paid out on insurance – they'll be fine. But even if they weren't being looked for at the moment, they wouldn't be able to re-open for months."

Sarcastically, she responded, "So, what? All three of us just hop on Astraea's Muse and sail off to — "

"Don't," he interrupted. "I don't want to know where."

Blair looked at him with a silly grin and said, "I think you're being a bit overly-dramatic. This isn't some movie or something."

Blaze shrugged his shoulders as he finally stopped messing around with his beard. Still fidgeting, he adjusted the flap-cap that was covering his head and then finally settled with crossing his fingers together above his knees as he squatted uncomfortably on the stone stairs alongside her. After weighing his words carefully, he answered, "You understand how this all plays out, right? I'm giving you an out here, and not because I'm a nice guy. I've talked to our people – our network and I've convinced them to over-pay for anything you're willing to sell. I don't know if there even is such a thing with as wild as the feed is right now... if the reaction we've seen so far is any indicator, maybe they're getting a deal, who knows. But – my point is - I need your help to get my brother and his wife out of here as well. The fire's already been started on this. You can bow out, and go at it alone – how long do you think that lasts? No feed, no money, and no one to trust. Once they eventually put your face to the name, if they haven't already, you'll be hunted everywhere you go. How many people went into that shop, saw the painting, and saw you? Even without wearing Blinks yourself, your face has been scanned thousands of times – any time you pass a stranger on the street and they look at you. They just have to connect the dots – put your face in the same place and same times as ΘN. That'll take days, maybe? Weeks if you're lucky. Maybe hours."

"And your... group... they're offering enough gold to... what? *Make* me disappear?" she asked.

"If that's what you want. The AMLA and the similar laws in Europe – they don't extend everywhere. You can trade that gold for local currency where you end up, so long as they still use paper money or coins or whatever," he said. "The commitment I got was one briefcase of gold coins per painting... they hold about forty-five pounds each... I figured you'd want coins – they'd be easier to exchange a few at a time."

"This is crazy," she said, rubbing her face with her hands.

"Yup," he grunted. "But hey, at least you know your options."

She rolled her eyes at his suggestion, knowing fully well how few options she actually had. After a deep breath and a prolonged sigh, she eventually relented. "When do you want to get the others?"

"I'll go there now and have the originals back on board tomorrow morning... Also, I spoke with old man Agnew, who has agreed to help move your boat to the municipal doc near the Arch. If we do it now, maybe they have a harder time finding you; they know you live at the marina. We go now and there's at least a chance we can avoid being noticed. Tanner and Lil will meet you there first thing in the morning along with supplies... I'd recommend saying your goodbyes today if there's anyone in town..."

Blair nodded her head, understanding the futility of trying to find an alternative. It was all happening so quickly it made her head spin and ache with nausea, but there was little that could be done. For his part, Blaze simply stood up from the steps of the OPO and walked off casually, as if nothing had transpired.

After he departed, Blair walked alone in the chilly morning air, ambling down the red bricked Main Street as tourists darted in and out of the shops. For all the friends she had made in town, she knew the only people she needed to speak with were the Andovers, and so she walked the short distance back to her old home.

By the time she arrived, it was nearing lunchtime, and both Zay and Bell were still at work. With Mia not yet released for the Thanksgiving break, the house was deserted. She made her way to the backyard where she found the door to her cottage, still beautifully painted in magnolias. *It will only be a matter of time before someone steals this too,* she thought. With nothing to do but wait, she found her old bed in the small cottage and laid down for a nap.

Some hours later, she awoke to a young girl's voice shouting, "Mom! Blair's here! Blair came back!"

The sweet sound of Mia's voice was enough to pull her completely out of her slumber, and in only seconds, Blair had raced into the yard where she found Mia, just outside of the door to her cottage. Without another thought, she scooped up the young girl in her arms and gave her a big squeeze, saying, "I've missed your face, Ms. Mia!"

"I've missed you too," Mia squealed. "Mama says we're going to get to see your boat soon – promise?"

"I'd... really, really like that. But I'm afraid I'm going to have to go on an adventure first. It may be some time before I can take you sailing," Blair answered, trying to fight back how difficult it would be for her to not have this extended family in the same town.

"What's this about you going on an adventure?" Bell called out as she exited the house. "Also, good to see you, Big Squirt!" she said as she gave Blair a hug while she still clutched Mia in her arms.

"Oh, well... that's actually why I dropped by. There's um... there's some stuff I need to do out of town... I'm going to be gone for a while," she answered, trying to communicate sincerely the seriousness of her situation without saying too much. All the Andovers wore their lenses habitually, and she realized at some point, this conversation would surface if they were looking for her. Any details she provided would then only end up aiding those trying to find her.

"That sounds... serious. I've never known you to just leave town – I don't even know how you would," Bell said, somewhat confused by what she was hearing.

"Um... It's probably nothing... Really, I'm fine," Blair answered. "But... you know... just in case. I just wanted to tell you all that I love you and I'll miss you terribly while I'm away."

"Is this about that arrest? The disturbing the peace thing? I thought Jax's attorney made all that go away?" Bell said, prying for more answers.

"Oh, no – it's fine. That all got resolved. It's an art thing, I suppose. There's a new opportunity that's opened up for me, and... I'm going to go try it out. See some more of what the world has to offer outside of St. Charles and St. Louis... An adventure," she said dispassionately.

"Hmm," Bell answered skeptically. Then dryly she offered, "You sound over the moon about it."

"Well, it's just a weird situation... I guess," she said, trying to not raise additional concern.

"Weird... like you're being pressured to do this, weird? Is Jax behind this? Some weird isolation and control thing he's pulling?" she asked. "You'd tell me, right?"

"No, it's not like that. Frankly, I haven't heard from him for a few days. We kind of had a thing... an argument; he's trying to figure his life out," Blair answered. "And the shop's going to be closed for a while at least, so there's not much I can do there. Sounds like a good time to go explore the world."

"What happened at the shop? I thought your friends were doing really well there – that was the last I heard," Bell asked with increasing concern.

"I... don't have all the details. Something happened to their building – vandalism, I think. And so, they're going to have to close doors for a while until it's all resolved," she answered, trying once again to evade as well as she could.

"Oh, I heard about that on the feed – there seems to be a whole string of it going around. Some hoodlums working for this radical from Europe... ΘN, I think they said his name was. But they made it sound like it was all in St. Louis – I hadn't heard anything about it here in the burbs," Bell said, blinking through her feed furiously as she searched for more information. "Here's one – they're saying someone stole the wall of the building in the middle of the night – maybe a prank or something?"

"Yeah, I only heard through a friend, so I'm not sure," Blair answered as she brushed a strand of her falling deep red hair away from her face. "Anyway, I'm pretty sure they have insurance and it will all be fine in the end. But... it's closed for now."

"That's too bad," Bell said. "And here in town, too. I don't think Old St. Chuck's seen anything that big in years."

"Probably not," Blair chuckled. "Anyway, I can't really stay long – I just wanted to see the both of you before I left."

Bell's eyes furrowed, studying her. Having lived with them for years and being treated as an extended member of their family, it felt weird for her to not know the full story. Blair knew any additional information might put them in danger or otherwise help those who were looking for her.

"You won't say where you're going, and you don't know how long you're going for. And your boyfriend isn't even going along," Bell said, recounting the facts as far as she knew them. "I'm worried about you, B."

"Don't be – I'm fine. I'll get word to you guys when I land somewhere, so you know I'm safe. It will be good for me, I think. I could use some time to clear my head, and I've spent my whole life here – it will be good to have a change of scenery," she answered, trying to sound more excited and optimistic about the change that was coming so rapidly.

"Okay... it sounds like you're committed to not letting me talk this out of you... You're a grownup, Blair – you get to decide these things for yourself," Bell answered. "I... just wish there was more you could say or something we could do to help."

"You all have already helped me so much – SO MUCH. I couldn't ask for a better surrogate mom and little sister. You both mean the world to me," Blair said as she hugged them both once again.

After saying goodbye, Blair began the long walk back to the marina. Without a bicycle, the eight-mile trip would take a few hours, but there was enough daylight left to make it home before dark. As she walked, she considered whether she should call Jax. Not having any other way to get ahold of him, she knew the cellular phone he provided would be the only option. While loathe to use it, she knew she couldn't just disappear without saying something.

She knew the line in the sand she had drawn between them likely wasn't fair to either of them, and her impulsive decision hadn't helped. It was simply the way things were unfolding. Still, of all the people in her life, in the months she had known him, he had always accepted her for who she was, as incompatible as it could be. He doted on her, concerned for her every need. While her art had become problematic, it wasn't the art itself that had caused the rift, rather it was the circumstances they found themselves in.

I need to call him; I can do that at least, she thought.

With new resolve, she continued on along the long country road that headed north out of St. Charles towards the marina, intent on finding the cellular phone she had hidden away somewhere on the boat.

When she arrived at the marina, she quickly headed towards Astraea's Muse, only to be stopped by the old pirate along the way.

"You talked to Blaze then?" the old man shouted abruptly as she walked down the main walkway between the boats. Even at a distance, she could see his eyes had narrowed as if he were busy at work on something serious.

"We spoke this morning," Blair answered.

"Good... good. Well, let's get a move on, then," he answered as he left Betsy's Bannermaid. As he walked towards her, she could see he was carrying several large cases, including the one she had seen him store his rifle in.

"That's a lot of gear," she said when she saw him carry the large cases off of his boat and walk towards her.

"It's a long trip," he said. "Holbox will take days, even with good wind."

"Holbox?" Blair said. "Blaze told me you were going to help me get the boat to the marina down by the arch. I don't even know what a Holbox is."

The old man gave a wry smile as he answered. "A Holbox is an island, of course, off the coast of the Yucatan.

"Yucatan – like Mexico?" she said, somewhat surprised at the idea, but having no reason to disagree with it.

"Unless you have a better plan – they don't care too much about Safe Speech and what not. You'd be free to paint whatever you choose, with no one to say different. And Holbox, in particular – the entire length of it can be reached by bicycle. Back in the twenties, it was a popular spot for tourists; I dated this hippy chick who used to talk about the art scene down there. Nowadays, it's less of a hotspot. Not too many people, but even so, there are still plenty of tourists and whatnot. It's pretty quiet, pretty good fishing too!" He paused for a moment, searching her eyes for any objection. It was obvious to her that the old man was feeling a need to help provide some order to the chaos that was recently enveloping her life, and she was self-aware enough to understand how innocently ignorant of the world outside she was. The old sailor paused abruptly from his otherwise rapid pace through the marina and looked with eyes that reflected a certain level of desperation as he said, "I'll sail you wherever you'd like, child. It's just when Blaze said you didn't have a plan of where to go... it popped into my head – seems like it'd be a good fit for you. But more to the point, I can't just let you sail an old 43-foot sailboat straight out into the gulf with no experience and only Tanner to help. You know the basics from books. He's spent a little time on the water, but it takes years of experience to pull off a trip like that."

Blair paused reflectively, knowing he was right, but troubled by the position she appeared to have put him in. "Ah... Cap'n... I'm sure we can manage..."

"Well, darlin', I happen to know you've never sailed down the Mississippi. I also happen to know you've never sailed in open water. And because today I just so happened to be the smartest one around, I JUST SO HAPPENED to know that boy Tanner ain't much better a deckhand than his brother," the old man said with a wink.

"I can't ask you to do that – that's way too much for me to ask a friend," she said apologetically.

"No, nonsense. You've become like a daughter to me these last few months; you've given this old man a chance to smile and laugh again. There's not a chance in hell I'm letting you idiots try to pull off this stunt – not without someone who has some experience in these things. Besides, past the confluence with the Missouri, the whole river is a wild ride – sand bars come out of nowhere. Tankers are like whales that would swallow up a little fish like your boat – forget the right of way, they wouldn't even see you and couldn't turn fast enough to avoid you even if they did. You don't have a chance without me," he said, then casually walked ahead of her towards her sailboat.

With a spryness that defied his age, the old pirate quickly climbed aboard the vessel, with Blair following just behind. He then handed the cases to her, saying, "Best keep the forward cabin for the married folk; I can sleep wherever you'll put me. But these... you'll need to find room for."

Once Blair took hold of the cases, she groaned at the weight of both. The rifle case she had expected, but the hard-sided suitcase must have weighed seventy pounds, sufficiently so that the wheels at the bottom appeared as if they would buckle once she set it down on the deck.

"Mind the goods, young lady. I'd rather have an insurance policy if it takes a while to make it home," he said as he saw her struggling under the weight.

Blair looked at him quizzically, pondering for a moment what could be so important and so valuable that he would bring it along. Then she realized perhaps he was smuggling the same contraband she was, just in a suitcase instead of briefcases.

"Better than burying it on a remote beach, I suppose," she said with a laugh.

"The thought crossed my mind," he chuckled playfully.

It took several minutes for her to store his cases in the lower berth, but as soon as she returned topside, the old man had already removed the mooring lines and started the auxiliary engine. Realizing their departure was imminent, Blair moved quickly to pull the small step ladder aboard and stow it in the compartment designed for it, securing the lock so it wouldn't open in rough weather.

"I'll pilot us out of the marina, dear. Just make sure your wares and such are secured downstairs – just like I showed you," the old man said as he slowly backed the boat out of the slip.

Blair descended into the cabin once again and began placing her art supplies into the storage compartments under the sofa benches. What few dishes she had went back into the cupboards, that latched with a horizontal slide lock, preventing them from opening when underway. She then secured the remaining doors and ran bungee cords along anything that could bounce in place once they were out on the water. With the cabin secure, she returned once again to the deck.

Captain Agnew had already navigated out of the opening of the small marina, and Astraea's Muse was finally on the open water of the wide Mississippi.

"Ah... the helm, my dear," he said, gesturing to large steering wheel that sat just back from midship.

"Me? You want me at the helm?" she laughed.

"Well, I didn't spend all that time teaching you how to run this rig for you to sit on the sidelines. We've got a lot of river ahead – you'll need to get a feel for her," the old man chuckled as he moved over to the side, relinquishing control of the ship to Blair. "Besides, we'll stay under motor tonight; I don't want to take a chance tangling the sheets in the dark. Tomorrow, after Tanner and his wife come aboard, we can see about setting the rigging."

They motored eastward along the Mississippi for several miles towards the turn in the river where it would soon flow southeast and then south. It would take hours, and the river was still and quiet in the newly darkened night.

"Cap'n, could you take the helm for a minute... there's something I need to do," she said, gesturing to the old man who had been occupied going through the hatches and inventorying space and the condition of their fittings.

"Of course," the old man replied instinctively.

Once she had returned below deck, Blair had to search through several containers until she at last found the old cellular phone that Jax had given her. When she turned it on, it took her several minutes to re-familiarize herself with how it even functioned. Then finally, she found the contact list with only one entry, "Jax".

In an instant, the speaker of the phone came alive with his voice on the other end. "Blair? Blair, are you ok?"

"I'm fine," she whispered through the microphone.

"What's wrong? You never use this thing, it must be important – has something happened?" he asked in a panicked tone.

"Well... it's just that I'm going to be leaving town for a while... I didn't feel right about the way it ended between us – it wasn't fair of me to ask you to walk away from your life because I want to have my own life... I'm sorry," she said softly, trying to fight back the raw emotions that hid just beneath her words.

The voice on the other end of the feed fell silent momentarily. With the cellular phone only connecting to the voice stream portion of his feed, Blair couldn't see his face, and likewise, she knew he couldn't see hers. The silence made it worse because she couldn't read his eyes; she couldn't tell what he was thinking.

"Blair..." he answered. "I think... Everything I've built here is something I can't trust – I don't know how much of it was me and how much was my parents pulling strings. After we talked last, I had time to think about what really matters. My work is to find talented artists – I found you. And in a weird blur, you quickly became more important to me than your work or my work. That's been difficult for me to sort through."

She listened intently to what he was saying, not sure she understood, or if she did, where that sentiment left them. Finally, she replied saying, "I only want you to be happy, Jax. I want to be happy being who I am, honestly and authentically. And if your work makes you happy, you should keep doing it. I understand."

"I'm selling the gallery," he responded abruptly. "I've already talked to Wells – there are interested parties lining up. I can't be here like this... doing my job... if I turn my back on the most talented artist I've ever found in my life. Even if it's just a business decision, I can't."

"So, that's what this will be then – a business decision?" she asked.

"No – god, I hope not!" he said frantically. Then, pausing for a moment, his voice softened as he said, "I love you, Blair. We long ago blurred the line between work and romance - we're both passionate about the same thing. I can't do this – I don't think I can continue working in the art world without you being a part of my life; I don't want to. It's... empty."

As she felt the tears fall down her cheeks, she fumbled for words, not knowing what to say. Through the tears, she answered, "I love you too, I think. No, I'm sure of it. But right now, I need to go. They'll be coming for me."

"Who's coming for you?" he said defensively. "Where are you? I'll come get you!"

"No, it's too late... the feed will explain more than I can – it's not safe to say more. It's all connected; they'll hear this conversation and know. Just be safe," she said, brushing away her tears.

"I'll find a way to you," he said frantically as the signal on the phone crackled with a loss of reception. Moments later, the call failed. She searched for the cable he had provided her and found an outlet to charge it, not knowing exactly how it worked or why the call had failed. *Perhaps it was for the best*, she thought. *If he came for me, they would follow him and we'd both be in trouble.*

Once she returned to the vessel's cockpit, the sniffles and tears betrayed her wrecked emotional state sufficiently so that the old sailor understood something had transpired. Rather than say anything, he simply raised one of his arms on the helm and gestured for her to join him, resting the arm around her shoulder in a comforting hug.

They rounded the bend where the river turned to the south, and not far beyond, they passed the confluence of the Missouri river that would lead back home to St. Charles.

Last chance, she thought.

Not far from the point where the rivers merged, they passed beneath a freeway overpass, then the Old Chain Rocks Bridge. Within a few brief minutes, the river widened slightly before splitting to cut around Mosenthian Island. Holding to the Missouri side of the river, they continued in the channel until she could clearly see the lights of homes and factories on shore.

"There's old Saint Lou," Agnew said, gesturing towards the city.

As they drew closer to downtown, she saw the Arch in the distance, lit up beautifully in the night's dark sky.

"The Municipal Marina is just north of the monument," the old man said. "If we have a view from there... I don't recall. But I wouldn't plan on walking all the way down to the park in the middle of the night alone, young lady. Some of this town can be a bit iffy."

Blair simply smiled, grateful to have her old friend always thinking of her safety and watching over her. As it turned out, there was no view of the monument from the marina, but she knew they would pass it in the morning. This gateway monument felt like it was ushering her on her own adventure, the same as it had for so many who had traveled west in search of their own future. Seeing it before she left felt appropriate, even necessary.

When they neared the marina, Agnew took control of the helm to steer the boat. Surrounded by other vessels, he refused to take chances. Then only moments later, Astraea's Muse pulled directly up to a public dock.

"Hop off and see to the bow and stern lines, kiddo," the old man ordered in a fatherly voice.

She did so enthusiastically, remembering for once exactly what was required. A few short figure eight knots around the dock cleats later, and the boat was secured. Then she heard the next order from the captain, "Head below. It's only a few hours until the others arrive. You'll need your sleep for the long run of ass kicking we're gonna take over the next week."

"Will it be that bad?" she asked as she climbed back aboard.

"Through the river, it won't be easy," he said with a heavy sigh. "And it will probably take the better part of a week to reach the gulf. Then before we make the crossing, we'll need to take on provisions and make sure we have any spare parts for this tub. Just to be safe... We'll be fine. Go get some sleep."

$$\sim 16 \sim$$

The day after Blair's disturbing call, he considered whether he should stay home from work. He hadn't slept at all that night, fighting a weird mixed drink of emotions. The coldness of his parents' manipulations infuriated him; the sweetness of her voice and the sharp burn of worry and fear all intermixed with a twist of an instinct for self-preservation.

They'll be coming for me, he repeated in his mind repeatedly. *But why now? It had to have something to do with the people making the prints.*

While his emotional state made his decision-making questionable, pacing back and forth across his loft wasn't productive or helping him sort through what was happening. As soon as the sunlight replaced the twinkling of building lights, he dressed and headed in to work.

Out of an abundance of caution, he'd kept his lenses out as much as possible the previous few days. And once he reached the curb of his building, he hesitated to put them in to call for a ride after the unsettling call from Blair. Nothing had monitored his morning routine to anticipate his departure time, necessitating a less automatic, more inconvenient effort to get a ride. He wondered for a moment if he should walk instead; it was at most a mile to the gallery. Then again, his habits and routines had long before been collected as data; there wasn't anything to be gained from walking instead of calling for a ride.

As he placed his lenses back into his eyes to call for a ride, headlines began crossing his feed addressing the vandalism crisis that was sweeping the city and the additional law enforcement presence that was happening in response to it. The attention it was getting was especially odd, and the threads and sub-threads he followed were flooded with commentary and links to related images and video. While he waited for the rideshare to arrive, he began digging deeper, trying to determine what happened that had the city buzzing. It didn't take long to find a video of a poster-sized print of a bald eagle, choking on a gold coin that had been pasted to the side of the Old Courthouse near the Arch. Another on a building next to the Sculpture Park off of Market Street. As he continued following links, he found others – there were dozens. At some point, either the AI or some unwitting art lover made a connection between the eagle print and Native princess prints that had been sold through the tattoo shop. The images had already been scanned or shared over a million times over the previous day with other videos of city works and law enforcement removing them.

He continued scrolling through the various connections until the rideshare arrived, looking for any analytics on how the stunt was being received. From what he could tell, the attention Blair's print was receiving appeared to be self-feeding; removing the posters only fueled interest.

A short trip later, he arrived at the gallery long before it officially opened. Instead, he headed straight to his office for coffee as his research on the feed continued, lost in a blur of time, caffeine, and feed hysteria.

It was the voice of Bruce that finally returned to any sense of normalcy in his morning routine. "Morning," he said, interrupting Jax's obsessive dive into his lenses. "You're here early."

"Couldn't sleep," he answered, sipping from his cup of now cold espresso.

"Right... Well, you have a waiting list this morning. A few of them are already waiting in the lobby," Bruce said with a touch of annoyance.

"More people looking for Omnis Nemo pieces?" he asked. Looking towards his assistant for confirmation of his suspicion, he sensed there was something else bothering him, something beyond the early morning appointments. "What's wrong, Bruce? What's the sour look for – walk-ins are part of the deal."

"It's not that – it's... Well, the final offer documents from Wells came through," he replied.

"Listen, I know it's a bit of a shock... I probably should have given you the heads up about what I was thinking so you didn't find out this way. I'm sorry for that." Jax answered, knowing he owed him far more than the courtesy of some open communication.

"Why sell it?" Bruce snapped. "I thought we made a great team here."

"We do," Jax said assuredly. "The reason is... personal, I guess."

"Hmph," Bruce grumbled. "Well, I guess I'd better polish up my resume then."

"Is that what's bothering you?" Jax asked. "I mean, I get it – I probably caused some unnecessary anxiety that you didn't need. But listen, you are the lifeblood that keeps this place running. I will do everything in my power to make sure whoever buys this place knows your value. I don't see any sane person wanting to let you go. Frankly, I don't think you have anything to worry about. Crush will still be here. It's the *me* part that will be missing."

His words seemed to have at least a mild effect on easing his assistant's tension, and while not altogether content, he refocused on the business of the day.

"Ms. Anderson is first in line," he finally answered, looking through the list of appointments on his feed. Then with a wink he added, "I'll give you five minutes head start."

"I appreciate you," Jax said. "Truly – not sure what we'd do without you."

"Mmmm hmmmm," Bruce replied, still working through the list.

After making a fresh cup of espresso, a message came through from Bruce indicating Ms. Anderson was on her way to his office. As soon as she reached his office, she abruptly demanded, "I need you to get me an original ϴN piece, Jaxson – your mother says Crush has access."

"I apologize for the miscommunication, Ms. Anderson; my mother is mistaken. Nobody knows who this new ϴN is – not the police, not the FBI, and not even me," he lied stoically.

"Your mother says *Omnis Nemo* IS ϴN – you featured her work at the gala, as I recall... that stunning redhead," she argued. "Now, let's not play games here. Money isn't a concern, obviously. What will it take?"

Jax paused for a few seconds, infuriated that his family had gone from causing the chaos that had ensued to attempting to profit from it. He knew he should be diplomatic and polite, but in a lapse of judgement, reckless anger poured out of his mouth in place of tact.

"Ms. Anderson – I appreciate you putting your trust in Crush – in my family. I am, however, sorry to inform you that due to my mother's wild accusations, that young woman has since fled the country," he answered, slamming his hands down on the top of his desk. He then looked at her directly in the eyes and said, "What will it take for me to get you an original work from ϴN? Even if I had that ability – even if I could – it would take an act of God – literally. And you know, I'm even a little concerned that God Himself could not convince me to help you. I don't want to. In fact, it's the opposite. Right now, there literally are unspeakable torments I would rather endure than help one of my mother's friends join the latest art trend!"

The appalled look on her face revealed his message had been received clearly, as Ms. Anderson stormed out of his office muttering to herself, "The audacity! I thought you were raised better..."

While he knew his explosion was tactless, the release felt cathartic. After taking a moment to straighten his tie and compose himself, he was surprised to find a man and woman, both in dark-colored suits, suddenly arrive at the top of the staircase with no announcement from Bruce.

"I'm Special Agent Krynski, this is Special Agent Wrilley – are you Jaxson Wadsworth, the owner of this gallery?" the woman said in a low, assertive voice.

"I am," Jax said stoically. "But before you begin, I've said everything I know to Detective Hernandez of the Saint Louis Police Department. My full statement is a part of the official record; I'd suggest you speak with the detective."

"We've seen the interview with Detective Hernandez, Mr. Wadsworth. We have some additional questions for you though, if we could encourage you to spare a few minutes," the man in the suit interjected.

"Look – if we're going to do this again, I want my lawyer," Jax answered, annoyed.

"That would be Mr. Henry Wells, Esquire, is that correct?" the Agent Krynski asked, scrolling through her notes in the feed as she blinked.

"Yes – call Henry," he answered. "Now, if you'll excuse me, I have work to do."

"Sir, Mr. Wells is presently in custody, facing charges of obstructing justice. Is there other counsel you would like to contact?" Agent Wrilley asked.

"What do you mean Henry's in custody? Obstructing justice?" Jax asked with a look of confusion.

"Sir, we can't, um... discuss the particular details of that aspect of the investigation. I'm sure you can understand," Agent Krynski answered. "Is there another attorney you'd like to call, or should we just get into it?"

Jax thought for a moment. The only other attorney he knew was Blair's friend, Xavier, although he didn't know what he specialized in. It would be a huge ask to involve them, but as he looked at the stern faces above the government suits in his office, he knew he had little choice. He was certain there was a good chance he'd be sitting in a cell next to Henry by the end of the day if he did not find some help and quickly; the level of interest in Blair's work was simply too high – there was too much visibility for it to be ignored.

"Yes – I can't say that he'd be available right now, but I can reach out. Would you care to have a seat?" he said cooly.

"Thank you," Agent Wrilley responded as he sat down on the leather sofa in Jax's office. Agent Krynski hesitated a moment, but followed suit once Jax began blinking through his contacts. Moments later, he linked with Zay.

"Zay – it's Jax. Apologies for the interruption – this is a bit impromptu for me as well," he said apologetically.

"No problem. I'm guessing you've heard from Blair and you've got some news you can share?" Zay responded eagerly.

"No, unfortunately, not yet at least," Jax said with a heavy sigh. "I do, however, have two FBI agents sitting in my office that have some questions for me... And my attorney was recently arrested, presumably for telling them to take a hike. Is there any way you can help? I'll understand if you can't – no hard feelings."

"I'm not sure how much help I'll be without any preparation, but I'm happy to try. Can we go remotely?" Zay asked. "I'm at the firm currently – over in Maryland Heights. With all the stuff on the news feeds, it would take a while to get there."

Turning towards the agents, Jax asked, "Counsel is willing to link in, if that's acceptable to you both?"

Both of the agents nodded in agreement, and seconds later, Zay's face appeared on all of their feeds, a fourth voice adding to a three-person conversation.

"Mr. Wadsworth, as I said, we've seen the notes from Detective Hernandez – we've heard your statement. While we do not at this time, have any evidence indicating you or the gallery to have done anything illegal, we are now certain that the woman you are acquainted with, Blair Huxley, is also known as 'Omnis Nemo', or otherwise the terrorist 'ΘN'. Can you confirm this for me?" Agent Krynski asked.

"I can't," Jax lied. Then, looking at Zay's face on the feed, he saw his attorney's eyes as wide as saucers, having only heard the accusation for the first time.

"And why is that?" Agent Wrilley asked as his eyebrows furloughed in frustration.

"Could you please be more specific, Agent Wrilley?" Zay interjected automatically. "Asking why a person can or cannot do something could be interpreted any millions of ways. Is there something *specific* you are trying to get at?"

After rolling his eyes, Agent Wrilley continued by saying, "Do you or do you not have specific, credible information that would prove Blair Huxley is, in fact, 'Omnis Nemo' a.k.a. 'ΘN'?"

"I do not," Jax replied calmly.

"Sir, this would work a lot better for you if you cooperate with our investigation," Agent Krynski added, trying to sound empathetic and relatable.

"Are you threatening my client, Agent Krynski?" Zay asked incredulously. "Are these intimidation Gestapo tactics you are deploying part of official Bureau policy, or are you just freelancing here?"

"I'm simply stating facts. There are high levels of political and public interest pointed squarely at ending the current circus, and all facts point towards this young woman," Agent Krynski answered.

"The facts? *What* facts?" Jax asked, cocking his head as he looked at the agent with surprise. "I'm going to apologize now, because I haven't had a lot of sleep, and I'm cranky this morning, even after two cups of espresso."

"Jax, maybe I should – " Zay interjected.

"No, no, Zay – I got this one," Jax answered. Then, turning to the agents, he assertively explained. "The facts are simple, really. I never personally saw Blair paint anything. You can look at images of the four pieces attributed to 'Omnis Nemo' that the gallery featured at the gala. I came up with that name to protect the artist's anonymity, but if you look closely, they're all landscapes and city landmarks. None of them are political, and not one of them is signed. Now, Crush didn't sell any of those pieces, as you know from the notes with Detective Hernandez; if we had, I'm pretty sure this would be a very different conversation. But think for a moment – IF the Omnis Nemo that we featured is the same artist that's all over the feed right now, isn't it odd their interests would simply change? You just, overnight, decide to go from landscapes to political commentary? And suddenly you start signing your work, where it didn't matter before? It doesn't add up for me."

"Sir, we're not experts in the art world," Agent Wrilley answered respectfully. "We wouldn't know if any of that is unusual or not for an artist. It's just not a compelling enough reason to dismiss the other evidence.

"So, you think there's no chance that after the attention Omnis Nemo received at the gala, and those landscapes being plastered all over the feed... no one decided to be a copy-cat and borrow the name to promote their own work? I mean, are you connected to the feed?" Jax asked somewhat sarcastically.

Agent Krynski looked skeptically at him as she answered, "Sir, be that as it may, the evidence we've seen –"

"What evidence?" Jax exclaimed, "People stealing content from each other and profiting off of it is an everyday thing on the feed; it's literally a business model. You take a beautiful woman like Blair, some clever branding like Omnis Nemo, and you can create an elaborate story for your own purposes. There could be any number of reasons why this played out the way it did. You asked if I had any evidence Blair is ΘN – I don't have ANY! What evidence do you have that says she is?"

"If she is not ΘN, why is everyone else convinced?" Agent Wrilley asked, taking notes on the feed as it streamed through his lenses.

"Well, I suspect my mother had something to do with it. She's already convincing her friends to contact me to illegally purchase original pieces from ΘN, or did you miss Mrs. Anderson storming out of the gallery a few minutes ago?"

"Why would you suspect your mother is involved?" Agent Krynski asked, suddenly less skeptical of what she was hearing.

"I know she was. From what I've inferred, she fed Detective Hernandez this lie about the gallery selling illegal paintings in an effort to help Caldo get out of a drug charge – she all but said it explicitly. She said she was trying to help him in order to protect her investment; you could pull the record. And when this ΘN thing started getting attention, she saw another opportunity! Pull the feed record from just before you came in – you'll hear Mrs. Anderson say as much," Jax reported. Then abruptly he added, "Have you asked Caldo?"

"The artist with the drug charge?" Agent Wrilley asked, shifting uncomfortably in his seat.

"Yes – there are several of his paintings downstairs," Jax said, nodding toward the staircase. "He's still a client here, so I don't want to speak ill of him. But... Now, this is just me... if I were trying to resurrect a failing career, this kind of stunt would be the way to do it. And we know my mother is trying to help him - the level of free marketing exposure ΘN is getting right now is priceless. You guys are the Feds – connect the dots."

Glancing at Zay's face in his feed, he noticed his impromptu attorney looked completely confused and out of his depth. *It would only be a little while longer*, he thought. *Hang in there, buddy.*

"If that's the case – if this is all Caldo and your mother's doing - why did you just tell Ms. Anderson that the young woman from the party had fled the country?" Agent Krynski asked, attempting to catch him off guard.

"Oh, so you DID pull the feed. Good. To answer your questions, I *assume* she has!" Jax exclaimed. "Wouldn't you? You're an unlensed, twenty-three-year-old with no money, no connections, and the cops – well, now the Feds too - everyone thinks you're this terrorist in the news – what do you do? Where do you go when your face gets plastered all over the feed?"

"So, you're saying you don't know for sure," Agent Krynski said, nodding her head slowly as her lips puckered slightly, revealing her frustration.

"Look, Blair and I dated for a while – she came to the gala. We spent some good times together. Frankly, not that it's any of your business, but I think I'm in love with her. The problem is we are just incompatible. I sell art; she makes art. But I can't sell the art she makes because she doesn't want to connect to the feed – she wants to stay living like it was the eighteen-hundreds or something. What am I supposed to do?" Jax answered, doing his best to convincingly mix as much truth as he could with the lie.

"That's not an answer," Agent Krynski responded.

"No – I do not know where she is or where she has gone. I have not had much contact with her; she just said she was leaving. She wouldn't say where," he said honestly.

The two agents looked at each other briefly, and Jax couldn't tell if they were still skeptical or buying what he was suggesting. In the end, there was nothing in his feed, transaction records, or any communication he had that would say otherwise. Unless there was some new information he wasn't aware of, he should be safe, he thought.

"Thank you for your time," Agent Wrilley said as he stood from the sofa, followed shortly after by Agent Krynski.

"My pleasure," Jax responded stoically.

As the two agents descended the staircase leading from his office, Zay finally spoke up, once again, "Hey, Jax?"

"Zay, I'm so sorry to have dragged you into all this," Jax said, apologizing once again for his desperate act.

"For Blair – I'd move mountains. Speaking of which, why don't you head over here for dinner this evening. We can catch up," Zay insisted.

"An offer impossible to refuse – I owe you after this," Jax laughed. "I'll give you all a heads up when I'm on my way."

With that, the feed ended and Bruce sent up his next appointment, Ms. Johansen.

When the eighty-something year old woman finally reached the top of the staircase, Jax greeted her warmly and apologetically offered, "Ms. Johansen – it's lovely as ever to see you. But I have to warn you up front, if you're here about any paintings related to ΘN or Omnis Nemo... I'm afraid I won't be able to help."

"We can pay you... off the books, so to speak," she interjected desperately.

"Thank you for the offer, ma'am. I'm afraid it's simply not possible," he answered apologetically.

Ms. Johansen began shaking her head in frustration and turned back down the staircase, having never even removed her hat or coat.

This is insane, Jax thought to himself. Then walking downstairs toward the main floor of the gallery, he called out to Bruce, "Hey, would you mind screening these appointments – if it's anything related to ƟN or Omnis Nemo, tell them I won't be available until next year."

"Next year? Won't the gallery be sold by then?" Bruce asked, then suddenly understanding he said, "Oh, got it."

"That's exactly right," Jax laughed.

Bruce chuckled slightly before relaying, "Your mother called the gallery line again. She says you're not answering on your personal feed."

"Also exactly right," Jax said with a smile. "You're two for two. One more and it's a hat trick."

"Well, I talked to her," Bruce said, shaking his head as he laughed. "She says she knows nothing about you selling the gallery. She's worried for you." Then, mimicking the old woman's voice said, "It will ruin his reputation, Bruce! He'll never work in this city again!"

"Ah," Jax answered. "What do you think, Bruce?"

"Me?" his assistant answered.

"Yeah, you've known me for years. You've seen this place grow and become successful. What do you think?" he asked.

"Honestly?" he asked.

"Yes – honestly. In a few weeks, I won't own this place anymore – be as honest as you'd like," Jax replied.

"I think you were a damn fool for letting that girl get away. And I'm a little surprised it took you this long to man up and tell that toxic old hag where she could go," Bruce said.

"Ouch," Jax laughed. "But probably fair."

"So why are you standing around here, then? Why aren't you going after her?" Bruce asked, gently berating his boss.

"I don't know where she is," Jax responded honestly as he held out his hands to his side in dismay.

Bruce nodded and ticked his teeth, adding, "Well, you sure messed this one up, didn't you?."

"I know," Jax answered. "But I'm trying to fix it. And on that note, I'm going to head out. Take the rest of the day off. Close the gallery. Hell – take the rest of the week off. Christmas is only days away – go spend time with your people."

In a few quick minutes, Jax was in an automated vehicle on his way to the marina where Blair's boat had been kept. It had occurred to him in the previous days that without lenses, flight travel would be more difficult, saving only privately owned planes. Likewise, trains or ride-share would be impossible. That meant she probably would have taken her sailboat. While she had called the day before and he assumed she had already left, perhaps there was a chance or a trace of her that could be found. Maybe the old man at the marina had seen her or knew something; he was teaching her to sail, after all. There was no way she could flee the country in that old tub, not without help.

When he eventually arrived at the marina, he found it lifeless and empty, even more so than it normally was. Not only was Blair's boat missing, but the entire marina sat quiet and still on the glassy water that surrounded the boats. Not even a duck or seabird appeared to have the courage to disturb the silence. Nothing looked particularly out of place. It was simply as still as a landscape painting.

He noticed many other vessels had been removed from the water for winter and were now stored in the marina's storage lot. They had recently been covered in a white plastic film that hugged the hulls, as if they had been vacuum sealed or melted around the hulls, hugging every angle and corner of each boat. As he walked down the ramp onto the docks, he soon observed movement on one of the few boats that remained in the water, a thirty-something foot powerboat with a black skull and crossbones flag hanging from the bridge. He thought for a moment he recognized the boat as belonging to Blair's old sailor friend, the man he was look-ing for. But then, as he came closer to the boat, he realized there was a different man on board, one whom he recognized.

"Blaze?" he called out.

"Oh, hey!" the man with the bushy black beard responded with a wave. "It's Jax, right? Blair's friend?"

"Yeah," Jax said uneasily. To hear her name mentioned so casu-ally after the hours he had spent worrying about her whereabouts and safety felt oddly surreal.

"Right," Blaze said. Seeing the look of concern on his face, he asked, "Hey, you alright, buddy? You good?"

"I... think so," Jax answered, unsure if he was or wasn't. "I... I guess I was just hoping I would show up here and find her sailboat still in the marina – just some trace of her, I guess."

"Uh huh," Blaze grunted as he began removing the shorelines from the dock cleats on either side of the powerboat. "Hey, you want to give me a hand with that one?" he asked, pointing towards the forward starboard cleat.

"Sure," Jax said as he hurried over to detach the rope. Then, try-ing to keep Blaze talking, he casually asked, "Is this one yours?"

"Nah, just getting her out of the water for the old man. We gotta get her winterized before it freezes. It's supposed to be a cold one," Blaze responded as he warmed up the motor.

"I thought Blair said the old man lived on the boat year-round," Jax said casually. "I was hoping I'd find him here, actually. Just... trying to see if anyone has any information about Blair."

"He does live on it year-round – just usually moves further south for January and February. Mud Island near Memphis or there's some spots down by New Orleans – he likes a change of scenery. What's the use in having a boat if you don't go anywhere, right?" Blaze answered with a friendly smile.

"But he's not here now?" Jax asked quizzically.

"Nope," Blaze answered.

"So, not staying aboard this winter, then?" Jax asked.

Blaze simply shrugged his shoulders and said, "I dunno – just know he asked me to get BB here out of the water for him."

"I'm guessing you haven't heard from Blair either, have you?" Jax said, suspecting the man was being intentionally vague.

"Nah, sorry friend. I'm sure she'll turn up," he said with a polite smile. With that, he pulled the levers of the powerboat's motor, shifting the vessel into reverse and slowly began to back out the slip. As he did, he gave a short wave to Jax, who remained standing on the deck of the marina, lost and alone.

He watched as the powerboat pulled away, heading towards either another part of the marina or a different marina. He couldn't say which. As he walked back up the dock towards the ramp, he considered whether the old man missing at the same time as Blair was a coincidence. He assumed it wasn't, and based solely on Blaze's ambiguous answers, he knew something happened that involved both men. He just couldn't say what.

By the time the rideshare arrived at the marina, it was early afternoon. While it was too early for dinner, he knew he owed Zay an explanation, and they were eager to know what he knew about what was happening with Blair.

When he arrived, he was greeted with a big hug from their daughter, who he heard yelling while he was still in the front yard, "Mom – Blair's boyfriend is here!"

"Zay said you'd be stopping by," Bell said as she greeted him at the door.

"Heard about that, did you?" Jax answered with a slight chuckle.

"Mmmm hmmm," Bell answered. "Sounds like there's more going on than we've heard. Zay's inside. Come on in."

"Thank you," Jax responded. "I suppose a second inquisition is warranted, given all that's happened."

As he entered the kitchen, where the family had gathered, Zay was just starting dinner, only this time, veggie burgers were on the menu.

"Ah, Jaxson – welcome back," Zay said, greeting him as he entered. "You're in for a treat – I make these protein patties with my own special recipe. Tastes just like the real thing!"

"I don't even remember what the real thing tastes like; it's been so long. I was just a kid when they issued the moratorium on animal proteins and dairy," he said with a shrug.

"Well, I'm older than you, and I DO remember what getting a nice, juicy double-cheeseburger was like – HEAVENLY! This is the next best thing, I assure you," Zay answered proudly.

"Can we just skip to the part where you fill us in on Blair?" Bell interjected, annoyed at the developing comradery between her husband and the man whose status in relation to Blair was questionable.

"Honey, don't be rude. I told you – he doesn't know. I was there on the call with the FBI; nobody knows!" Zay responded.

"I'm happy to fill you both in on everything I DO know," Jax added. "But that's probably something we should take offline."

"Offline?" Bell scoffed. "You mean, no lenses?"

"It'd probably be safer, I think?" Jax answered, sounding unsure. "I... I'm not sure what I know and what I don't anymore. And eventually those agents are going to track down this conversation, and I don't want to accidentally leave clues that might lead them to believe something that isn't there."

"I think that's fair, don't you, Bell?" Zay said, nodding in agreement with Jax despite the stern stare on the face of his wife.

"You both sound paranoid." Bell answered, shaking her head in disbelief. "Why on earth would anyone want to track down THIS conversation? Why would the FBI even be interested?"

Jax hesitated to respond and instead remained motionless, waiting in their kitchen. Seeing his reluctance and with a heavy sigh, Bell finally relented, removing the devices connected to her eyes and saying, "There. Happy?"

Zay followed suit, and then turned to Mia, who was coloring at the small table in the kitchen, saying, "Little love, why don't you color upstairs while the adults talk?"

Mia grumbled indiscernibly at being kicked out, citing a need to know what had happened, but she was dismissed all the same.

"Now then," Bell asked. "Why is the FBI coming to your gallery? Why do they suspect this has something to do with those posters that are popping up everywhere?"

Jax took a deep breath, attempting to figure out exactly how much information was enough for them. He then explained as best he could, "When Blair came to the gala, we showed several of her pieces – not for sale, but just to showcase her work as an artist. We attributed them to Omnis Nemo – to be safe. Well, all the attention she got made some powerful people jealous, for lack of a better word. And so, they made allegations against the gallery, against Blair, against me – all of it. My attorney stepped in to help resolve the initial wave, but when this whole thing with ΘN started up..."

"Is Blair... ΘN?" Bell asked directly.

Jax sighed, fearing he would say too much. Even without her lenses, if she knew something, it might slip while she was wearing them. He knew he could trust the Andovers to protect her as best they could, but if they knew the truth, he wondered if they'd even be able to protect themselves. They had housed and harbored her while she completed the paintings, after all. They hadn't known their content violated Safe Speech laws, but if they were later questioned and revealed they knew she was ΘN, it would only be a matter of time before they'd be facing charges as well.

"So that's a... yes? No?" Bell asked.

Zay interjected himself, seeing his wife was getting frustrated, saying, "Jax explained to the FBI that he has never directly seen

Blair paint anything, or sign her name, or sign 'ΘN' to any painting. Unless that was a lie, Jax?"

"Not a lie," Jax answered.

"What kind of crap is that? That's lawyer speak, for *I don't want to answer your question!*" she spat, annoyed by the two men's elusiveness.

"Let me ask you a question, Bell," Jax answered, brushing aside her annoyance. "Would you love her any less?"

Bell looked visibly discomforted by the question and bit her lower lip as she shook her head in understanding.

"So, do you really want to know then? Maybe next time you see Blair, ask her – preferably somewhere where Safe Speech laws don't exist," Jax said.

The annoyance on her face was unmistakable, but she clearly understood his reluctance was intentional and meaningful rather than some aloof game he was playing. "Alight... fine," she answered. "But where then?"

"I dropped by the marina on my way here, just to see if her boat was still there – maybe to see if she'd come back, if anyone knew. I don't know," Jax answered with a shrug. "Safe, I hope. She called me and said she was going away for a while, but she wouldn't say much else. I'm hoping there are some clues – something. But the only guy I saw at the marina said he hadn't seen her or Old Man Agnew, her boat neighbor, if that's the right word for it."

"You think he's with her?" Zay asked, deducing the two might be connected.

"She told me he had been teaching her to sail. Now she's gone, he's gone, the boat's gone... and she got the boat from Tanner and Lillian – but from what I can tell, their shop was vandalized. Folks on the feed think they're caught up with ΘN; they had a painting in the shop by ΘN. They were selling prints of it," Jax answered. "But that's about the extent of what I have been able to put together. I'm not even sure the FBI knows about the connection with

Agnew or Tanner and Lillian – and I'm certainly not volunteering it. I just thought the two of you should know. I think she's with friends. I think they're sailing for... friendlier shores, I guess. Wherever that is."

"Good," Bell answered. "If she's safe, that's all I really care about. And I'm sorry for... verbally assaulting you like that. I just worry about her."

"We all do," Jax answered. "But if there's a record of what we suspect, if they know who's important in her life, every call – every written correspondence – every purchase you make... it's all going to be under a microscope. I think we just have to trust that she's going to figure this out and let us know when she comes up for air."

Zay nodded, understanding the complexity of the situation, and even Bell looked more relieved.

Jax stayed for dinner and they chatted mostly about all that was happening with the posters in the media, the hype that it had created, and what it meant for the artist who painted them. Throughout the course of the day, the sensation they were causing had only grown.

"From what I've seen, at some point in the early morning, some new posters were discovered, pasted to the walls of several libraries, churches, and even a police station. It's pretty ballsy..." Bell explained over a glass of wine.

"I saw one pasted on a freeway overpass as I was coming home from work. Not even sure how they would get up there to pull that off, but there it was," Zay answered.

"I was digging into it this morning, but with everything going on throughout the day, I haven't really caught up," Jax answered.

"Well, it sounds like it's only getting bigger," Bell said. "For better or worse, probably both. There are talks of people meeting up... silent marches and what not. Even since you've been here, there's new reports of delays to the robocars, operations being limited. I guess we'll see."

"We will," he shrugged. "I just hope it doesn't turn into something... worse."

He didn't stay long that night, fearing the rideshare could take hours to get back to his home from St. Charles. After it finally arrived, and he started the journey home, it quickly became clear the reports of delays were understated. At several points, the automated vehicle re-routed; one segment of Interstate 70 had been shut down completely, causing backups on Interstate 170 and Interstate 64. The trip ended up taking a full two hours instead of the simple thirty-minute ride he'd grown accustomed to.

Once he reached his loft and found his bed, he was exhausted. Despite his desperation for sleep, he thought he'd take just one more look to see if any new information was available that would help piece the puzzle together. Instead, he found only political commentary. The democratic socialists were already pointing towards the Native princess painting in an effort to co-opt the influence of "ΘN", decrying government negligence in underserved communities, which must have been a product of capitalist greed.

That's quite enough of that, he thought. Then, after removing his lenses, he quickly fell asleep.

~ 17 ~

The muddy Mississippi was as calm as it had been that morning as they reached the outskirts of New Orleans. Tanner had been at the helm throughout the night, and once she had brewed a cup of tea, Blair joined him on deck to take over.

"That for me?" Tanner asked hopefully.

"Can be, but then you won't sleep," Blair laughed as she extended the ceramic travel mug towards him.

"Haven't been getting much of that anyway with all that's going on," he replied, taking the mug. He then looked at it hesitantly and handed it back to her. "Nah, it's ok."

"Hey, I know you're worried," Blair answered. "We all are. But I promise you, when we get where we're going, I'm going to make it right by you guys."

"Stop," he replied, shaking his head. "I don't blame you for all this, neither does Lil. We're the ones who made the prints; we wanted to hang the painting in the shop. That was all our call – we practically talked you into it. This is just all rolling out in a way none of us saw coming."

"Still, the shop – all the work you put into it, and it was really taking off – it's just... horrible," Blair answered empathetically.

"It's just a building, B. Just a building. My home, my entire world, is that lusty, dark-haired woman below deck. So long as she's safe, it doesn't matter where we go," he answered as he continued staring downriver behind the helm. After a few minutes of silence, he added, "What am I doing? It's your turn!"

Blair laughed as she took her place at the helm, steering their small vessel as it crawled through the muddy brown water. A large cargo ship was traveling towards them several hundred yards off the port bow, and she needed to ensure it had plenty of clearance and distance. By the time the ship's wake began rocking her sailboat, Tanner had already descended below deck for sleep.

The Old Man had insisted they resupply again before they reached the gulf, and it was her job to get them closer to the marina before he'd take over bringing the ship in. As they inched closer and closer towards the city, traffic on the river became more noticeable and hectic, but after several days of practice, she felt like she was capable of at least not running into anything.

Nearing the hub of the city, off to the port side, she was surprised to see enormous cruise ships hulking above the waterline. Even from a distance, their size was intimidating, but fortunately, Lillian and Agnew joined her on deck before they reached the heart of the city, and the old sailor quickly took control of the vessel to be safe.

"Be a dear and lower the mainsail, Blair," he said as he took her place behind the wheel.

Blair jumped to, attaching the line of front sail to the winch as she began cranking to lower the sail. "Are we going under power for a while?"

"The river bends northeast for a bit and then back to the south. It's squirrely around the city, so rather than repeatedly resetting the sails, I think it's best. We'll top off fuel when we get to the marina," the old man replied instructively.

Blair nodded her head, understanding his reasoning, and then carefully set herself to ensure the lowered sail had not folded unevenly and the ropes were untangled. As they trudged along, she sat with her legs dangling off the bow, enjoying the view of the city as an old paddlewheel boat came into view, followed by ferries that moved people from one side of the river to the other.

"The French Quarter is off that direction, not sure if you can see it," the old man shouted towards the front of the boat where she sat sightseeing.

"I wish we could stop and enjoy some of the music," she shouted back wistfully.

"Maybe in better times, dear," he answered as he continued to steer the vessel.

As they rounded the twist in the river that nearly encapsulated the old city, Lillian joined her at the bow, and the two giggled as they dangled their feet over the edge of the deck playfully.

"You good, doll?" she asked quietly as they sat together enjoying the morning.

"Sure," Blair answered. "It could be a lot worse."

Lillian nodded with understanding as she answered, "Still a long way to go."

"Yup," Blair responded. "Still plenty that can go wrong... but I'm glad I'm here with friends."

Lillian reached over and wrapped her arm around her friend's shoulder, giving her a gentle hug as they remained in silence with their lower legs and feet dangling over the edge of the boat.

As they stared off into the distance, Blair began noticing more pilot ships and tugboats were filling the river. Agnew must have seen her studying them as eventually he called out, "They're for helping the bigger ships avoid the shallows; shouldn't be too much of a problem for us. We're fairly nimble."

Blair nodded, thinking she understood. There was still so much to learn about this adventure they were committed to, and the enormity and complexity of their undertaking made her feel naïve for her previous comments that they would somehow make the trip without his expertise.

Within the hour, they began heading south once again, and the old man pointed off to the starboard bow, saying, "That's Belle Chasse up ahead... We'll find a place to dock and take on supplies.

Why don't you head below deck and stay out of sight for a bit? Lillian can help me tie her up."

"You bet," Lillian answered, still sitting beside her.

The sailboat turned slightly, almost unnoticeably as the small buildings in the distance grew larger as they grew nearer the southern suburb.

"That's my cue," Blair laughed as she finally rose from her forward perch and carefully made her way to the aft of the ship.

"I'm bringing her up on the starboard, Lil. Be ready with the bowline," Agnew called out as she descended below deck.

From within the cabin, she could hear the change in the motor as the ship slowed and then puttered at a crawl as they neared the dock. After several more minutes, the motors cut entirely, and she could feel the weight of Lillian rock the boat as she leaped onto the dock and began tying off.

Once the ship was secured, the hatch of the cabin opened to reveal Lillian's smiling face as she said, "Agnew says we'll be a few hours tops – need anything?"

"Nope," Blair answered. "Just be safe – maybe wear some sunglasses or a hat or something?"

"I don't think it's my face they'll be looking for, doll. But I promise we'll be careful," Lillian answered warmly. "Just hang tight, relax. It'll all be fine. Tanner's going to sleep for hours, but wake him if something happens. The old man says he has some friends here, so..."

"Of course he does," Blair laughed uneasily.

With her painting supplies packed away to make room for passengers, painting was out of the question. Instead, she looked around for a book, and found one Tanner had brought along, Hemmingway's *The Old Man and the Sea.*

"A little on the nose, isn't it, Tanner?" she chuckled to herself as she sat down to read. As the hours passed, she soon became disinterested in the story, lacking any appreciation for fishing or discussions about baseball. It was something to do to pass the time.

Eventually, she heard a commotion from the dock nearby and peered out the window, searching for signs of their return. Sure enough, Lillian was quickly spotted, carrying several large bags of groceries toward the boat, while the old man followed on her heels. Then, just before they reached the boat, she heard the unfamiliar voice of a third man speaking.

"Good morning," she heard the voice say faintly through the walls of the cabin.

"Mornin," Agnew replied gruffly.

As she once again peered through the window, she noticed the unknown man was wearing a blue, military style uniform. Looking further, she observed a medium-sized metal powerboat with an orange bottom. Along the hull, she saw the words COAST GUARD written in large, block lettering.

"Sir, do you have a moment?" the voice asked Agnew, who had continued walking after exchanging pleasantries.

"Sure, how can I help you?" Agnew answered gruffly.

"I'd like to link you over an image of a suspect we've been looking for. She's reported to have a sailboat just like that one you're headed towards," the uniformed man said loudly enough for her to hear.

"Sure thing," Agnew answered. Then moments later he said, "Whew! SHE IS SOMETHING. Can't say that I've seen her, but I sure hope I find her before you young fellas!"

She heard the young officer laugh in response, and some indistinguishable comment was made in response. For several seconds, she couldn't make out what exactly was being said, but eventually she heard Agnew's voice once again saying, "Nah, that's the issue – this one's Astrea's Muse. Named her myself when I picked her up after my last tour."

"Oh, where'd you serve?" she heard the officer ask.

"Panama, mostly," Agnew answered gruffly.

"I've heard that was a rough haul," the officer answered.

"We all do our part," Agnew answered.

Several more indistinguishable comments were made before she felt the boat shift under the weight of someone climbing aboard. When the hatch finally opened, Lillian was smiling and moving calmly as if nothing had just transpired, as calm as the glassy water that surrounded them.

Without even looking at Blair, who was hunched down on her hands and knees on the small sofa within the cabin, Lillian began slipping the bags of supplies they had purchased into the lower cabin. As soon as she was below deck, she quietly added, "Just stay there, and stay still."

One by one, she brought the bags of supplies into the cabin, as Agnew started the motor and began working on casting off the lines that held the boat against the dock. Then they were once again underway.

Blair waited several minutes for the tone of the motor to change, a signal they had returned once again to the river's channel. Then, carefully and cautiously, she opened the hatch to the cabin and peaked out.

"All clear, dear," the old man called out from behind the helm. Returning to the deck, she looked around for Lillian, who was back at the bow, preparing their sales. "So, everything went ok then?" she asked.

"Ah, never you mind that," the old man said with a wink. "Just some puddle pirates doing their job."

"So, I'm guessing we have everything we need, then?" she asked cautiously.

"Yes, ma'am," Agnew answered with a smile. "We should reach the gulf by sunset, and we're just about to raise the sails. Maybe you could give Lillian a hand?"

"I'm on it," Blair answered as she moved forward to assist her friend. While Lillian appeared to be just about finished, she took a moment to see if she could weasel out more information than the sparse amount she had received from Agnew.

"So, no big deal then?" she asked as she helped straighten the sheet to prepare for the winch.

"Looks like it," Lillian responded without confidence. "My heart about beat out of my chest there for a minute when those Coast Guard boys started in. But hey, relax. It's all good. We're good. Everything's fine."

"I about died!" Blair exclaimed suddenly. "I was trying to peek out the window, and I had my ear pressed up against the hull trying to hear what was being said. I was sure they had us!"

Lillian took a second to stop and adjust the red bandana that was holding up her hair. To Blair, it looked almost habitual, as if she was exercising the nervousness that she still felt. Then, after she had finished, she simply smiled and said, "Hey, we're good. The worst should be behind us now... Let's get this sail up."

As they made their way to the stern, Blair soon found the crank tool and began working the winch as the sail gradually climbed up the mainmast. Next, they situated the sheets for the mizzen sail, and raised it as well.

"Well done, young ladies," Agnew shouted. "I'll make sailors of you both by the time this journey is over."

"Thank you, Cap'n," Blair said with a smile. "Do you think the wind will hold?"

"Should be fine. We've got broad reach for the moment. Forecast says it should hold for a least a few days... it just takes the time it takes," he answered.

"Look at you sounding all pirate-y!" Lillian laughed.

"I've been practicing!" Blair answered giddily. Then, turning back to Agnew, she asked, "Would you like me to take a turn?"

"Be my guest, young lady," the old man answered with a smile.

Under full sail, the weight of the boat felt light in her hands, even as the water became choppy as they continued further south down the river. After a few hours, the various channels and outlets of the river began making it intimidating for her as she began second guessing which part of the river was the channel. The small patches of farmland that surrounded them were so low-lying she could barely see them from their short height above the water. Agnew stayed by her side diligently the whole way, only gesturing here and there when she looked at him for reassurance.

At last, she realized they were about to hit open water, which was still brown and muddy for some time as the contents of the river emptied into the gulf that lay beyond. The only land that remained consisted of long lines of rock jetties that lined the shipping lane, eliminating any mystery of where the channel ran in the brown soup like water. "I think we're close!" she shouted excitedly.

"Just about there," Agnew answered behind her. Then gently patting her on the shoulder he said, "You did well – that's no easy stretch of water. I'm proud of you."

Blair blushed at the compliment, still feeling it was undeserving. She knew she probably would have panicked had he not been within reach the whole way, and without thinking, she turned from the helm for a moment and hugged him tightly, saying, "Thank you, Agnew."

"Happy to, dear," he answered with a warm smile. "Now, let's get the hard part done. Just up ahead, where the water starts to blue, check your compass and point her dead south."

"Yessir!" Blair exclaimed as she quickly returned to having both hands at the helm.

Tanner, who had snuck onto deck some time earlier in the afternoon while Blair was concentrating, sat at the bow with Lillian as the two held hands while the boat sailed forward. "You did it, B!" he called out as he looked back towards her.

"Woo-hoo!" Lillian cried out next to him.

"Next stop, Mexico!" Blair shouted excitedly back at them.

The small group celebrated mildly into the early evening, talking and laughing and telling stories from back when Tanner used to sail. Eventually Agnew's stories of trying to teach a younger version of Tanner came up as he explained, "He wasn't nearly as eager to learn as you were, my dear. A head full of rocks, I used to say."

"No denying that," Tanner laughed. "I just never had the memory for all the terms and names for things. But I think I have a good feel for it – I'm a little rusty, but I think it started coming back somewhere around Memphis."

"Oh, Memphis, huh?" Lilian asked. "Then what happened that one night... where were we? It was near that battlefield and the big casino—"

"Vicksburg," Blair chuckled quietly.

"That's it! What happened at Vicksburg, babe? That thing with the tanker?"

"What? We didn't hit it. I just got distracted by the lights, is all. No harm done," he said defensively.

"Oh, oh, ok, babe. You're right," Lillian answered as she gently rubbed his shoulders.

They continued on for a while until Blair drifted off in her seat at the back of the cockpit. "I'm going to call it," she finally said. "But wake me up if you need me."

"I'm the night shift, B," Tanner answered dutifully. There's a whole bunch of ocean in front of us. So long as we avoid the lights of other ships, I'm not sure there's a good reason we all won't get some sleep."

"Okay, good night then," she answered, too tired to insist otherwise.

The next day and several that followed they sailed on uneventfully. Tedium and the boredom of simply sailing gradually began to take its toll on the small group, but there was little to be done.

The vast blue emptiness of the ocean was a marvel Blair had never seen before, but after several days of staring at nothing, it too lost some of its luster. Fortunately, the early December water of the gulf was relatively smooth, and the wind stayed mostly consistent. At first, they busied themselves taking turns playing card games, until at some point a gust of wind carried several of the cards overboard. Eventually, Blair dug a sketchbook out of one of her stored boxes and began working on portraits of each of them, more to keep her hands busy when they weren't at the helm. Tanner and Lillian used their free time to draw as well, only they focused on new tattoo designs they could use down the road. For his part, the old man seemed perfectly at peace on the water, needing no diversion other than watching the horizon ahead.

On the morning of the sixth day, a few hours after Blair had taken her turn at the helm, Agnew joined her on deck as usual, and after greeting her said, "Not far from here, we should be coming up on Scorpion Reef."

"Oh yeah? I was beginning to think we might be lost," Blair said jokingly.

"Nah," he answered in a low, raspy voice. "I know exactly where we are."

"And where's that exactly?" she asked playfully.

"Just a bit of ocean. South of Louisiana. North of the Yucatan," he said with a smile.

"Oh, silly me for doubting," she laughed. "So this scorpion reef... are there scorpions?"

"Not that I know of," he said without providing further explanation as to the name. "Just keep a lookout for breakers. Only a few parts of the reef are above the waterline. It'd be a shame to run aground so close to our destination."

Realizing the potential seriousness of running into a reef, her lackadaisical demeanor from the last few days suddenly vanished as she again focused on the task at hand.

"What's got you spooked?" Lillian asked as she joined Blair on deck from the cabin below.

"Cap'n says we need to watch out for a reef up ahead. Scorpion Reef," she answered, scanning the horizon for any sign it may be closer than she expected.

"Why Scorpion Reef? Is it full of scorpions or something?" Lillian asked, confused.

"That's what I asked!" Blair laughed in response.

"Dumb name if there's no scorpions on it," Lillian said with a shrug.

Within the hour, Blair saw small white lines on the horizon ahead, and as they came closer, it was clear she had found the reef system Agnew had spoken of. Without hesitation, the old man came up beside her and began pointing out how she should go about navigating it and where they should drop anchor.

"Are we stopping?" Lillian asked from her seat at the rear of the cockpit.

"We don't have to," Agnew answered. "But the water here is some of the nicest in the Caribbean. It's uninhabited, save for an occasionally manned Mexican Navy outpost... I thought you ladies might enjoy a swim as a change of pace."

Blair looked at Lillian, smiling wildly at the idea of getting to swim in the beautiful turquoise water before them. Lillian's response was equally ecstatic, and she quickly disappeared below deck in search of a pair of binoculars with which she could see the potential diversion that lay ahead. A few moments later, she was standing on the bow, staring into the binoculars and gesturing toward the western end, just as Agnew had suggested.

"It looks like there is a small island... a beach, even. If we can get close enough..." she shouted back at Blair behind the helm.

"Let's drop the sails and go in slow," Agnew said as more of a suggestion than a command. "You'll want to stay to the west of her until we get close. Then keep a close on the depth finder as we crawl in."

It took some attention and patience to bring Astrea's Muse close to the island. To ensure they wouldn't damage the keel, they dropped anchor while they remained in fifteen feet of water, still dozens of yards from shore. As Angew provided instruction on lowering the anchor, Lillian disappeared below deck briefly, only to return a short time later with a shirtless Tanner in tow.

"I heard it's time for swimmin!" he yawned, still half asleep from his long night behind the helm.

"Almost," Blair laughed. "We just need to check the anchor caught and we'll be set."

"You need sunscreen first, babe," Lillian interjected as she began rubbing lotion over her husband's chest. "You too, B. That porcelain white skin will fry out here."

After checking the anchor and finishing their personal preparations, they appeared ready to enjoy an afternoon in the sun. Only Agnew declined the opportunity, saying, "I'm happy to stay aboard and get some rest... this old man hasn't been around so many people in years. It'd do me some good to have some quiet."

"I'll bring you back a scorpion," Tanner responded with a smile.

"Look hard, Tanner. I hear they're sneaky," the old pirate laughed.

Without warning, Tanner took a few quick steps and jumped into the ocean, sending a splash that sprayed up onto the deck.

"Yup, definitely staying here," Agnew said with a smile. "You kids have fun. Just... better be safe and be back by sunset. We can stay here for the evening."

Lillian followed, jumping into the water in a tank top that covered her undergarments in place of a swimsuit. Blair did the same.

When she hit the water, the cool, refreshing saltiness washed over her. It had been years since she had been swimming, and for a moment, she struggled to keep her head above water. Then a large foam object fell from above, striking her on the head.

"Wear it," the old man shouted. "We didn't come all this way to see you drown at some spit of sand a hundred miles from nowhere."

Blair fumbled for a moment, embarrassed at her overconfidence, but with a little effort, the life preserver was secured around her chest and snapped in place. Then, as quickly as she could, she quickly began kicking in the water to catch up with Lillian and Tanner, who were gradually making their way to shore.

Even with the floating vest, getting to the beach took some effort, but fortunately, the sandbar extended further than she imagined. Still dozens of yards from shore, she found herself able to stand. Then, after several steps, while delicately avoiding large pieces of coral that rose from the sand, she discovered the water was only waist deep. As she continued, it gradually became shallower until she was less than knee deep and nearing the shore.

The small island was sparsely covered in small grasses and driftwood that had found its way ashore; the island and the beach were teaming with wildlife. Pelicans and other seabirds seemed unbothered by their presence, and even wading in the water, small schools of fish rushed by their legs ambivalently.

"Paradise," Lillian said as Blair approached behind her.

"It's beautiful," she answered. "I... wish Jax was here to see it."

"Me too, kiddo," she said, putting her arm around her friend as they wandered the remaining distance up onto the sand, where Tanner had sprawled out after swimming the distance as quickly as he could.

Leaving Tanner to relax where he had fallen, heaving and out of breath, Blair walked a way with Lillian at her side, enjoying the sunshine and laughing at the odd little crabs that scurried along the sand everywhere they went.

"Must be harder for you," Lillian said abruptly after they neared the end of the tiny island.

"What's that?" Blair asked.

"Leaving him... leaving your mom, the Andovers... it's been your entire world. At least I got to bring mine along. I can't imagine having to walk away from all the people that I love," she said pensively.

"Just for now," Blair said, kicking away a small piece of driftwood with her sandy toes. "When we get there, I'm going to figure out how to get word back to them... to let them know where we are."

"How do you plan to do that exactly? Have you figured it out yet?" Lillian asked casually.

"Maybe a treasure map of sorts," Blair laughed. "Best I can think of."

"Hm," Lillian mouthed in response. "I suppose we'll just have to see how clever this man of yours is... I could tattoo turn-by-turn directions on Tanner's palm, and he'd probably still not be able to find me."

"Just gotta have faith, I guess. Maybe some hope and luck too," Blair sighed, staring off into the clear turquoise water that lay just beyond.

~ 18 ~

Three weeks have passed without word, he thought. *He should be hearing something.*

As he showered before work, he used his lenses briefly to check for updates, but it was more of the same. The protests against government surveillance had grown. Transportation had been shut down completely to prevent more people from gathering in the city, and he realized he'd be walking to work once again.

"That's enough of that," he said aloud, removing the lenses from his eyes as he finished his morning routine and looked for something to eat for breakfast. Without wearing his lenses regularly, there had been no grocery deliveries and his refrigerator was near barren. On that morning, a questionably aged jar of pickles would have to suffice.

When he reached the bottom floor of the building, he wasted no time looking for a ride; there were none to be had. Instead, he began walking the mile as he had for at least a week.

At least its exercise, he concluded as he made his way northward, up the block that was lined with townhomes and condo complexes that catered to affluent urban professionals. After the second block, he reached the outskirts of Forest Park. Cutting through the park saved time, and from the past few days, he'd learned this route could mostly avoid the large groups of protestors that had been forming at different landmarks throughout the city.

Unfortunately, as soon as he reached the roundabout near the zoo, he was stopped by a group of National Guardsman who had blocked the entrance to the park with their large, tank-like armored personnel carrier.

"Can't go this way, sir," the Guardsman at the front of the group said as he approached. "Forest Park's closed."

"It's never closed," Jax responded stubbornly.

"It is now, sir. I suggest you find another way around," the Guardsman replied sternly.

"Can you tell me the best way to get to Central West End, then? What's open, what's closed – I have no idea..." Jax said with a frustrated side.

"Closures are all posted on the City's feed in real time, sir. Check your feed," the Guardsman answered in a curt voice, signaling it was the end of their conversation.

"Great," Jax answered, faking a smile. "Much appreciated."

Returning the direction he came, Jax turned eastward down Oakland Avenue as he began walking the long way around the southern edge of the large city park, paralleling the interstate that was also closed. As he passed the Science Center, he discovered the parking lot was empty.

Must be closed too, he thought.

Then, a block further, the parking lot of the high school was similarly barren.

With a deep sigh of frustration, he returned to South Kingshighway Boulevard, where he once again turned north toward the eastern end of the park. Yet as soon as he crossed the overpass, it too was blocked by recently erected barriers and large groups of National Guardsmen.

"Great," he said aloud to himself, as he turned around and headed south once again. Then, from the height of the overpass, he noticed an old pedestrian walkway that passed over the interstate, and more importantly, several people were using it to cross from Forest Park Southeast into Central West End. He knew it was his best chance, and reinvigorated, he began walking down the grassy hill next to the freeway on-ramp until he was on the small street that ran between the nearby red brick townhomes and the freeway. By that point, his socks were soaked from the wet grass, which made the trip even more annoying, and just before reaching the pedestrian overpass, he took a moment to clean the small cuttings of grass from his otherwise pristine dress shoes. As he did, he heard a voice behind him say, "You going to the gathering, too?"

Looking up, he discovered an older teenager, dressed in baggy black clothes and carrying a backpack. The young man's face was acne scarred, and his hair looked greasy like it had not been washed in days. "Afraid not," Jax answered politely as he finished wiping the remaining debris from his footwear.

"You're missing out, man... We could use more suits down there. It's mostly just been kids... college students and other rebels," the young man answered.

"Maybe some other time," Jax answered with a polite smile.

"Suit yourself, man," the young man answered as he passed him by, continuing over the overpass.

Jax followed behind him a short distance, not wanting to be directly associated with any of the trouble the city was currently seeing; he had received enough attention and didn't need more. Yet, as soon as they reached the far side of the overpass, the young man quickly disappeared into a large crowd of people that was marching down Clayton towards the US Government building located a block or two away.

As the large group of protestors moved en masse, he began hearing slogans being chanted within the crowd. Most were wearing masks, which he assumed were their attempts to avoid facial recognition in the feed. Many had hoods with bandanas covering all but their eyes. While their chanting was not particularly clever, they were loud, and they were many.

"TURN *ON* FREEDOM! TURN OFF SURVEILLANCE!" they roared as the column slowly moved down Clayton Avenue.

Jax turned westward, attempting to move away from what was likely to be another disastrous altercation like those he had seen hundreds of times over the past week on the feed. The protests were in every major city and many of the smaller ones as well. He wasn't even sure if it had anything to do with ΘN at this point. From what he'd seen, Blair's work may have sparked the situation, but the administration's response was like gasoline for that spark. As he walked away from the large march behind him, he knew it would end the way they all had — rubber bullets, batons, and dogs. Eventually, someone in the mob would throw something serious – maybe a brick or a flaming bottle of liquor. That seemed to be the line that had to be crossed before the drone swarms appeared.

After turning north once again, he found himself at the southern corner of the large hospital complex at the southern end of Central West End. As he passed by, snow began falling to coat the road and the autonomous emergency vehicles labeled with the names of districts around the city. They arrived at the hospital in a steady trickle, one or two at a time; they were the only vehicles he had seen operating for days. As they pulled into the emergency services area, he watched as the wounded were hurried indoors.

Still several blocks to go, he thought.

When he eventually arrived, he found Bruce sitting at his desk quietly.

"Why bother?" he asked as he came through the doors.

"Nowhere else to be... and I'm pretty sure I don't get paid for sitting at home," Bruce answered glibly as he blinked his way through the feed.

"Can I just pay you to stay home until this passes? Does that work?" Jax said, only half joking.

"I mean, you could... but even with all of this, there's a business to run, I think," his assistant answered with a laugh.

"Any news on the escrow, funding, any of that?" he asked as he removed his coat and headed toward his office.

"Funds should go through soon, from what I can tell. I just sent over the final documents we received last night – the final numbers, the disclosures, it's all there," Bruce answered. Then breaking his concentration on his feed for a moment, he looked to Jax and with a subtle smirk and said, "In other, *positive* news, the new owners have decided to make me an 'Operations Manager' for the gallery, in your absence."

"What does... what exactly is an Operations Manager?" Jax asked as he started up the stairs.

"I think it means they want me to do your job, but not pay me the kind of money you make... that's the gist of it, I think," Bruce sighed, joggling his head in amusement. "Still sorting out the details, but at least I still have a job, right?"

"I told you not to worry about it; they'd be fools to lose you," Jax laughed as he continued his way toward his office. Then, looking back, he said, "Hey, talk them into letting you have my office. I bet they'd go for that."

After making his espresso, he sat down to review the details surrounding the sale. He made more from commissions in a year than he would selling the business, but in the end, the price was fair. As he continued looking through the details of the deal, Bruce appeared at the top of the stairs, saying, "Hey, not sure you saw this. I know you've been disconnecting with all the junk on the feed right now. But this um... package arrived for you last night. Air courier left it outside; even the drones are acting scared right now."

Jax looked up briefly at the long cardboard cylinder that he had carried with him to the office, and with little thought, he said, "You can just... set it on the sofa or something."

"Do you want me to just open it for you? I'm not doing anything else... it's not like we have appointments in all this mess," Bruce asked.

"Knock yourself out," Jax answered, returning the paperwork related to the sale.

As he read the last of the terms, he worked out how much he would pay in commission to his agent for the sale from the price. Even then, the proceeds were sufficient for him to start over somewhere, he figured.

"Um... boss... Jax!" Bruce said, attempting to get his attention.

"Yeah," Jax answered, only half paying attention.

"You're probably going to want to see this yourself," Bruce answered as he moved towards Jax's desk and began unrolling a canvas across the surface. When he unrolled it, he discovered the painting was from the perspective of someone looking down onto a young woman with crimson hair standing in knee deep, light blue water surrounded by flamingos. She was scantily clad in a white negligee, but looked more the style of innocence or purity than sexuality.

It's not the ocean, he thought. More like a lagoon.

"Is it from... her?" Bruce asked, careful not to name the artist as they both were currently connected to the feed.

"Maybe," Jax answered. "Was there a return address?"

Bruce returned the cylindrical tube in which the painting had been sent and began inspecting it, only moments later to answer with, "No luck."

Looking closer into the image, Jax knew there had to be some clues or indicators of some kind. Blair was smart and well read; she was too clever to make it obvious. As he looked carefully at the painting, he saw the woman was holding a conch shell in her outstretched hand, from which a burst of light was radiating. It was central in the image and unmistakably a riff on the goddess Astrea.

"What am I missing?" he muttered to himself as he continued looking.

It was then he noticed an odd, secondary light source in the form of a light greenish blue that emanated from the water. It caused the birds nearest to it to appear pinker, while others in the background remained as dark silhouettes.

"I think those are flamingos," Bruce interjected as he examined it at his side.

As he continued looking, far off in the background behind the central figure, in the top right corner of the painting, he noticed the faint silhouette of a Mayan style pyramid, barely discernible from the remaining dark background. The top of the pyramid was unmistakable; he knew he had seen it before in pictures or videos – somewhere on the feed.

As quickly as he could, Jax began scanning the feed for images of Mayan pyramids, and the first image that appeared was one of the most well-known.

"Chichen Itza", he whispered to himself.

"I don't want to hear anything too specific, just in case," Bruce said as he stepped away from the painting. "I'll leave you to it. Maybe I can see about booking you a flight to go see that big Mayan pyramid; you could use a vacation..."

"Thank you, Bruce – I really appreciate it," he answered as his assistant made his way down the stairs.

"Okay, Blair – somewhere with a lagoon in the Yucatan. And it's known for some bioluminescent sea life and flamingos..." he said out loud to himself.

Returning to the feed, he searched for any combination of "Yucatan," "Bioluminescence," and "Flamingos." The first result that appeared referenced Isla Holbox, a small island known for its art community.

Having found his answer, Jax rolled the painting back up and returned it to the tube in which it had arrived. He then immediately headed downstairs, painting in hand.

"I need a flight to Mexico," he said as he reached the gallery floor.

"Already done. I just linked it over," Bruce answered. "You'll have to stop in Dallas, and once you get to Merida, you're on your own. It leaves late this evening, so there's time."

"You're a gem – a true jewel," Jax said, pointing at his assistant excitedly.

"I know," Bruce said emphatically. "Just keep me in mind once you have your new thing going... I like margaritas too!"

"You got it," Jax said, heading for the door. Then suddenly he turned and said, "How am I going to get to the airport? There's no ride service right now."

"Well, like my mother used to say, you could always use the wheels that God gave you," Bruce suggested.

"It's got to be six or seven miles... in dress shoes with wet socks... and all this madness going on," Jax answered, considering the difficulty he was facing.

"The things we do for love..." Bruce answered with a dramatic sigh.

"Indeed," Jax laughed. "I'm linking over to you a power of attorney. The escrow info is all in the paperwork; the final documents just need a signature and the funds will transfer. Help me out on this, and I'll send you a nice Christmas bonus when I get where I'm going."

"Sure thing – happy to," Bruce said with a sincere smile. "And no special bonus is needed. Just keep me in mind..."

"You have my word," Jax answered as he stormed out of the gallery.

As he began his trek westward, the daunting hike he had ahead of him weighed on his mind as his wet socks sloshed and squelched in his leather shoes. After two blocks, he saw a coffee shop he was familiar with in the short distance ahead, and as he came closer, he noticed one patron who had recently entered the shop parked and locked his bicycle just out front.

Jax stopped in front of the small shop and waited for the college age man to exit, only to immediately stop him with a proposition.

"I will pay you ten thousand dollars for the use of your bicycle – are you interested?" he said directly to the man who looked at him like he was mad.

"Get real, man. This is some kind of scam. Nobody pays that kind of money for a bike," he said, shaking his head as he moved to unlock it.

"Send me your link info, and I'll pay you right now. Easy money. I need to get to the airport; I'm kind of desperate," Jax answered him, trying to convey his seriousness.

The man stopped for a second and looked at him, trying to figure out what the catch was in this offer. Having just finished with the combination lock on the cable, he pulled the cable together and reattached it along the bicycle's crossbar, eyeing Jax as he did. Then, just before he climbed aboard, he looked at him and said, "Okay... send me the money. And if it comes through, it's all yours. Worst case, I get scammed out of a bike I bought for three hundred at a thrift store."

"That's quite a markup," Jax said through his teeth.

"You offered it, man. Unless this is some kind of scam," he replied, still uncertain if his time was being wasted.

"Send the link – I'm Jaxon Wadsworth the fourth. Should pop right up," Jax answered.

Moments later, the man's contact information appeared on Jax's lenses and he initiated payment. "Ibrahim, it's been a pleasure doing business with you," he said as he took the bicycle from the man with a smile.

"Holy crap, dude. You were serious?" the man answered as payment came through.

Ungracefully, he attempted to climb onto the machine with Blair's painting tucked under his arm, only to nearly toppled over. He then recalled his last experience and immediately climbed off the contraption to tuck his pant legs back into his socks and loosen his tie. Then, after securing the painting, he was off.

"Thanks again, dude," the man called out as Jax rode on.

He followed Lindell Boulevard westward along the northern end of Forest Park. While the National Guard was posted at the entrances, he hoped he would encounter less difficulty moving away from the city than he had moving through it. That hope faded fairly quickly as he came to the university.

Still a few blocks away, a large group of students had gathered on the lawn outside of the university's art museum and the western border of Forest Park. Likewise, one of the armored personnel carriers turned onto the street directly in front of him. Taking no chances, Jax turned up the same street to head the opposite direction. Then, several blocks into the nearby neighborhood, he turned left again and continued westward along the parkway. By the time he reached Melville, the north-south road his lenses were navigating to, he could hear the buzzing of drones above.

"Focus, Jax," he said aloud to himself as he continued peddling.

Only a few blocks later, he passed through Del Mar Boulevard, intersecting the road at the exact location as a famous, historic and cultural landmark known for its live music. *Chuck Berry used to play there*, he thought as he suddenly remembered the song that the small venue was named after, an early, bluesy piece of rock 'n' roll from many generations before.

"Who sung that?" he said to himself, searching his mind for the answer at the tip of his teeth. "It's an old song... Franky Dominico? Frank Domingo? Blair would know..."

Then, peddling ever harder towards the airport, he began singing the melody as loudly as he possibly could, "BAH dum bah dum... bah...bah-dum-ba-da-dum..."

One block further on, just ahead on the sidewalk, an elderly woman exited a corner store with arms laden with bags of fresh produce. Swerving slightly to avoid her, Jax continued incorrectly singing what he could remember as loudly as he could muster, while she stared back at him half-amused and half-unsure, "Though Blair's so far... she thinks of me stiiiiiill... for she is my world..."

As he passed by, she smiled and subtly waved at the crazed man in the business suit as he loudly sang his song, peddling hard on a thrift store bicycle. And yet, the absurdity of the spectacle didn't bother him. He was on a mission, and his heart was overjoyed at the chance of finding her safe and away from danger.

With the minor detour only slightly prolonging his journey, he reached the airport after about an hour of steady peddling. "Not too shabby, Jax," he said to himself as he found a place to park the bicycle near the departure terminal. There was no bike rack, of course; instead, he simply dropped the kickstand and left it on the sidewalk as he continued on.

For once, the line through security was short, and as he reached the officer screening passengers, he linked his flight information, waiting for the signal to move forward.

"Jaxon Wadsworth the fourth" the agent said as he matched the contact information with the records in the flight system.

"That's me!" Jax responded casually.

The officer paused for a moment and then, with a slight gesture, called over another officer, whom Jax assumed was his supervisor. After a few minutes passed, the supervisor said, "Sir, you've been selected for a random search. Could you step this way?"

Jax frowned, knowing the randomness of the search was likely the result of something to do with the ongoing investigation of his family, the gallery, and the suspected links to the supposed terrorist ƟN. Dryly, he responded, "Oh, goody."

As long as they let me board the flight, he thought to himself as the officer used a small handheld imaging machine to scan the length and breadth of his body. Then, once complete, the officer asked, "So, what's in the tube?"

"Art," Jax replied.

"Sir, please remove the item from its container for inspection," the officer said.

"Sure thing," Jax answered, as calmly and ambivalently as he could. He then moved to a nearby steel table and pulled the plastic cap off of the cardboard tube. After several shakes, the tip of the canvas within slid forward. He then removed the canvas and unrolled it onto the table. The supervising officer looked at the work carefully for several long minutes before saying, "Hmph... it's pretty."

"I think so too. A friend made it for me," Jax said politely.

"Thank you. You may go," the officer answered.

Jax then re-rolled the canvas and placed it back into the cardboard tube as casually as he had removed it, thankful Blair hadn't signed the piece and its subject was not political.

A short walk to the gate later, he sat down in an uncomfortable chair in the waiting area. He knew he'd still need to wear his lenses until he boarded the plane, but having grown used to the peace that came with being disconnected, the anxiety of the noise that flooded his lenses began to build.

"Patience, Jax. Nearly there," he whispered to himself under his breath as he closed his eyes.

The couple that sat down next to him quickly ended what little chance of peace he hoped for as he awaited his flight, loudly snipping at each other as they awaited the same flight.

"I already told you – I don't know how long the delay will be in Dallas; there's nothing on the feed about it," the white-haired older man about his parents' age said to the woman next to him. "I've just seen the reels, and the damn right-wingers are even worse in Texas than they are here!"

"Well, I just don't understand why the protests would delay an airport. They're not protesting on planes!" the well-dressed older woman spat tersely.

"Pilots have to fly the plane. The luggage guys have to load the three large suitcases you had to bring with you! There's people on the runways, the flight controllers – they all have to be able to get to work," the white-haired man argued.

"They should just arrest them all... or shoot them. Whatever it takes for life to get back to normal," she said with a confident nod.

The white-haired man simply sat back in his chair, ignoring the comment.

Trying to distract himself from the conversation, Jax took one last look into the threads, only to discover those on the right and left end of the political spectrum were still blaming each other for the unrest of the past few weeks. The only thing they agreed on was the need to restore the integrity of the Safe Speech Act; it was vital to national security.

When a voice overhead announced they would begin boarding soon, Jax had nearly finished looking through videos of the most recent violence that had erupted. As he linked over his boarding information to the gate attendant, he looked at one last reel, a commentary piece from some political science professor who was explaining the meaning behind one of Blair's pieces.

The professor in the video then explained, "This ΘN, whoever he or she is... Well, they're clearly depicting an innocent young woman dressed as Lady Liberty being dragged through the street by a brutish, devilish rendition of Uncle Sam. She appears to have been brutalized in some way, perhaps violated... I'm no expert in art, of course, but I think it's pretty clear this is commentary about toxic masculinity and its role in shaping our present society."

Not even close, Jax thought as he found his seat and at last removed his lenses.

~ 19 ~

"Feliz Año Nuevo, Señor Ramos!" Blair said, as she looked away briefly from her work. Having been in town for a week, she felt like she was finally making some inroads with the locals. They were kind to her, calling her "*Pelirroja*" where pronunciation of her name sounded more like "BLAH-IR" when they read it out loud, or "BLAR" when she tried to correct their pronunciation. The nickname stuck, and it felt fitting in the costal paradise.

In the warm morning air, the small island town was bustling with American tourists, mostly hipsters, backpackers, and other nomads in town for the holiday season. Peak season for bioluminescence or whale shark tours wouldn't come until the summer, she learned. But the winter weather was far milder, and the humidity was bearable. The regular sight of American and Canadian travelers eased the language barrier some, and it gave her a chance to catch up on news from back home.

"So, you're settled on this design, then?" Lillian asked, after she returned from her morning stroll to the corner *panaderia* for sweet rolls the locals called "Conchas".

"Well, it's your shop, Lil – I'm only a silent partner or investor or whatever," Blair answered with a shrug. "I just don't see American Traditional being a big thing down here; most of the murals in town are more ethereal and mystical. I kind of thought this would draw in the tourists... it's this or a flamingo with a gold chain and boxing gloves, but I can't figure out exactly how a flamingo would wear boxing gloves... so."

"Nah, I think it's fitting," Lillian laughed. "Seems like she's become all of our icon at this point – not just yours. I just hope no-one steals the wall off of this place once they find out you painted it."

"Well, that's the good thing about a small island, I suppose. There aren't cars... or trucks. You'd need like thirty people and a boat that could back right up to the beach – and that's a few blocks away," Blair said, contemplating the logistics involved.

"Seems pretty safe then," Lillian chuckled.

"Yeah, pretty safe... pretty safe," Blair echoed.

"Good. Well, why don't you set those brushes down for a minute and come inside for breakfast? Tanner wants to go over the plan for our grand opening on the second, if we can swing it," Lillian said, as she turned back toward the small, newly leased shop off of Calle Palomino.

After passing *conchas* around, Tanner began discussing their business plan, which mostly consisted of doing tourist tattoos – sea turtles, flamingos, flowers, and other oceanic symbols. They'd specialize in low-cost, fixed price flash that would be quick and easy, rather than large custom pieces.

"It's not really our forte or style, I suppose. But we should do ok – there's plenty of demand for it. And people pay in cash here, which is a plus," he explained.

"Did you speak with the immigration officials?" Lillian asked, still concerned that their spontaneous change of countries would be problematic.

"We have to show sufficient monthly income and an adequate net worth. I had the Native Princess painting appraised for insurance purposes and gave a copy of the appraisal to immigration as evidence of assets," he said with a laugh. "There's still paperwork. We'll get a temporary visa and then apply for residency. With the lease documents for the new shop, the business plan, and our tax records, it should be enough to make it happen. If it's not, we'd need to leave the country for an overnight trip every sixty days or so. Or maybe it was ninety. I forget."

"And you, B? You spoke with them, right?" Lillian asked, turning her attention to her friend, who was attempting to dust off the pink sugary crumbs that had collected from her breakfast treat.

"It's going to be a bit more difficult for me, I think," she answered as she wiped crumbly sweet remnants from the corner of her mouth. Then slightly embarrassed at the mess she had made with the pastry, she added, "I went to the immigration office, but because I don't have any records on the feed, they recommended I go to the Commission for Refugee Assistance, which is a few states over, apparently. There's a bus I can take from Valladolid or Chiquila, but it'll probably be a several day trip."

"There's no... special process for VIP political refugees or anything?" Tanner asked. "Like a 'World-Famous Artist Lane' or something? Mexico seems like the kind of place where that would be a thing."

Blair shrugged her shoulders and said, "Not that I've heard of, but you never know. I was thinking I could hire an attorney to help – we could use the legal advice, all of us."

"Probably smart," Lillian said, nodding in agreement. "And the Captain – what's his plan?"

"I thought he was still planning to head back to St. Chuck," Tanner answered. "But he's been spending most of his time with some old señorita he met, so I haven't heard much from him."

"He told me yesterday he was planning to spend Christmas with her in Bacalar," Blair said with a smile. "Apparently, she has a house on the lake and a small fishing boat."

The remark made Tanner grin with admiration as he said, "Good for him! I guess when you're that age, you don't waste any time."

"And Jax? Any word?" Lillian asked, ignoring her husband's burst of misogyny.

"Nothing yet," she sighed. "The painting should have reached him by now. I dunno... maybe he's not coming after all."

"He's coming, B. It's probably all the crazy that is keeping him," Lillian answered as she placed a comforting arm around her friend and gave her a gentle, reassuring squeeze. "He loves you. Give him time."

After finishing breakfast, Tanner and Lillian spent most of the day preparing the new shop for its grand opening celebration. Ordering the supplies they needed was complicated slightly by logistics of getting things to the island, and there was work to be done cleaning, painting the interior, and stockpiling the various inks and cleaning supplies.

Outside of the shop, Blair continued work on the mural they hoped would be a signature landmark for tourists. The mural's outline and most of the base paint had been completed, showing the image of a winged Astraea that stretched the length of the wall. In her outstretched arms, she held a brass scale in one hand and in the other, a sword. The face of the virgin goddess looked up to the heavens while a bright star shone down, illuminating her face against the deep blue sky of the background. She had been working on the piece for days, starting only after the building owner gave permission; many other buildings in town were decorated with murals from local artists. Why not his, he said.

That evening, after an unusual dinner of a local delicacy, pizza topped with lobster, she took a long walk along the beach, alone. The sound of revelers in the small city center was an ever-present reminder of the festivity available only a few blocks away, should she desire to join in. But while she had spent her whole life wondering what it would be like to join the hustle and bustle of the nightlife, in her loneliness, celebrating simply didn't feel right.

In the moonlight, the beauty of the island held a solemn quality. The ocean became black, whereas in the daylight it was the lightest of blue because of the sandbar that ran just off shore. With the tide out, she knew the sandbar stretched far out into the water before dropping into depths that couldn't be walked.

Slowly, she stripped off most of her clothing and waded into the dark ocean until she was knee deep and a sufficient distance from shore. There she stood in the water, silent and alone with her thoughts.

Looking up into the night sky, she wondered if Bell and Mia were ok; she missed them dearly. Once things were settled, she would fly the family down, she told herself. With all the gold she had exchanged for the rights to her paintings, money wouldn't be an issue anymore. She still had the originals, of course, and if things became desperate, she supposed she could sell them too. For the time being, she was just happy to have her art safe and at home without fear of anyone coming to take her or them away.

She wondered if her mother ever had the chance to stare into the night sky from prison. Unsure of whether her mother's cell had windows, or what her life looked like each day, she couldn't say for certain. But the beauty of this island would have endeared her mother to the place as much as it had her.

After several more steps, she was waist deep in the water, standing on the soft, squishy sand of the long sandbar that ran along the north side of the island. She stayed there for more than an hour, watching the stars and wondering what had become of her life that she should so awkwardly and fatefully end up in par-adise surrounded by friends. For all that providence had provided, she was grateful, but lonely all the same.

Having lost track of the time, she eventually realized the tide was coming back in when she noticed the water had risen slowly and silently around her, nearly to her shoulders. She turned, sad to leave the night sky behind, and began her retreat towards shore. Although it was the end of December, it was still warm enough outside to be comfortable, and with the tide moving in quickly, she clumsily attempted to dive towards the shore, trying to swim with the current to hasten the effort.

When she finally reached the beach, she was completely soaked, but she wasted no time in donning her now sandy clothing, which clung tightly to her wet, slender frame as her long, red locks dripped feverishly on the sand. She did her best to wring the saltwater from her hair and then twisted and wrapped the salty mess in a somewhat organized pile on top of her head. Both wet and sandy, she began her slow walk back to the small two-bedroom villa they had rented close to the new tattoo shop.

As she ventured back down Calle Palamino, she passed several small hotels with their palapas and white adobe frame, and then the small school surrounded by the decorative, white concrete walls that sat next to the new shop, which was followed by an open air *taqueria*.

"Some *Pastor*, Ms. BLAR?" the taco vendor asked. "You are all wet – maybe hungry too?"

"Thank you, Jorge," she answered. "I already had dinner."

"You sure?" the portly man asked. Then he continued by saying, "That painting of yours is already driving in business – *la comida es gratis para ti*. That's uh... free food for Miss BLAR, *complimentaria*."

"You are too kind, señor," she laughed. "Maybe tomorrow."

Then, from the rear of the open-air restaurant, she heard a familiar voice, "That's a shame. I was hoping I might snag a date with a beautiful woman – I've heard this place is sort of known for... what's the word you taught me, Jorge?"

"*Señoras guapas*," said the portly taco vendor with a smile, using his hand for emphasis.

"That's it - *Señoras guapas* – thank you, Jorge," the voice responded. Then, stepping into the street light of Calle Palamino, her suspicion was finally confirmed.

"JAX!" she shouted excitedly.

"Hi," he said sweetly. "No, wait, it's '*hola, buenos noches*'," he answered, paying particular attention to correct pronunciation.

Without reservation, she jumped into his arms and began kissing him frantically in the middle of the street as tourists and locals passed by, unphased. She held him tightly for a long while, afraid to let go as she wept tears of joy at being reunited.

"Hey, what's wrong... what is it?" Jax asked when he felt her crying in his arms.

"You said you'd find me," she said as she pulled away slightly and smiled as she looked into his eyes.

"And I did. Of course I did – how could you have ever doubted?" he asked as he kissed her salty forehead.

"Well, what took you so long?" she suddenly stammered before pulling him back towards her and laughing.

"This painting you sent – it led me right to you," he answered warmly as he gestured toward the cardboard tube he carried along with a small leather bag. He then began explaining, "I didn't bring any clothing or anything – just the painting you sent. I just came. And it all seemed perfect until I was delayed in Dallas for a few days. I didn't leave the airport; I just waited. And by the time I got to Merida... Well, let's just say that suit will need a miracle worker... It just took a bit of time... then the train... then the cab. But a few hours ago, when I got off the ferry, I just asked some locals if they had seen a fiery red-headed artist – it didn't take long after that."

"Señor HAX, I have wrapped up your meal for you," Jorge said from deep within the taqueria. "I made *mas para la Señora* BLAR, *tambien.*"

"Gracias, Jorge," Jax said with a smile, as he received the foil-wrapped meal from the man. Then, reaching for his wallet, he heard the man answer, "No, no-no. *Es gratis para la Senora* BLAR. Free for Miss BLAR. *Gratis para amor.* For love. *Buenos noches.*"

"*Buenos noches,*" Blair answered. "And *muchas gracias, señor.*"

They walked for a short distance until they reached the small villa Blair had rented along with Lillian and Tanner, and when they entered through the front door, the look on Lillian's face showed only relief.

"Well, look who made it!" she interjected.

"Honey, who's –" Tanner said from within the kitchen, then with understanding he added, "Well, look at you! Finally!"

"I know… I know… but here I am. I didn't even wait for the final paperwork on the gallery; Bruce is sorting it all out. I came as soon as I figured it out," he said, gesturing to the cardboard tube he carried tucked between the handles of a small leather bag that looked new. "Of course, I couldn't send word because you all have been offline since you left,."

"You sold the gallery?" Lillian asked. "I mean, Blair said you told her you were going to, but… Well, we hadn't heard anything – we didn't know if it went through, if you found someone…"

"Several offers, actually. Nothing crazy, but it should be enough to start over," he replied confidently.

"Enough… for?" Tanner asked.

"Well, that remains to be seen. For now, I kind of just want to enjoy being here – being with Blair after everything that's happened. For now, rest," he said with a heavy sigh of exhaustion.

"Ah," Lillian said with a knowing look. "Well, we were just on our way out to the cantina – weren't we, babe?"

"We were?" he asked, confused. Then, understanding the two needed some time alone, he corrected himself, saying, "That's right – *Mezcal* tasting. You'll be here tomorrow, right? You're not disappearing anytime soon?"

"Tomorrow… the day after that… until she gets sick of me," Jax laughed.

"Good – we'll catch up in the morning then. I discovered a chorizo spot that's to die for — real meat, too. REAL MEAT, none of that soy-based crap they have back home," Tanner exuded with excitement.

"I'm looking forward to it – even if it takes some time for my stomach to get used to it again," Jax said with a smile.

Once Tanner and Lillian excused themselves to allow the couple some privacy, the pair decided the first order of business was to catch up on all that had transpired, while Jax ravenously feasted on the tacos.

In between bites, she asked, "So, how did the gallery sale sit with your parents?"

"I didn't bother to ask them – I just did it. I sold my share of it, at least. They had a small stake – they still do. And now they can sort it out with the new owners," he said, squeezing lime over his carne asada.

"Just like that? I can't believe the police let you leave the country," she said as she grabbed his knee right next to hers, verifying with her hands he was real and there and not some imaginary manifestation she had conjured from the ether. Then suddenly and spontaneously, she dashed to the refrigerator to find him a beer, which she opened and set in front of him.

"Well, I may have suggested to the FBI that my mother was trying to get me to sell ΘN paintings to her friends, and that all this may have started because she was trying to influence law enforcement to protect their investment... Might have also suggested that a certain known drug abuser may or may not be the infamous terrorist ΘN," he said swallowing down a cold beer alongside his meal.

"Wait, you said what?" she asked, shocked at his revelation.

"I only suggested he might be... they'll investigate... it'll cause some headaches," he answered. Then, after finishing the first taco, he added, "It's petty, I know. This tit-for-tat playing the police against each other, but it felt just, and it bought some time. In the end, they'll investigate and it will probably come to nothing. They have money and influence enough to not get into too much trouble. But it will cause some hand wringing in the meantime. I guess I just got tired of being pushed around, especially by people who are supposed to love me... But it's done now."

Then, after picking up the second taco, he said, "Tell me about your adventure – you literally sailed across the Gulf of Mexico with an old pirate. And it was your first time taking the boat out. How'd that go? Obviously, you're safe, but – tell me."

"Well... it was wild, I guess. We made our way down the Mississippi with only minor issues. Old man Agnew had done it several times before, which helped. We stopped briefly outside of Memphis for supplies, and then again south of New Orleans, where the Coast Guard was looking for us. But it ended up fine. Then, after several days sailing through the Gulf, we stopped to swim at this beautiful reef – it's like a day or two from here. It was amazing! I'll have to take you back there sometime soon – just gorgeous. Anyway, when we finally reached Isla Holbox, I used some of the gold to pay for the lease of the tattoo shop for a year... and a few months for this place until we figure the rest out."

"The gold?" Jax asked, confused by what she was explaining.

"Yeah, Blaze's people, the ones I sold the rights to the paintings to, they paid me in gold coins... turns out it's pretty portable and oddly enough, pretty easy to convince people to take in lieu of the digital money," she explained with a smile.

"How much gold are we talking about, if you don't mind me asking?" he said.

"A lot, I think. It feels like a lot. There were five briefcases, and they were all pretty heavy," she said with a shrug.

Jax's eyes grew wide with surprise, and after he swallowed a bite of taco in a hard gulp, he asked, "Just for the rights to reproduce the paintings — not for the originals themselves?"

"Oh, no – all the originals are upstairs in my room. They paid to make the prints. I mean... I now know they were using my paintings to kick off all this mess that everyone's been talking about," she answered. "I... I didn't know how bad it would get – just off my paintings. I didn't think it would be this bad. It's almost like it was back when my mom and dad were... Well, what's done is done now."

"How do you feel about it now that it all turned out the way it did?" he asked, studying her as he asked.

"Well, I'm not sorry about selling my work. I won't apologize to anyone for that. No one has the right to silence any else's voice – especially not people in power," she said, as dedicated to her beliefs as ever. "It's harder for me when I think about the people who were hurt... people that have died in everything that's happened since. They were standing up for the cause I believe in, and I'm just... hanging out in paradise."

"Some guilt there?" Jax asked.

"A little," she answered honestly. "But we can't all be revolutionaries like my parents. I'm an artist. Maybe it is finally time for change, and it will be worth it... I never told anyone to act violently – I never said it was good. I... simply wanted to say something. I wanted to tell people that this whole system they've created to control people isn't right... Maybe inspire people to say they've had enough."

"They certainly did that, for all the good it has done so far," Jax said rather solemnly as he recounted the scenes of violence and civil disorder that flooded the feed in the past weeks.

"Anyway..." she said, a bit saddened by the thought of all that had transpired. "Did you happen to hear from Bell or Zay? I worry about them."

"They are fine. I checked in with them not long after you left. I told them I'd keep searching, and I'd let them know when I had more," he responded, returning to the plate of tacos in front of him. "I didn't want to take the chance of drawing too much attention on my way down here, but now that I've found you..."

"I'd love to have them down here sometime soon. Mia would love the water here – it's beautiful," she answered.

"We can make that happen," he said confidently. "It sounds like between the gallery sale and your treasure horde, we shouldn't have too much of a problem getting established here. Flying the Andover's down won't be a big deal, so long as we stay... cautious."

"Good – they're smart. I'm sure we can figure out a way to get them word," she answered. "That just leaves my mom."

"I don't know what we can do to help her," Jax responded empathetically. "I mean, maybe with the right lawyers, there could be some movement. But with everything the country is going through right now, unless policy changes, I can't see how anyone would allow a known dissident back on the streets."

"I was thinking the same thing... but I have to try. If I can use some of the gold to help her – I'd even sell some originals, if that's what it took. I... I just can't abandon her there without trying," she answered. Then abruptly she said, "You have a little salsa on your... here, I'll get it."

She quickly picked up a small paper napkin and wiped the drip of salsa that had gathered at the corner of his mouth, and the two of them laughed gently, thankful to once again be together.

"Well, you're not going to stop painting, right? And here, you could do it without an issue – there's no Safe Speech Act in Mexico. You're safe," he said.

"Of course I'll keep painting," she laughed, shocked by the absurdity of his question. "That's why I still need you!"

"Oh, I see – make me do all the work then?" he chuckled.

"Yup," she said with a smile. "Have you ever thought about opening a gallery in Holbox?"

"Only recently," he said with a smile. "But honestly, there's only one client I'm interested in working with."

"Oh... that sounds exclusive... maybe lucrative too," she said coyly.

"Well, this client is really talented. Sort of famous too," he answered stoically. "So as long as Deidra is willing to make the trip down here... I don't see any reason I shouldn't –"

Blair's shock was followed an instant later as she slapped him gently, saying, "Deidra? Really? I mean, I love her work, but..."

"Of course not!" he laughed. "I've every intention of working for the best... Maybe Deidra too, if she's willing to jump ship – it'd be nice to see her again."

"I LOVE her work," Blair answered. "She's brilliant."

"So, that... sounds like what you want to do? I'll run a gallery, and you'll provide the art?" he asked, studying her for confirmation of her intent.

"You'd be the exclusive dealer for ΘN... that sounds pretty fancy... edgy even," she said with a smile.

"You... still want to go with ΘN – not paint under your own name?" he asked curiously.

"I think I like being able to just be me, and not have to worry about folks tearing down my walls because they think it's worth something. ΘN may be wanted in the US, but nobody seems to know who he or she really is. I kind of like that – it's mysterious!" she said playfully, dramatic.

"So... something like 'ΘN on Holbox'... No, that doesn't work," he said, finishing the last bite of his taco. "Maybe 'ΘN Isla Holbox'?"

"Let's sleep on it and come up with more ideas in the morning," she said as she took his hand and began leading him towards the staircase.

"Hey," he said suddenly, squeezing her clasped hand.

"Hey what?" she said as she turned back toward him.

"Thank you," he said in a sudden, serious tone.

"For what?" she said, shaking her head.

"For having the courage to have a voice that was all your own. For staying true to it, despite all the danger and fear and the consequences. For inspiring me to be as courageous as you are. Thank you," he said, trying to contain his emotions.

"Thank you for loving me," she answered. "Now let's go to bed... Maybe a shower first; I'm all sandy!"

BLINK-BLINK